PIECES OF YOU

As a shy teenager, **Ella Harper** found a way to escape by learning foreign languages, and imagined she might eventually get a glamorous job speaking French. After completing a BA in French and Russian Studies, she found herself following in her father's footsteps into banking instead, seduced by the excitement and glamour of that world. But after climbing her way to Assistant Vice President, Ella started idly mapping out the beginnings of a novel on an old laptop. When she realised her characters were more real to her than dividends and corporate actions ever could be, she left her job to become a writer. Eight years later, and Ella has published four hugely popular novels under the name Sasha Wagstaff. *Pieces of You* is her first novel as Ella, inspired by a personal loss and fertility issues suffered by friends.

For more information about Ella, find her on Twitter @Ella_Harper, and on Facebook at /EllaHarperBooks.

ELLA HARPER

Pieces of You

AVON

AVON
A division of HarperCollins*Publishers*
77–85 Fulham Palace Road,
London W6 8JB

www.harpercollins.co.uk

A Paperback Original 2014

1

First published in Great Britain by
HarperCollins*Publishers* 2014

A catalogue record for this book is
available from the British Library

ISBN-13: 978-0-00-758110-8

Set in Sabon LT Std by Palimpsest Book Production Limited,
Falkirk, Stirlingshire

Printed and bound in Great Britain by
Clays Ltd, St Ives plc

MIX
Paper from
responsible sources
FSC™ C007454

Acknowledgements

There are many people I would like to thank when it comes to this particular novel. Mostly due to their support and friendship, but for many other reasons that I'll keep to myself to avoid sounding gushy.

Those people are as follows:

Jeni, as ever, for being there whenever I need you, with your wisdom, sanity and guidance, despite being in Australia.

Donna, for your expert help with all the hospital stuff . . . thank you for taking the time to do so much research on my behalf and sending me such huge emails with the exact information I needed.

Thanks to the EEB girls for being excited about my books and rearranging them at airports tirelessly. Naughty but brilliant . . . I love it.

To my parents, for being there for me always, whatever drama I'm going through.

And to Ant, Phoebe and Daisy . . . just because.

Two very important mentions – to Ketters, otherwise known as Kate. For being such a great friend and for supporting me through this entire process . . . you know what I'm talking about. And to Claire, an equally good friend who deserves the same level of gratitude and thanks for the very same reasons. Both of you . . . you're awesome.

Thank you to my wonderful agents Diane Banks and Kate Burke. Special thanks to Kate for her tireless hard work and commitment to this novel . . . invaluable.

Thanks to the lovely team at Avon, headed up by Sammia Hamer, who believes so passionately in what I am doing; it spurs me on.

Thanks to my fab friend Alexandra Brown, to the wonderful Adele Parks and to lovely, lovely Gemma Burgess (two special mentions for you – Errol and 'Hey Ho'). To the very sweet Veronica Henry and also to my idol Fiona Walker (we met at last!), for such incredible support over the years, for championing me on Twitter and suchlike, and for 'keep going' type emails.

Also, thanks to all fans, book bloggers and readers who have been excited about this new novel and the change of genre – and as a general comment, to all who have kept me going with fabulous emails.

This novel took a while to come to fruition and I consider myself extremely lucky to have such a fantastic support team around me. Heartfelt thanks to all of you.

This one goes to my excellent friends . . . you know who you are.

CHAPTER ONE

Lucy and Luke

February

'What are we doing here, Harte?'

If I sounded impatient, it was because I felt it. I'd been standing outside Luke's hospital for about fifteen minutes and my toes were beginning to seize up. It was one of those crisp, frosty mornings where pavements and branches of trees looked as though demented elves had gone crazy sprinkling sugar all over them; pretty enough, but also bloody freezing.

'Just hang on a bit longer,' Luke frowned, checking his watch. 'What time do you have?'

'It's nine-fifteen and your mother is going to be cross if I'm late for work.' I grabbed his wrist, pulling at the battered metal strap of his watch. 'I know you love this thing, but seriously, it has terrible time-keeping issues.'

'I know, I know. But it's my dad's . . . you know I can't take it off. It's the law.' Luke straightened. 'Ah, here's the person I've been waiting for.'

I sank my chin deeper into the warmth of my scarf and blew on my hands as a pretty girl approached us. She was smiling and proffering a wrapped package. I felt a flicker of intrigue, but chilliness prevented me from displaying too much interest.

The girl stopped in front of Luke. 'Luke Harte? Sorry I'm late. Here it is.'

'Great! Thank you; you're a life saver.' Luke handed over an envelope which the girl pocketed. He looked ridiculously pleased with himself, in fact. 'God, I love it when a plan comes together.'

'What sort of plan?'

He touched my nose. 'Don't look so suspicious. It's Valentine's Day! You know that, right?'

'I'm aware.'

I sounded prim, but there was a reason for that. I had Valentine's Day wrapped up and sorted. I had ordered in some lovely food rather than trusting my own cooking (for very good reasons, I hasten to add), I had wine, I had candles and I had vague ideas about a massage-type thing for Luke at the end of the night.

'So go with it, okay?' Luke's eyes met mine and I could tell he was indulging me. The man knew me well.

'Now I know we usually save things until later, but I've been tracking this gift down for you. It's a good 'un, even if I say so myself. Are you going to open it? I can't wait to see your face.' He thrust the package into my hands.

'No pressure then,' I smiled, dropping my eyes. 'I know you and your surprise gifts. They're usually amazing and then I worry that I've only, you know . . . thought of dinner with candlelight.'

2

Luke waved a hand. 'That's all I want, so you're spot on . . . can't wait. Open it, go on.'

I turned the package over in my hands. Was it chocolates? No, Luke wouldn't be so obvious. Nor would chocolates require personal hand-delivery. Was it a book? I peeled back a section of wrapping paper. Books were the perfect gift for me; I adore them. Perhaps it was another copy of *Wuthering Heights* – I collected them; the older the better. Old novels with illustrations and dedications written in the front pages in fountain pen, scratchy, illegible marks steeped with meaning.

I tore the rest of the wrapping off, discovering a hardback with a torn, tarnished sleeve – or wrapper, as they used to be called. *A Book of Delights*, I read. 'How lovely. Er. What is it, exactly?'

Luke opened the book. 'It's an anthology of poetry and quotes and stuff. Romantic things.' He flipped the pages. 'I mean, it's probably mostly pretentious rubbish, but apparently there are a few really nice poems in there.'

'You old romantic, you.' I was impressed.

'That's not even the best bit,' Luke said.

I flicked my eyes over him. The man was practically preening.

'There's an inscription at the front . . . read it. This is absolutely the best bit.'

I found it. It read: *To my darling wife, with all my love, Luke. 14th Feb, 1954.* '1954? What the—? I don't understand . . .'

'Some other Luke wrote in the book all those years ago.' Luke was practically beside himself at this point. 'The other Luke wrote that to the wife *he* loved. Isn't

3

that amazing? I've had someone on the case trawling through old books for ages, looking at inscriptions. I was hoping for a "To Lucy", but this one appeared and I just knew it was perfect.'

I traced my fingers over the writing. It was neat and well-formed – nothing like Luke's actual writing which was chaotic and sprawling. I flipped through the pages and found a poem called 'Captive'. It made me smile. Luke leant over my shoulder and read it.

> *I did but look and love awhile,*
> *'Twas but for one half-hour;*
> *Then to resist I had no will,*
> *And now I have no power.*

Luke laughed. 'Ha ha, brilliant. That's you and me.'

'Is it? Wow.' I closed the book and stroked the cover. 'Just . . . wow. You're unbelievable.'

'Too much?' Luke's shoulders hunched and he screwed his face up. 'I know you hate surprises.'

'No. No, it's not too much. It's perfect. Just . . . perfect. You're . . .'

I was overwhelmed.

'I love how you crumble in the face of anything truly romantic,' Luke said, placing a hand on my neck. 'It's one of the most adorable things about you.'

Against my better judgement, I started to cry. What an idiot. Buy me a soppy book with an achingly romantic inscription and I become a dribbly mess. Well, in fairness, my tears weren't just about the book today, but I was still mortified.

Fear gripped my insides in an icy vice. I thought about the vitamins, the acupuncture, the doctors, the therapy, the alcohol avoidance, the hope, the joy and the disappointment. And about what might be ahead for us if nothing else worked.

'It will happen, Luce,' Luke said, reading my mind as he gripped my shoulders. 'We *will* have a baby.'

I couldn't meet his eyes. When we first met, eight or so years ago, I wouldn't have questioned our chances. Eight years ago, I didn't know the half of it. At the beginning of our relationship we'd been reckless about contraception, because we both wanted children from the outset. We'd been rewarded with an early pregnancy that we hadn't expected . . . and then punished when the dream had been cruelly snatched away. And that hadn't been the only time our dreams had been trodden underfoot.

Luke lifted my chin and kissed me. 'It will happen. Without a shadow of a doubt.'

He was emphatic. I was cautious. It was how we rolled. He was the carefree optimist; I was one of life's natural worriers. My extreme need for tidiness and order led my best friend Dee to introduce me as 'Monica from *Friends* and then some' to new acquaintances; accurate, but not the most charming of introductions.

Luke placed a warm hand on my neck, ducking his head so I had no choice but to meet his eyes. 'Don't even think we won't succeed at this, Luce. Because we will.'

'But we've already lost . . . What if we can't . . .'

'We will.'

'How do you . . . ?'

'I just do.' Luke kissed my forehead and drew me closer. 'I love you and you love me. There is nothing we can't achieve together.'

I leant into him, inhaling his strength, breathing in his positivity. He was right. We could do this. I clutched my beautiful book and I held on to Luke and, in that moment, I knew everything would be all right. It was Valentine's Day and I had a thoughtful husband, an amazing gift – and I had the most important thing of all; I had hope.

CHAPTER TWO

Lucy

September

A woman strode efficiently into the consulting room. I felt panic set in. I didn't recognise this person. Where were the other ones, the ones who knew what we'd been through, how much this meant to us? Someone had obviously decided that today we should come face to face with the only fertility consultant in Bath we weren't on first name terms with.

I shifted in my chair, unequal to the challenge of dealing with a stranger. The consultant began hastily perusing our file to familiarise herself with our case, allowing us a brief smile.

A professional smile, I observed with weary expertise. Non-committal, reserved. Not so different to the other consultants, then. They were able to produce an entire repertoire of smiles for each occasion – cautiously hopeful, compassionately apologetic, not-sure-yet-neutral. I studied this consultant. It was a game I had taught myself to play during the agonising waits we were always subjected to when it came to IVF appointments. Don't get me wrong, the NHS has been superb, but waiting is de rigueur. Bad news might be on the horizon – or not, as the case may be. Either way, sitting patiently wasn't in my nature.

I settled back in my chair. Did this one have children? Her well-cut suit was spotless, the shoulder pads decorated with shiny buttons rather than milk stains. One tick for non-parent. The freshly-dried mane of dark hair looked as though it hadn't ever had clumps of Weetabix mashed into it not this morning or any other morning.

Another tick, I thought with a sinking heart. Unlike most of the others, this consultant bore zero tell-tale signs of a hasty exit from home. It shouldn't matter but, for some reason, it did, very much. Because if anyone was going to snatch my dream away, I would prefer it to be someone who knew how utterly crucifying it was. How it would feel like the end of . . . well. I didn't want to think about that.

As the minutes ticked by silently without a word from the consultant, I felt a strange, silent scream building inside. I'd been behaving irrationally recently; I knew that. I'd been distracted, emotional . . . that and probably far, far worse. I was spiralling inside, chaotic. I glanced at Luke. His jaw was tight and his hair was messed up, but as he turned to me, he managed a grin. The man actually managed a grin. He had put up with so much from me I wasn't quite sure how he had coped. The mood swings, the hysterics, the anger . . . a lesser man might have crumbled. Or, at very least, run a mile.

I guess the fact that he wanted this as much as I did saved him.

Sometimes, I wondered what Luke saw in me. Unlike him, I wasn't especially funny. I mean, I could be highly amusing after a few glasses of wine, but only moderately so without.

Looks-wise, I had dark hair, direct, brown eyes that needed several coats of mascara to bring them out and a slim but rather boyish figure. Based on comments made by friends, I had deduced that I was pretty enough, but in a non-threatening way. Meaning, presumably, that the boyfriends/husbands of my female friends enjoyed my company – may even have found me vaguely attractive – but they didn't necessarily feel obliged to bend me over the kitchen counter passionately if caught alone with me by accident.

I rubbed my forehead, my fingertips weirdly cool in the sultry heat. And what about all the baby stuff? I reckon the baby stuff had made me seem a little crazy. More than a little crazy.

I watched Luke drumming the fingers of his other hand on his thigh. He was apprehensive, maybe even more so than me.

The consultant looked up apologetically. 'I'm so sorry, I normally get to grips with new patients before I meet them. Teenage daughters who dawdle all the way to school are a perennial hazard.' She rolled her eyes to garner our sympathy and returned to the file. 'Please bear with me . . .'

I exchanged a glance with Luke, noticing his eyebrow cocked pointedly. I ignored his rubbish Roger Moore impression. Yes, yes; I had presumed that the consultant was childless, but instead, she had older kids. Hence the pristine appearance. I·shrugged tetchily. The consultant was still a slow reader. Dee's daughter Tilly was faster with *The Faraway Tree*.

Luke tightened his grip on my hand. 'It's going to be all right,' he whispered firmly. 'This time, everything is going to happen the way it should.'

I nodded. It was one of life's ironies that the only fly in the ointment, the only tiny but irritating flaw that prevented us from being complete, was that we were here in this office, waiting for a consultant we didn't know to tell us if our baby might stick around this time. A tedious but excruciating fact: we couldn't conceive a baby. Not one that stayed put for longer than twelve weeks, anyway.

One in four women experience a miscarriage at some point in their lives and one in five pregnancies end this way, but having eight of them had eclipsed everything else in our lives. We hadn't conceived a baby naturally for years . . . at least . . . no, wait. We didn't talk about that. We never, *ever* talked about that. It was the one thing that had caused a major rift between us.

Losing so many babies had changed us irrevocably. 'Character building,' Luke used to say bravely, tears streaking down his face as he gathered me up and held my heartbroken body in his arms for the umpteenth time.

Yes. Character building. We had done much of that over the years.

A few years ago, I remember Luke playing with Dee

and Dan's youngest daughter Frankie in the park, using her as a human Subbuteo, swinging her chubby legs and roaring with laughter as they scored a goal. It was an image I still held in my head, although I was no longer sure that it would become a reality for us.

The clock on the wall ticked steadily, mockingly, echoing my biological timer. In my ears, the rhythmic ticks gathered pace, rather like sand slithering at high speed into the bulb of an egg timer.

If only they had been able to find something wrong. But Luke had superb sperm by all accounts, and my ovaries, womb and fallopian tubes were perfectly ripe and healthy. Yet somehow, the stench of failure had been firmly but unfairly placed at my door, or rather, at my womb. Because if I couldn't conceive, it must mean that *my* body was at fault. Terms like 'foetal rejection' and 'hostile environment' had been carelessly tossed on to the table as explanations.

'Hostile environment' – have you ever heard such a thoughtless, cruel term? It made me want to scream. It was an onslaught to my womanhood and everything I felt I should be capable of, but what was the point? Everyone would just think I was crazy or hormonal. Or both.

And so it had begun. Three bouts of IUI – intrauterine insemination – that hadn't worked and, due to my age – thirty-seven, ancient in baby-making terms – we had started IVF immediately afterwards. Hormone injections, accompanied by the dreadful side effects everyone talked about, multiple ultrasound scans to check the size and maturity of my eggs and injections to 'ripen' my eggs. The best ones (Luke liked to call these the 'Eggs Benedict'

11

of my offerings) were mixed with his sperm (spun, washed and carefully selected, Luke would comment in amusement, as if describing a washing cycle) and these were then hopefully fertilised before being placed back inside my body.

Smear tests had nothing on IVF treatment, I thought ruefully. I'd spent more time with my legs in the air and my parts on show than I cared to admit. Ultimately, all dignity and modesty had been annihilated. My womb had been discussed and scrutinised in such intimate detail over the past few years I almost felt I should give it a nickname. Luke had a choice few, all unsuitable for general consumption, but they made me laugh.

Speak, I pleaded with the consultant mutely. Tell us it's all right. I pulled at an unravelling thread on my trousers, feeling an affinity with it. We had missed out on the magical moments most parents surely revelled in, such as the deliciously important task of choosing names. (For the record: Jude for a boy, Bryony for a girl.) But such a thing had fallen by the wayside, as had daring to have a preference when it came to the sex of a baby. A preference? Pure self-indulgence. Healthy, that was all that mattered. Just . . . healthy.

I bit my lip. Recently, instead of flattering talk about what incredible parents we would be, friends and family had mentioned egg donation and surrogacy and, astonishingly, buying a dog. Yes, obviously, we should forget about babies and get a chihuahua. Dee . . . even *Dee*, had even suggested giving up. *Giving up*. It had caused the only major row we had ever had, and it had taken a while to forgive her.

It was difficult for me to explain, but I yearned to carry Luke's baby. I had this inner ache that I felt only our own child could fill. Luke understood, I thought, although I did have a sense deep down that he might have been more than happy to discuss other options, should we have needed to. I couldn't think that way, though. I had to believe that this would work.

The consultant finally sat back. 'Well, everything looks healthy this time round,' she remarked rather cheerily. 'Obviously we're not out of the woods yet and you've had quite a journey, but this is the furthest you've come, so there is every chance that this pregnancy will develop as it should. Fourteen weeks . . . this is fantastic.'

The consultant's gaze softened. 'Regular scans and check-ups, of course. But that's all part of the process, as I'm sure you're aware. Here you are – another set of scan photographs for you to keep. Lovely ones. Look at this one of the baby's feet.'

I took the photos. I was shaking.

'Really? Everything looks all right?' Luke's elation was evident; his heart on his sleeve, as ever. He crushed my hand accidentally and I loved him for it. My own euphoria tended to be rather more contained these days – a casualty of the process – but Luke was endearingly positive.

The consultant gestured to the test results in the file. 'It does. The baby is healthy, the heartbeat is strong and all of your tests came back with great results.'

'A perfectly good oven, as it turns out. I bloody knew it.' Luke snaked an arm around my neck and spoke into my ear. 'I told you that old guy didn't know what he was talking about, Luce. I knew it; I just knew it.'

13

I burst into tears. An aged, male consultant had once breezily described my womb as a 'broken oven' some years back and I had never quite got over it.

'Let's just get through the next couple of months, shall we?' The consultant's professional demeanour was firmly back in place. She headed for the door. 'Good luck, both of you, and I'll see you again soon.'

Was that 'good luck' because we needed it, or was she just wishing us well? I caught myself. Would the ball of tears in the back of my throat, caught like a frozen waterfall, ever thaw? I just wanted to feel normal. I wanted to be able to glance at doll-sized baby grows pegged on a washing line without dissolving into tears. I wanted to be able to hand a lonely-looking teddy bear I'd found on the supermarket floor back to its owner without biting my lip until it bled. The sweet scent of downy peach fuzz on the head of a friend's newborn as I cradled a tiny body? Instant hysteria. Snot, heaving chest . . . the works. Cue awkwardness all round and cautious comments about it being my turn soon. Yes. My turn.

I traced a finger along the baby picture, outlining its perfectly formed leg. Perhaps this baby wanted us as much as we wanted him or her. As we walked into the heavy summer air, Luke placed a tender hand on the swell of my stomach.

'Didn't I tell you to trust me? Didn't I say it would all work out eventually? We just had to wait for the right baby to come along.' He was thrilled. 'This one is special . . . this one wants us to be her parents. His parents. Whatever.'

'God, I hope so.' I touched his face. 'I've been a nightmare, haven't I? Absolutely barmy.'

Luke caught my hand and held it. 'Not barmy. Clinically insane. Make that certifiable – joking!' He doubled over at the bicep punch I threw him, his expression sobering. 'You want this badly, that's all. We both want this badly. This one wants to stay in your perfect, *perfect* oven. This is it, Lucy. This is *it*.'

I held Luke's hand against my stomach. A baby of our own – part me, part him. After eight years of trying and after eight, sad little boxes in a cupboard, a baby of our own. At last.

CHAPTER THREE

Patricia

Sitting alone in the florists, Patricia found herself staring down at her notepad. She should be making a funeral wreath for tomorrow morning, but she had been putting it off. It was getting dark outside and Gino, busy putting the chairs inside Café Amore for the night, noticed her from across the street and waved.

Patricia slowly held a hand up in response. She felt weary. And desperately alone. True, she *was* on her own – in the physical sense – having sent Lucy home hours ago to plan an elaborate anniversary dinner (although with Lucy's track record, Patricia privately felt more than one evening's practice might be in order), but still. She felt alone in all senses of the word. Isolated, forlorn, solitary. It was unnerving after all this time to be knocked sideways by this familiar, suffocating feeling, Patricia thought. She steadied her hands on her notepad.

She had felt so disconnected since Bernard's death. Even after all this time. It was as if she felt set apart from other people much of the time, unable to fully get involved in her surroundings . . . or involved in life, in fact.

It was Luke and Lucy's fifth wedding anniversary on Sunday. Their *fifth*. Five years without a . . . Patricia forced the thought away and focused on Lucy. She loved Lucy. Not in a 'you're-the-daughter-I-never-had' way, of course, because she had Nell, but there was a genuine closeness between them. Wasn't there? Sometimes Patricia wondered if she had prevented a real connection from growing. She didn't mean to be aloof, but she found it hard to be openly affectionate. Patricia wasn't really sure why. Was that because she had lost Bernard? Had the lack of physical contact made her cold towards others? It was possible, she supposed.

Working together helped; she and Lucy had forged a good relationship over flower arrangements and awkward customers. Lucy had only started working at the florists after meeting Luke as Patricia had needed an extra pair of hands and because Lucy was at a crossroads, career-wise. But she had stayed and she seemed to love it.

And now Lucy was properly involved in the business. It irked her that Lucy moaned about the lack of a credit card machine, as did Lucy's desire for order and symmetry with everything. 'Getting with the programme,' Luke jokingly called it and although he took a gentler, more persuasive line, he obviously agreed with Lucy.

The truth was, Patricia didn't trust modern technology. You always knew where you were with cash and cheques; that was what Bernard used to say and he was spot on. But she was doing her best to embrace new ideas – like those flannel flower baskets Lucy had shown her some months back. It had taken her a little time to see them as a viable prospect, but she was in her fifties; she liked to mull an idea over before she could get her head around it.

If only Bernard were still here; he'd know what to do about all these . . . Patricia faltered. If only Bernard was still here. Not just to listen to her reservations about the state-of-the-art business ideas she was struggling to understand, but to stop this awful loneliness.

Patricia rubbed a hand over her eyes. She felt faintly foolish. Funeral flowers always did this to her. Despite the length of time Bernard had been gone, she missed him. Every single day. She would wake up each morning and, as she'd read in some of those women's magazines where they always went on about deceased partners, there would be seconds of blissful, sleepy forgetfulness. Then the haze would clear and she would remember. He was gone. And the anguish would consume her. And she would miss the smell of him, the sound of his laughter and, most of all, the easy history they shared.

They had been a cliché of sorts: childhood sweethearts, married young, devoted to one another. Their lives had lacked notable drama or incident and that was just the way they had liked it. Bernard had worked as a GP in their local surgery, with just the right blend of kindly firmness. He had been well-liked in the community and she had been happy to bring up their three children and be a traditional housewife. When the children were older, Bernard had inherited a sum of money after the death of his parents and, knowing how much she loved flowers, he had bought an empty shop space for her. Patricia had taken a floristry course, even though taking such a step had filled her with anxiety, and *Hartes & Flowers* had been born. It had been the single most romantic thing Bernard had ever done for her. She thought of him each time she opened and closed the shop. Each time she trailed her fingers along the cream, distressed-effect counter he had chosen.

What made it so difficult was that Bernard had dropped dead one day. Just like that. No warning, no prior symptoms, no goodbye. Just . . . dead. In a flash, in a heartbeat. Or not, as the case may be. The doctors said Bernard had had an undiagnosed heart condition, that his condition had made him the equivalent of a ticking time bomb. Patricia detested this expression; it made Bernard sound like some sort of sinister terrorist threat. Apparently, it was quite common for people in the medical profession to miss their own health problems – they couldn't see what was under their own noses.

Thank goodness for Luke, Patricia reflected. Quite simply, he had been the lynchpin of the family since Bernard had died. He shouldn't have been, but he had stepped up admirably when Ade couldn't. Just for a nanosecond, Patricia's heart ached at the thought of her eldest son. But she steeled herself and put that feeling right back in the box it belonged in. Ade was gone and he wasn't coming back.

But Luke. Luke had gritted his teeth and got on with it. Barely twenty-one and probably ill-prepared for the responsibility of supporting his mother and younger sister through their grief, Luke had knuckled down and coped.

It had been Luke's idea to send Nell to a therapist when all of her problems had started, and thank God they had. Thank God.

Patricia placed the wreath carefully in the fridge in the back office and paused, her hand on the cool, metal door. Her life seemed to be on hold at the moment, had been for some time, in fact. She always seemed to be waiting.

As Patricia drifted back into the shop to tidy up, she noticed a harassed-looking woman wielding a futuristic-looking pushchair with a baby in it. A stroppy toddler tugged at her hand, whining loudly, neither of them noticing when he dropped his cuddly Buzz Lightyear toy.

Patricia dashed outside and picked it up. 'You dropped this, sweetie.'

The boy took it sulkily, saying nothing as his sticky fingers closed around the green and white figure. The mother turned, frowning. 'Say thank you,' she reminded her son, tiredly.

'Thank you,' the boy mumbled.

Patricia smiled. 'You're welcome. Lovely evening, isn't it?'

The mother half-smiled. 'Will be when these two are down for their sleep,' she replied. 'Come on, Josh. Let's go. Say bye to the nice lady . . .'

Patricia leant against the doorframe and watched them. After Bernard had died, she had hoped and prayed for a distraction. A baby-shaped one, not a new man in her life. A baby she could smother with all the pent-up love she could feel swirling inside, the love that had nowhere else to go. But it hadn't happened. She had tried to find out what was going on, of course; Luke was her son but he had seemed reluctant to elaborate. Patricia felt helpless. Of course, it hurt a little that Luke didn't seem to want to confide in her. Thinking about it, that had pretty much stopped when Bernard had died. Patricia guessed they had all been affected in different ways by his absence, but it was a shame, because Luke had always been so open.

Patricia gathered up her bag and locked the shop door. The fact of the matter was, she had this prickle of resentment she didn't know what to do with, and laying it at her daughter-in-law's door for not giving her a grandchild gave the feeling a more comfortable home. It was unfair, of course it was. And it might not be accurate. But with Nell in her early twenties and far too focused on her fashion degree to think about kids, Luke and Lucy were Patricia's best bet.

Patricia pushed all thoughts of a baby to one side. She was being selfish and that wasn't fair. She needed to keep busy – she needed a few projects of her own to focus on. Patricia glanced back at the shop window. The pots really were beautiful. Perhaps she could do a course, making pots and dishes and things she could use when she baked. Yes, a course of some kind. That would keep her busy.

CHAPTER FOUR

Lucy

'It's *ridiculously* hot,' Dee said, fanning her pink face with Dan's worn straw hat. 'It's September; it shouldn't be *this* hot. I was hoping for sunny with a light breeze. God, this is what the bloody menopause is going to be like, isn't it? Mood swings, hot flushes and vaginal dryness. Bloody *hell*.'

I glanced at her in amusement. We hadn't even hit our forties yet. Besides, Dee had a cheek moaning about the heat. I was absolutely roasting in a loose-fitting purple maxi dress with one of those elongated cardigans over the top. Paranoia about someone spotting my tiny bump was to blame for my sweaty hairline, but honestly, I was about to melt.

Hearing my mobile beeping, I groped in my handbag.

'Who's that?' Dee jammed Dan's hat on her head, squashing what I knew to be an expensive blow dry. She looked ravishing in it, as she did in everything she wore. 'Not Luke cancelling, I hope. Frankie's got her heart set on playing swingball with him all afternoon.'

'He wouldn't miss it for the world. No, he's just going to be a bit late.' I took out my sunglasses. Perhaps I could slip off my cardigan when everyone had downed a few of Dan's pungent sangrias.

'I suppose, now that Luke's a senior paramedic, he can't always just dash out of the door, even for Frankie,' Dee drawled. 'Why can't I have a hero for a husband instead of a gallery owner? It doesn't sound half as sexy. Art . . . saving lives. There's no comparison.'

'Being a paramedic isn't sexy. Luke comes home covered in blood most nights.'

'Don't spoil it. But seriously. You two are such a couple of romantics.' Dee sounded wistful.

I glanced at her. 'You and Dan have a brilliant time together.'

'Oh yes, we have fun,' Dee replied vaguely. 'But still . . .' She turned her attention to Dan, who was holding court on the patio wearing torn Bermuda shorts and a navy T-shirt. 'Look at him. He's a bloody caveman.'

I studied Dan. He was wielding a beer and a ridiculously large pair of tongs as he told a joke to a group of men in matching short and T-shirt combos.

I smiled. 'He's definitely "Man in Charge of Fire".'

'Ug, ug. When Luke gets here, there'll be lots of references to "man tools".'

'And about his gigantic barbecue being compensation for a tiny knob.'

Dee's mouth twitched. 'Men,' she said indulgently.

'Men,' I agreed. We laughed.

Luke and Dan were proper mates. Although their friendship had been brought about by the closeness of their wives, it was a union in its own right nonetheless; games of pool, putting the world to rights over beers, jokey texts at all hours that caused them to snigger like schoolboys. Standard stuff, but there was genuine respect and affection there too . . . Maybe even a teeny bit of 'hetero man love', as Dee called it.

Dee flapped her face once more. 'Right. More people. I need to air kiss and host. I might even proper kiss a few of them, if they're dishy.'

I watched her as she set off down the lawn, her hot-pink prom dress flouncing around her knees. I sighed a breath of relief; Dan's sangria was legendary – laced heavily with booze, vodka-spiked fruit bobbing in it – and I couldn't possibly drink it. Dee was practically a member of the booze police and I knew she would be the most challenging person to keep my pregnancy-dictated avoidance of alcohol from, because drinking was a thing we did together, but, luckily, she was too busy circulating and introducing people as though they were on speed dates to notice.

My friendship with Dee – or Delilah, as she was known back then – began eight years ago, the summer I'd begun working at a book shop. We met in the deli next door, bonding over deliciously pungent houmous, and we cemented our friendship on a night out, working our way through the cocktail menu in a local bar. This, I learnt, was a normal night out for Dee, but it wasn't for me. I rarely drank in those days, nor was I much of a girl's girl. I wanted to be, but I struggled, and Dee was the extrovert required to bring me out of my shell. She introduced me to grown-up drinking: Porn Star Martinis ('because they come with a champagne chaser – it's the future, darling') and Salt 'n' Peppa Vodkas (neat vodka, with three olives providing the salt element, and a sprinkle of black pepper). Better still, she introduced me to her gaggle of loud friends and, after a few months spent in their company, I found I had gained confidence, although I'd never be Dee.

I glanced around Dee's sprawling garden. It was reasonably well looked after and, like their house, it was very much a family space. Dominated by climbing frames, swings and, the *pièce de résistance*, a vast treehouse, erected with much ugging and hammering by Dan in another macho moment.

I waved at Patricia and Nell as they strolled into the garden, glad to see people I recognised. Dee charmed men and women effortlessly and, being the total opposite myself, I envied Dee her enigmatic allure.

I was one of life's 'growers', a person others tended to need to get to know, rather than instantly warmed to. Dee had a number of opinionated theories about why this was the case, most of them blaming my 'kooky' parents and lack of siblings. She probably made a good point, but, whatever the reason, I was still really shy, despite the boost knowing Dee had given me. This, I'm told, translates to 'stand-offish' on initial contact. This fact distresses me – it's not the way I want to be seen – and I have tried to work on it, but it feels forced. And I admit: it's sometimes easy to forget to make the effort when Luke has enough charisma for the both of us.

Dee joined me again, raising an eyebrow at my still-full glass. Damn. I should have tossed it in the bushes.

'Drink up, Luce. You're lagging behind.'

'Sorry.' I made to sip it, close to blurting out my baby news. But we had agreed not to talk about the baby until the twenty-week scan this time. Our secret weighed heavily on my shoulders; Dee was my best friend and it didn't feel natural to keep this from her.

I glanced around for a suitable conversation point to distract Dee. I spotted a woman in a low-cut dress that showed off a plethora of daring tattoos and knew I was safe for the moment.

'Who's *that*? I haven't seen her at one of your shindigs before.'

Dee obliged with a peppy observation. '*That* is the wife of one of the artists at Dan's gallery. She's about to feature in her husband's explicit nude collection, would you believe?' Dee flipped her sunglasses down on to her nose. 'I must've been drinking champagne at one of Dan's events because I don't even remember inviting her . . . don't say it, Luce; I know I can't handle the bubbles. But honestly. We can see her bum cleavage from here, so I'm not sure the nude paintings will show us anything new. Apart from her fairy parts, perhaps – do you think she has those tattooed as well?'

I snorted. Fairy parts? For such an extrovert, Dee could be surprisingly prudish when it came to sex talk. I felt a sticky hand on my arm.

'What's bum cleavage?' Frankie's brow wrinkled. She wore a tiara at a rakish angle, giving her the air of an off-duty princess. 'And fairy parts?'

Dee looked vexed. 'Franks, you do have the most incredible timing. Can't you ever appear when I'm talking about school schedules?'

'You don't talk about school sched . . . whatever you said,' Frankie responded with the brutal honesty of a three-year-old.

'Are you wearing sun cream?' Dee fretted, expertly checking Frankie's shoulders for redness. 'And where's your hat?'

'It's gone.' Frankie's expression darkened. 'Not talking about it.' Ignoring her mother's look of agitation, she turned to me. 'Where's Uncle Luke?'

Where indeed? I checked my watch. 'He's working, sweetheart, but he promised me he'd be here for your Swingball championship.'

Frankie looked unimpressed. 'When I grow up, I'm not going to work at all. I'm going to be just like Mummy.'

'Charming.' Dee took a long, exasperated sip of sangria.

I hid a smile. 'Mummy does work, Franks. She works hard bringing up the three of you.'

I frowned. What was that? I had felt an odd sensation in my stomach. This pregnancy was scaring the hell out of me. I'd had a few strange twinges in my groin over the past few days, and was concentrating hard on not worrying about them.

'We're not *work*, Auntie Lucy.' Frankie shot her mother a withering look. 'We're just *children*.' Catching sight of her brother and sister terrorising a neighbour's child, she tore after them.

'Just children,' Dee echoed faintly. 'If only. I'd be amused if I thought she was joking.'

I watched Dee's three children charging down the garden, bellowing and galloping like wild animals.

Somehow, Dee and Dan had managed to divide their gene pool equally, giving Jack, their only son, Dee's height, blonde curls and clear blue eyes. Tilly, their second child, had Dan's expressive features, his unruly dark hair and the heavy-set jaw more suited to a man than a young girl. And Frankie, the child they hadn't planned, had inherited a rather exotic blend of them both, giving her dirty-blonde curls and heavy brows that Dee was already itching to wax.

Was our baby a boy? Would he be like Jack, boisterously confident, destroying everything in his path? Or perhaps a girl like Tilly – thoughtful and creative, but still prone to bouts of excitable shrieking and yodelling? Maybe we'd have one of those 4D scans everyone seemed to be having these days, the ones Dee said made babies look like freaky little aliens with webbed fingers.

'They're so very *loud*,' Dee continued, clutching her hair. 'They actually make my brain rattle sometimes.'

I felt something familiar struggling to break free and I squashed it down, hard. It wasn't just Dee's languid charm I envied. Her life seemed so perfect, so complete. The house, the garden, the fact that she and Dan were entirely suited – no, that wasn't it, because so were Luke and I. But the *children*. I closed my eyes briefly. If only I could be blessed with half . . . a *third*, of Dee's luck. Easy conceptions, smooth pregnancies, no major heartaches along the way.

I need to be clear about this: I loathed myself for the acrid ripples of jealousy that often poleaxed me without warning. Dee was my best friend and she had been supportive, sympathetic and downright heroic during the endless miscarriages and the ensuing heartache.

But somehow, Dee's ripe fertility left the stench of failure all over me. Two major events had rocked our friendship. The first had been the time Dee had admitted that she and Dan were pregnant again, by accident. Frankie's unexpected arrival had caused a new kind of grief. The choking kind that left a ball of spiky thistle in the back of my throat. An accidental baby? One that hadn't required temperature-taking, vitamins, injections or side effects? Dee's apologetic hug when she'd told me had almost tipped me over the edge and we had clung to one another wordlessly. What was there to say?

The second event had been more recent, the time Dee had cautiously suggested that I consider 'letting go' of my baby dreams. My fingers involuntarily curled around my glass of sangria at the memory, those feelings clawing at me again. Ferocious rage, screaming frustration and an urge to strike Dee had been so violently strong that I had been forced to stalk away at high speed. We hadn't spoken for a month and I had grieved for our friendship, certain we would never speak again. Dee had left countless pleading messages on my mobile, followed by some drunken ones accompanied by tuneless singing to the soundtrack of that old TV show *The Golden Girls* – we used to watch it constantly after nights out back in the day – and after the fifteenth rendition of 'Thank you for being a frrriiieeend', I had finally relented. I knew deep down that Dee had suggested giving up on our baby dreams because she cared. To underline the hideousness of the whole sorry episode, we had lost our second IVF baby shortly afterwards, and Dee had been almost as devastated as we had been.

Dee interrupted my reverie. 'Let's go and join Dan at the barbecue; he's looking forlorn.' We strolled towards the patio together.

'Good lord, who's that?' Dee said, waving to someone.

'Haven't a clue. Did Dan invite him? Nell looks gorgeous, doesn't she?'

She did. Luke's sister was naturally stylish with bobbed hair, the same chestnut-brown shade as Luke's. She was wearing what looked like one of her own creations, a stylish tea dress with an unusual hemline. The print was bold, but it suited her.

'That's Nell's friend Lisa,' I informed Dee, 'from school, I think. She owns about five clothes shops already. She's the archetypal business woman.'

'Wow. Five shops. That's so cool.'

Dee always admired other women who ran businesses. I had a suspicion she might harbour secret dreams of becoming the next female Richard Branson, if only she could find a slot in her children's busy social schedules.

'That guy she's being chatted up by is cute,' Dee said. 'Her type? . . . Oh, no, maybe not.'

Watching Nell politely brush the guy off, we waited for her to join us. 'Hey,' Nell said warmly. 'What a perfect day for a barbecue.'

'It's too bloody hot,' Dee grumbled, wiping her brow. 'This is what the menopause will be—'

'Ignore her; she gets crabby in the heat.' I turned to Nell. We really needed to get our friendship back on track – somehow we'd drifted lately. 'Listen, do you fancy

30

coming over for coffee tomorrow morning?' I intended to hide behind the kitchen counter and distract Nell with some bad cooking. Sweltering in the heat, I pulled my cardigan round my tummy to disguise the swell.

Nell seemed pleased. 'That sounds great. Oh dear, look at Mum. She's being chatted up by a man with a beard. She has a thing about beards. And not in a good way.'

'Who does?' Dee shuddered and waved Nell away. 'Go, rescue her.'

I put a hand on my stomach. There it was again. A tiny flutter inside. Like butterfly wings beating. It was the baby, it was moving. It was too early, surely? I gasped, turning away from Dee. The baby was stretching its limbs, wriggling, kicking. Relief coursed through me. There was nothing wrong. Everything was fine. My baby was growing and moving and it felt magical.

'Are you all right, Dan?' Dee frowned as Dan started frantically poking the sausages. They looked cremated.

He groaned. 'It's all gone a bit . . .'

'Pete Tong?' Luke appeared, putting his hands on Dan's shoulders. Wearing navy shorts and a crumpled white shirt, he looked as though he'd recently stepped out of the shower. 'Desperado, you are truly awful at cooking. Do you need some help, sweetie?'

'Finally, the cavalry arrives!' Dan clapped his hand on Luke's back in a display of manly camaraderie.

Luke noisily kissed Dan's cheek then did the same to Dee. 'Look at the size of that barbecue.' He turned back to Dan and rubbed his chin gravely. 'You know what they say about men and their barbecues don't you, Dee?'

Dee giggled as Dan handed Luke a beer.

'Shut up, you arse. And don't you dare mention my man tools.'

'Tongs.' Luke shook his head. 'You are *such* a girl, Danny boy.' He caught sight of me and immediately came over. 'Hey you,' he said in my ear. 'Everything okay?'

I nodded. I wanted to tell him about the baby moving but now wasn't the time. I leaned in and gave him a kiss. He hugged me, his hands on my back. There was something about the way Luke touched me that made me feel completely cherished. Or turned on. Depending on the type of touch on the given day.

'I missed you,' he said, pulling back to look into my eyes. 'That's totally naff, isn't it? I've only been at work.'

'Yes, it's totally naff. You're adorable though. Never stop saying stuff like that.'

I felt Dee watching us, but when I looked at her properly I wasn't quite sure what to read from her eyes.

I pushed Luke away jokingly. 'Go. Go and help your boyfriend.'

Luke grinned and strolled back to the barbecue. 'Hand your tongs over, boy,' he told Dan. He started to fork sausages on to a plate or into the bin, depending on their blackness.

The food was disappearing as fast as they were cooking it. I picked at an avocado salad and helped Frankie dissect a rather charred sausage she kept describing as 'dirty'. Dan was drunk and taking all the credit for the cooking. 'Well, my sausages might have been a bit burnt, but it's probably going to be better than Lucy's dinner tomorrow.'

I flicked his bare thigh hard, gratified when he yelped.

'Ouch!'

Luke handed the tongs back over. 'For that, my friend, you are on your own. No one disses my wife's cooking, not even me.'

'But it's really, really bad . . .' Dan protested.

'Enough! Bring me one of those burgers if it's a shade lighter than noir, would you, serving wench?' Skipping out the way of Dan's slap, Luke put his arm around my shoulder. 'Are you sure everything is all right? You look lovely, by the way. That purple thing is nice.'

'Really? My stomach shows under this cardigan and my boobs look massive.'

'Every cloud.' Luke tightened his grip. 'Not long now until the next scan. Counting the days.'

'I think Dee might have guessed about the baby but I haven't said anything.' I gestured to my untouched glass. 'But listen. I felt the baby move. Properly. I was panicking because of those twinges, but then it felt like something fluttering around inside me.'

'Christ, what have we got in there if it's got wings?' Luke went to laugh then stopped. 'God, that's amazing, Luce. What did it feel like? Tell me everything. Every single thing.'

I willingly described the extraordinary sensation, several times, in minute detail. I felt so incredibly happy and, as the night drew darker and the air chillier, I gratefully wrapped my cardigan around my stomach, keeping our secret that way for as long as possible.

Laughing as Luke and Dan danced to One Direction, even though they should have known better at their age, I allowed myself to relax. I chatted to Patricia briefly – the

33

usual chit-chat – but I was probably distracted by the baby sensations I was feeling. My arms ached – *ached* – at the thought of holding our baby, but this time it was a good feeling. A beautiful feeling. I could barely wait.

CHAPTER FIVE

Nell

Nell watched Lucy peering anxiously into the oven. She had some dodgy-looking meringues in there and, apparently, they were her fourth attempt. Nell couldn't imagine bothering to cook something twice, let alone four times. She might re-cut a pattern fifteen times until she got it right, but that was different; that was her passion. She guessed this anniversary meal must be enormously important to Lucy, especially since she detested cooking so much.

Nell glanced around the small but homely kitchen. It was immaculate, with everything in its place. With Lucy in charge, how could it be anything but? There was a huge bunch of fragrant yellow flowers on the windowsill, brightening the room. There were always flowers in the kitchen; it was Lucy's thing – well, Luke's thing for Lucy.

Nell watched her, wondering why she had been

cold-shouldered over the past few months. They were close and had been ever since Luke introduced Lucy to the family, so it was inexplicable. Upsetting, too.

Nell rolled her shoulders. It didn't matter. Lucy was being friendly again; they would be back on track in no time. Besides, was it only Lucy's fault they hadn't talked much recently? Nell had her own reasons for not challenging the distance that had developed between them.

'They won't cook any quicker if you stare at them, you know,' Nell found herself saying to Lucy. 'God, I'm turning into my mum. Stop me if I start banging on about the WI and poking my nose into everyone's business, won't you?'

'Nell, I don't think you're in any danger of *that*.'

This was followed by a semi-snort and Nell wondered if she had imagined the slight edge to Lucy's tone. Perhaps not. Her mum was horrendously nosy – they berated her for it all the time – and Nell knew that Lucy was a very private person.

Lucy straightened, her face flushed from the oven. 'So. I'm cheating a bit with a tomato bruschetta starter and I think I can just about cook the herby lamb things. It's just these awful, pissing meringues.' She wiped her furrowed brow. 'I mean, how is it possible to undercook them, overcook them and, my best one yet . . . turn them into shrivelled cowpats?'

'You know this is like the blind leading the blind?' Nell picked up the iPad Luke had left on the counter. 'How to cook the perfect meringue,' she began, skim-reading the page. 'Right. Apparently, you need to use a glass bowl, you mustn't get yolks into the whites and it's imperative that you use cream of tartar. What the hell is cream of tartar?'

'Buggered if I know,' Lucy replied, looking crestfallen. 'This was a really, really bad idea.'

Nell spotted a recipe on the internet page. 'Why not make Eton mess instead? If you have a meringue that's even vaguely decent, you could smash it up, smother it with cream and slap some berries on top. Luke won't even know he's eating a cowpat.'

'Genius. I'm sold.' Looking relieved, Lucy took a seat on a bar stool, her movements measured and careful, Nell noted. Why? What was that about?

Lucy pointed at the magazine Nell was thumbing through. '*Vogue*. That's probably a fashion student's bible, isn't it? Too many adverts for me, I'm afraid.'

'I'd kill to feature in one of those adverts. My fashion line, I mean. That's the plan . . . one day.'

'The next Vivienne Westwood.'

'Just . . . the new Nell Harte.' Nell felt herself flushing. She probably sounded pretentious. 'You know what I mean, though. I don't want to be compared to anyone else. I just want to do my thing.' She needn't have worried; Lucy hadn't noticed, seemingly preoccupied, if in a rather vague way, with a carton of coconut water.

'So, what's new with you?'

'Me? Not much. You know my life is dull. Do you have any news?'

Lucy shook her head, casting her eyes down. 'Not really. Obviously I got married five years ago today, but apart from that . . . nothing much to report, I'm afraid.'

Nell considered her sister-in-law. There was something different about her. She was wearing a new top, a floaty, floral effort, which wasn't her usual taste, but it wasn't just the clothes. Lucy had a great figure for fashion – slim, not remotely busty, slight hips – but actually, there seemed to be a fairly substantial bust there today. And the hips . . . Were they a little fuller? It was possible Lucy had put on a few pounds since they'd last had a proper chat, but Nell decided it suited her, career as a fashion model notwithstanding.

'Would you like some?' Nell gestured to the coconut water.

'Ummmm, no thank you.' Lucy pushed it away. 'It smells gross.'

'It doesn't taste much better than it smells,' Nell said, sipping it and gagging. 'All the rage, but like many fashions, style over substance.' She dumped it in the bin, noticing Lucy's expression flicker. Was something wrong? Nell felt anxious, but as Lucy's features settled, she relaxed again.

'Patricia was popular at the barbecue yesterday,' Lucy commented. 'Chatted up by all sorts of . . . by all sorts.'

'Yes, but she wasn't having any of it. I don't think she can see herself with anyone but Dad. I don't want her to replace him or anything either, but it would be nice to see her happy again.' Nell pulled a face. 'Not sure she gives off the right vibes though . . . she's a bit . . .'

'Detached?' Lucy offered.

Nell shrugged. 'I guess so. Yes.'

Lucy nodded distractedly. 'It must be hard for her.

I've only been married for five years, not the thirty – thirty-three?' She glanced at Nell who gave a nod of agreement. 'And I can't imagine being with anyone else but Luke. And I'm not just saying that because you're his sister.'

Nell smiled and chewed a stubby fingernail. She didn't know much about marriage, or relationships for that matter. She'd had a few boyfriends on and off since she was fifteen, but nothing serious. Not until now.

She was desperate to confide in someone and Lucy was here, now. Nell faltered. But maybe Luke was a better person to talk to about this. A man's perspective. She could guess what the woman's perspective would be. Actually, Nell mused, did she want to confess this particular deed to anyone at all? She already felt ashamed of herself and she wasn't sure she could handle more judgement.

Hearing Luke returning from his run, Nell edged herself off the bar stool. 'This has been lovely, but I'd better be off. I've got an evil new lecturer who thinks I need to work on my fashion portfolio, even though I've only been back at college for a few weeks.'

Nell suddenly noticed how pale Lucy looked and her brain kicked in. Swollen boobs, slightly fuller in the face, flinching at pungent smells. Of *course*.

'That *is* evil,' Lucy agreed. 'Poor you.' She stood up but remained behind the counter. 'Thanks for the meringue advice.'

'Any time. Thanks for the chat.' Nell walked around the counter and pulled Lucy into a warm hug. Yes, she was definitely right about her sister-in-law. That was a firm, pregnant stomach, all right. Nell felt a shiver of apprehension. This time. Let it happen for them this time.

'You're not leaving?' Luke strolled in wearing shorts and a damp-looking T-shirt. 'I've got to do an extra shift this afternoon, but you can stay for a bit, can't you?' He sniffed an armpit. 'Do I smell that bad?'

'Your feet do,' Lucy said, pulling a face.

'I have to do some work. Yuk . . . how do you put up with him, Luce?' Nell danced out of the way of his sweaty embrace and headed down the hallway.

'You dropped this.' Turning, she found Luke holding out a piece of paper.

She took it, feeling idiotic. 'You didn't—'

'Of course I didn't read it, Nell.' Luke's eyes assessed her. He was concerned, not judgemental. 'You still do that?'

Nell gave an off-hand shrug. 'Only now and again. That's an old one. I – I only do it when I feel a bit, you know . . . anxious.'

Luke nodded, seeming to accept what she said. 'Makes sense.' He put his hand on her arm. 'But you know you can talk to me about anything, don't you? Anything at all?'

'Yes. I do. And thank you. Don't worry about me, Luke; I'm fine. Enjoy your anniversary dinner, won't you? Even the cowpats.'

Leaving him to ponder that gem, Nell closed the door and leant against it. Why hadn't she said anything to Luke? He had given her the perfect opportunity to open up about it and she had chickened out. Maybe it was

40

okay to have a secret. Like them with their baby, maybe it was okay for her to keep this to herself.

Sitting in her bedroom later that afternoon, her portfolio open and untouched on the desk in front of her, Nell fidgeted. The vintage dressmaker's dummy she'd found in the shop in Camden – the delivery had cost more than the purchase price – stood regally next to her desk, wearing a half-finished pinafore. Nell wished she hadn't decided to add patch pockets; they were a nightmare to sew and she kept putting it off.

Sorting through some swatches of material, Nell tried to concentrate. Aside from the whirl of feelings that seemed to be paralysing her, her focus kept being splintered by crashing noises downstairs. Her mother, sorting through her cake tins, presumably to find the perfect size for whatever she was planning to create next. She sounded as though she was auditioning for *Stomp*.

Perhaps baking was like taking drugs for some people? Perhaps it dulled the pain the way alcohol or cocaine did? Nell couldn't remember her mother baking as much as this when her father had still been around, but maybe she was mistaken. God, she needed her own place. She started as she heard a knock on the door. Luke appeared.

'Hey. What are you doing here? I only saw you earlier on . . .' Nell half stood up.

'I was worried about you. Sit down, sit down.' Luke came in and closed the door pointedly. 'I'm on my way to my shift but I wanted to come and see you.'

Nell was touched. 'That's really nice of you.' She sat down and gestured to the bed. 'Sorry I can't offer you a spot on the sofa in my new pad,' she added wryly. 'The bed is the best I can do.'

'Still gagging to get your own place, then.' Luke threw himself carelessly on the bed, the way only a brother would.

'Is it that obvious?'

Nell smiled at the sight of Luke sprawled across the bed. It reminded her of the old days when they used to talk into the early hours of the morning before their mum stomped down the landing and scolded them.

'Yeah, it is. And I don't blame you. There's nothing like having your own flat or whatever, but it will happen, Nell. These things take time and you're only young.' Luke changed tack and cut to the chase, as was his way. 'So. The letters to Dad. I know you said that was an old one I picked up earlier, but was it?' His tone was gentle. 'I don't mean to pry. I just want to know that everything is all right with you. I mean, I know why you started writing those letters to Dad in the first place.' Luke's eyes dropped to Nell's wrists.

It was involuntary, but Nell found herself rubbing her left wrist. The right wrist bore matching scars but the left was far more deeply scored. She was right-handed; it made sense. The skin felt gnarly beneath her fingertips, a stark reminder of her past. The old feelings came rushing back. Her mouth suddenly felt parched. That inner panic, the feelings of appalling fear and apprehension were swirling in her stomach, gathering momentum. She fought them, hard. It took a minute or so, but she finally gained control again.

'I – I . . . honestly only do it now and again,' Nell

confessed. 'Write the letters, I mean. And only when something is on my mind.'

She stared up at her noticeboard. It was covered with torn-out magazine pictures, vintage postcards and quotes by Chanel, Lagerfeld, Valentino. It was her inspiration board, full of her passion. Nell couldn't understand why recently she wasn't moved by it. She hadn't been since she'd met . . . ever since . . . something had changed. She expelled air, wishing she could release the tension in her heart as easily.

'What's on your mind, Nell?' Luke sat up and gave her an intense stare. 'There can't be anything going on in your life you can't talk to me about, surely? This is me. Nothing shocks me and nothing will make me think worse of you. You know that.' He reached out and touched her knee. 'You're my little sis. I'll always be here for you.'

Moved to tears, Nell bit her lip. She wanted to unburden herself. But what could she say? That she had met someone? Someone who was not a 'long term prospect' as Ade would say, mostly because he spoke and wrote as though he was approaching a bank with a business plan, but *someone*, nonetheless. Someone she shouldn't have met, someone she had no right to be with. Nell shut the words down inside. She couldn't. She loved Luke and she trusted him with her life, but her woes weren't any of his concern right now. It was Luke and Lucy's wedding anniversary – hardly the time for Nell to be dropping her own rather unsavoury bombshell. And with Lucy most likely pregnant again, it felt even more distasteful to own up to her own, rather shady secret.

'Another time?' Nell offered weakly. 'I – I don't know if I'm in the mood for talking today. You go and enjoy your anniversary dinner. After your shift, anyway.' She checked her watch. 'You'd better make a move, hadn't you?'

Luke stood up. 'Yeah. If you're sure. But you know where I am, okay?' He bent and kissed Nell's head. 'I don't want you to feel alone ever again. Not like you did before. You have me and you always will.'

'I know that. Thank you.'

'Okay. I'll catch you later . . . I'll be in trouble if I'm late for my shift.'

Nell watched the door close behind him. Luke was right. She didn't need to feel alone. She had people she could talk to. She had her friend, Lisa – although Nell was fairly certain what Lisa's reaction would be to her news. Touching her wrist again briefly, Nell tugged her portfolio towards her and re-read her assignment. She had a lot of work to do. She'd be far better spending her time doing that than dwelling on her love life. There would be time enough for her to discuss her relationship woes with Luke. She'd tell him next time she saw him.

CHAPTER SIX

Lucy

'The food was amazing, really.' Luke took my hand across the table. 'I loved the Eton mess. *Loved* it.'

'Are you sure?'

I wanted to believe him, but I actually thought I'd burnt the meringues. Luke had (very sweetly) asked for seconds, but that was only because he had impeccable manners. Only an utter gentleman would have made such a furore over a couple of soggy bruschetta and a plate of over cooked herby lamb.

I sighed. I had no idea why I had bothered to try and cook. Neither of us were drinking, as I couldn't and because there was a chance Luke might have to go back to work. It might have helped wash down the terrible food I had cooked. I fervently hoped Luke didn't have to go back. We needed this meal, this time together. It was our wedding anniversary and we'd both been so stressed about the pregnancy.

But, cooking aside, I had come up trumps on the gift

front this time. I'd bought Luke an oak chopping board with 'Antihero' carved into the side which was a literary joke about his job. It had cost me an arm and a leg, not that I cared about that.

'Aaah.' Luke looked sheepish. 'I don't have your gift yet. I mean, I have a card and the gift will follow, if that makes sense.'

'Oh. Okay. No problem.'

I admit it; I was taken-aback. For Luke not to produce a gift was unlike him, out of character.

As he opened his chopping board, I drew his card out of its envelope.

Darling Lucy
Another incredible year together. I'm proud to call
you my girl every single day and I know we will
soon be holding our baby and moaning about sleep-
less nights. I long to moan about sleepless nights!
Your gift will be here soon, and it's a good one, I
promise!
  Love always, Luke x

'Awww.' I was touched. It was a lovely message . . . the best.

'I love this,' Luke said, turning the chopping board over in his hands. 'Antihero. Ha ha, brilliant!'

'Better that you do all the cooking in future.' I pulled a face at the burnt meringues and stood up to start clearing the plates.

'Don't be daft. Hey, sorry about the delay with the gift, but honestly, it will be worth the wait.' His face was

46

earnest. 'You know I always get on board with the whole present thing. But this gift took a bit longer than I thought it would and I have one thing left to do to make it perfect.'

I shifted in my seat. I had vague backache but our chairs were notoriously uncomfortable.

'You look amazing, you know that?'

'Do I?' I glanced down at my dress. I'd made an effort with a teal-coloured jersey concoction with capped sleeves and a deep V-neck that made the most of my new-found cleavage. It was a romantic dress for what I was determined would be a romantic night. The process of IVF was curiously neutral. Intimate in its own freakish way, but not between husband and wife. I wanted tonight to be about myself and Luke – about reconnecting – and most importantly, about remembering why we got together in the first place.

Luke turned in his chair and pulled me closer so I was standing between his legs. 'That dress is lovely, but it's not that. I haven't wanted to say this to you before now, because of . . . well, you know. But pregnancy suits you. You look beautiful. Really beautiful. It takes my breath away just to look at you.'

I was lost for words. Completely lost. I felt Luke's hand on my waist. He moved it across my stomach, across my swollen bump.

'I'm so excited about our future,' he said, his eyes clouding over with emotion. 'This is going to be the best thing that's ever happened to us, I just know it.'

'Me too.'

I felt such an intense rush of happiness, it threatened to blind me. This was going to be the making of us. This baby was everything we had ever wanted and I was going to do my very best to enjoy the final months of my pregnancy, to embrace this experience. I had wanted to so badly, but fear had held me back. I covered Luke's hand with mine so we were holding my bump together.

Luke stood up, cupping my neck. He kissed me, a sweet, gentle kiss that became more urgent. I kissed him back, sliding my arms around his waist. I knew his back was super-sensitive, so I ran my hands across it, smiling as he flinched with pleasure. He groaned.

I smiled, bending to kiss him again. I liked making Luke groan.

'No, it's my phone,' he said, reaching down and drawing it out of his pocket. 'It must be work.'

'Ignore it?' I said hopefully, resting my forehead on his shoulder. Oh, the frustration.

'I can't. Shit.' Luke checked the message. 'I need to go in. Christ. Talk about bad timing. It's only a four-hour shift, but still. Sorry, Luce.' He gave me a kiss, the kind that had a ring of promise. 'Let's reconvene later. Or in the morning. Shall we?'

I nodded. I could wait until then. Reluctantly, I let go of him, our fingers touching until the last second.

'We are such saps; I love it.' Luke headed out of the room, throwing a grin over his shoulder. 'Laters, dude.'

I held up a hand in farewell, the other wrapped around my tummy.

Five hours later
My back felt tight and cramps spiralled through my groin. I slowly lowered myself on to the bed. I hadn't

imagined it. That burning sensation I had been feeling earlier down one side of my groin was becoming more acute, the pain thrumming through my body. To think that earlier, all I was worrying about was burnt meringues and leathery lamb. Now, my adrenalin was pumping like crazy and I could hear rushing in my ears.

Where was Luke? I had left him a message, just a brief one, calm and without a hint of panic, but I hadn't heard back from him. The panic I had hidden was taking hold, gripping me round the throat. I needed to talk to someone, but it was Sunday; my midwife didn't seem to be on call today. I'd left her a message, too, not bothering to hide my terror this time.

I took some deep breaths, trying to work out whether I could move. There wasn't any blood; that had to be a good sign. The other times, there had always been blood. Blood before any proper cramps. I was tired, I had morning sickness from dawn until dusk and I was suffering from crippling migraines. But these were symptoms of a normal pregnancy; I had been assured of this.

Where the hell was Luke? His shift was a four hour one, I remembered him saying that. It had been five hours now and he still wasn't back.

My entire body felt icy with fear. The fear gripped me like a hand around my throat, choking me, squeezing until I could barely breathe. I was trying my best to stay calm, not to think the worst. But the pain was increasing with every passing second. My gut was telling me that something was very wrong. I needed Luke. Luke was the only person who could ever support me in these situations. He was the only person who understood me, who knew how to pull me out of the pit of despair I was spiralling into. Or to catch me if the worst happened.

I gasped as another painful cramp consumed me. I scrabbled for my mobile again. I could call Dee. I needed to speak to someone, to be reassured. No, I needed to get to hospital. Although I knew that if something had started to go wrong, there wasn't much that could stop it. I had been here before, so many times. But still, I needed to go. I just . . . didn't want to move. I just wanted to hold off a tiny bit longer, cling to the dream for a few more seconds. As soon as I called someone, it would become real.

Another sharp cramp shocked me with its force and made me reach for my mobile. This wasn't right; it didn't feel right. As a strong cramp tore through me, I bent over and screamed.

Twelve hours later
'Sweetheart, are you all right?'

I opened my eyes to find an unfamiliar face looming above mine. The eyes were full of sympathy and there was a hand holding my shoulder firmly. I was in a bed, but it wasn't mine; it was hard and unyielding and there was a starchy sheet pulled up around me, the cotton crisp.

'You were crying in your sleep,' the woman said, patting me. 'It's totally understandable in the circumstances. I've just started my shift, so I'll be here all night with you. Just call if you need me.' She moved away quietly, tending to someone else in a bed nearby.

Crying in my sleep? I blinked. My eyelids felt heavy and sore. I was in a hard bed with stiff sheets and the woman – I checked out the unflattering uniform – was a nurse. I was in hospital. What was I doing here? Where was Luke? I shifted myself up, beginning to feel scared. I felt bruised, inside and out. I moved my hands tentatively until they were on my stomach. It wasn't flat and it still felt firm-ish but I could tell it was . . . hollow. Empty.

I felt a sob rising in my throat. The memories came back in a rush: the pain, the frantic phone calls to the midwife, to Luke, and eventually, to Dee, who must've called the hospital. I gripped the sheet. Doctors, nurses, my clothes being removed, a gown being tied. My hand being held tightly by someone (Dee? A nurse?) and screaming for Luke. But he hadn't come. And I had . . . God, I couldn't even think about what I'd had to go through. Stillborn, they said. Just one of those dreadful, regrettable things, they said, stroking my sticky hair from my face.

My beautiful, four-month-old baby . . . the baby we had longed for, was gone forever. They said it was a girl. This, I had taken in. A girl. A girl who should have had stars on her ceiling and a pretty, lilac bedroom.

I put my hands on my face and started sobbing, chest heaving, shoulders shaking.

'Oh, darling.' Dee appeared carrying two paper cups with lids. Her blonde hair was in disarray and she was wearing a pair of Hello Kitty pyjama trousers and a massive grey Transformers T-shirt that must have belonged to Dan. 'I'm so desperately sorry.'

I started to cry again, hating myself for being such a girl. But it mattered, it mattered so much. The pain was unbearable. Not the physical pain, the other kind.

Dee put down the coffee. 'I guessed your news at the barbecue when you didn't drink Dan's sangria.' She took my hand and squeezed it. 'I don't even know what to say to you because it's so bloody cruel. I'm so fucking *angry* that this has happened to you again.'

'Where's Luke?' My voice sounded croaky.

Dee shook her head. 'I don't know. I've been so worried about you, I left it to Dan. He's been calling and calling, but he can't track him down.'

'Did you check my phone?'

Dee bit her lip. 'No. Sorry, Lucy; I didn't even think . . . it's all been so dramatic . . .'

'It's okay. I'll have a look. Where is it, Nurse?'

The nurse turned back to us. She picked up my notes and then her expression changed. 'Lucy Harte? I'm sorry, I didn't realise. You're Luke Harte's wife.'

'Yes.' I sat up. 'Has something happened?'

Dee stood up, her eyes darting around. 'What's going on? Please tell us.'

The nurse hung the notes back on the bed, her mouth tight. 'I'm going to get someone to come and see you. Wait here please, and I'll be back as soon as I can.'

I turned to Dee urgently. 'My phone . . .'

She rummaged in the bedside cabinet and found it. 'Here. Jesus, there are tons of missed messages. Are they from him?'

'No. Oh my God. I can't . . . Dee.' I listened to one of the messages. 'They're from Joe, Luke's partner. Christ, he's been in an accident – a serious one . . .' I put a hand to my mouth. 'We have to find him, now. Dee, help me . . . *please.*' I flipped back the sheet and swung my legs over the side of the bed, trembling as my feet hit the cold floor.

Dee stood paralysed. 'Shouldn't we just wait? Oh fuck it, we're doing this. I brought you some clothes . . .'

'No time. I want to find Luke.' I was petrified. What had happened to Luke?

'I get that, but . . . hang on.' Dee tore off her T-shirt, revealing a pink vest top. 'Put this on. And these.' She grabbed a pair of my flip flops from the side cabinet and threw them down by my feet. Grimly determined in spite of my fear, I led the way and we took a lift, two sets of stairs and meandered down several corridors. Dee kept trying to thrust me into empty wheelchairs that were lying around, but I refused, pausing only once to ask someone the way. The slap, slap, slap of my flip flops on the scrubbed hospital floor was driving me nuts, the sound incongruous against the relative hush of the corridors.

We were given directions to Luke's room and my heart threatened to leap out of my chest. I felt Dee reaching for my hand and I curled my fingers around hers.

We went in together, almost bumping into a youngish doctor – or was he a consultant? He had some notes in his hand and he was talking to a nurse. They were in the way of the bed and I couldn't see Luke.

'Mrs Harte? I was just about to come and find you. I'm Dr Wallis, Luke's consultant.' He seemed surprised to see me, but he was calm and pleasant.

I squeezed Dee's fingers. My terror was barely

contained; it simmered just below the surface. I could feel the blood pumping round my body, was suddenly aware of its ebb and flow.

Dr Wallis turned to me. 'This will probably be shocking for you, but I'm going to talk you through what happened to Luke tonight, okay?'

I think I nodded.

I stared past him, trying to catch sight of Luke. When I did, I felt as though I'd been knocked sideways. He didn't look like himself at all. His lovely face was caked with dark, dried blood, especially round his mouth. Someone had tried to clean him up but there had obviously been more important things to tend to.

'Luke was brought into A&E some hours ago,' Dr Wallis was saying. 'He was assessed by the trauma team and he was immediately referred to the general surgery team. The most life-threatening condition that needed to be dealt with was Luke's ruptured spleen.'

A ruptured spleen. I searched my memory, trying to recall Luke's study notes, the ones he used to recite aloud before exams. A ruptured spleen was dangerous but it might heal on its own or it could be removed.

I glanced at Luke again. His body was still, bizarrely so. Luke was never still; he was constantly talking, laughing, goofing around. He had bandages binding almost every limb, halting him, keeping him inert. He looked completely broken. Broken; as though he was made out of china, not from bones and organs and skin. What the hell had happened to him?

The specialist's voice swam into my consciousness. As well as the ruptured spleen, Luke had several broken bones, including ribs, both legs and collarbone. Damage to the spine, full extent of damage not yet known. A head injury resulting from a shaft of metal from the front grille of the lorry sticking out of Luke's head like a chocolate flake in an ice cream cone. Surgery to remove the metal.

'Luke also had a cardiac arrest when he was brought into A&E,' Dr Wallis said gently. 'We think this was as a result of hypovolemic shock, brought on by his ruptured spleen. Spleens bleed like you wouldn't believe,' he added, 'which in turn means there is a high risk of this kind of heart attack.'

'This kind of heart attack?' Dee asked, looking dazed. 'Is there more than one kind?'

Dr Wallis smiled at her. 'Yes. But I won't bore you with the details of the other kind. The only other thing I must add, Mrs Harte, is that we are monitoring Luke closely as he is at high risk of developing a blood clot. We call it an embolus,' he said, I think for Dee's benefit. 'Luke has undergone extensive surgery and now that he is immobile and in a comatose state, this is something that can be a concern.'

Really? A possible 'embolus' was cause for concern? Jesus. My brain couldn't compute any of this. I flinched inwardly from the onslaught of information; I had to break it down. Broken bones could be mended – or operated on, worst case. The spleen had been dealt with. Comas were beyond my comprehension though, not something I could drag from my memory bank.

I walked slowly to the bed. Luke was hooked up to lots of machines. They were beeping intermittently, overlapping one another with shrill monotony.

I reached out a hand. It was shaking horribly. I wanted to touch him. Would he feel cold to touch? No, how silly. His chest was rising and falling rhythmically, accompanied by artificial sucking and blowing noises, which would have sounded comical, except that they were anything but. I took Luke's hand. It was warm. Warm, but motionless. I gripped his hand, willing him to respond. His face remained immobile, his eyelids not even fluttering at the touch. He wasn't Luke.

Dr Wallis was still talking. 'The next few days will be critical. How Luke responds to his injuries early on will be a key indication of his overall recovery, but there is much for him to get through. If he stays in the coma for a few days or more, we'll probably run a CT scan. This rules out bleeds or infarcts.' His expression, when my utter bewilderment gave away how little I was following, was apologetic. 'As traumatic as this is for you to see, Luke's coma is probably helping him right now.'

I nodded. That I remembered. The coma was protecting Luke from the pain – it was the body's way of shutting down and coping. The specialist murmured a few more words to Dee, then left. The nurse stayed. Protocol in ICU; I knew that.

'He's going to be all right,' Dee said, putting her hand on mine. Her voice sounded artificially bright and I knew without turning round that she was crying. 'He's going to pull through and when he does, he's going to tell us to stop being so silly and emotional.'

'He . . . he doesn't know about the baby, Dee.' My chin quivered. 'Should I tell him about the baby? What do I . . . ? I don't know what to do.'

'Oh, darling.' Dee bent down and curled her arms around my neck.

I felt her rest her face against my hair, her cheeks wet. I swallowed, twice. I could feel something rising up inside me and I knew that, when it took hold, it was going to overwhelm me. I willed Luke to wake up and make my world right again. He didn't and it wasn't.

My heart clenched. I had lost our baby. I had lost our baby and my best friend, the one person I needed to talk to about it, was lying in a coma. I needed Luke's arms around me. I needed him to tell me it was all going to be all right, even though I knew it wasn't. I just wanted to hear his voice.

When Joe – Luke's paramedic partner – urgently dashed in and started telling me what had happened, I found myself unable to be brave any longer. Hearing Joe's earnest, apologetic account of the ghastly details, I broke down and sobbed.

CHAPTER SEVEN

Patricia

Thirty minutes later, Patricia arrived at the hospital. Inside Luke's room, she stopped abruptly in front of the bed. She wasn't prepared . . . she hadn't known what state he would be in. Lucy had left her a garbled message and, as soon as she had received it, Patricia had pulled on some clothes and driven to the hospital. But she hadn't expected this – she hadn't anticipated seeing her son looking as though he'd been broken in half and battered with a hammer.

Patricia felt hysteria coiling up inside her. *My boy. My beautiful boy.*

'What happened? How could this have happened?' Her voice became shrill even though she wasn't sure who exactly she was addressing. A nurse looked up. She was unperturbed by the emotional outburst and seemed about to speak, but when someone else entered the room she placidly returned to her notes.

'Mrs Harte. I'm so sorry.'

Distraught, Patricia turned. The young man who had just entered the room was vaguely familiar, but she couldn't place him. She willed her brain to catch up.

'I'm sorry. Have we . . . do I know you?' Patricia noticed that he was wearing the same teal outfit Luke wore. He was a paramedic.

'I'm Joe, Luke's partner,' the man explained. He was pale and his uniform was streaked with blood.

Patricia stared at it, sickened. Was that her son's blood? She put her hand to her mouth. She was in danger of throwing up all over Joe's trainers if she didn't concentrate with every fibre of her being. Patricia turned away. She focused on Luke again, trying to make sense of everything.

This wasn't right; she wasn't meant to see her son's life hanging in the balance like this. If anyone should leave this earth first, it should be her. Not that he was going to die. She wouldn't allow it. She would gather him up in her arms and bloody-well breathe for him if it came down to it.

Patricia was stricken. What could she do for her boy?

'I – I drive the ambulance,' Joe said, raising his voice a little. He rubbed a hand over his neck, seemingly unable to tear his eyes away from Luke's inert body.

'Were you with him when this . . .' Patricia waved a shaky hand in Luke's direction, 'happened?' Her vision swam and she was grateful when Joe guided her into the chair next to the bed, worried she might faint. She couldn't seem to stop shaking.

Joe took a deep breath. 'Yes, I was with Luke. I – I can't believe this.'

'Tell me what happened.'

Patricia knew she sounded peevish but she wanted to know the details.

Joe started speaking in an uneven tone. 'We were driving to a house on Charlotte Street . . . a woman had fallen down the stairs, suspected broken leg. We were almost there and I was about to turn . . . I checked both ways. Right, left, right. It's automatic, isn't it? I do it twenty . . . forty times a day.' He paused, the horror of the accident reflected in his eyes. 'I turned, with plenty of time to avoid oncoming traffic and this lorry came out of nowhere. It was going so fast, but I saw it and I tried to avoid it. I nearly made it, too; it was only a glancing blow.' Joe wiped a sleeve across his eyes. 'It ploughed into Luke's side, Mrs Harte. Right into it. The ambulance spun round once, maybe twice and then it tumbled right over and we hit the side of a house.'

Patricia sat numbly, gripping her handbag in order to contain herself. She sat primly, her knees and ankles rigidly locked. She was sure she must look frightful. Her hair was uncombed and she wore a crumpled top and skirt, the first thing she had happened upon when she had got Lucy's message.

Patricia could hear Joe speaking, but she could barely register what he was saying. In the distance, Patricia heard a piercing cry and she panicked that she had voiced the horror spiralling up inside her. But no, it was someone else in another room. Patricia relaxed fractionally. Her

60

agonised shrieks were still under wraps. Just about suppressed.

'I'm just so sorry, Mrs Harte,' Joe was saying, wringing his hands. 'I keep going through what happened in my head, reliving it to see if there was something I could do differently.' He shook his head. 'But I honestly don't think I could.'

'I'm sure it wasn't your fault, Joe,' Patricia replied automatically. She had no idea whose fault it was, but she felt the need to reassure this poor man who clearly blamed himself.

'Get yourself a cup of tea,' she told him, feeling that he might appreciate some motherly concern. It was the best she could manage, in the circumstances.

The nurse nodded. 'She's right, Joe. Get some rest. There's nothing more you can do here.'

Clearly dazed and perhaps realising he was superfluous, Joe left the room.

'What's going to happen to my son?' Patricia asked the nurse. 'Can someone please tell me? I'm . . . I'm thinking terrible things . . . I just . . .'

'Of course.' The nurse smoothly reassured her. 'Dr Wallis, Luke's specialist, has already been through the details with your daughter-in-law and I'm sure you'll be spoken to as well.'

Patricia nodded dazedly.

'Your daughter-in-law should be back soon,' the nurse reiterated. 'She's just gone for some final checks and then she'll be discharged.'

Final checks? Discharged? Puzzled, Patricia stared after the nurse. Lucy hadn't been with Luke in the ambulance,

61

so what on earth was the nurse talking about? Turning back to Luke, Patricia found her mind focused only on him.

My brilliant, funny son, she thought. Luke had been her rock when Bernard died. Clichés were clichés for a reason, as Bernard always said, and this one was true. Luke and Ade had shouldered the coffin together with the pall bearers at the funeral and when Ade hadn't been able to manage reading their father's favourite poem Luke had taken over. He had politely ushered everyone out of the wake when he noticed his mother crumbling and had put his arm around her when Ade couldn't.

'Do stop crying now, Mum,' Luke had said, dabbing clumsily at her face with a tissue. 'You look like Alice Cooper. Dad couldn't stand him.'

'I know. He always said he looked like a panda in drag.'

Luke smiled. 'Yeah, that was it. Look, you know you'll always have a plus one while I'm around, Mum. I might not be as handsome as Dad but I'm a much better dancer. Dad was the king of jive, but I do a mean Time Warp.' He had tightened his grip around her shoulders. 'Which is far cooler, when you think about it.'

She had soaked his jumper sleeve with tears at this, grateful for his support. Ade was the eldest, but he hadn't shown half of Luke's gumption and when – to her surprise and intense disappointment – he had let them all down for the last time, Luke had been left to pick up the pieces.

Patricia felt the familiar flash of resentment. Someone needed to tell Ade about Luke. Would he come home?

He deserved to know, he might want to come back. And where was Nell? Nell should be here; Patricia had called her as soon as she had received the call from Lucy. And where was Lucy? Patricia had no idea.

Unable to suppress it any longer, Patricia let out a heartfelt cry of anguish at what had happened to her beloved son.

CHAPTER EIGHT

Nell

Nell felt a warm arm snaking around her body. A male arm; solid and reassuring. Hairy, too. She opened her eyes blearily, wondering where she was. She snuck a look to her right. Ah, yes. It was all coming back to her now. She leant on her elbow and checked her watch. It was 4am. 4am on a Monday morning.

Nell lay back down with a jerky sigh. After struggling to concentrate on her portfolio the night before she had headed out for a few drinks with friends. It wasn't something she normally did on a Sunday night, but for some reason, she had felt the urge to let her hair down. And somehow, she had ended up here. Nell shifted slightly, hearing Cal stir.

Nell stared at the ceiling. She hadn't bargained on receiving a phone call from him asking her to come over to his flat late last night. Such a thing hadn't figured in her plans and she had surprised herself by hesitating. Or rather, she had been taken aback that she had hesitated for only the briefest of moments. It had been a booty call, but she hadn't been able to help herself. Which meant that she was weak. And stupid.

Did Cal deserve this, this instant acceptance of his request? Nell bit her stumpy fingernail, then abandoned it. He had barely spoken to her over the past few weeks. He had just about acknowledged her at college, but only because it had been unavoidable.

Nell knew she should feel guilty. She should feel used. But she didn't. She felt desired and loved and beautiful. She felt horribly guilty, too, but the other feelings were outweighing the bad stuff and that was what she was struggling with. Last night had felt special, just like the other times. It probably wasn't though – at least, not for him. How could it be?

Nell glanced round the room, not sure she liked what she saw. It was inherently masculine with dark furniture and old-fashioned drapes she suspected had come with the flat. The classic 'man cave'. But, on reflection, perhaps the fact that it lacked a woman's touch was for the best.

'Hey.'

Nell turned over. Cal's blonde hair was tousled and his eyes were a murky green in the faded light. He wasn't handsome, by any stretch of the imagination. He had a crooked nose, his face was a craggy map of wrinkles and he really needed a shave because her chin was ripped to pieces. He was also nearly thirty years older than her. And that wasn't the worst part.

Nell studied Cal. It was his mind she admired, his intellect. He was older, wiser, experienced and . . . yes, he was caring. He really was. Other women definitely found him sexy – she had heard some of her friends discussing him in lectures. Not that he actually conducted many these days. Since he'd been promoted to the title of professor, he told Nell, his days were spent wading through paperwork with the 'odd, joyous moment of teaching' thrown in.

Yes, Nell decided. Cal was sexy. But there had to be more to it, otherwise she was going straight to hell. She didn't have a current reference – the only one she could come up with was to liken Cal to the actor, Richard Burton. Maybe it was the Welsh thing; Nell wasn't sure. Or the charisma. Or the . . .

'I'm glad you came over.' Cal reached out and stroked her thigh.

Nell leant over to grab her T-shirt, pulling it over her head. 'Where's my phone? I thought I heard it in the night.'

'Haven't a clue.' Cal yawned. 'Check the floor. Most of your stuff ended up there.'

Nell got out of bed and gathered up her things. Finding her phone, she frowned, noticing a number of missed calls and texts. Feeling a shiver of apprehension, she listened to one of them and, in a heartbeat, she was galvanised into action. Pulling her clothes on haphazardly, she grabbed her handbag and threw on her jacket.

'Is something wrong?' Cal sat up, his eyes radiating concern.

'My brother . . . I have to get to the hospital.'

'He works there, right?'

Nell urgently headed towards the door. 'He's been in an accident. It's serious.'

Concerned, Cal padded over to her in his boxer shorts. He wore surprisingly trendy underwear for his age. 'Is there anything I can do?'

'No. No thanks. I'll be fine. I'm sure I'll be back for your lecture next week . . . especially as you don't lecture much these days.' She held something out. 'Here.'

Cal's fingers curled into a fist and his expression was rueful. 'Call me later. I know how much your brother means to you.'

A sob caught in Nell's throat. She wasn't sure Cal had the first idea how she felt about Luke; their feelings about the importance of family hardly tallied. No, that was unfair. He did understand. And he did realise how important family was, which was why he was beating himself up about what they were doing.

Cal caught her arm suddenly, pulling her close. Their noses touched. 'You know there has never been anyone else, don't you? I've never done this before. It's you . . . it's only because of the way I feel about you.'

Nell nodded, feeling a flash of pleasure. She left Cal standing in his boxers clutching his cold, abandoned wedding band and started frantically combing the streets for a taxi.

'Mum, calm down. He's going to pull through.'

Nell tried to take a full breath but found that she couldn't. She had tried hard to imagine how awful Luke might look on her taxi ride to the hospital, but this wasn't what she had expected. The sticky, rust-brown blood, the machines, Luke's dreadful pallor. It was shocking to see her brother, such a vital person, reduced to this.

'How do you know that? How can you possibly know that Luke will pull through?' Her mother was a mess, both physically and emotionally. Her hair was all over the place and she could barely string a sentence together. Pacing from one end of the room to another, she couldn't sit still for a second and it was putting Nell's nerves on edge, like someone stroking a cat the wrong way.

'I don't know, Mum,' Nell admitted. They were both shell-shocked, but for some reason, she felt that she should be the one saying all the right things. She hadn't cried yet, but she wanted to, just for the sheer release it would bring. 'I'm just trying to think positively, is all.'

'Where the hell have you been, anyway? Why didn't you come as soon as I called you?' Patricia's tone was accusatory, but she probably didn't realise how she sounded.

Nell opened her mouth then thought better of it. What could she say? That she'd been in bed with a married man – a professor at her college, no less? No. It was unthinkable, especially right at this moment.

Nell glanced at Luke. And to think she had waited to confide in him about Cal. Why had she waited? What was the point? Now it was too late. Not too late; what a stupid thing to think. Luke was going to come out of this, but Nell cursed herself for leaving it, for feeling the need to be secretive, even for a short while.

'Lucy.' Nell was stunned at the sight of her sister-in-law. She wore a grey Transformers T-shirt and a pair of flowery flip flops. Her cheeks were as grey as her top and her legs, naked up to mid-thigh, looked pale and vulnerable.

68

Nell stared at her, thinking how young Lucy looked without make-up. She looked out of place, like a student who'd wandered downstairs for breakfast after a heavy night.

Catching sight of her, Patricia spun round. 'Lucy. You must be distraught. Are you all right? And what are you wearing?'

Nell stared at Lucy. There was something strange about the exhausted slump of Lucy's shoulders, about the empty look in her eyes. Something else had happened. Something terrible. Nell's eyes dropped to Lucy's stomach. It looked oddly deflated. Nell felt a cry rising up and she clapped a hand to her mouth to keep it in.

Lucy slid into the chair next to Luke's bed, tiredly leaning her head against the wall. 'I – I was pregnant. Nearly sixteen weeks.' She wavered, clasping her knees with her hands.

'Was?' Patricia's hands started to shake.

'I'm afraid so.' Tears slid down Lucy's cheeks but her eyes seemed strangely glazed. 'I lost the baby in the night. They don't know why. They . . . they never know why.'

Patricia let out a strangled gasp.

'IVF, last attempt,' Lucy managed. 'A . . . a little girl.'

'No. Oh, Lucy, no.' Patricia shook her head repeatedly, back and forth, back and forth. She made to step forward, but her movements were wooden.

Nell took Lucy's hand. It was small and cold, like a child's. She hated that she had been right, that Lucy had been pregnant. And worst of all that she wasn't any more. Four months, four whole months. That only made the loss all the more tragic. And now Luke was in a coma. Poor, poor Lucy.

Nell felt something ripple up inside and she struggled to hold it back. Now wasn't the time for a panic attack. That would be selfish and inappropriate. Lucy was suffering a double tragedy; she was only suffering one. She simply had to breathe. In, out, concentrate, focus. Wasn't that what her therapist always used to say?

Nell saw her mother open her mouth, begin to say something. Almost in slow motion, Nell urged her to say nothing, to think before she spoke. Her mother wasn't known for her tact and Lucy had already been destroyed.

'Please don't,' Lucy said, before any words – right or wrong – could be uttered aloud. 'Patricia. Please. Please. I . . . I can't . . .'

Nell glanced at her mother, seeing the words freeze in her throat.

It was too much, too much for anyone to bear. Nell couldn't imagine how Lucy must be feeling. Losing their final IVF baby and now this, Luke, in a coma. Nell wanted to say something, but the right words wouldn't come.

Nell tried to ignore the sterile air that was permeating her nostrils, doing her best to put the image of Luke's rust-stained head out of her mind. Luke was going to be all right. He had to be. They needed him. They all needed him. Nell's thoughts shifted uncontrollably to her father and Ade. She had lost them, both of them. One had died, one had run away. Nell shrunk inside, transported to her teenage years. She was out of control, floundering, and now she was on the brink of losing another anchor.

Not Luke as well, not Luke as well . . .

Nell gritted her teeth. All she had to do was breathe. She couldn't fall apart and she couldn't act like this was worse for her than it was for anyone else. She simply had to breathe. Simple.

CHAPTER NINE

Lucy

There hadn't been much change to speak of. They said it was to be expected after such a severe accident and it was only the following day, so I shouldn't be downhearted about Luke's vitals looking pretty much the same.

Vitals. Vital signs. In Luke's case, in the state he was in, the description seemed to underline how very . . . un-vital he was. His body was too still, as if his dynamic energy and spirit was being held down beneath the sheets.

The hours since discovering him in ICU had limped past with agonising, unremarkable slowness. Another trip to surgery, the promise of a CT head scan which would reveal any bleeds or larger blood clots, but no real change.

The kindly Dr Wallis had been replaced by another consultant, or rather, a surgeon; a man with enormous teeth like tombstones. Apparently, this was all very normal; patients in a state of trauma were dealt with by a team of people, the lead changing as each different issue was dealt with. And this new consultant seemed incompetent by comparison. Perhaps he simply lacked Dr Wallis's excellent bedside manner, but when he evenly stated that Luke's leg was 'shattered', I couldn't help shivering. Shattered. Was that the finest choice of words? Was that the diplomatic best a consultant could come up with? Shattered was a word most people used to describe a broken glass. On the upside, not that the consultant described it that way, Luke's spinal injury was not as bad as they had first thought.

'Oh, hello, Mrs Harte,' a nurse said, coming in with a trolley. 'I need to change Luke's dressings. You can stay if you wish . . . ?'

I shook my head. I hadn't presumed myself squeamish, but when it came to Luke, I was. I'd rarely seen him bleeding before, a situation that had only come to my attention in the past day or so. Sure, Luke had cut himself when he was chopping vegetables or whatever, and he'd taken a tumble while running once – an amusing incident involving a fox and a badly lit alleyway. That time, he'd come back with a cut knee, a grazed elbow and a slightly sheepish expression, full of anecdotal details about the 'bastard fox' that had felled him. But that was it. He'd gone from childish knee-scraping to full-on gore in the space of a day. I wasn't used to seeing Luke's body falling apart. He put people back together, or at least he started to. At the scene of an accident, Luke leapt out and started the process of re-assembling and healing.

'I have to change his catheter now,' the nurse said. She looked cheerful rather than embarrassed, but was giving me the heads up if I wanted to leave. 'I can do this blindfolded; it's you I'm thinking of.'

I left. Luke gave me enough backchat for barging into our ensuite bathroom at home. 'Can't a man pee in peace, Stripes?' he'd yell as I apologetically giggled and backed out of the room with my hands over my eyes. The man had an absolute horror of being watched during seemingly innocuous toilet rituals.

God; even trivial memories of Luke made my heart feel as if it might explode. What was wrong with me?

I drifted into the waiting area. It was a dismal space; stark and unwelcoming, which was strange considering the amount of time friends and family of seriously hurt people spent in it. I realised the hospital budget didn't run to accent cushions and brightly coloured wall prints, but the hard, plastic chairs were unforgiving and not for long-term use. I sat on one of them and brought my knees up to my chest. My stomach felt . . . vacant. It was still rather wobbly, but the skin was contracting quickly. I'd spent however many years of my life without a baby inside me but now, everything about not having one there felt wrong to me. I closed my eyes, pushing back hot tears that I knew would fall if I let them. In a final act of cruelty, every pregnancy symptom had disappeared, almost immediately, in fact. My breasts were no longer tender, the intense nausea had dissipated, and with it, the special glow I had felt inside at harbouring a new life. And that unique fluttering sensation . . . I fumbled over this. That incredible, joyous feeling of my baby moving and stretching inside me had gone and I could barely remember what it felt like. I even missed

74

the hideous nausea because it had been such an inherent part of my pregnancy.

I gripped my knees. The sorrow I felt for our lost baby was overwhelming and, without Luke, I couldn't make sense of it. Was it my 'hostile environment' that had caused this to happen? Or was there some other reason this last little IVF baby hadn't been able to stick around? I had called my parents to let them know and they had been concerned, but predictably detached – or perhaps I felt detached from them and their well-intentioned, but somehow neutral, reaction to both bits of shocking news.

Did I want them to come down from Scotland, my mother had asked? I told them not to, that I would contact them if . . . when, Luke's prognosis changed. I couldn't see the point; my mother would be caring enough, but unable to offer me much in the way of emotional support, and my father would pat me woodenly and look uncomfortable. No, I was better off with Dee and Dan – with Nell. Patricia, even. Although things were still a little strained between us. That unspoken reproach of hers towards me over the baby stuff jabbed at me bitterly. Perhaps I was imagining it, but I had rather too much to worry about in terms of Luke's future right now to stress about Patricia's motives.

I felt bleak, but I couldn't help thinking that Luke would be urging me to pull myself together and be optimistic. Whatever happened, Luke always tried to see the positive in things. I wandered back into his room, certain the new wee bag must be in place by now.

The nurse absently smoothed the bed sheet into place.

'Have you and your husband . . . Luke, been together long?'

'Five years. No, sorry. We've been married for five years, but together for much longer than that.'

I took a seat next to Luke. He had been properly cleaned up and his freckles were visible beneath his fading tan. The bruise on his forehead was developing into a spectrum of impressive colours, as if Tilly or Frankie had been making his face up with eyeshadow. Most of his body was still tightly bandaged and the machines continued their monosyllabic blip and chhhh noises, over-compensating for Luke's complete silence.

It was so unlike him, to be silent, I thought, as I sat on the edge of his bed. Ever since we'd met, Luke had been at the centre of everything.

CHAPTER TEN

Lucy and Luke

June, eight years earlier

'Please come,' Dee pleaded. We were sitting in the tiny garden of her flat on the outskirts of Bath drinking very strong gin and tonics. 'It's a party; what's not to like?'

'Whose party?'

I adjusted my chair. It was one of those fold-up things that made one's backside sweaty and one's posture inelegant. Recently boyfriendless, I wasn't in the mood to hear about a party, let alone go to it. I berated myself for being so grumpy.

'Liberty's.' Dee pulled a face. 'She's pretentious, I know, but her parties are *fabulous*, Luce. Champagne in the bath, trendy live music.'

I glanced at her. There had to be more to it than that. Champagne and trendy live music were two a penny in the circles Dee moved in, even if Liberty's parents did own a gorgeous stately home thing just outside Bath. There was a man involved; there had to be.

I pulled at my hair, which was in desperate need of some sort of hair product. Heat made it frizz up like those bright orange crisps, Nik Naks. My hair wasn't orange, you understand. Just . . . full of kinks.

'Who's going?' I asked. It was a pointed question.

'Dan Sheppard,' Dee admitted, knowing there was no point in denying it.

I smiled. Dan Sheppard was an arty type Dee had recently met at her brother's barbecue. Usually cool about men she had a thing for, she'd talked about him non-stop since they'd met and that meant that Dee was *serious* about him.

I gulped down my gin and tonic. I knew I'd be going to the party, because my friend needed a wing-woman. But I was feeling rather low right now. Lack of boyfriend aside, I'd been working in a book shop for almost a year at this point and the literary degree I'd finished seven years ago felt like a distant memory. I felt as if I had lost my way a bit because, even though I wasn't overly ambitious, I did want to do something fulfilling with my life, something I enjoyed.

'I don't have anything to wear,' I offered lamely.

Dee leapt out of her fold-up chair – no mean feat – and kissed my cheek. 'Thank you, thank you, thank you! And I have plenty of clothes you can borrow. Let's go and find you a dress . . .'

And so it was that I found myself at Liberty's party, wearing a too-short, black-and-white-striped dress of Dee's that had me yanking the almost-pointless hem down over my bottom every two minutes. I made suitable murmurs of appreciation at the magnums of

Moët nestling in ice in the marble bath, and I dutifully agreed that the rather shouty live band Liberty had hired would be fantastic at Dee's brother's wedding in the autumn.

Sitting outside clutching a glass of champagne, even though I would have preferred a gin and slimline or one of Dee's Salt 'n' Peppa Vodkas, I nudged her. Liberty was heading over with a brown-haired man wearing slouchy Levi's and a Foo Fighters T-shirt. Whoever he was, he wasn't Dan Sheppard. I sighed. I was terrible at small talk.

'This is Luke Harte,' Liberty announced, pushing him forward like some sort of trophy wife. 'He's funny, charming and ridiculously clever, so I knew you'd both want to meet him.'

Luke Harte pulled a face. 'Holy shit. I'll never live up to *that* introduction. I'm not even remotely funny, for starters.' He grinned, Dee laughed and Liberty melted away, job done.

Luke Harte had managed to commandeer a beer, despite everyone else being forced to drink champagne, I noted rather sourly. He looked unabashed. 'Sorry about that. Liberty always says such embarrassing things. Hey, do you really think she's called Liberty?'

Dee eyed him approvingly and straightened the bold, off-the-shoulder floral dress she was wearing. 'I'm Dee. Delilah, actually,' she said. She held her hand out.

Amused, he took it, giving it a firm, non-flirtatious shake. 'You're shitting me. Parents Tom Jones fans?'

'Something like that.'

'You must get fed up with people chorusing "Why, why,

why" at you when they're drunk. A bit like being called Eileen when "Come On, Eileen" comes on. Nightmare.'

Dee was eyeing Luke appraisingly, almost as though she was wondering if he might be a better option than the elusive Dan Sheppard.

Luke's eyes drifted to me. 'What about you? Are you named after a song as well?'

I shook my head. 'Sorry, no. Nothing nearly as exciting.'

I didn't offer up my name at this juncture; what was the point? You know – we all know – when you've met someone who is out of your league.

Luke Harte was good looking. A nice chin, lovely eyes. I couldn't see the colour; it was too dark outside, but they looked friendly, sexy. He wouldn't be interested in me. Or was that my low self-esteem talking? My last boyfriend hadn't been a nice chap, as it turns out. Controlling and arrogant, I had recently struggled to work out why I had been attracted to him in the first place. I hadn't expected him to cheat on me twice, or for him to finish with me citing my 'anal retentiveness' as the reason.

That said, I possessed enough self-awareness to know that I was pretty enough. But I wasn't dazzling. And Luke Harte was one of life's dazzlers. It wasn't really about his looks – he exuded good humour and his wide smile and chatty style suggested he was used to being the life and soul of the party. Judging by the way he was leaning against the wooden post of the gazebo with a wide, chilled-out smile, Luke Harte was totally at ease in social situations and, if not arrogant, then he was confident in the extreme.

Luke looked genuinely disappointed though. 'That's a shame,' he responded lightly. Well, if you won't tell me your name, I'll just have to give you one. I hereby name you . . . Stripes.' He made the announcement rather grandly and gestured to my absurd dress.

I looked down, feeling self-conscious. 'This? It's too short and it's not even . . .'

'It's gorgeous,' Dee interrupted, getting to her feet. 'Doesn't it suit her? I told her it shows off all her best assets.'

'It certainly does.' Luke's eyes didn't leave my face.

I felt like a fraud. The dress wasn't even mine. Liberty had been right about Luke. He was certainly charming.

'Oooh, there's Dan.' Dee adjusted her dress. 'I'll go and say hi and grab us some more drinks.' She teetered away in the high heels that always gave her crippling blisters and we heard her loudly introducing herself.

'Right. That's my cue to leave.' I put my now-warm glass of champagne on the table and mustered up a polite smile.

'You're not serious, Stripes.' Luke straightened and placed his beer can on the table next to my champagne flute. The two drinks looked curiously intimate together.

'We've only just met,' Luke added. 'Stay. Talk to me.' He sounded almost flirtatious.

I wasn't equal to the task. 'I'm afraid I'm not very good company tonight.'

'Really?' He regarded me, seemingly concerned. 'What's up?'

I shrugged. I was sure Luke Harte didn't want to hear about my relationship issues. 'Oh, you know. Men.'

He smiled and rubbed his chin gravely. 'Ah, *men*. I'm familiar with this topic. I have a younger sister, Nell. She's told me some horrific tales about these beings.'

I couldn't help smiling back. 'Yes, well. I'm sure there are some nice ones out there, but my last boyfriend wasn't one of them.' To my surprise, I found myself giving Luke a quick run-through of key events, culminating in the humiliating confession-of-cheating-but-you're-dumped-anyway saga.

Luke frowned. 'What an idiot your ex is. I can only apologise on behalf of my species. We're not all like that, I promise.'

'I'm sure you're right.' I glanced over my shoulder to check on Dee and found her sitting on Dan's lap. She was fine, job done.

'I can prove it if you like,' Luke offered, his eyes creasing at the edges.

'Prove what?'

'That we're not all like him. Like your idiot of an ex-boyfriend.'

Was he asking me out? Surely not. I felt panicked. I wasn't ready for another relationship . . . or even a date. And with Luke Harte? I stared at him, realising he was younger than me, perhaps by five years or so. Dee would think it was brilliant if I dated a younger man, but I really wasn't sure I was up to it.

The romantic in me gave me an inner nudge. Was this one of those moments? One of life's opportunities that shouldn't be missed? I just didn't want to get hurt again.

'Come out with me,' Luke said, meeting my eyes. 'For

a drink. Dinner. The cinema. Bowling, if you're feeling competitive. I'm a master bowler.'

'I'm . . . I'm not very good at bowling.' It was lame, but I didn't know what else to say. I had a feeling I was blushing madly and wished I could duck out of the bright light that hung above us.

'Dinner then,' he said lightly. 'Surely you're good at eating dinner?'

He was mocking me, but only gently. I bit my lip. 'We'd have absolutely nothing in common,' I blurted out. I was mortified. Why had I said that? I sounded ridiculous.

He burst out laughing, unruffled. 'And what, pray tell, brings you to that conclusion?'

I had to justify myself after such a statement. 'Well . . . I'm shy, you're outgoing. I alphabetise my books; you probably stuff them into bookshelves any-old-how. Not that there's anything wrong with that,' I added to soften the blow.

Luke Harte held his hands up. 'Wow. You've definitely got me pegged. I *do* shove all my books on to the shelves in random order. How did you know that? Do I look like a messy, couldn't-care-less kind of a guy?'

As he moved under the gazebo light, I noticed that his eyes were a very nice shade of blue.

'Erm. I don't know. I just guessed about the books. Or rather, I just know that I'm weird compared to most people when it comes to these things.'

'Quirky, not weird. And opposites attract, remember. Clichés are clichés for a reason, as a very wise man once told me.'

I noted a wobble in his voice and I was intrigued. 'A wise man?'

'My father. He . . . he died a few years ago. We're all still reeling from it. My family, I mean. It's literally the worst pain I've ever felt in my life.'

'Gosh. I'm so sorry.'

Luke nodded. 'Thanks. It was grim, but we're all moving on now. Mostly. Anyway, are you close to your parents?'

'Not at all, unfortunately. I'm an only child . . . not planned, I think. I always felt a bit . . . superfluous.' I rolled my shoulders. 'But hey. They're okay, really. They live in Scotland now.'

'That's a shame.' He seemed genuinely sympathetic. 'Are you going to tell me your name now? I feel at a disadvantage. Especially now that we've . . . you know. Shared things.'

I managed a teasing glance. 'I don't think I will. Besides, there are plenty of other, prettier girls here for you to chat to.'

'Is that so?' A furrow appeared in his brow. 'What if I said I liked girls in short, stripy dresses who alphabetise their books?'

I felt laughter approaching. 'I'd tell you it was a phase. One I'm sure you'll grow out of very soon.' A giggle escaped.

'Ouch! That hurt, Stripes.' Luke clapped his hands to his chest, miming pain. 'But that just shows that you haven't got me pegged, after all.'

'Oh?'

Luke leaned against the post and folded his arms across his chest, decapitating the Foo Fighters. 'Because if you knew me better, you'd know that I don't go in for phases. Things I care about, I stick with. My family and my career, to give you a couple of examples.'

I considered him. He was definitely younger than me, in his early twenties, I would say at a guess.

'I'm a paramedic, for my sins.' Luke's mouth twitched. 'Soon to be, anyway. I know, I know; you think I'm doing it for the glory. I expect you think I support Man United, too.'

I was impressed; I admit it. Which was ridiculous. He saved lives, but so did lots of people. It suited him though. It gave his good looks and charming patter credibility. Which made him seem even more attractive. Dammit. How very annoying.

'If you'd seen some of the things I've seen . . . injured children, domestic abuse, stuff like that.' He looked serious for the first time, his mouth settling into a sober line. 'But enough about me . . . what do you do?'

'I work in this book shop.' I cringed, thinking this must sound rather rubbish compared to being a paramedic. Luke looked interested, however, so I carried on. 'It's lovely and my boss is this sweet, old guy who's really nice to me and pays me far too much, but it's not necessarily my vocation, you know?'

'Do you know what that is?'

I shook my head and laughed. 'No! Not exactly. I studied literature, but I'd really just be happy to do something that made me feel . . . uplifted. It doesn't have to be something incredible like being a paramedic, but something fun. Something . . . positive. That probably sounds strange. Sorry.'

'No, it doesn't.'

Luke's mouth curled up as if he was thinking about something and he drummed his fingers on his arm. I wondered if it was a habit that might become annoying, then decided that it wasn't. And that I was getting ahead of myself.

'I know this might sound a bit weird, but if you really want a change, my mum could do with an extra pair of hands in the family business. It's a florist.'

A florist? I faltered. I thought about it. I supposed it could be rather lovely working with flowers. Apart from condolence ones, presumably. I had always loved flowers, but I was relatively clueless about the different kinds.

'Think about it,' Luke said. He added a casual shrug. 'It's in the centre of town and the pay isn't bad at all. I know my mum could do with some help, so if you're really pushed, it's an option.'

'Okay. Thanks. That's really kind of you.'

'I'm not being kind, if I'm honest. The job is real, but I'm also trying to engineer a situation where you won't be able to reject my advances so easily.'

That lovely smile again. I was seriously in danger of becoming smitten with Luke Harte.

'I should go . . . Dee's calling me over . . .' My voice registered my regret.

Luke stopped me by taking my hand. 'Listen. Stripes. You're the most fascinating girl I've met in ages. You're funny, you're super-organised – which I love, incidentally – and you're beautiful. Quirky-beautiful. That's the best kind, by the way.'

That did it for me. Luke Harte was too much for me. When had anyone told me I was beautiful, let alone 'quirky-beautiful'? I was scared. Petrified, in fact.

'I – I have to go,' I mumbled, stumbling away from him. When I reached Dee, I stole a glance over my shoulder, my heart beating a bit more quickly than usual. But Luke Harte had gone; melting into the darkness like a ghost. It was almost as if our chat hadn't happened.

I spent the next month thinking non-stop about Luke bloody Harte. About him asking me out, about me saying no. About me telling him about my idiot of an ex-boyfriend and about him opening up about his dad. I don't think I'd ever spoken to a stranger about myself so much.

Then one day, he just turned up. Dazzling Luke Harte turned up in the little book shop I worked in, wearing his teal paramedic's outfit and claiming, with a mischievous smile, to be in the mood for book-buying.

'Fill your boots,' I said, delighted to see him. I watched in amusement as he carefully selected books about caring for gladioli, the Second World War and the practicalities of owning a greenhouse.

'Actually, I'm not really here to buy books,' Luke sheepishly confessed after presenting my boss with a twenty pound note, with the change to go in the charity box on the desk. My boss gazed at him adoringly.

'No?' I said.

'No. I'm here to ask you out again and I'm not taking

no for an answer.' He grinned. 'I'll stage a sit-in, if I have to.'

'Goodness. A sit-in. How passionate you are.'

'You have no idea.' Luke laughed at his own awful joke. 'Seriously. You name it, we'll do it, date-wise. Decorating cupcakes, feeding monkeys at the zoo . . . shopping for clothes.' He covered his face. 'God. That's how desperate I am. I'm offering to go shopping for clothes. I'm a disgrace to men the world over.'

I melted. Who could resist such an advance? 'I'm in,' I told him with a stupid grin. In reality, I was more than 'in'. I was hurtling, fast-falling, utterly bowled over. Despite being terrible at bowling.

Later, Luke told me that he had spent five weeks tracking me down, the delay caused by Liberty being sent on a month-long cruise with her least favourite aunt as a punishment for the wild party.

Our love story, as Dee liked to call it, was kind of old-fashioned. Cosy dinner dates, endless chats into the early hours of the morning. A slow, heady burn between us that had taken my breath away in the early weeks and that swiftly turned into body-shuddering passion. I gave up my job in the book shop and I started working at Hartes & Flowers. I loved it and I loved this man that had come into my life like a whirlwind, with his romance and his eyes and his words.

And at the point, pretty early on, where Luke quietly said: 'Lucy, I'm so in love with you, I can't even bear it,' I felt an exquisite rush of relief. I had fallen in love with him long, long before that moment and the agony of worrying that he didn't feel the same way had almost killed me.

Being chased by a man like Luke had turned my life on its axis. Losing him really wasn't an option.

CHAPTER ELEVEN

Nell

September

Nell balanced the notepad on her lap, but her nervous, jiggling leg kept knocking it off. She glanced over her shoulder, certain all the other students sharing the grassy bank with her must have spotted the state she was in, but they were oblivious. Smoking, chatting, reading, exclaiming over something outrageous in *Tatler*. The last thing they were doing was paying any attention to Nell or her inner panic. They were all at college for a meeting to collect coursework notes and information about their final year, but Nell couldn't stop thinking about Luke. What if he woke up and she missed it?

It was a beautiful day, sunny and clear, she observed. The kind of day that brought everyone outside for a breath of fresh air and the feeling of warmth on skin. The world was still turning and she couldn't help resenting it. Luke had almost died. Luke might still die. Yet everyone was continuing with their lives without a care in the world. Even *she* was continuing with her life. It had only been two days since Luke's accident, but, frighteningly, there had been no change.

Nell made an effort to still her jiggling leg. She needed to talk to someone. There had to be someone else she could speak to rather than doing this, surely? But her closest friend Becks had moved away and phone calls weren't the same thing as face to face. She had other friends like Lisa, but she was so busy with her shops . . . besides, Nell didn't feel comfortable speaking to Lisa about Luke; it felt too personal. Which was ridiculous, but Nell wanted to keep what had happened to Luke wrapped up in a bubble, close to her heart. At least until they knew what the outcome was going to be.

Nell thought about talking to Cal. She hadn't seen him since she left his flat the other night. She hadn't been into college until today and she could hardly ring him at home; his wife might answer. Or one of his kids – an awful thought. He used his mobile to contact her but he had actively discouraged her from contacting *him* that way. Which left her in no man's-land, basically. Out of contact and out of control. She could try him at the flat she had stayed at the other night – it used to belong to Cal's uncle and he stayed there a fair amount during the week, as he lived an hour or so away by car. But Nell didn't want to approach him . . . it felt too forward, too needy.

The guilt about Cal's wife and children threatened to suffocate her every time she thought about them. But Nell wasn't about to feel sorry for herself. She deserved to feel guilty – she had done a bad thing. More than once. She pulled the notepad closer, knowing what she was about to do. Was it weird? Maybe, but it had helped her all those years ago . . . perhaps it would help her now. Nell didn't feel she had a choice. He was the only person she could talk to right now.

Dad,
It's me. We haven't spoken for a while, so I thought I'd check in. You don't mind me writing to you, do you? That therapist thought it was a good idea when I was a kid, a way for me to 'get my feelings out when I couldn't vocalise them'. I didn't. I was so angry, I called her a name a twelve-year-old shouldn't say out loud and the therapist was terribly understanding about it. I was livid. How dare she be so sympathetic and insightful?

The thing is . . . I have news. Not good news. And you're pretty much the first person I wanted to talk about it with. Here goes. Luke is in a coma. Lucy lost their last IVF baby. Read that again. I know. It's horrendous. I can't compute it, can't even understand how this can have happened. It's the sort of thing that happens to someone else, isn't it? And just one of those things, not two at the same time.

Really, Dad, I hate to sound trite, but if you know anyone with any clout up there, kick them in the bollocks, will you? Because this is really, really shit and they don't deserve this. Lucy and Luke are good people – the best.

To make matters worse, when it all happened, I was in bed with someone. A married man, Dad. MARRIED. And he's one of my lecturers at college.

Yeah. I know. I can imagine what you're thinking.
Not what you want to hear about your little girl,
but you don't have to tell me how stupid I am,
because I already know. Trouble is, I think I kind of
love him. That sounds juvenile. I don't 'think' and I
don't 'kind of'. I just do. Love him, that is. And it's
scary. I've fallen hard and quickly – the worst way
to fall, right? Especially when you know that person
isn't right for you. I haven't told anyone yet, by the
way. Not even him.

Listen, I've emailed Ade to tell him about Luke
and I think he's coming home once he's sorted a
few things out. He was devastated . . . really
shocked. I'm not sure how Mum will feel about Ade
possibly coming back; she doesn't even know Ade
and I are in touch, albeit sporadically. They haven't
spoken for years . . . since Ade left, in fact.

Anyway, that's it, Dad. A lot to take in, I know.
If I can just leave it with you, you know, the
kicking in the bollocks bit? Thanks. I wish I
could . . .

Nell broke off, feeling someone peering over her shoulder. She screwed the piece of paper up into a ball.

'What's that?'

It was Cal. He looked rather professorial in a jacket with those weird leather patches at the elbows. Surely rather warm on a day like today?

'Are you starting your new assignment already?'

'Er, no.' Nell shoved the balled-up letter into her bag. 'Sorry. What with Luke and everything . . .'

'Of course, the accident.' Cal shifted the stack of papers he was carrying from one arm to the other. The sun made his golden hair appear dappled. 'Yes. How is he? Any change? I'm worried about him. About you.'

Nell felt as if she was basking in the glow of his concern and she felt a flash of something inside. No. She tried to push it down. She didn't want to love Cal. She wasn't allowed.

'No, he's the same. So, he's terrible, basically. He's in a coma and my sister-in-law lost their baby the same day. She was four months pregnant.'

Shock registered on Cal's face. 'Darling. That's horrendous.' He gave a courteous nod to another senior-looking lecturer before squatting down beside Nell. 'You've been through hell. Are you okay?'

Nell shook her head. 'Not really. No, I'm not. He's . . . Luke's broken.' She sniffed. 'I mean, literally. He's broken almost every bone and they think he might have brain damage. He's not responding to anyone and the doctors keep doing that thing where they deliver the same news over and over again, something in their manner telling you to prepare yourself for the worst, you know?'

Cal's brows knitted together. 'Really? You get that from them repeating the same prognosis?' His eyes, when they met hers, were gentle, kindly. 'Are you sure you're not reading too much into things, Nell? Just because it looks bleak at the moment doesn't mean that your brother won't get better. I've been in a few situations like this . . . not as awful, obviously,' he added hurriedly, 'but I really don't think you can assume all that from them repeating a prognosis.'

94

Nell felt unconvinced, but she supposed Cal probably had more experience of these kinds of things than she did. 'It will be all right,' Cal assured her, standing up again. He flexed his back slightly as if it hadn't taken kindly to squatting down.

Nell joined him. 'It just feels as though everything has fallen apart.'

'Not everything.' Cal leaned in as close as he could without touching her. 'I'm here. For you. And I hate seeing you like this. What can I do to help?'

Nell shook her head helplessly. 'Nothing. There's nothing you can do. At least . . .'

She looked up at Cal, noticing how tanned his crooked nose was. Perhaps he marked assignments in his back garden while his children bounced on a trampoline and his wife brought him a cold beer. Nell closed her eyes, banishing the image as well as the ugly jealousy that came with it. She had no right to that feeling. Cal didn't belong to her; he belonged to someone else.

Nell turned the subject back to Luke. 'I'm going to visit him later. Come with me? I could do with some moral support.'

Cal rubbed his stubbly chin. It made a rasping sound. 'Er, well. That could be tricky. I mean, I want to, but I'm not sure I can.'

Nell brushed grass from the hem of her dress. 'You're busy . . . I understand . . .'

'Well, it's not so much that.' Cal hoisted his papers up again. 'It's just . . . Nell, you must know that people can't see us out together? My marriage, my career – there's an awful lot at stake.'

Nell's hand, still dusting off shards of grass, halted. 'Oh. I see.' She let out a bitter laugh. 'And there was me worrying about you being tied up with lectures. Don't worry about it, Cal. As you say . . . there's an awful lot at stake here.' *My brother's life, for one,* she thought, distraught.

'Nell—' Cal put a hand out, almost dropping his stack of assignments. 'Don't be like that. You mean the world to me; you know you do.'

'It's okay. Look, I have to go. I need to email my brother.'

'Your brother?' Cal looked perplexed.

'Yes, my brother. Not Luke; Ade . . . obviously.'

'Who's Ade?' Cal looked even more bewildered. 'You've never mentioned Ade before.'

Nell glanced at him, astonished. Surely she had told him about Ade? How had she missed that bit of information? She supposed she was touchy about Ade . . . it was one of those subjects she didn't offer up unless she really trusted someone. She thought she trusted Cal. Perhaps she had kept something back after all.

Cal shook his head. 'Before you berate me for my lack of support and for being human enough to worry about my job and my home life, despite the way I feel about you, ask yourself how much you've even let me into your bloody life, Nell. I'm taking massive risks every day for us and you don't even talk to me about the important stuff. This is the first time I've ever done this . . . ever had an affair . . . and it's beginning to feel like a one-way street.' He stalked past her, leaving behind an air of injured indignation and a waft of Hugo Boss.

Nell, aware that a few nearby fashion students were eyeing her curiously, put her head down and carried on walking. Cal had a cheek talking about how much she'd let him into her life. *She* didn't have a wife and children. *She* wasn't the one saying they couldn't be seen in public. At her brother's bedside, of all places. *Really?*

Flame-cheeked, Nell stormed out of college, despite having a full day of lectures.

CHAPTER TWELVE

Lucy

Sent home to take a break and have a shower, I hesitated outside the front door. They had allowed me to sleep on a pull-out bed next to Luke's so I hadn't been home since Luke's accident two days ago. Since . . . the miscarriage. My breath caught on that word, a word I had hoped never to utter again, even in my mind. I leant my head against the door, trying to lift my aching heart. If only Luke was here.

Sorrow is a heavy, suffocating feeling that we have probably all been familiar with at different times in our lives, but I was taken aback at how cumbersome a burden single-handed grief was proving to be. Aware that I probably looked like a crazy person, I lifted my head from the door and reached for my keys. My neighbour, an elderly man named Errol, paused whilst hoisting his shopping from his car boot. He bobbed his head in my direction and I caught a sob in my throat. Having lost his beloved wife of fifty years a few months back, I guessed Errol knew all about single-handed grief. I was touched, but unequal to the task of responding, so I held up a trembling hand. I struggled with my front door key, my fingers fumbling with the lock. I paused, collecting myself. I had to do this. On the upside, I wasn't likely to trip over baby stuff. We had still felt superstitious about the pregnancy, so we were planning to leave everything until the last few months, when we felt more secure. Was that wrong? Did that mean that deep down we hadn't believed we were actually ever going to be holding this baby in our arms? I didn't know any more . . . the right or wrong approach to making my pregnancies last had gone beyond me.

Opening the door, I suddenly wondered if I might actually have found this easier if there was the odd baby thing for me to cling to. A baby grow, perhaps; something to sob into, just to vent some of this pent-up emotion. It was difficult enough to deal with Luke's presence in the house. He was absent, but at the same time he was everywhere . . . the imprint of him, at least.

Closing the front door, I felt his absence acutely. His car keys were strewn across the table rather than hung up on the hook on the wall – of course; Luke had an anathema of putting things in their rightful places. His battered, slightly stinky trainers lay underneath the table, abandoned, as usual, the second he returned from a run and tore them off. I had often threatened to put them in the washing machine or, worse, throw them in the bin, but in this empty house they were an echo of him. I could almost see him bursting through the doorway, exhilarated from his run, the trainers the first thing to come off and be messily tossed aside.

'Don't bin them, Luce,' Luke would beg. 'I've broken them in . . . moulded them to my freaky toes. You wouldn't deprive a man of his favourite running shoes now, would you?'

I would elbow him away, smiling, wishing he was tidier. Some hope. Without entering the kitchen, I knew there would be a half-finished sachet of the strong coffee beans only Luke could tolerate next to his beloved DeLonghi machine. Not in the cupboard above the machine, but next to it . . . open and aromatic. There was. The kitchen smelt strange, though, and I realised there were no fresh flowers. Of course not. Luke always bought those for me.

I walked up the stairs slowly, knowing that in our bedroom I would find a pile of worn T-shirts flung carelessly on the chair, despite the linen basket keeping the chair company in the corner. The walls had been stripped of paper months ago and there were several paint samples marked on the walls; various shades of beige – my choices – and a few brighter colours like emerald-green, coral and a blue I can only describe as electric. This was Luke's way of trying to get me to be more daring, not as 'vanilla', as he put it. But we hadn't yet agreed on a colour scheme, and Luke detested painting. I was a dab hand with a paintbrush, but I wasn't any good at fixing wardrobes or putting up shelves. Mind you, neither was Luke.

I heard a bleep and took out my phone, but there were no messages. I removed Luke's phone from my other pocket. There were two messages; I must have missed the earlier one. They were all from someone called 'Tiggsy', not a name I was familiar with. I opened the most recent one. It said:

Feel better soon, thinking of you.

I read it again. Tiggsy. No, it didn't mean a thing to me. Luke hadn't mentioned this person before. Male or female? I couldn't tell from the text. It was brief, neutral. It must be someone Luke was close to, otherwise he wouldn't have given them a nickname. Although . . . whoever this Tiggsy was, he or she didn't know the extent of Luke's injuries, which was weird. I experienced a moment of uneasiness but it was soon forgotten when I noticed that the baby manual I kept on my bedside table had been moved. Had Patricia or Nell taken it? Had they used a spare key to come round and remove all traces of the baby Luke and I were supposed to have? I looked around. Nothing else had been moved or removed. Everything else was the same. Except . . . in the exact spot the book had been was the key to the spare room – a large, old-fashioned key that looked as though it should open a grand, magical room from a fairy-tale.

The spare room was full of Luke's medical journals, and a huge pile of clothes and old childhood stuff he hadn't got round to sorting; hence the reason it tended to be locked, so I could do my best to ignore the muddle and clutter.

Why was the key here? Did I really want to go and look at Luke's medical books right now? But I had to know why the book had been moved and replaced with the key; it would irritate me otherwise. Sighing, I headed across the landing and unlocked the door.

I switched the light on and my hand slipped off the

door handle. Luke's books, clothes and childhood crap were nowhere to be seen. The spare room had been turned into a nursery. Painted a neutral cream with touches of yellow, a blackout blind already rigged up and an ivory cot tucked into one corner; it took my breath away.

A Winnie-the-Pooh mobile lay unmade in the cot and a soft-looking yellow blanket had been carefully folded and placed on the mattress. A matching dresser was home to a huge, smiley teddy bear and next to it, a bookcase containing brightly coloured baby books. On the top shelf, there was a bundle of books tied together clumsily with a green ribbon, a random selection that wouldn't mean anything to anyone apart from me and Luke. A book about greenhouses, another, hefty tome about the Second World War and a really boring one about gladioli. A note was attached to it. It said: 'How Mummy and Daddy Met – A Fun Tale for When You're Older.' A few aged copies of *Wuthering Heights* from my collection. And there was my baby manual, next to it. I felt a strong tugging sensation in my chest.

Taking in the rest of the room, I turned around. On the opposite wall, there was a narrow wardrobe, with one door ajar.

I saw something hanging in it and, feeling my stomach curl, I took slow steps towards it. There were two baby grows, one baby-blue, one pale-pink. On the chest of each were the words 'I Love Mummy'. Blue for a boy, pink for a girl. It didn't matter which we'd had; Luke had been prepared for both. Either. My gaze blurred and I put a hand to my face. Tears. More tears. Bittersweet ones. My heart splintered as I reached out and touched one of the baby grows. The pink one. Oh God. I still had to sort 'arrangements' at the hospital. A funeral. I was dreading it. But I had to do something; a shoe box wasn't going to cut it this time.

Something else in the bookcase caught my eye. A card. 'Happy Anniversary, Stripes,' it said. Luke. *Luke*. Proper tears came then, ones with big, racking sobs and snot. He hadn't forgotten our anniversary . . . He'd been planning this surprise. He hadn't doubted that our baby would arrive. Luke had been hopeful, confident, *certain*. He had wanted me to see this, to see how much he believed we could be a family.

When had Luke done this? It had to be the weekend I visited my parents in Scotland – I hadn't been out of the house long enough for Luke to have pulled this off otherwise. But that had been a long time ago, six weeks ago at least. I had spent the entire weekend there, and I had been petrified my parents might spot my pregnancy, but I needn't have worried; they had both been far too preoccupied with the damp problem in their house and the horrible Scottish weather to even bat an eyelid at my blooming stomach and growing chest.

I sat on the floor, holding the card. I lifted it to my nose, hoping to catch a whiff of Luke's aftershave. I didn't; it smelt of card. I put it down and took out Luke's phone. I realised I could hear his voice if I wanted to, by listening to his answerphone message. Would that be weird? Maybe, but I couldn't resist doing it. I heard Luke's jokey voice telling the caller to leave a message on the 'Bat phone' and there were even a few *de ne ne ne ners* for good measure, with Luke's laughter cut off at the end. I listened to it three more times before I felt stupid and stopped. Luke wasn't dead. He hadn't gone. He was going to come out of his coma and he was coming home.

I jumped as Luke's phone bleeped in my lap. Jesus. My nerves were shot to pieces. I glanced at the screen. It was the mysterious Tiggsy again. Feeling voyeuristic for some reason, I read the text.

Luke, I'm back, working at the hospital again.

Sorry. Coming to see you.

I checked Luke's phone once more, reading the history of messages from 'Tiggsy'. There wasn't anything incriminating; they were either about meeting up, or talking about 'stuff'; jokey and innocuous.

Leaning back, I laid down on the floor, staring up at the yellow light fitting that Luke had put up.

I stayed there for a long time gazing up at that wonky lampshade, tears sliding into my ears. Luke had done this for me and I wished I could rewind time and replay this scene the way Luke must have planned it. Us, opening the door to this room together. Me, surprised, moved and delighted, grinning as I threw my arms around his neck to thank him. Luke, thrilled at my reaction, happy that he had surprised me and given me hope that this pregnancy was the one that would work for us.

I sat up and wiped my eyes. What a difference a few days could make. A few days ago, two healthy, happy people were planning for the arrival of a baby. Today, two broken people, their lives shattered beyond recognition. With a sigh, I got to my feet and tucked the baby grow back in the cupboard. Taking one last, lingering look at the nursery Luke had so thoughtfully created, I closed the door and headed for the shower. I just wanted to get back to the hospital.

CHAPTER THIRTEEN

Patricia

Patricia smoothed down a page of *Woman's Own*. It was four days since Luke's accident and there was no change. He'd had a CT scan to rule out bleeds and infarcts, and that had all been fine. The doctors had no idea what state Luke was actually in, as the level of brain activity could only be assessed in the basic terms of 'normal function/reaction' while he remained unresponsive. Patricia had gleaned that the quicker the patient woke up, the better their overall recovery. This gave her a sense of mild panic and, as each day passed, the level of panic increased.

Consultants kept using the acronym 'GCS', which apparently stood for the 'Glasgow Coma Scale'. Lucy had told her this, because Dee had interrogated one of the consultants about it. It was something to do with movement, the opening of eyes, speech.

Patricia was fairly certain that Luke wasn't exhibiting any of these things, which terrified her. She knew this

106

meant that Luke was in a deep coma, not one of the shallow ones which allowed a patient to respond with speech, for example.

Patricia put a hand to her mouth. It was all so awful, so incredibly unreal. She suddenly became aware that the nurse who was always present in the room was staring at her in that benign, concerned manner that usually preceded kindly questions about how she was coping and an offer to help. How the nurse who changed Luke's wee bag and checked his vital signs could help a mother stop worrying about the long-term prospects of her son's health and well-being was anyone's guess.

Patricia had sent Lucy to the canteen for something to eat; the poor girl was almost on the brink of collapse. Her parents had stayed over for a couple of nights before heading back to Scotland this morning and Lucy had seemed exhausted afterwards, perhaps with the effort of appearing strong in the face of everything she had been through.

Patricia felt anxious about Lucy. Things still felt a bit awkward between them . . . rather strained. They were united over their concern for Luke, but they were somehow at odds with each other. The aloofness that had always been present between them seemed more acute. They were sharing the bedside vigil along with Nell, but Lucy was doing the lion's share and Patricia was sure she wasn't sleeping or eating much. Patricia couldn't blame her; the restorative benefits of a good sleep and some decent food were evading her, too. As Lucy must, Patricia craved normality, but they were all living in a strange hiatus right now.

Patricia deliberately turned back to her magazine. She'd heard that reading to coma patients helped them, so, in the absence of anything more practical, this was all she could think of doing. Luke couldn't speak, but she was assuming that he could hear and understand her and that he would welcome something – anything – to distract him from the boredom of lying there inert. She would occasionally help to wipe Luke's face or hold his hand . . . today she had even brought in some family photographs from home. Silly, really. His eyes were closed so how could he see them? She had described each picture, of course – regaled Luke with as much detail as she could to jog his memory or connect with whatever part of his brain might be listening. The hardest thing had been not crying, especially when she had shown him photographs of Bernard. But Patricia thought that it was probably best to keep her voice normal. Comforting, familiar.

Drained, Patricia put a hand to her head. She had arranged for Jane, her cover at the florist's shop, to stand in for herself and Lucy. She wasn't capable of dealing with the customers and she knew Lucy wasn't either. How could she be?

Patricia had been sitting with Luke for an hour now and she had read all the baking-related articles and interesting, real-life stories. Some poor girl had a tumour the size of a baseball in her stomach and couldn't have children.

'What do you think about that, Luke?' she asked him. She sounded aggressive, not like herself. Perhaps confrontation would jolt him out of his silence because Luke wasn't used to hearing his mother challenging him.

'Well? What do you think, Luke? You could answer me, you know.' Patricia swallowed. 'You could . . . I don't know . . . flick a finger, grab my hand, move your eyelashes.' She broke down and pleaded. 'Do something, Luke. Please, do *something*.'

Patricia brushed a tear from her cheek. All she could hear was the beeping machines and the puffs of the breathing apparatus. It was torture. The noise from the machines and the lack of noise from Luke. She could barely stand it. Tears rushed up again and stung her eyes, but Patricia refused to give in, not yet. It was early days – wasn't that what everyone said? People came out of comas every day. Well, maybe not every day, but you heard stories, fantastic stories about people surviving worse accidents than this.

She looked up as the door opened.

'Oh, hello, Mrs Harte. Is the other Mrs Harte around?'

It was Luke's consultant, Mr Moriarty. Patricia studied him, placing her magazine on the bed. Luke was an avid Sherlock Holmes fan. He would think that having a consultant named Moriarty was brilliant, even if the consultant wasn't a professor.

'Sorry . . . the other Mrs Harte?' Mr Moriarty repeated with a brief, professional smile. 'I went through this with her earlier, but I just want to make sure that we're all on the same page as far as Luke's prognosis is concerned.'

'She's gone to the canteen,' Patricia replied. She felt irritable, but she knew she was being irrational. It was just . . . sometimes she felt as though she was being treated like a second-class citizen, medical staff halting their prognosis update in Lucy's absence.

Mr Moriarty glanced discreetly at his watch, but his eyes, when they connected with Patricia's, were kindly. 'Right. Well, as I explained to your daughter-in-law earlier, we all need to be aware that the longer Luke remains in this coma, the more likely it is that he will need some sort of rehabilitation plan. Please try not to worry . . . I know that sounds frightening, but it's actually the best thing for Luke . . . that we are all aware of what we're dealing with and how to move forward.'

Patricia concentrated on what Mr Moriarty was saying. She heard him say something about 'lack of mobility' and panic set in. Why couldn't anyone tell her anything positive? Where was the other consultant, the one who had seemed more upbeat about Luke?

On the face of it, though, as Mr Moriarty reached the end of his prognosis, it wasn't awful. It wasn't cheery, but it could be far worse. Luke's spine injuries weren't devastating, but the coma was causing the most anxiety. Whilst Luke remained in a coma, there was no way of telling how well his brain was functioning.

Lucy arrived just as Mr Moriarty came to the end of his rather sombre speech. She glanced at Luke, her eyes registering pain. She knew he didn't look much better; they all knew it. Luke was there, but not.

'Do you have an update?'

Mr Moriarty patiently began talking through the prognosis again. 'Not really, I'm afraid. As I explained to you earlier, what we need to see from Luke is some sort of response. We're running tests, but so far we haven't seen his eyes opening or any response to pain.'

Patricia assessed Lucy as she tried to quell the panic

in her stomach. Her skin seemed unnaturally wan, almost waxy, as if all colour and light had drained away. Her eyes were threaded with crimson, bloodshot and puffy from weeping. Poor Lucy.

'That's bad, isn't it?' Lucy wrung her hands. 'The longer he stays in this coma, the more likely it is that he'll be . . . that he'll have . . .'

Mr Moriarty put a reassuring hand on her arm. 'It's scary, I know. But we won't know what the extent of the damage is – if any – until Luke comes out of this coma. His responses will give us an indication of any brain injury and we'll be able to check his residual symptoms.'

'Residual symptoms?' Lucy looked pained. 'Do you . . . you don't mean physical disabilities?'

'Yes, I'm afraid I do, but really, we can't tell at this stage.' Mr Moriarty was nothing if not honest, but it was difficult for both of them to hear.

'Can't people stay in comas for years? Don't they sometimes suddenly wake up and they're fine?'

'They do in films,' Mr Moriarty advised. 'In real life, that's a fairly rare occurrence. The best we can hope for is that Luke comes out of this sooner rather than later.'

Lucy nodded, but she seemed unsteady on her feet.

Patricia ached inside. Her daughter-in-law had been through hell. They all had, but Lucy was the one who had lost a baby and, in a different way, a husband, all in one day. But Patricia didn't know how to be with Lucy. They were close, affectionate even, but there had always been a hint of tension that kept them apart, like opposing magnets. That tiny sliver of friction sat between them now, preventing Patricia from embracing her daughter-in-law and providing the support that Lucy must surely need. Patricia wanted to do it. She wanted to help Lucy by being a substitute mother. The question was, would Lucy let her?

Suffused with guilt, Patricia's eyes dropped to Lucy's stomach. There was no trace of the baby now, none at all. Lucy's midriff was flat and she'd lost the flattering bloom that Patricia had failed, unbelievably, to attribute to pregnancy. A grandchild. There had almost been a grandchild. Patricia closed her eyes. A girl, Lucy had said. A little girl they could all have cherished and spoilt and adored.

Patricia felt something heavy pushing down on her, an uncomfortable prickle that was both familiar and alien. Grief? It seemed extreme, and it couldn't be close to what Lucy must be experiencing, but Patricia felt the loss all the same. It was horrible. The baby that was a part of Lucy and a part of Luke had gone. The timing was excruciating.

Patricia opened her eyes.

'Thank you,' Lucy was saying routinely, her eyes cast down. 'Thank you for the update.'

'I'm sorry I can't be more optimistic,' Mr Moriarty responded. 'I mean, there are some good points here, but the coma isn't something we can ignore. We're running some more tests, so I'll come back to you on those shortly. For now though, that's the best I can offer you, I'm afraid.' He withdrew.

'His bedside manner isn't that great,' Lucy said, turning away from Patricia.

'No,' Patricia agreed. She knew Lucy was crying and she felt helpless, pointless, even. What on earth could she do – what should she say? Did she sympathise about the baby or about Luke? Which was worse for Lucy? The baby had gone forever, but Luke's coma was ongoing and agonising.

Knowing she should put her arms around Lucy, Patricia said instead: 'Mr Moriarty. What would Luke think of that?'

'Luke would think it was cool,' Lucy offered, wiping her nose. 'Especially if Mr Moriarty was a—'

'Professor. I thought the same.' Patricia met Lucy's eyes. 'I lose track of what makes a "Dr" and what makes a "Mr".'

'"Dr" is a consultant, "Mr" is a surgeon. I think.' Lucy's hand fluttered to her hair, but she didn't touch it, her hand dropping redundantly. 'I had no idea I would ever know such things. I learnt a lot of useless stuff from Luke when he was studying, but this is a whole new level.'

Patricia took a step forward. She wanted, needed, to embrace her daughter-in-law.

Patricia loathed herself for a moment. Why couldn't she do this simple thing for her daughter-in-law?

'Lucy, I'm so sorry about . . .'

Lucy sucked her breath in sharply, as if sympathy smarted. She froze, folding her arms. The unconscious barrier. Patricia faltered, uncertain. She wanted to do something, she should do something. They stood facing one another, paralysed.

'Mum.'

Patricia jumped, making Lucy start. Their heads

whipped round to the bed. Luke had spoken. Luke had *said something*. Lucy clutched Patricia. Patricia let out a whimper. *You heard it too*, her eyes said. They both stared at Luke, but he was quiet, inert. Had they imagined it?

'Luke,' Patricia said desperately. 'Please . . .'

Lucy glanced over her shoulder. 'Patricia,' she began.

'Mum,' said the voice again.

Patricia stood, rigid, her jaw clenched. That voice. So much like Luke's, but it wasn't. It was deeper, with a twang that hadn't been there before. Patricia slowly turned towards the doorway, feeling herself welling up. She steeled her nerves. She wasn't ready for this. She simply wasn't ready.

Ade. Her eldest son. There he was, standing right in front of her, for the first time in years. Patricia drank Ade in, indulging herself. He looked good . . . tanned, healthy and dynamic. Tall, taller than Luke, with more freckles. Her son. Absent for ten years.

Ade stepped forward, his eyes flickering from Patricia to Lucy. 'We haven't met, at least not properly,' he said to her. 'Skype isn't the same as face to face, is it?' He kissed Lucy's cheek and stretched out his fingers, just connecting with her arm. The gesture was tentative; they were essentially strangers, after all.

'I spent the flight from Australia trying to think of the right thing to say and I didn't come up with anything good. Apart from sorry. I'm really, really sorry about your baby. And about Luke.'

Lucy nodded, her teeth trapping her lip. She was staring at Ade, jolted perhaps by his resemblance to Luke. She was seeing the freckles and hearing the voice.

And she was looking at Ade's eyes. They could almost be Luke's. Almost.

Patricia watched them, her heart thumping. Skype? Ade and Lucy had chatted on Skype. It was unexpected, shocking. How didn't she know this? Why had they kept it from her?

'*Woman's Own*?' Ade picked it up, his eyes on Luke. His lip quivered, as though he might break down. 'Surely not Luke's favourite publication, Mum?'

'What would you know about that?' Patricia barked. Her eyes smarted, but she held the tears back. 'We haven't seen you for nearly ten years. *Ten years*, Ade.'

'I know. I'm sorry, Mum.' Ade's voice cracked slightly. 'Nell told me what happened and I came straight here. I came straight . . . home.'

Patricia wanted to hug him, more even than she had wanted to hug Lucy minutes earlier. Patricia took a step closer and her arms lifted fractionally, but she wasn't able to carry the motion through.

Ade gave her a jerky smile, as if he could sense her thoughts. 'As soon as I heard, I handed my business over to a friend and I got the first flight I could. I just wanted to be here for you, Mum. I wanted to see Luke and I wanted to be here for you.'

Because I wasn't last time. The unspoken words hung in the air. Patricia wanted to hug him fiercely, to breathe in his scent, but at the same time, she wanted to strike him, she wanted to beat his chest and scream.

Lucy had returned her gaze to Luke and Ade moved to stand next to her. His body language was sensitive, supportive.

115

Lucy started to cry again and it was Ade who put a hand out and squeezed her shoulder.

'I just can't stop thinking about him,' Lucy said in a hoarse voice. 'Our wedding, how we met, moving in. It's like my life is being played back to me in slow motion.'

'I'm sure that's completely normal,' Ade replied, soothingly. 'If I were you, I'd enjoy those reminders. Think about Luke, remember the good times and plan his return home.'

Patricia bristled. How was it that Ade, who'd been absent for so long, could say exactly the right thing? She hung back uneasily. She felt as if she had swapped one son for another. She wanted both. She needed both. Not Luke in exchange for Ade. It wasn't fair. It just wasn't fair.

CHAPTER FOURTEEN

Lucy and Luke

October, eight years earlier
'You're not. Are you really? Oh my God. That's . . . really? I can't even . . .'

Luke was dumbfounded and he was struggling to hide it. I didn't blame him. I felt pretty staggered myself.

Not sure what to say, I fixed my gaze on the trees by the side of the hospital. Their leaves were mostly a riot of russet and yellow but one drooping tree had those spectacular burgundy leaves you see on glorious adverts for New England and, as I stared, a lone red leaf spiralled to the ground. I felt empathy for it. I too appeared to be cartwheeling through the air with a complete lack of control right now. I just wasn't sure I was about to calmly float to the floor when a crash might be more in order.

I realised that a strange silence had settled between Luke and I. It was uncomfortable as well as unusual . . . we rarely spent any space of time together without one of us starting a conversation about something.

I took a shaky breath. I should say something. I knew I should say something. I had metaphorically hit Luke round the head with a baseball bat; it was down to me to try and make things right.

'Listen, Luke. There is absolutely no need to feel . . . I'm not telling you this to make you . . .' I faltered. Overcome by what was happening, my ability to string a sentence together had gone out of the window.

I tried again. 'I realise this must be a massive shock to you. It is to me, too. Actually, calling it a shock is an understatement. This would be better described as a terrifying bombshell . . .'

My legs buckled and I started to sink. I put my hands out to steady myself, grateful when Luke grabbed them and guided me on to a nearby bench. He sat down next to me, still holding on to my hands.

Wincing, I braved it and glanced at Luke properly. I had learned that his eyes, besides being fairly remarkable in their own right, gave away his inner feelings whether he liked it or not. I checked them. I believed he was feeling concern, but his expression, now that my words had sunk in, seemed calmer than I would have expected.

Luke squeezed my fingers. 'It *is* unexpected, but I wouldn't call it . . . terrifying.'

I let out a short laugh. Now I knew he was being kind. Not terrifying? We'd been dating for around four months and it had been intense and heady, and pretty damned brilliant. And now I had just turned round and told him that I was pregnant. Pregnant. That was scary shit for anyone, even someone as cool as Luke.

'Don't get me wrong; I wasn't expecting you to tell

me that today.' Luke let go of one of my hands to rub his chin briefly. 'I mean, wow. That's . . . that's . . .'

'Terrifying,' I nodded, dropping my head. I felt a little nauseous, but I guessed that was probably more to do with shock than anything pregnancy-related. I was only four or five weeks along – very early days. I felt a rush of elation. God, I wanted this; I really, really wanted this. I hadn't been one of those girls who'd planned out my entire wedding with a folder full of floaty dresses, flowers and centrepieces, but children had always been on my radar.

I glanced at Luke who seemed momentarily distracted by the same trees that had caught my attention earlier. It suited me, gave me a moment to collect my thoughts. The thing was, I knew that Luke was equally keen to have children. It was a conversation we'd had relatively early on, perhaps even in the first few weeks of meeting. It had come about in a relaxed way – nothing forced or heavy – just a general chat about hopes for the future. Not necessarily together, just . . . hopes and dreams. I couldn't deny that Luke's enthusiastic agreement about children being more important than marriage had sent my heart soaring, because I had already fallen head-over-heels in love with him by that point, but I hadn't meant for this to happen. I started as Luke took my hand again. He looked emotional . . . did he look emotional? I was on a knife edge, not knowing how this was going to go. Either way, I knew I wanted to keep this baby. It was just that part of me – most of me – yearned to have Luke by my side when I did so. I forced myself to look Luke in the eye.

'Okay.' Luke started. 'This is definitely unexpected. But it's the best news. The *best* news.'

'Is it?' My voice broke slightly. My heart didn't know what to do with itself. It, like my mind, wanted to believe what Luke was saying, to believe he was genuine, but I was terrified to trust my gut instinct.

'Are you just saying that?' I had to know. 'Because you really don't need to . . . I know this is scary and weird because we've only been seeing each other for a while, so please don't feel that you—'

Luke stopped me. 'I'm not just saying it, Lucy. Look, I'm going out on a limb here, okay?' He cleared his throat. 'I know we haven't been together for that long, but I've totally fallen for you. I mean, in a big way. And – and I'm hoping you feel the same way because I'm putting myself on the line here, but this news . . . this is . . . God, it's just incredible. I'm so happy!' He broke into a smile that nearly made my heart explode.

'You – you are?'

'Of course I am!' Luke lifted a careless shoulder. 'I don't care that it's happened this soon, because you and me . . . we're meant to be, aren't we? It's not like we're not going to stay together. This is the next chapter in our lives together.'

'I . . .' I was rendered speechless by his words and his openness. It was everything I had wanted to hear. I could hardly believe it. I fell into his arms, allowing myself to fully feel the joy. We were having a baby. A baby. Together. And we both wanted it. Luke stroked my hair out of my face with such infinite tenderness, I very nearly came undone. How had I got so lucky? How had I ended up with this man, and a baby too?

I smiled as Luke's hand dropped from my hair to my stomach. I listened as he said hello to the baby – to our baby – and I laughed when he excitedly gathered me up in his arms again.

Together, we were invincible, and I knew that everything was going to be all right. Our future was set. I don't think either of us had ever been as happy in our lives.

CHAPTER FIFTEEN

Nell

September

'I can't believe you have a brother I've never met,' Lisa said, taking a seat at a nearby table, one of those bottle-green metal things you could barely fit an ice bucket on.

Nell placed a bottle of rosé and two glasses on the table, a wobbly leg causing wine to slop out of the bottle. She picked everything up again and put the bottle and the spare glass on a nearby wall. She'd finally decided to tell her friend everything. Well, nearly everything.

'Yeah, I know. Luke's in hospital and now Ade's back. Everything's gone weird.'

Lisa poured out a glass of wine and handed it to Nell. 'I'll just keep you company until he gets here, okay?'

Nell nodded. She was glad of Lisa's company, she was a good friend. They had stayed in touch since school, but in a rather sporadic fashion because Lisa had been busy setting up her empire. Five clothes shops was a magnificent achievement at her age, but Nell wondered if Lisa's love life had suffered as a result. Nell still hadn't told her about Cal; she kind of wanted to, just not right now. Not with all this other stuff going on; she simply wasn't strong enough to weather a possible negative reaction.

She sipped her wine. Her mum had sent her out for a break after she had completed a long shift at Luke's bedside that day, longer than normal. Nell didn't mind; she wanted to sit with Luke. She was due back at college soon so she would have to do it in shifts around her lectures. Or she might have to ask for a leave of absence or something. The trouble was when she wasn't with Luke, Nell spent the entire time worrying about him and texting her mum and Lucy (whose phones were usually turned off) for updates.

'It's buzzing here tonight,' Lisa commented, sitting back in her chair. 'You can't breathe for trendy bars and cafés popping up all over the place at the moment.'

'Full of bloody students, too,' Nell agreed with a brief grin. Feeling humid in the sticky air she wondered if a storm was brewing. She didn't care about the weather. She was on edge and her nerves felt sparky, as if they could go off at any moment.

She was meeting her brother for a drink; that was all. Her mother was being very bossy about her and Ade having time off from sitting with Luke, but Nell knew it was the right thing to do.

'You don't smoke!' Lisa said as Nell took out a cigarette.

Nell felt idiotic and she flushed. Cal liked her to smoke; he said it made her look sexy. Like Marilyn Monroe, he had whispered in her ear. Had Marilyn Monroe even smoked? Nell hadn't a clue if that was a full-on 'come to bed' line or a vague truth, but for some reason, she liked it, even if she was more Audrey than Marilyn. Wasn't that what they said in the TV show *Mad Men*? That women were either an Audrey or a Marilyn. Simplistic. Unrealistic. Misogynistic. Anyway, Cal made smoking seem glamorous, tucking stale breath, wrinkles and possible cancer into a box in the back of a cupboard. Did it also prove that he didn't really know her if he categorised her as a Marilyn?

God, she wished she could stop over-thinking her relationship. Most likely Cal just thought Marilyn Monroe was sexy and that was that.

'I didn't know you smoked.' Ade was there, leaning against the wall. It was a casual enough gesture, but he seemed extremely nervous.

Nell put the cigarette away. 'I don't. Not really. This is Lisa.'

'Hi, Lisa.' Ade gave her a genial smile.

'I hope you like rosé wine,' Lisa commented, standing up. 'Nell bought a whole bottle.'

'Am I an honorary girl for the night?' Ade smiled. 'Go for it. I'm in. I don't like to discriminate; I drink any shade of wine. It was nice to meet you, Lisa. Are you sure you can't stay?'

'Thanks, but no.' Lisa looked regretful, but it was fleeting. 'I have an appointment with some accounts. Thrilling stuff. Speak soon, Nell.'

'Bye, Lise. I'll call you tomorrow.'

Nell poured a glass and observed her brother warily. It was startling how much he reminded her of Luke. His freckles, the blue of his eyes. His voice was similar, but of course now he had that Aussie twang. Strong, distinctive, un-Ade-like. And when it came down to it, he was anything but Luke. As the past curled up and settled around her shoulders, Nell felt her insides hardening.

'So. How are you, Nell?' Ade relaxed, sipping his wine. If he hated it, he hid it well.

'Pretty awful,' she answered, feeling the urge to take out the cigarette again. 'How do you think I am?'

Ade nodded, seemingly keen not to rile her. 'Of course. It's terrible. Luke . . . Lucy. This is all such a nightmare.'

'Not so much for you. You haven't even been here. You don't know what they went through to get that baby.'

Ade dipped his eyes for a moment. 'Yes. I deserve that, of course. But Luke emails me. Quite a bit, actually. And we Skype occasionally. I know most of the history.'

Nell shrugged jerkily. She knew all this. Luke told her he and Ade Skyped and emailed. She and Ade emailed too – what of it? It didn't mean Ade was suddenly able to lay claim to the pain she was going through. That kind of pain was earned from being physically present, from being a proper member of the family.

Ade ran his fingers along the stem of his wine glass. 'Lucy seems lovely.'

'She is.' Nell drained her glass and filled it again. She took the cigarette out and looked around for a light, leaning towards a group of nearby students. She started when Ade took out a lighter and did the honours. 'You smoke?'

'Yes. I haven't completely changed, you know.'

'Really? I don't remember enough about you from back then to know.'

'Ouch.' Ade wasn't laughing. His eyes flickered as they met hers. 'Fair enough, Nell.' He changed the subject, probably because he knew they were veering into dangerous territory. 'So. You and Lucy get on?'

'Yes. She's socially backward and so am I.'

'Socially backward? Is that how you see yourself?'

Nell let out a shuddering puff of smoke. 'I'm shy. And not very good at talking to people. Something to do with some shit that happened to me in my teens. That's what my therapist said.'

Ade looked stricken. He lit his own cigarette and blew a curl of smoke into the air.

Nell wondered if he was buying himself some time. But perhaps she was being cynical.

'So, what about you, Nell?' Ade leant forward. 'Aside from everything that's happening with Luke, what's going on in your life? You told me in an email that you were enjoying your fashion degree?'

Nell's mouth tightened. And now he was making small talk. 'I was. I can't seem to get excited about it at the moment.'

'Again, understandable. You've got a lot on your mind.'

'I suppose.'

'A boyfriend? Do you have someone in your life, Nell?' Ade seemed genuinely interested.

Nell met his eyes. She didn't trust him. How could she after what had happened? Perversely, she wanted to test him, however. See if he could keep up the facade of playing nice and polite in the face of her shady life.

'Yeah. You'd probably describe him as . . . Well. Not a "long-term prospect".'

126

Ade sucked on his cigarette. 'Ah. Married.'

'Married.' She stared him down, daring him to judge her. Ade wasn't Luke. Her mother had told her this, over and over. It was etched on her brain like a tattoo, so Nell was fully expecting a barrage of abuse, or at the very least, a slightly scornful stare. She received neither.

'That's a shame,' Ade commented lightly.

Nell waited and watched. He drank rosé and smoked.

'That's it? That's all you have to say on the matter?' She was being deliberately confrontational, but she couldn't help it. She felt some residual resentment – no, more than residual – towards Ade for leaving just when she needed him the most. Nell didn't want to feel the way she did, but it was the first time she'd spoken to him properly in years.

'What do you want me to say, Nell?' Ade flicked ash from his cigarette and sighed. 'I can't offer my congratulations, because the guy is married and who knows where that will end. I don't want to put a downer on it, because I know you must have feelings for him if you know his background and you're still going ahead with it. But if you're waiting for me to judge you or pour scorn on your relationship, you'll be sitting there for a very long time.'

Nell watched her cigarette tip glowing. She wasn't so much wafting it about the way Cal suggested, but drawing on it like an addict. Not very Marilyn-like. She stubbed it out, confused about who she was supposed to be. She was also aware that she'd had too much wine.

'What do you want from me?' Ade asked. He didn't demand, he asked. Pleaded, even. 'Whatever you want, Nell, you can have it.'

With permission, suppressed fury unleashed itself. Nell turned on him.

'Oh, what do you know, Ade? You walked out ten years ago. You don't know anything about me or about Lucy – or . . . or Luke. You're acting all chilled about my relationship, because you don't know anything about having an affair.' Nell jerkily slopped more wine into her glass. 'Dad died and you couldn't cope and you walked away and left us all to pick up the pieces. You left Luke to pick up the pieces.'

Ade looked shocked, but when he stubbed out his cigarette next to hers, his movements were slow and considered. 'Okay. I guess you're right. About one thing, at least. I don't know anything about having an affair, but my marriage is over.'

'Is it?' She was taken aback. 'I mean, I don't know anything about . . . Tina, isn't it? You met her over there . . . you haven't really talked about her that much.'

'I know. Not that me not talking about her means anything. I loved her for a long time. She was the main reason I stayed in Australia.' Ade looked sad.

'Did she cheat on you?' Letting her guard down, Nell put her head in her hands. 'I'm going to feel even more awful if she did. And just . . . I'll feel awful for you.'

'No. She didn't cheat and neither did I. It's a bit more tragic than that.' He raised his eyebrow and Nell almost gasped because he looked so much like Luke. It was unnerving, yet she felt oddly reassured at the same time.

Ade didn't notice her gasp, nor would he have understood it if it had registered. 'We just . . . fell out of love. We have a business together and we have money and a great house. We just didn't fucking love each other enough for all of that to be enough.' He caught the surprise in her eyes and he didn't capitalise on it. 'And as for leaving Luke to pick up the pieces . . . I guess you're right about that. I did that and I'm not proud of it.'

Ade carefully placed his wine glass on the nearby wall. 'I hate that I'm back because of what has happened to Luke, Nell. I wish I'd come back before now. This isn't . . . this isn't how I planned it.'

'Did you have a plan? About coming back?'

'Not as such. I mean, I did. But I knew I needed to sort everything out with Tina first. I wanted to come back here when everything was sorted, when I could come back because I wanted to.'

'Rather than like this.'

Nell drank some more wine. She could understand that. Ade felt as though his visit home had been forced, that it wasn't of his choosing. Probably a little like the way she had felt when he had walked out all those years ago, leaving her floundering, without her rock to cling to. Nell felt herself closing up again.

'Well we can't always control the way things happen, can we, Ade? Sometimes the shit hits the fan and we're left to get on with it.'

Ade regarded her unhappily. 'I guess you're right, Nell.' He stood up and, after hesitating briefly, leant over to kiss her cheek. 'But I'm here now. However I got here and whatever happened before, I'm here. For you. And for Mum. And I know I'm going to have to earn your trust back, but I'll do it. I promise.'

Nell watched Ade walk away. Her hand shook and she couldn't seem to grasp her wine glass. She took out her phone and dialled Cal, forgetting that she wasn't supposed to call him. He answered quickly.

'Nell? Are you all right?'

'Not really.' She started to cry. 'I just had a drink with Ade and I think I made him feel bad . . . I think I wanted to make him feel bad. And now I feel terrible because he was telling me stuff and I realised that he's had a hard time too.' Nell clumsily took out another cigarette. 'He's getting divorced. And I didn't even know. Jesus, I'm such a bad person.'

'You're not.' Cal exhaled, sounding sympathetic, if cautious.

'I'm just so worried about losing Luke because I lost my dad and I lost Ade and now he's back but no one knows if Luke is going to make it.' Nell hiccuped.

'He's going to be all right,' Cal assured her in hushed tones. 'Listen, Nell; I can't really talk right now . . . I'm . . . My wife is—'

'Of course. Sorry.'

Nell ended the call. What was the point? Cal wanted her to open up – he'd slammed her for not sharing more of herself – and the second she did, he threw his wife in her face. No, that wasn't fair. Cal was lovely. He loved her. He was just in a difficult situation right now.

Nell stumbled away from the bar. She had a date with her notepad and pen. It was pathetic, but that was her life.

Dad,
I'm drunk and I shouldn't be doing this. But I need
to talk to someone. I saw Ade tonight and he told

me his marriage was over. I wanted to hurt him the way he hurt me, but I think he's in pain anyway, without me trying to wound him.

I'm just so worried about losing Luke the way I lost you. And Ade. You left and then Ade left and Luke – Luke saved me, Dad. When Ade ran away and left us to cope with Mum being a loony, Luke was there. He was there for me when no one else was.

I – I tried to kill myself, Dad. Did you know that? I cut my wrists and I meant to do it and I was livid with Luke for finding me. I just couldn't handle life. Not without you. And Ade. But Luke fixed me. He sent me to a therapist and he spent time with me and he listened, even though I was such a little hater in those days. I needed him. I still need him. He's going to make it, right? Tell me he's going to make it?

Cal doesn't like it when I get emotional. What does that say about him? I AM emotional. I'm a former suicide attempter and a professional, emotional wreck.

Night, Dad. I can't even read my own writing. Sorry for being drunk and needy. I miss you. I really miss you.

CHAPTER SIXTEEN

Lucy

I wiped my eyes. It had been one of the most awful days of my life and most of my recent days had been pretty horrific. I took a tissue from Dan, trying to mop my face. I was sick and tired of crying; my eyes hurt, my lips felt swollen and I felt utterly spent. I had done nothing but sob, snivel and wail for the past fortnight, but I didn't know what else to do.

'I should have worn waterproof mascara,' I hiccuped. I must have looked a mess, but it's not every day a girl has to brave the funeral of her stillborn baby while her husband lies in a coma.

The ceremony had taken place in a chapel close to the hospital, mostly arranged by Dee. After the hospital staff had moved my baby (it makes me choke to say this) from the ward to Rose Cottage – this, apparently, is a hospital term for a mortuary – Dee arranged certificates and funeral homes and everything else. She also gave me the number for an organisation that supports parents dealing with baby bereavement, but I'm not up to speaking to anyone right now.

Patricia and Nell had both attended the service, which was lovely of them. But they had discreetly withdrawn at the end, leaving me alone with Dee and Dan. I was surprised by this and could only assume that Nell had suggested slipping away. Either way, I appreciated it. For some reason, I felt that Dee and Dan were the right people to comfort me at this time; besides, I would see Nell and Patricia later when they came to visit Luke. But I wasn't sure how I felt about that. Would they be awkward with me? No one knew what to say to me any more.

'That was so sad. So, so sad.' Dee looked shell-shocked. Wearing a black sundress with peep toe heels, she looked rather dressy, but I appreciated her making an effort. Even Dan, clutching a tissue cube, had turned up in a dark suit, despite the fact that I knew he detested wearing them. He'd be sweltering when he headed outside; it was late September but it was oddly warm. We started taking the short walk back to the hospital, shoulder to shoulder.

Dee mopped at her face, allowing Dan to hand her another much-needed tissue. 'That tiny coffin.'

Dan swallowed, on the edge of tears. 'Sorry, Luce.' He placed a hand on my neck, rubbing it awkwardly. 'Things are horrible right now. We're here for you. Whatever you need.'

I nodded, touched by Dan's tenderness because he was usually so jokey and brash. It made me well up again and I took another tissue.

'I did the right thing, didn't I?'

Dee sniffed. 'Of course you did. You had to do this

133

now, and we don't even know what's happening with Luke yet.'

Perhaps seeing my stricken expression, Dan cut in. 'What she means is that we don't know when Luke will come round. He will, but you had to make this decision now and you've done the right thing for sure.'

Dee looked appalled at herself. 'What he said, Luce. That's exactly what I meant. I wasn't saying Luke wasn't going to come round – I just meant that – sorry . . .'

'I know, I know. Dee, stop it.'

I squeezed her hand to cease the apologics. I seemed to have become one of those people for whom practically every topic is an elephant in the room. My husband, his progress – or lack of progress, more accurately – and our lost baby. Even my best friends were struggling to appear normal. But I didn't blame them. We were all living a surreal existence; we were all wading through a nightmare.

I felt Dan's hand in mine and, taking Dee's, we headed inside the hospital, my second home. As we walked towards Luke's room, it occurred to me that we looked faintly ridiculous. Three grown-ups holding hands like children. In a hospital of all places. I could only assume that the recent traumas we had all suffered had stripped away the usual social restraints that adulthood dictated.

'Christ, look at him.' Dan released my hand and went into Luke's room. 'He doesn't even look like himself.'

Dee cleared her throat. 'I miss him. I really, really miss him.'

'Me too.' Dan noisily used one of the tissues he had

brought along for everyone else. 'I keep thinking he's going to wake up, laugh his head off and tell me to stop being such a girl for crying all over the place.'

'You big girl's blouse, he'd say,' Dee said with a short laugh.

I didn't comment. I wished more than anything that Luke would open his eyes and say something. 'Luke would have approved of the service,' Dee reassured me, mistaking my silence for anxiety over my choices. 'It was really beautiful.'

I expelled a hiss of air in place of replying. Perhaps because of the repetitive suck and blow of Luke's ventilation pipes, I had become oddly aware of my own breathing. Sometimes, it felt as though the only certainty in my life was the fact that both of us would breathe in and breathe out, even if Luke's process was artificial.

'Thank you for coming,' I said mechanically, sounding like a bride greeting guests in a line-up. I'd start telling Dan and Dee to help themselves to the buffet in a minute.

Dee kissed my cheek, guessing that I needed to be alone with Luke. 'We'll leave you to it, Luce. Come on, Dan.'

Dan hugged me. 'Call us if you need anything. Or if there's any change.'

'Of course. Thanks, guys. Speak later.'

I stared at Luke. I wanted to speak to him properly and I knew I probably should do, but I conducted many of my conversations with him in my head. It felt ridiculous having a one-way conversation about such serious issues, especially with a nurse always present in the room. I reverted to my mental line of questioning.

Did I do the right thing, Harte? Was it okay for me to go ahead with the funeral? I had to do something . . . I had to make a decision. Forgive me if I should have waited. If you come out of this coma tomorrow, I'll wish I'd waited and you won't make me feel bad but I'll make me feel bad.

I was relieved that Ade was absent. We had spoken several times since he had come back, but I was finding it difficult. He reminded me so much of Luke, it made my heart ache. They probably weren't that similar, but there was something about Ade's laugh, about the way his eyes creased when he spoke, the very direct way he had with words. They were all haunting reminders of what I was missing while Luke was stuck in this coma.

'Oh, I'm sorry. I'll come back.'

A blonde woman peered into Luke's room. She wore a white coat and her stethoscope was draped artfully around her neck, the way another woman might wear a statement necklace. She seemed flustered by my presence. Was she flustered? I seemed to be imagining all sorts of things at the moment.

I stood up wearily. 'No please. Come on in. I'm used to people checking Luke's progress.'

'Right. Yes.' The woman hesitated. 'Well, as long as you're sure.' She came properly into the room and positioned herself at the end of the bed. She seemed uncomfortable but I didn't pay much attention. I noted a dove-grey pencil skirt and a crisp, white blouse, but nothing else registered. I was used to the staff change-overs here. 'I'm, er, Stella,' the woman said.

Stella. How familiar. In my experience, consultants and surgeons wore their titles like trophies. As well they might, I supposed. They worked long enough and hard enough to get them.

Stella, as she obviously liked to be called, remained at the end of Luke's bed. I felt her eyes on me and I felt her concern. Most of the doctors and nurses who came into Luke's room did this – assessed me silently, as though they were able to check my mental state by the state of my clothes or how red my eyes were. I could only think they imagined I might be suicidal after what I had gone through, but contrary to their assumptions, there was no way I would leave Luke.

Stella was staring at me again. Not just looking, staring. 'I just wanted to see how he was. I really shouldn't be here.'

I rubbed my temples with my fingertips, my skin clammy to the touch. Something about this exchange felt off, but I couldn't place it. I felt tired and overwrought and my brain wouldn't seem to work properly.

'Sorry. Why shouldn't you be here?'

I turned to face her. Stella was youngish, mid-twenties, probably. Pretty, slim and there was a glint of intelligence in her blue eyes. She didn't look old enough to have qualified yet, so perhaps, inadvertently, I had been correct about her being a trainee.

'I just . . .' Stella paused. 'What I mean is, I don't work in this department.' She was staring at my stomach, her mouth parting slightly.

Was she *shocked*? Why? Why had the sight of my flat stomach caused this woman to reel? No one knew about my pregnancy.

I followed her gaze to my stomach, placing my hands upon it. 'You know I was pregnant?' I asked. Uneasiness caught me in the throat like an errant fish bone.

'You lost the baby.' Stella's tone sounded even, expressionless.

'Yes.' My tone matched hers. The atmosphere shifted.

How did she know about my baby? About to probe more deeply, the words died as Stella emerged from behind the end of Luke's bed.

She was pregnant. Ripe, rounded – four or five months, perhaps? Four, I would say. My own bump had been on the small side during my most recent pregnancy, but I was knowledgeable about the size a stomach should be. I always felt that pregnant women were everywhere, *everywhere*. Especially near me, especially when I had just lost a baby. My life was plagued by women flaunting their beautiful, perfect bumps.

'Four months?'

'Around that. I didn't know I was pregnant for quite a while . . . I . . . God. Sorry. Sorry.'

People were predictably contrite when it came to careless pregnancy stories. Dee, regular customers who came to the florists, random women in cafés and supermarkets. I recalled Dee's agonised expression as her announcement about Frankie hit home all those years ago and I could see the same emotion mirrored in Stella's eyes. Stella fiddled with her stethoscope, her movements erratic. There was silence in the room apart from the aggravating beep, beep, beep of Luke's machines.

'Listen, I hope Luke pulls through.' Stella nodded, seeming to almost deliberately avoid looking at Luke. 'I mean, I'm sure he will. I just hope it's soon – for your peace of mind.'

'Thank you.'

I wanted to ask how she knew him, what she was doing here. 'What are you—'

'Listen, I wish you all the best, Lucy,' Stella said before I could finish my sentence. She faltered, as if she wanted to say more. Seconds later, it seemed she had changed her mind and she headed for the door.

I felt desperate. *Stop!* I wanted to say. Who are you? How do you know my name? Who told you about my baby?

I was unnerved by the arrival of Dr Wallis, the kindly consultant who'd tended to Luke when he first had his accident. 'Do you know that woman?' I blurted out. God, I sounded mental.

Dr Wallis surprised me by calmly answering as if I was a sane person, not a deranged one. 'The one who just left? Yes, she's a trainee doctor. She worked here for a year or so, then she left a few months ago. I believe she's been transferred back again – it happens sometimes.' Dr Wallis frowned as he glanced at Luke and spoke again, absently. 'I didn't realise she was pregnant, I must say. I always thought she was ruthlessly ambitious. A career girl, you know?'

A pregnant career girl. Something didn't ring true here. 'Why did she leave?'

'Haven't a clue,' Dr Wallis replied cheerfully. 'Trainee doctors often move around a bit; they need the expertise, and sometimes, there just isn't the work.'

'Right, right.' That made sense. I relaxed. What had I been worried about?

Dr Wallis picked up Luke's notes. 'Stella Tiggs, pregnant. Who'd have thought it?'

I placed my hand on Luke's bedside table. Stella Tiggs. Tiggs. Tiggsy. Stella was the mysterious person – the mysterious *woman* – leaving messages on Luke's phone. And she was four months pregnant. No. No way.

I glanced at Luke's beautiful, rested face. My mind was shooting off in a million directions and, if I wasn't careful, it was going to alight on a theory and call it a gut instinct or women's intuition. I caught myself. This was my husband. This was *Luke*. I trusted him. Absolutely and completely.

'I'm actually quite pleased with Luke's progress,' Dr Wallis smiled. 'Obviously we need to get him out of this coma, but I'm confident that when he does, we'll be able to assess his mobility and set up a comprehensive programme to aid his recovery. Rehabilitation, that's the key in these situations.'

How I had missed Dr Wallis's sanguine optimism! His positivity buoyed me up and I almost put Stella Tiggs out of my mind. Almost.

CHAPTER SEVENTEEN

Lucy and Luke

March, six years earlier
'I can't believe it's ours.'

'Me neither. I hope you didn't have to sell yourself to get it.'

'Only a bit. The best bit, obviously.'

'What, really? You sold your chin?' I leant my back against his chest, wrapping his arms around my waist. 'Oh wow, I'll miss that dimple.'

Luke pinched me and I wriggled away. 'It's called a cleft, woman. A *cleft*. Jeez.' He jangled the keys, his breath causing puffs of white. 'I'm going in. Are you coming? The removal people must be on their way.'

I thrust my hands into my coat pockets, shivering. 'They're carrying precious cargo in there. My crappy three-piece suite and your mum's old dining room table. I hope they drive carefully.'

'I'm sure they will. A bloody dimple indeed!' Luke

huffed, fingering his chin as he crunched through the frost on the pathway.

I stayed where I was, grasping the view and allowing it to form a memory. The house was perfect. Well, it was perfect for us. Dusted today with a scattering of snow like a gingerbread house, it was set in the best location for our needs; close to the hospital and also, to a charming primary school we had our eye on for the future. Aside from that, it was a Victorian terrace with three bedrooms, one of them not even large enough to swing a gerbil in, let alone anything else. I was wondering whether to use it as a laundry room, but I had a feeling Luke had plans for a man cave. Xbox, stinky armchair, that kind of thing.

I joined Luke at the front door.

'I love the kitchen,' I said, sliding my arm around his waist.

'I know you do,' Luke replied, his expression mocking. 'God only knows why, because you can't cook for toffee. You are to cooking what Gok Wan is to . . . to carpentry. Probably.'

'Indeed. But I do like a contemporary kitchen. And it's lovely and sunny in there. You'll look good chopping and creating in there, Harte.'

We were lucky the old timers who lived there before had a wealthy daughter who wanted them to have a pretty kitchen. The rest of the house was hideous, a shrine to casino carpets and naff fireplaces. It was in need of some updating, but that was how we'd managed to afford it. Knowing that the old couple who had lived there before had been married for sixty years – sixty years! – had given us a romantic view of the house. It was very obviously the ideal place for happily married people to have children (the couple had squeezed four into this teeny abode) and to take some time renovating and updating. That last part was definitely us.

'May I?' Luke scooped me up in his arms, almost slipping over. 'Dammit. Frost isn't the best of surfaces for big, romantic gestures.'

'Did you put the key in the lock already?'

'Shit!' Luke put me down again. 'This isn't going according to plan.' He fumbled with the keys, slotting the right one into the lock finally.

'Shall I carry you over the threshold?' I giggled. 'Might be easier.'

'Stop it.' Luke scooped me up again, planting a juicy, rather invasive kiss on my mouth. 'Me man, you woman and all that. Okay, serious speech time, Stripes.' He cleared his throat. 'Well, we've only been together for a year, but this feels very right to me. Hopefully to you too, otherwise we have a biiiiiggggg problem. Namely a mortgage.' He looked down at me, his eyes dancing. 'This is a new start for us. A home. A family home for us to – you know. Make babies.'

I sighed happily. 'God, yes. I really, really want us to make babies, Luke.'

'Me too.' Luke laughed, then looked thoughtful. 'I love you, Luce. And now I'm going in because I'm so cold, my balls are shrinking into the abyss.'

'Too much information, boy. And . . . we're *in*.' I set my feet down on the revolting hallway carpet. I couldn't look at it for too long; it made my eyes go funny. 'This is so exciting! Let me look at the kitchen again.' I ran to it, soaking up the sunshine and dancing around like a child.

'We should always have flowers in here. Always.'

'I'll leave the feminine touches to you.' Luke watched me, as if he found my impish delight amusing.

'It's just so great,' I said, turning to face him.

'*You're* great,' he said, pulling a face to show he knew he sounded soppy.

I watched him opening cupboard doors, peering inside.

'I could put my granola in this one,' he said, straight-faced.

'Granola? What are you, Harte – a *girl*?'

'Yes, didn't I tell you that? Oops, sorry. Too late.' Luke tugged me over by the waist and slid his hands into my coat. 'Warming my hands, nothing more.'

'Yeah, yeah.' I kissed him. 'I've heard that before.'

Luke kissed me back, his hands roaming. 'Is this cleft in my chin really my best bit? Really?' He pushed his hips against mine to make a point and I started laughing against his mouth.

'Okay, I was wrong . . . you have other best bits . . .'

Our kisses became something else, something rougher and more urgent. Luke shrugged my coat off my shoulders and I helped him by quickly pulling off my huge jumper – it was one of his. I shivered as cool air hit my skin and Luke made a growling sound and buried his head in my neck, breathing me in. He trailed a hand down my chest, carefully avoiding my bra and I ached for him to touch me. He moved clumsily as I tugged at his jumper, eventually yanking it and his shirt over his head in one, inelegant movement. Wrapping his arms around me, he warmed me up with his body, his mouth searching for mine again.

'The removal men are due any minute,' I breathed. I didn't care; I couldn't resist him. God, I loved that cleft – and everything else. I couldn't get enough. I literally could not get enough of this man.

'I only need a minute. Maybe two . . .'

Luke met my eyes and they were glazed with lust. That did it for me. There is nothing more attractive to my mind than a man – my man – with lewd thoughts etched across his face. I undid his jeans, not taking my eyes from his. I wanted him. Now. Every time with Luke, it felt like my present and future colliding because I knew this was the man I was meant to be with for the rest of my life. I backed towards an old table the previous owners had left behind. It looked unstable and not up to the job, but we were going to risk it.

Luke lifted me up on to it, steadying it with his hands. He pushed my skirt up around my waist and pulled my legs around him. I sank my hands into his hair, arching my back as he lifted my hips towards his.

Ten minutes later, we realised how lucky we were that the removal men got lost on the way. And that the wobbly table was more robust than it looked. It had taken quite a pounding.

'Jesus.' Luke's voice was unsteady. 'That was . . . amazing. My legs are shaking. They are *shaking*, woman.'

'So are mine.' I smiled into his shoulder. My cheeks were flushed and my skin hummed and throbbed all over. I could still feel Luke's mouth everywhere, like an imprint on my skin that I didn't want to wash off. It was as sexy as hell. If we'd had time, I'd have been up for having him again.

'Well, I think we can safely say we christened the kitchen.'

'You can say that again. I won't be able to nibble a slice of toast ever again without remembering *that*. This. You.'

I kissed him longingly and reached for my jumper. 'Or when you munch on your granola.'

'Ha ha.' Luke smoothed my skirt down, restoring my dignity. 'God, Luce. This feels so right, doesn't it? You, me, this place?'

I nodded. It was everything I'd dreamt of when we first got together. Almost everything. Not now. I pushed those memories away. This moment was too precious.

'It's going to happen,' Luke murmured in my ear. He had read my mind. How did he always read my mind? 'I promise it will happen for us.' He pulled my jumper over my head and stroked my hair into place. 'We might have even scored a goal just now, fingers crossed.'

He struggled with his shirt and jumper, pulling them on together, mussing up his hair. 'That sounds like the removal men. Okay, let's check. We look intact. We're fine. No one will know.'

Luke went to the front door and let the removal men in, joining me in the kitchen again.

'Any chance of a cuppa once we find the kettle?' one of the removal men asked, poking his head through the doorway. 'And maybe a biccie?'

'Absolutely,' Luke said, casually picking something up off the worktop. 'That box is clearly labelled, so we should be in business soon.'

'Great. Us men can't work on an empty stomach, you know . . .' He headed out into the hallway, calling out directions to the removal team.

'You might need these,' Luke whispered, uncurling his hand to reveal my knickers.

Blushing scarlet, I snatched them out of his hand. I stuffed them into my pocket just as another removal man arrived, brandishing the box containing the kettle and biscuits. Luke couldn't hide his glee.

'Yay!' I cried with unnecessary enthusiasm. A giggle escaped.

The removal man looked at both of us and eyed the wonky table thoughtfully. 'Lucky that didn't snap in two,' he drawled, giving me a huge wink.

Luke burst out laughing and I nudged him, mortified. My cheeks were *flaming*. Throughout the morning, the removal man caught my eye knowingly and I winced with agonised embarrassment. Long after the removal van had pulled away, we unpacked box after box and every so often, we smiled at one another, our bodies tingling at the memory.

As it grew darker, we ate a takeaway in the kitchen, cracking up laughing as Thai green curry slopped on to the floor, despite the wedges of kitchen towel squashed under two of the table legs.

'Christ,' I said, catching sight of a book poking out of a box in the hallway. 'Why on earth have you brought those stinky old books about the Second World War and greenhouses?'

'Those?' Luke took a look over his shoulder. 'They remind me of you, that's why. I bought them when I found you in that cute little book shop you worked in.' He grabbed my fingers. 'Those books remind me of the way we met. It'll be a good story to tell our kids one day.'

I grinned. 'My elderly boss nearly passed out when you bought that stack of books. He'd never taken so much money in one day. I think he fell a bit in love with you. He wasn't the only one.' I pulled a face. 'Yuk. How slushy.'

Luke grinned back. 'Awww. But hey, it was the least I could do, barging into the shop like that and asking you out. It was like something out of *Notting Hill*.'

'I dig men who are into greenhouses . . . always have.' I leant across the table and kissed him. The table beneath us creaked obligingly, almost as though it was having a chuckle at our expense.

It was a beautiful, memorable day. I knew that whenever we ate at that wobbly old table, we'd remember it. Because our lovely new house was perfect – for us and for our children, whenever they came along. They were going to come along, weren't they? Yes. Glancing at Luke, I placed a hand on my stomach, full of hope. Children would be the icing on the cake for Luke and me. A dream come true. It was going to happen soon, I just knew it.

CHAPTER EIGHTEEN

Patricia

October

'Is it too warm for a roast? It's too warm for a roast,' Patricia fretted. Truthfully, she wasn't really fretting about the roast dinner, she was agonising over the fact that she had left Dee and Dan with Luke. Patricia didn't like leaving other people with Luke, even though she trusted Dee to call immediately if anything changed. It made her feel nervous. Luke would want to see herself or Lucy when he opened his eyes, surely?

It was just a lunch, she told herself. A lunch. They could head straight back to the hospital later and take turns again.

Patricia opened the oven and stepped back from the gust of hot air. 'I should have made a salad. Or we could have had a barbecue, couldn't we? Although I'm not sure how to get that thing working. Luke's the expert and well— He's not—' Her voice cut out, but it didn't matter.

The only person in the room was Nell and she was staring out of the dining room window distractedly.

Patricia prodded the chicken, sending juices sizzling into the tray, as she tried to control the tears that were pricking at her eyes. If Lucy and Ade were any later, she was going to be serving dry chicken and overdone potatoes. And Patricia prided herself on her roast potatoes; they were restaurant-worthy, according to Luke. She boiled them for a strict twenty minutes, drained them, shook them vigorously with the lid on before placing them, individually, into hot duck fat with a sprinkle of flour on top. Luke described them as 'legendary'.

She didn't really need to make dinner; her WI friends had dropped off so many casseroles and pies, the fridge was heaving. What else could a person do in a crisis, but bake? Patricia removed the chicken and turned the oven down a fraction. 'I did tell them one o'clock, didn't I, Nell? Nell?'

Nell said nothing, chewing a fingernail as she stared into space. She sat huddled on a dining room chair, as a person who felt the cold might sit, yet the dapple of sunlight leaking through the long, embroidered nets must surely be cloaking her with warmth.

Patricia put down what she was doing for a second and went over to Nell. 'Are you okay?' She put a hand on Nell's shoulder.

Nell looked up at her in surprise and Patricia realised that she really didn't show Nell how much she loved her often enough.

'I'm fine, Mum. Thanks.' She put her hand on Patricia's, briefly, then turned back to stare out of the window.

Patricia sighed and went back to make some gravy,

scooping most of the hot fat away from the chicken pan and adding flour as she fired up the hob. Mashing up the vegetable trivet her mother had taught her to use long before Jamie Oliver waxed lyrical about it, Patricia tossed a glass of white wine in, turning to check on Nell again.

Nell had been withdrawn since Luke's accident and despite a few, brief attempts to get her to open up, Patricia had all but given up trying to get through to her. Nell always went into herself in a crisis; she shut down like a defunct power station and it was unrewarding work trying to prise her open again.

Patricia briskly stirred stock into her gravy. She and Nell had been inseparable before Bernard died. They had always been like mother and daughter, rather than having the 'besties' type friendship some women self-consciously spoke of at the WI, but they had been close. Shopping trips to buy clothes together, ice creams at the local café and a shared love of reading in the garden when the sun was out, that kind of thing.

But when Bernard died, everything had ground to a halt. It would be convenient and conscience saving to point the finger at Nell for this lapse in effort, but Patricia knew she could only blame herself. Just when Nell needed her most, Patricia had ducked out. Not out of life, but she had shut down and she had shut everyone out. And when Ade had left, Nell had fallen to pieces, only allowing Luke in. Patricia wished her relationship with Nell could go back to what it was before, but she had no idea how to even make tracks.

Nell had silently and rather haphazardly laid the table earlier, but she seemed reluctant to chat, certainly going by what had just happened. Since placing all the cutlery the wrong way round like a person who didn't know her left from her right, she had been content to stare out of the window at who knew what.

'Sorry I'm late, Patricia.' Lucy seemed flustered when she arrived. Thinner, paler and somehow faded. Without Luke by her side, Lucy seemed colourless and lost, even though that wasn't a very nice thing to think. Patricia contemplated this as she managed a watery smile and she wished she didn't immediately feel a stinging pain over her son's predicament whenever Lucy was in the room.

Lucy held out a bottle of white wine apologetically, as though she had been planning something better but had run out of time. 'It's warm. The fridge at the petrol station had been raided.'

'Thank you. I have some white in the fridge already, so we'll pop that one in there for later, shall we?'

Lucy nodded and, after a moment, leant forward to kiss Patricia's cheek. Startled, Patricia turned away and instantly regretted what must seem like a rebuff. Was it the first physical contact they had shared since Luke's accident? Why was it so hard to accept? She should be gathering her daughter-in-law up in her arms. They should be sharing the despair they were both feeling and they should be consoling one another, united in their hope for Luke's speedy recovery. Patricia watched Lucy and Nell embrace, jealous of their easy friendship. Shouldn't she be able to embrace her daughter that way, her daughter-in-law?

Lucy straightened, holding her arms awkwardly across her body.

'I . . . listen. Do either of you remember Luke mentioning someone called Stella?' She stumbled slightly

152

over the name. 'Stella Tiggs. She's a trainee doctor at Luke's hospital. She left a few months ago, but she's back. Working there again, from what I understand.'

Nell stood up and headed to the fridge. 'Stella Tiggs. No, I don't think so.' She opened the bottle of white wine and poured three glasses. After a pause, she reached for another and filled it. 'Why do you ask?'

Lucy ran a pale hand through her hair. 'Well, it's silly, really. I found these texts from someone called Tiggsy and I didn't know who it was.'

'Tiggsy?' Nell handed her a glass of wine. Her tone remained casual, but her eyes were watchful.

'Yeah. I know. A nickname.' Lucy sipped her wine too quickly. 'Anyway, I met her, yesterday, this Stella. She came to see how Luke was getting on.'

Patricia checked the clock and decided to go ahead and carve the chicken. Ade wasn't spoiling this duty lunch, or whatever Nell kept calling it. She wasn't even sure she should have arranged it. She'd had half a mind to hold Ade at arm's length for a while, but, perversely, now that he was actually here, she was like a junkie needing a fix.

'What's the problem? Surely Luke has the odd friend you don't know about? Especially at the hospital.'

'Sure.' Lucy shrugged, but her jaw remained rigid. 'I'm probably over-reacting.'

Ade arrived at that point and Patricia left Lucy chatting to Nell as she greeted him. She was determined to make an effort today, to welcome him back into the fold. His arrival at the hospital that first time had caught her by surprise and she knew she hadn't acquitted herself well.

Ade looked good, unfairly so. 'Unfairly,' because Luke obviously looked anything but good right now. A white shirt, expensive-looking dark jeans and loafers had transformed Ade into a grown-up version of the man Patricia remembered. The tan turned him from nice-looking to handsome, drawing out his freckles and lending him a suave air.

'Ade. Lovely to see you.' Patricia knew she sounded formal. On impulse, thinking of the way she was being with Lucy and Nell, she leant forward and kissed his cheek.

'You too, Mum.' He looked openly delighted and he thrust a large bunch of purple freesias into her hands. 'Sorry, coals to Newcastle and all that. I did bring some rosé wine though.' He met Nell's eyes as if they were sharing a private joke, but Nell seemed caught up in whatever Lucy was saying.

Ade's face fell a little, but he gave his mother an amiable smile. 'What smells so good? A roast? Oh wow, you're spoiling me. I've dreamt about your roasts, Mum.' He flushed. 'I mean that; I have.'

'Well, isn't that nice?' Patricia didn't know how to take his comment. 'Let's sit. Shall we sit?'

Ade hesitated.

'Here,' Nell said, coming to his rescue and perhaps sensing that Ade didn't want to accidentally commandeer Luke's usual chair. 'Sit next to Lucy.'

Lucy smiled, but her face was taut. Perhaps she was struggling with Ade's presence, too.

Ade flicked Nell a grateful smile and accepted a glass of wine. 'Should I carve?' he offered.

'I've already done that,' Patricia called from the kitchen. 'I couldn't wait any longer.'

'Oh dear. Not a good start,' Ade muttered under his breath to Lucy, as Patricia sailed back in with the chicken. 'I was at the hospital,' he added, probably to justify his tardiness. 'I met Dee and Dan . . . they're lovely, aren't they? And I was chatting to Luke's consultant.'

'Any update?' Patricia asked, in an overly-bright voice. Her stomach was in knots every time someone else came back from visiting Luke because she had no idea what she was going to hear. She bustled around, bringing the roast potatoes to the table, followed by a large selection of hot, buttered vegetables and her prized gravy.

'Not really. I mean, he was upbeat, but until Luke comes out of this coma, I don't think anyone can really say for sure what we're dealing with.' He passed the potatoes to Lucy, his eyes softening. 'How are you doing, Lucy? "Bearing up," that's the British phrase for it, isn't it? In Australia, we just say "How's it going?" and hope you get our drift.'

Patricia dropped her carving knife with a clatter then snatched it up again. Her eyes met Ade's but she said nothing. She disliked the way he talked about Australia as his home.

Lucy gazed at the potatoes. 'Thanks, Ade. I'm all right. I'm . . . I'm coping. We're all just coping, I suppose. It's it's hard, isn't it? Without Luke. I just hate seeing him like this. He's not himself. Not remotely.' She managed a rueful smile.

Ade helped himself to gravy. 'I know, it's awful.' He sniffed, then seemed to pull himself together. 'This chicken is great, Mum. And the roasties. Legendary.'

Patricia's eyelids fluttered at Ade's unintentional echo of Luke. 'Thank you. I'm glad you're enjoying them.'

It hurt to hear Ade using the words Luke would have used. And she couldn't help wishing Ade was here under different circumstances. This wasn't how she had wanted it. She had had vague thoughts in her head of bringing the family together, but now she wondered if it was too soon for any of them to accept Ade. To adjust to Luke not being here.

Nell made a point of clearing her throat. 'I thought I'd read *Great Expectations* to Luke during my visits. Better than a *Woman's Own* sorry, Mum. What do you think, Luce?'

Lucy managed a wan smile. 'Great idea. That way he'll have no choice but to listen to one of my favourite novels, like it or not.'

'That was my plan.' Nell nodded, eyeing her mother.

Patricia was only half-listening. She struggled to keep her thoughts on an even keel, despite the easy chatter going on around her. Luke was missing, and every time she looked at Ade or heard his voice, she was thrown back to the past – to when Bernard died. She couldn't help it.

Ade had left them. Left them when they were all broken and bleeding. She wanted to forgive and forget but the wound was so raw, especially with Luke in hospital. Patricia knew she was picking at a scab, but she didn't know what else to do because the hurt, the pain she felt just from looking at him was overwhelming.

Patricia watched Nell drinking too much wine, her eyes never straying far from Ade's face, but the implication behind her gaze was masked. Patricia watched Lucy toy with her food, managing the odd morsel that she chewed for indeterminate periods. Ade was cheerful throughout, helping himself to seconds and waxing lyrical about the food. It all felt forced and stilted.

Patricia started to clear away, keen to move to dessert. She presented a lemon meringue pie rather grandly, confident that it was perfect. Supremely light meringue, a squashy, tart lemon filling without a soggy pastry bottom in sight.

'Your favourite, Ade,' Patricia announced, hoping to reach out to him somehow.

Lucy looked up quickly, meeting Nell's eyes across the table.

Ade cast his eyes down and fingered his wine glass. 'Er, no. Mum, that's Luke's favourite.'

Patricia abruptly sat, almost missing her chair. 'Oh. Yes, yes of course. Silly me. I can't believe I did that. Your favourite dessert is treacle sponge, Ade. Treacle sponge and custard. And flapjacks. You like flapjacks.'

Ade reached out and covered Patricia's hand with his own. 'It's fine, Mum. I understand. I've been away for a long time and Luke is very much in your thoughts right now.'

Patricia burst into tears. 'He is. He is!' She whipped her hand away and coiled it into a fist. 'I can't stop thinking about him. He should be here . . . this isn't right. Luke was – is – everything.'

Lucy stood up, tight lipped and ashen. 'Was? He's not *dead*, Patricia. Stop talking about him in the past tense!'

Patricia recoiled at Lucy's obvious anger. She hadn't meant to cause that – that wasn't what she meant.

An ugly flush appeared in Lucy's cheeks for the first time that day. 'He's in a coma and his consultants are hopeful that he will come out of it soon.'

She pushed her chair back, knocking it over with a clatter, and swept her bag up. Without a backward glance, Lucy stalked out of the house. The front door slammed shut, the sound reverberating loudly into the dining room.

Nell almost stood, but seemed to think better of it. 'Don't take that to heart, Mum. Lucy has a lot on her mind at the moment. She doesn't mean to be rude; she's just under an awful lot of pressure.'

'We're all under *pressure*,' Patricia snapped back, regretting it instantly. Inside, she was horrified at what had just happened. She softened her tone. 'I just mean that we are all under pressure. You, me, Lucy. Ade.' The final mention was a politeness, an afterthought, and they all knew it.

'Oh, not me, Mum,' Ade said lightly. 'What pressure could I possibly be under?'

Patricia's eyes narrowed, her mouth twisting to form an acerbic, lemon-sharp pucker. What did Ade want from her?

Ade drained his wine, his head nodding slightly. His body was coiled up tightly, tension rigidly evident in his shoulders. 'I get it. I'm fine and all of you are suffering, right?' He put his napkin down carefully, getting to his feet.

'Well, I'll just bring you up to date, Mum. My marriage has fallen apart, irretrievably. My business is going well, but my heart isn't in it any more, which is why I've left it in the hands of my partner. My brother is in a coma and, contrary to what you all think, I love him – and all of you – very much. I hate seeing you both like this, seeing Luke's wife in absolute bits with everything she's going through.'

Ade swallowed hard, as if he was struggling to remain composed. 'I'm back home, but I feel like an outsider and, worst of all, I have this feeling, this really strong feeling, that you'd rather it was me lying in that bed than Luke. Because as you said, Mum, Luke is *everything*. Say I'm wrong. Say it.'

Patricia stared at him, speechlessly, and she hesitated. Just for a few seconds. A few long, heavy seconds that hung in the air and left a bitter aftertaste. They all felt it and they all wished they hadn't. Patricia rushed to defend herself, but it was too late. 'I—'

Ade gripped the back of his chair, his tanned knuckles briefly turning white. 'A suitable punishment for letting you all down when Dad died, right? Thanks, Mum. Thanks a lot.'

Patricia watched Ade's retreating back, consumed with regret. *Oh God. How dreadful. Poor Ade. What on earth is wrong with me?* Nell stood up too. Patricia's heart pounded and she felt a scream threatening to rip through her. 'Please don't leave as well, Nell.'

Nell looked aghast. 'Mum, that was *awful*. Poor Ade. You paused. You actually paused.'

Patricia wiped a smudge of lemon from the edge of her pie, wiping her trembling finger on her napkin. 'I – I wasn't thinking. I – he caught me off guard. Of course I don't wish Ade was in Luke's place.'

Nell picked at her fingernails, leaving tangerine chips on the tablecloth. 'Don't you, Mum? Are you sure? We both feel resentful towards Ade, don't we? If we're honest?'

Patricia let out a sob. Her shoulders shook and her hand went to her mouth. 'I don't want to feel this way; I don't. But I blame him. I blame him for leaving us all in the lurch like that and for what he made you feel, Nell. Can *you* forgive him?'

'I don't know. I – I have to take responsibility for myself. I did this to myself, not Ade.' Nell held her gnarly wrists out.

Patricia turned away. 'Don't, darling. I can't bear it.'

'Mum, we have to stop blaming Ade for everything. I couldn't cope with Dad dying and neither could you. Neither could Luke probably, but someone had to hoist us up and stop us from losing the plot.'

Patricia used her napkin as a tissue, blowing loudly. 'I know, I know. But the thing is, he's back and Luke's in a coma and it feels wrong. I just want Luke back.'

Nell stood up, awkwardly coiling her arm around Patricia's shoulders. 'We all want him back, Mum.'

Patricia leant against Nell, sniffing. It felt good to be in her daughter's arms. Her closeness, her warmth almost made Patricia come undone. It felt like the old days again.

Nell finally withdrew. 'I don't remember Lucy ever walking out of a lunch before.'

Patricia stared out into the garden. 'I owe her an apology. I shouldn't have talked about Luke that way.'

Nell pleated a napkin, her creative fingers fashioning it into a skirt shape. 'I think there's more on Lucy's mind than that. She's being irrational, but she's allowed; she's living in a nightmare.' She screwed the napkin up into a ball. 'We all are, to a degree. But we have to let Lucy take centre stage on that front, right?'

Patricia nodded. Letting out a big sigh, she picked up the pie and carried it to the kitchen.

Ade . . . and Lucy. The way they had left like that. Patricia swallowed, realising she was in danger of alienating the most important people in her life. She loved Ade. She adored Lucy. And she had been vile to both of them. Patricia's shoulders tensed as she allowed herself to cry, quietly, so Nell didn't notice. Her daughter didn't need to see her falling apart. She needed to be strong for her family – each and every one of them. Ade was just as much her son as Luke was, and Lucy was so terribly vulnerable right now.

Patricia tipped the lemon meringue pie in the bin. She'd make it again when Luke was back home and not before. Until then, she was going to check in with Dee, and then she was going to eat some much-needed humble pie. There were two people who needed apologies from her.

CHAPTER NINETEEN

Lucy and Luke

December, six years earlier

'Go on, open it. It's your last present. And, if I say so myself, it's stupendous. Like, off the scale *awesome*.'

'Bigging yourself up there, Harte. Creates unnecessary anticipation followed by inevitable deflation. Schoolboy error.'

'I'm feeling cocky and rightly so. You'll see.'

Luke handed me a gift the size of a large book. He looked absurdly happy, as if he might have pulled off something really cool, if a man who resembled a ten-year-old boy could somehow look that way. Let me be clear: Luke's outfit *du jour* consisted of pyjama bottoms Rupert Bear would have been proud of and a Star Wars T-shirt with Chewy on it, saying: 'It's Not Wise to Upset a Wookiee.' Enough said.

Don't get me wrong; I hardly looked adult myself. I was wearing a pair of striped pyjamas an aunt had bought Luke for his birthday and they pretty much neutered me.

I'd counter-balanced the asexual look by putting on a red satin thong with white faux fur underneath, for Luke to find later. Mrs Santa or some such nonsense. I wouldn't have contemplated such a thing before meeting Luke.

'Open it, open it,' Luke whined, pushing my leg. He started drumming on it, knowing it would get my attention.

'Stop it, you silly man.'

I lingered over the gift, turning it over in my hands. It was our first proper Christmas in our new house, because Luke had been forced to work during the first one we'd shared here, and I was dragging the morning out for as long as I possibly could. We were due at Patricia's for a lunch that would consist of six satisfyingly stodgy courses, heated rounds of charades that were as competitive as a professional golf tournament and, for anyone who could manage it, a buffet-style tea fit for the queen (post-speech). But, until then, we were making the most of sitting in bed with a pile of smoked salmon, hot buttered toast and a bottle of Moët that Luke had won in the hospital raffle.

Christmas at the Harte household was always a surprisingly festive affair, but today I wanted to savour this special moment away from it.

Luke jabbed me once more. 'Lucy, open it. I chose it especially for you. It took me ages. *Ages.*'

I rolled my eyes at him, mainly because he once told me it made me look 'alluring'. 'What am I?' I'd asked waspishly. 'A nineteen-fifties pin-up?'

'More nineteen-forties,' he'd deadpanned, making reference to me being older than him, the git.

I held the gift up. 'The fact that it took you ages to choose. Does that mean it's actually pants and I'll hate it?'

Luke gave me the arched eyebrow. 'I'm doing the guilt trip thing up front to cover myself. Just in case, you know.'

'God, I hate it when people tell me a gift took them ages to choose,' I grumbled. 'I feel all pressurised and stressed out. If I hate it, do I tell you? Or do I go all wide-eyed and gushy and chunter on about—'

'Just open it,' Luke interrupted, beginning to look impatient. 'Or I'll open it for you and that's going to spoil the whole bloody thing.'

'Okay, okay.' I tore the paper off. It was a box, made to look like a book. A first edition, perhaps, with frayed edges and faded lettering. Original and truly, the perfect gift for a book-lover like me. The man had done good.

'I love it! I'll keep my jewellery in it.'

'Not this, I hope. I'd rather you wore this.'

Luke reached over and with shaking hands, opened the box. Inside, there were crumpled sheets of red tissue paper and nestling amongst those, another box. A small, velvet one. One of those little black boxes of a certain size that make a girl's heart skip a beat or two, however cynical she might be. And I wasn't actually that cynical; I just didn't overly rate marriage. But my heart did the skippy thing, nonetheless.

I was also rather flabbergasted. I thought we were convention-free, chilled out and not part of the married gang. But we could be. I went with it, feeling giddy inside.

Luke fumbled a bit, opening the box and thrusting it under my nose. I squinted, held my breath a bit. I know

164

a girl shouldn't worry about the look of an engagement ring, but I was gripped with anxiety. I genuinely hadn't visualised such a thing before now; my relationship with Luke had always felt solid without marriage and we had agreed that we wanted kids first and foremost. But it tells a woman that her man really knows her when he gets it right, right?

I opened my eyes and relaxed. It was right. Thank God, thank *God*. An emerald, discreet and pretty. The man – *my* man – knew me. All was well.

Luke scratched his head. 'I had this little speech planned. Nothing fancy, but it was definitely heartfelt.' He started laughing. 'Gosh, I'm so hungover, I can't even think straight. Bollocks. Talk about ruining a moment. Sorry, Luce.'

'It's okay. I can't take you seriously when the Wookiee is perving at me.' I held my hand out grandly. 'Put it on me, please. If it's the right size, I will duly faint.'

Luke did the honours and, of course, it didn't fit. The ring slipped all the way round and we laughed. I have tiny, child-like fingers, so it was no surprise, nor was it a disappointment. Luke snuck an arm round my shoulders, tugging me into his armpit.

'Look, I know we've always said that marriage didn't matter to us, that we just wanted each other and our children, when we're lucky enough to have them.' He felt me stiffen and he took my hand, his grip firm and sure. 'And that's still true and still what is in our future despite the past few years.' His eyes met mine. Neither of us needed to mention those seven little boxes. 'But, I don't know. I had an old-fashioned moment and I thought of my parents and I wanted that too. Do you mind?'

'Do I mind? With this rock on my finger? Slipping off my finger—' I caught it and kissed him. 'You old romantic, you. I love that.'

I carefully placed the ring on the bedside table and slid my hand under his T-shirt. 'What a truly stupendous gift that is. Makes my Xbox look like – like just an Xbox.'

'An Xbox is a hundred times better than an engagement ring,' Luke corrected, rolling me back under the duvet. 'But I'm a gentleman, so I won't talk about how many months' salary it was . . .' He started pulling my T-shirt over my head. I helped him. My skin rippled with goose bumps as my bare skin met the air.

'Mmmm, nakedness . . .' Luke's mouth was on my chest.

I held him back for a second. Something had occurred to me. 'You do realise this means we can never, ever have sex with anyone else for the rest of our lives?'

'I do.'

The declaration was solemn, but I could feel his smile against me, warming my skin. I held his head and lifted it so he was looking at me. 'Marriage – it's different, Luke. What would we do if one of us fancied someone else?'

'Impossible.' Luke bent his head to my stomach, teasing it with his tongue. He peered into the waistband of my pyjama trousers.

I lifted his head again. 'All right. Not fancied, but I

don't know. Drifted. Ended up in a compromising posi-tion? Doesn't that happen to people who are together for a long time? You know, to married people?'

Luke shifted, gazing at me affectionately. 'You really do have terrible timing, Stripes.' He groaned, realising I was being serious. 'Okay. Let me think. If one of us started to stray, we should talk to one another.'

'Nothing more distasteful than confessional chit-chat about lust for another over the shepherd's pie,' I agreed.

'I mean about what might be going on in our relationship.'

'Like a pact?'

'Yeah, a pact. A fidelity pact.' Luke nodded. His eyes were still bleary with sleep and he rubbed them, knowing I needed him to be present for this conversation. 'If we're having problems and something happens, we talk. Like we always talk.'

'I like it.' I was decisive. 'Let's do it.'

'I'm hearing *that*.'

Mariah Carey starting singing about all the things she wanted for Christmas in the background and I knew that the cheesy song would always be more meaningful from today. Dammit.

Luke tucked my hair behind my ear, his expression sober. 'I love you, Luce. Happy Christmas.'

'Soppy bastard.'

I slid beneath the duvet and yanked him under there with me. 'Hey, we have a Christmas song now. Not just a song, but a Christmas one. Mariah will forever be in our hearts.'

'This is the best Christmas ever,' Luke said, sliding his hands around my waist. 'Wow, you're dressed like Mrs Santa under there.'

'A little surprise for you. Hey, Harte . . . I don't know how you're going to top this next year.'

'Me neither,' he agreed. 'I've used up all my brownie points in one go.'

Later, my body still tingling from Luke's touch, I stared down at the emerald on my finger. This ring, this moment with Luke – it was right. *We* were right. I hadn't even been bothered about getting married, but now I realised that it was exactly what I wanted. Marriage itself wasn't important as such, but marrying Luke was. This was one of the happiest days of my life. And to think I'd never really enjoyed Christmas before I'd met Luke.

Hearing Luke calling for me get a move on because we were late for lunch at Patricia's, I wriggled into a black velvet dress and hurried downstairs.

CHAPTER TWENTY

Nell

October

'So, do you think my coursework is okay?'

Nell wasn't sure why she had asked that. She wasn't even sure why she was back at college. Her mum, Lucy, Ade – they had all insisted, because they thought it was important that she continued her studies. Nell could see their point, but she wanted to be with Luke. She had only agreed on the basis that she was allowed to be part of the rota system her mum had efficiently drawn up as Luke's coma lingered on. Nell would take her turn at sitting with Luke and reading to him, even if it meant doing so when she should be getting some sleep.

Cal smiled at her gently, guessing she was still devastated about Luke. 'It was brilliant. Obviously. You know what I think of your designs. Not that I'm the person you need to impress with this stuff.' He flipped her file open, his finger tracing the curve of an elegant red dress. 'I love this. The shoulder detail is sublime.'

'Thank you. I liked it, too.'

Nell trailed her hand through some wild grass. They had taken an afternoon away from college to take a stroll in a park on the outskirts of Bath. Nell had felt guilty about it – she felt guilty about everything right now – but this outing was unheard of for Cal. She wasn't about to question it; she relished the time she had with him. Although deep down, Nell couldn't help wondering what it meant. What did it mean? Something? Nothing?

I must not nag him, she told herself mutely. She was, God help her, the 'other woman'. Rules for the other woman stated (somewhere) that questions about the relationship and where it was going should remain unspoken, at least in the early stages. As should any misplaced curiosity about wives, children and anything else that could trigger the defence barriers into lockdown position.

Nell swallowed her thoughts about where the relationship might be going or what Cal's request to spend more time with her might mean. If she was being honest, she had also needed to get away from the two oppressively suffocating camps she seemed to live in these days; home and the hospital.

Nell checked her phone, something she had started doing in frenetic bursts since Luke's accident. She didn't have any messages. She slipped the phone back into the pocket of her jacket, relaxing slightly.

'I haven't been concentrating on my studies recently. I thought my designs were – I don't know. Sub-standard.'

'Even your sub-standard is better than the not-so-illustrious efforts of some of your fellow students.' Cal looked pained and he tucked her file back under his arm. 'But not everyone is as talented as you, sadly.'

'So my designs were sub-standard?'

'No, no. That's not what I meant.' He glanced over his shoulder then slid his free arm around her shoulders. 'They were superb. You know I'm always honest with you about your work.'

Nell shivered with pleasure. Cal rarely touched her in public. She could have done without the awkward, remorseful privacy check beforehand, but she knew she shouldn't spoil the moment by saying anything. She wondered if they looked strange together, she in her early twenties, him in his – his early fifties. Her fresh-faced, him craggy and weather-beaten.

Nell shrugged the thought off. Who cared what they looked like? They were together and that was all that mattered. Cal so rarely put his arm round her in public, she was going to enjoy the rare and rather lovely sensation.

'So, how's Luke?' Cal asked, turning the conversation away from her studies.

Nell leant against his shoulder, enjoying the warmth of his body against hers. 'I don't know. It all feels pretty stagnant. Nothing has changed . . . he's still unresponsive.' She breathed in Cal's scent and wondered if person-addiction was a 'thing'. Sometimes, she felt overwhelmed by her feelings for Cal, as if she couldn't get enough of him. It made her feel out of control, vulnerable.

'You must feel as though you're in limbo,' Cal commented. 'As if you can't focus on anything else fully until you have results. Because whilst Luke is in limbo, so are all of you.'

'Exactly. That's exactly how I feel.' She gave him a brief smile, touched that he seemed to understand her. He was so wise; that was one of the reasons she'd fallen for him.

Cal stopped and turned her round to face him. 'I'm sorry, Nell. I really want you to know that I'm here for you.'

Only when your wife doesn't need you, Nell thought, unfairly. She let him kiss her and her mind cleared. Everything seemed to make sense when they connected. Perhaps that was why she felt so dependent on him. She needed him – maybe a little too much.

Cal turned and started walking again, his arm loosely around her shoulders. 'And what about your other brother? Ade, is it?'

'Ade, yes.' Nell told him about their drink and the lunch. 'I just can't trust him yet. It's too hard. He . . . he let me down.'

Cal gestured to a quiet-looking café near the gates. 'Let's get a drink.' They found a table and sat down. He put her file on the table between them. 'Iced tea?'

'Is it Long Island?' Nell pulled a rueful face. 'Sorry, yes. Iced tea is fine.' She nodded to the waitress, who had matted dreadlocks and studs through her nose and eyebrows. They looked painful. Nell felt distracted. 'What was I saying?'

Cal toyed with a menu. 'You were talking about how Ade couldn't take care of you when your dad died.'

Nell watched him slot the menu between salt and pepper pots shaped like skittles, his fingers stroking it into place. She drank him in, feasting her eyes on him the way someone else might when faced with their favourite food. Cal's blonde hair was attractively tousled, as usual – bed hair. It was either natural or it had been teased with wax; she hoped the latter.

Cal's eyes, that murky, sexy shade of green that contacts couldn't recreate, met hers. He rubbed his crooked nose, waiting for her to speak.

She was charmed by his interest. It made her more open. After the iced tea was placed on the table, she spoke again.

'When Ade left, I tried to kill myself.' Nell discreetly exposed her wrists, laying them flat on the table. 'And I meant to do it. It – it wasn't an accident.'

Cal reached across and gently turned her arms over. 'I guessed. I've seen your wrists, Nell. I've seen every part of you.'

She blushed and clasped her hands around her iced tea. He had noticed and not commented; how sweet of him. She had wondered if he had noticed the distorted flesh, but she knew now that the scars hadn't flown under his radar.

Heartened, Nell carried on. 'I was in therapy for years – Luke sent me. I don't know what would have happened to me if Luke hadn't been there.'

Cal sipped his iced tea. 'What you went through sounds traumatic. And I think what you're going through now is horrendous.'

Nell nodded, but she wanted more than a statement of fact. She wanted empathy and sympathy and everything in between. She wanted everything Cal had to offer her.

'I wish I could take your pain away,' Cal told her, reaching out to take her hand. He rubbed his thumb across her scar tenderly. 'I wish I could take these scars away and I wish I didn't have to witness the pain you're in right now, with Luke and Ade and everything else.'

Nell started to cry. She could feel herself spiralling, spiralling again.

Cal linked his fingers through hers. 'There's so much more to you than what happened all those years ago. It's not who you are; it's what you experienced.'

Nell blinked. He was right. She wasn't her suicide attempt. It was just something she did a long time ago. Snatching her phone out of her jacket pocket, she quickly answered it.

'Lucy. What's wrong? Is it Luke?' Nell listened, her eyes cast down. 'He's going to be all right, okay? You have to stay strong.' She spoke again, her voice muted, then ended the call.

'What's happened?' Cal signalled for the bill. 'Has Luke taken a turn for the worse?'

'No.' Nell bit her lip. 'Lucy was just having a panic about him. I don't know why, exactly. I think she just gets scared sometimes. We all do.'

'It's understandable. Christ, I have to go.' Cal glanced at his watch, looking panicked. He tilted his head apologetically. 'I need to get back to the university . . .'

'Sure.'

'I wish I could stay.' Cal bent his head and kissed her.

Nell was shocked. It was huge for Cal that he had done that in public. She watched him leave, her heart torn in two. She wanted to give it fully, but she couldn't. She couldn't. It was too big a risk and she might end up with it handed back to her in painful little pieces.

Nell put her head in her hands. An affair with a married man. Luke in a coma. Nell struggled for a breath. Panic was rising and it was gathering momentum. She needed an outlet. Holding one hand to her pulsing chest, Nell dug a pen out of her bag and flipped her file open to a clean page.

Dad,

I'm scared. Really scared. Life is . . . upside down. Ever since Luke's accident, everything has gone wrong . . . everything feels wrong. I feel lost without him and I reckon all of us feel the same. Mum, Lucy . . . even Ade – all of us feel strange without him.

Why can't we cope without Luke, Dad? How did we all become so dependent on him? What scares me most is what might become of us if he doesn't make it. That's what keeps me awake at night, Dad. That's what has me writing these stupid letters to you every time something bad happens. Because you're all I have. Without Luke, I've come to realise that you, my Dad who isn't even here any more, are all I have.

I know this is wrong, because I have friends, and I have Mum and Lucy . . . And Ade. And I have Cal. He should be the one I run to, right? Not you, Dad. Because as much as I still love you, you're not here any more. At least . . . in some ways, you're here for me more than Cal is.

You're here for me more than Cal is.

Nell re-read her own words, staring at them numbly. Abruptly, she tore the page out and screwed it up. It was all too complicated to think about right now. Right now, the most important person in this whole scenario was Luke.

CHAPTER TWENTY-ONE

Lucy

Noting the IVF consultant's much-used, but genuinely caring smile, I paused in the doorway. I would miss the spectrum of smiles those consultants were able to produce. That last one, however, was a killer. Sympathetic, kindly and brutally final.

I gently closed the door behind me. Talk about poignant symbolism. Whatever happened with Luke now, whatever state he was in after his coma, this part of our lives was over. IVF was no longer an option for us. I had felt the need to formally update the team about my miscarriage and about Luke's accident, even though I was sure they must already know. News travelled like wildfire in this hospital; Luke always said it was a hotbed of gossip and speculation, but I had been brought up on a strict regime of manners and good form. My mother would be impressed that I had remembered to cross the 't's and dot the 'i's, even in what she would no doubt describe as my 'state of devastating grief'.

I put a hand to my chest. It felt heavy, constricted. Sorrow, it seemed, was a weighty old emotion. I needed some air. This was a common theme for me these days, the desire to be outside. Away from the sterile claustro-phobia of the hospital, for sure, but it was more about the necessity of sucking down air into my lungs, as much as I could manage.

This quest had led to the discovery of a small garden at the back of the hospital, the area essentially made up of a hard wooden bench, a small strip of grass and not much else. It afforded me some much-needed solitude, a few moments of privacy and general peace and quiet. Perfect for 'someone in my position' (Patricia's expres-sion), it had become my sanctuary. I sat down and drew in a long, cleansing breath, allowing my mind to mull over the events of the morning.

I thought Luke had more colour in his cheeks, but the nurse in charge didn't seem to agree. I mean, she tried, but she wasn't hugely convincing. Perhaps acting lessons should become a standard part of medical training, the pass mark dependent on the ability to feign enthusiasm and to jolly relatives out of a pessimistic mindset.

Actually, Luke's consultants seemed fairly upbeat. They didn't dwell on uncertainties, because I suppose they couldn't put a plan together if they didn't yet know what Luke was going to need.

I was also concerned about Patricia. We had been civil to one another when we met up, but I was conscious of my actions at Sunday lunch. I shouldn't have reacted that way. I wondered how long the dual tragedy of losing our baby and having a husband in a coma would excuse my deplorable manners. Probably not for much longer.

I stared at the hospital, watching junior doctors and nurses bursting out of the double doors, immediately reaching for cigarettes as they swigged bottled water. How very *Grey's Anatomy*. I imagined them discussing Luke, the women shaking their heads at the idea of such a vital, handsome man in a comatose state, the men impatiently shrugging off the issue of looks and bringing the debate back to his diagnosis. Actually, that was probably terribly sexist of me; did female doctors and nurses even notice if a coma patient was handsome? Unlikely, when they were intimately acquainted with his bodily fluids.

I choked down a sob. It wasn't fair. He was so much more than that. God, I had to stop crying all the time. Even Frankie, Dee's daughter, had kindly demanded that I pull myself together yesterday. Perhaps I should succumb to the well-meant invites of the bereavement organisation. Perhaps they could get me to stop snivelling like a six-year-old searching for a missing kitten.

I sniffed and stared at the gaggle of doctors and nurses. One of the white-coat wearers looked familiar, her blonde hair lit up by the watery sunshine that was attempting to break through the clouds. She wore a dove-grey pencil skirt and a crisp, white blouse, the stethoscope coiled around her neck. It was Stella, Stella Tiggs; the woman who had earned a nickname from my husband. My husband, the man she liked to text from time to time.

She leant against the wall, presumably to ease her aching back. My eyes slid to her swollen stomach, the bump that was home to her baby. The usual, tired envy reared its head, but it was a numb kind, clouded by something else. Confusion. An itch. An unanswered question. And even though I was convinced it was innocent, I needed . . . something. Closure.

As if she could feel me staring, Stella looked up. She saw me and hesitated. Looking back, it was that fleeting hesitation that did it for me. If she'd simply waved and turned away, I might have let it go, but the hesitation made me take action.

'Come over,' I mouthed to her.

Stella straightened. She swallowed and smoothed her skirt over her bump. She seemed uncomfortable, reluctant. I didn't realise they did such professional-looking pencil skirts for heavily pregnant women; I'd never got that far with my own pregnancies before. I watched her thrust her hands into the pockets of her white coat and she entered the small garden, dawdling the way I imagined Frankie might if Dee dragged her to the dentist.

'Lucy.' She said my name shakily.

'Stella.' I caught my lip between my teeth and went for it. 'Tiggsy.'

She tugged a hand out of her pocket, placing it on the wall. It was smoothly done, but a tell-tale tremble alerted me to the fact that she was steadying herself. Once again, I was struck by how young Stella was; at least a decade younger than me. A few years older than Nell. Aside from some medical chit-chat, what could she have had in common with Luke?

'Are you working here?' I asked her. This wasn't the main question I had for her, but I had to start somewhere.

Stella paused. 'Yes. I . . . it's not what I wanted, but I was transferred back here. Only a few weeks ago, actually. I hadn't seen Luke for – for ages before his accident,' she added.

'How do you know Luke?' I asked her. I'm nothing if not direct these days. I blame Luke's accident. This time, Stella visibly flinched.

'We were friends. We *are* friends.' She corrected herself.

I waved a hand. Even Patricia slipped up with the past tense. 'I realise that. I just can't understand why he didn't tell me about you.'

Stella's mouth twitched and twisted. It seemed to have a mind of its own, perhaps working in line with her brain as it searched for the right words. As for me, my mind was telling me I was way off tangent but my stomach was doing the opposite. I was beginning to feel rather sick. I either had a bad case of indigestion or something momentous was about to happen here.

'Is there . . . I don't even know what I'm asking you. You and Luke—' I stopped. Stella looked agonised. I had this ringing in my ears, a kind of humming noise that seemed to drown out everything else.

I stood up, my hands curling into fists. I uncurled them, but it was an effort – not because I felt angry, but because I was on edge. Stella lifted her blue eyes to mine. I don't know what was reflected in my eyes, but hers were guilty, guilty, *guilty*. The rapid thump of my heart

181

joined the humming drone in my ears until they were both at screaming point.

Stella gave in. 'We – we used to talk. Luke used to talk. About the baby stuff.'

The baby stuff? She might as well have slapped me. Those three words relegated mine and Luke's tragic journey to a bland conversation piece. It hurt, deeply, but I'm not sure she meant it to. I could hardly bring myself to ask the next question, but something inside me was urging me, pushing me on to what seemed to be an inevitable conclusion.

'And when you were done talking about the baby stuff?'

I reckoned this was one of those moments you see in films. The ones where cameras on wheels rotate around the main characters to lend an air of suspense, to create tension. And where one of those characters makes an unconscious gesture that says more than a thousand words could. I, the other main character, watched a cliché in (slow) motion as Stella's hand lifted from the wall. It paused, in mid-air, before resting, fingers splayed, on her bump. On her baby. The message, however unintentional, hit me squarely between the eyes. It jabbed me in the heart. When Stella and Luke were done talking about babies, they had made one. My legs buckled, as if I'd been physically struck.

Suddenly, Stella starting gibbering, if that's the best description for lots of incoherent sentences that didn't mean anything.

'Lucy, I'm so sorry. I didn't mean for any of this to

happen. I – Luke – we – this is such a mess and I feel awful. Forgive me, please . . . forgive me.'

I found myself in a state of dazed, ear-piercing devastation. Stella was crying hard, tears streaming down her cheeks. I don't think I was crying, but I had lost all sense of reality by this point.

'You have to know that this was an accident – that Luke isn't to blame, not the way I am.' Stella tried to pull herself together, dabbing at her face with a tissue she found in her pocket, but she started crying again, her eyes red and squinty-looking. I shook my humming head, trying to clear it, trying to shake the poison out of it. She was talking about Luke. My Luke. Luke Harte, who proposed to me in a Wookiee T-shirt on Christmas Day. He wouldn't do this to me, he couldn't. Not after everything we'd been through together. Not when we meant what we meant to one another.

'I – I . . . it's not what you think,' Stella stammered, urgency burning bright in her eyes.

Why do people say that? *It's not what you think*. Doesn't that mean that whatever has happened is exactly what you think it is? I stared at Stella, aghast. I wanted to hit her. But I couldn't. She was 'with child'. If I was to believe what she was telling me, she was with Luke's child.

I couldn't see. Why couldn't I see? Either shock had blinded me or I was crying even more than I had cried to date, and that was saying something. I put a trembling hand to my eyes. They were blurred, blurred with a deluge of tears.

'Please let me explain – you don't know the full story—'

I stopped her, unable to hear any more. The 'full story' would be more than I could handle. God, I felt sick. I felt as though I could throw up all over Stella's pristine shoes.

'We had a pact,' I cut in tonelessly. I probably sounded cold, but I hoped my double tragedy would excuse me. Inside, I was literally falling apart. My insides were crumbling, my heart felt as if it had had a hole punched through it. And it hurt like crazy.

Stella blinked. She didn't know what I was talking about. I was thankful for that, at least. From what she was saying, she knew enough of my business.

'You don't understand,' Stella called as I stumbled past her. 'It wasn't an affair; it was just one . . . Lucy, please—'

I couldn't hear her for the rushing of blood in my ears. Anger and anguish apparently caused short-term deafness. I ignored the stares of the *Grey's Anatomy* gang who were all agog – something else to gossip about, no doubt – and I charged into the hospital at high speed. My hearing had returned but I could barely see for tears. Why were my faculties letting me down? I just needed to get to Luke's room and being able to see was pretty much a basic requirement. I took a second and wiped my eyes. My anger didn't dissipate, not even by a fraction, but I sorted myself out and starting walking quickly up some stairs. I strode past the grey plastic chairs and went straight into Luke's room, stopping only when I reached his bedside. He looked strange; he was now being ventilated via a tracheostomy – a way to wean him off the main ventilator, apparently. A tube down the middle of the throat seemed worse than the one in his mouth had, but I supposed it was more civilised in some ways.

'Do you remember?' I murmured, my voice sounding smaller than expected. The break in my voice kick-started the tears again, much to my fury.

The nurse checking Luke's obs looked up enquiringly.

'Do you remember what we said that day? Christmas Day. It was our first one in the house. Well, second. You'd just proposed, I'd accepted. You were wearing your stupid *Star Wars* T-shirt.'

I moved closer. Luke's face seemed different; the freckles were familiar but he now possessed sharply sculpted cheekbones that Kate Moss would covet. He seemed less vital – more beautiful Greek statue. I wanted to slap him out of his coma right now, however model-esque he looked.

'We talked about this, about what we would do if this might happen.' I willed him to speak, to defend himself, to reassure me. My breath was coming out in jerky gasps. 'You didn't do this, did you? Say you didn't.'

Luke said nothing. The machines predictably answered in his place, but unfortunately, a monosyllabic ssh or beep counts for shit when you need serious answers.

I felt tears splash down on to my hands. The opposite of someone with super powers, I had morphed into some sort of one-woman flood, my special gift the ability to drown anyone within ten feet. I stood rooted to the ground, unable to leave Luke's side. I was still angry, but devastation had taken over. I felt weak and frail and completely vulnerable.

'We had a pact, Harte,' I mumbled. 'We . . . we had a bloody pact.' I put my head down on the bed and wept as my heart cracked into tiny pieces.

CHAPTER TWENTY-TWO

Patricia

'I hope she likes them. Have a good day.'

Patricia smiled mechanically and tucked the cash in the till. She wasn't sure working at the florists was the right thing to do, but she supposed she should keep herself busy while someone else was sitting with Luke. Nell and Ade had both hinted that she should get back to work and, for some reason, Patricia's feelings were hurt, immeasurably. She felt unimportant, irrelevant. Wasn't it her job to be there for Luke?

A light breeze swept through the shop and, feeling a chill, Patricia hurried to close the door. As she turned away, the door opened again and she summoned up an automatic smile, amazed that she was able to function so efficiently with everything else that was going on in her life.

Turning to greet her customer, she saw that it was Ade. He stood in the doorway, his hands twitching apprehensively.

'Can I come in?'

'Yes, of course,' Patricia said, motioning for Ade to close the door. 'It's getting really chilly, isn't it? I mean; it's October, but still. It could be December.'

'You're telling me.' Ade shivered. His jacket was too thin to cope with the temperature. 'This feels positively sub-zero to me.'

How British; they were discussing the weather.

'I suppose it probably does.' She nodded, fighting the urge to rub his arms and warm him up, the way she had done when he was a child. But he was a grown man now; such antics would seem ridiculous. 'I'll put the kettle on.'

She headed into the back office and mechanically set about preparing tea and biscuits. She and Ade had barely spoken since that awful lunch. They had met by Luke's hospital bed, the medical equivalent of the water cooler these days, and they had exchanged pleasantries, but not much more.

'Tea?' she called, having already brewed a pot.

'Coffee, if you have it,' he answered.

Patricia tipped the tea away. Like Luke, Ade had always preferred coffee. She would join him, a show of solidarity. She tipped digestives into a bowl. Did Ade like digestives? She couldn't remember. Patricia felt aggrieved. She should know what biscuits her son liked; she should remember whether he preferred tea or coffee, if he took sugar.

Patricia watched Ade moving around the shop, gently touching the petals of a carnation, gazing at the cash desk. He rubbed his fingers on the head of a lavender

188

stalk, inhaling the oil as if it reminded him of something. Patricia picked up the drinks tray, then set it down again.

There was so much she wanted to say to Ade. There was the apology, of course. That hesitation the other day had spoken volumes, volumes she didn't mean and that she hadn't meant to convey. Patricia regretted it bitterly. Her son's feelings must be hurt and, whatever he had done in the past, he didn't deserve that. He didn't deserve to think that his mother would rather he was lying in a coma than her other son. It was reprehensible and it was untrue.

And what about Ade's business? His marriage? Patricia had no idea what was going on in Ade's life, not really. She knew about the logistics of his divorce, but not the emotion behind it. She was aware of his business dealings in a factual sense – he was an entrepreneur, apparently – but not in a literal sense. What did being an 'entrepreneur' actually mean?

Should he be staying back at the house, with her and Nell? Patricia wasn't sure it was the best move for her or for Ade, not the way things were. His bedroom had been turned into a spare room long ago, although not as quickly as Ade might have imagined. Patricia had kept his room like a shrine for four years after he absconded to Australia, in the desperate hope that his defection had been temporary, a whim.

Eventually, she had been forced to accept that his absence was permanent and, with a heavy heart, she had enlisted Nell's help to pack up the medical study books that were gathering dust in Ade's bookcase, the books he had abandoned before his family. Together, they had taken down the student-style music posters that adorned his forest-green walls and they had slathered on a neutral biscuit shade that had erased Ade irrevocably.

'How's that coffee coming along?' Ade's face appeared in the doorway. He was smiling; his hands thrust into the pockets of his jeans.

'It's ready,' Patricia trilled. Why did she keep speaking in a ridiculously bright voice around him?

'Great, thanks.' He picked one of the mugs up and wrapped his hands around it. His hands were larger than Luke's, Patricia noticed, with more freckles. Yes, she knew that. A scene flashed into her head: Luke and Ade, in their teens, sitting at the breakfast table, grappling over a box of Shredded Wheat . . . Weetabix, maybe. Ade winning because he had secured a better grip.

'What a surprise,' Luke had grumbled, folding his arms in a mega sulk. 'Of course he got there first; he's got hands like a frickin' *baboon*.'

'It's the guns that make it possible, brother,' Ade had crowed, pumping his arms up to mock Luke with his muscles.

'This place hasn't changed a bit,' Ade was saying as he strolled around the cash desk.

'Really?' Patricia bristled inwardly. 'I guess I don't like change much.'

Ade nodded. In agreement? As a criticism? Patricia detested the way she kept second-guessing Ade's sentiments.

'This place has always had bags of charm.' He swigged his coffee and helped himself to a biscuit.

Patricia glanced around the shop, attempting to see it

through Ade's eyes. What did he mean? That the florists was old-fashioned and grossly out of date, was her first thought. Perhaps possessing 'bags of charm' was Ade-speak for 'appealing' or 'magical', but somehow, Patricia didn't think so. Her thought process was backed up by Ade's next comment.

'You don't use a credit card machine?'

She felt her teeth grinding. 'You sound like Lucy. She goes on at me about that all the time.'

Ade shrugged. 'It's just one of those things that modern businesses tend to need – it's an efficiency thing more than anything else.' He gestured with his coffee cup. 'But the shop itself has such a great vibe. I could see a whole chain of these. A traditional florist's that delivers modern arrangements. You could have *Hartes & Flowers* shops all over the country if you wanted. Certainly another in Bath to start with.'

'Oh, I don't know about that . . .'

'It's just a thought.'

'Is this what you do in Australia? I mean, what do you do, exactly?' Patricia sipped her coffee and winced. She wanted to like coffee, but she just didn't. So much for solidarity.

'I'm a consultant. I help companies maximise their profits. Businesses like this that have something special about them; businesses that could be huge.' Ade drained his coffee. 'If that's what the owner wants, anyway.'

Patricia listened and chatted, but she suddenly found that she couldn't hold her apology in any longer. 'Ade. I'm sorry about the other day. I didn't mean to make you think that I would ever—'

'I know. I know that.' Ade put a hand out and covered hers. 'Mum, it's fine. We've both said things – and done things – we regret. This really isn't how I planned on coming back here, Mum. In fact I—'

They both looked up as the door opened. A blonde woman came in wearing a cream jersey dress that was stretched to its maximum capacity across her pregnant tummy. The woman started when she saw Ade.

'Gosh. You look just like Luke.'

He smiled faintly. 'Well, as Luke has a halfway decent face, I suppose that's a compliment. I'm Ade, Luke's brother.'

'Of course. Ade. Luke's talked about you a lot.'

Ade didn't bother with the 'only good stuff, I hope' line, instead turning to Patricia with his eyebrow raised. 'Has he? That's nice.'

Disconcerted at the Luke-like gesture, Patricia lifted a shoulder; she had no idea who this was, either. 'Can I help you?' she offered the woman, not sure what else to say. 'Some flowers, maybe?'

The woman shook her head. 'Oh, no. Sorry. I was looking for Lucy. She wasn't at the hospital, so I thought . . . Luke told me she works here, so I thought it was worth a try.'

'Are you a friend of hers?'

'Not as such. No.' The woman shook her head, her eyes darting around uneasily. Patricia glanced at the woman's pregnant stomach then looked away. She still found pregnant women difficult to deal with; God only knew how Lucy was coping.

The woman's eyes unexpectedly filled with tears. 'I, er

'. . . sorry, I should – I shouldn't have come.' She started to back towards the door.

Patricia and Ade stared at her, nonplussed. The woman suddenly began to sway and the colour drained from her face, causing Ade to quickly step in and guide her to a chair. Removing a potted orchid and dusting the chair clean with one smooth movement he set the woman down and gripped her gently by the shoulders.

'Take a deep breath,' he told her, his voice soothingly calm. 'Breathe and steady yourself. Everything is fine. Breathe with me, in . . . out . . .'

Patricia watched him, feeling a curl of something in her chest, something she hadn't felt for Ade for a very long time. Instead of seeing Luke when she looked at her eldest son, she saw Bernard. She couldn't put her finger on why, exactly, but she wanted to. It was . . . the composed manner, the low, reassuring voice. The confidence with which Ade had taken control of the situation without seeming bossy or overbearing.

Patricia felt the beginning of tears at the edge of her eyelids, but she pushed them away. She hadn't felt pride for Ade in a long time, but she was beginning to realise that she had been grossly unfair.

The woman dutifully took a few breaths. 'I apologise. This pregnancy . . . I get a bit breathless sometimes.' Her eyes met Ade's then quickly slid away.

Ade frowned, then went out the back to fetch a glass of water.

'Would you like me to pass a message on to Lucy?' Patricia offered, remembering the woman's comment when she first arrived. 'I haven't spoken to her for a few days; Nell – my daughter – usually covers the shift before Lucy's one. At the hospital, I mean.'

The woman sipped the water and shook her head. 'Oh, no. No, that's fine. Not to worry. I'll – I'll try and catch her at the hospital. It's not important.' She struggled to her feet rather clumsily, still seeming unstable.

'Are you sure?' Ade asked, reaching out a steadying hand. 'You seem very upset about something.'

The woman caught her breath. 'No. I'm . . . it's . . . oh God.' She started to cry again and Ade threw Patricia a flummoxed glance. Patricia shrugged her shoulders in bewilderment and leant over to grab a tissue from the box on the counter.

'So, you're not a friend of Lucy's, but you need to speak to her. Sorry; it just doesn't make sense to me.'

The woman nodded slowly and bit her lip, her eyes downcast.

Patricia felt a flicker of something unpleasant in her stomach. She had some sort of gut instinct that something strange was going on.

The woman let out a shaky breath and put a hand on the counter.

'How – how well do you know Luke?' Ade asked, drawing the words out reluctantly.

The woman blinked and brushed away the fresh tears that appeared.

Ade's eyes dropped to the woman's stomach and he turned pale. 'I'm probably way off beam here . . . I must be. But you and Luke. You didn't – you haven't . . .'

The woman burst into proper tears this time, abruptly covering her face with her hands.

Ade turned to Patricia, who was pale with shock.

'What?' she said. 'What's going on?' It couldn't be. There was no way. She stared at the woman's swollen stomach. 'Luke is – he wouldn't . . .'

Ade sat the woman down again. 'What's your name?' he asked her gently.

'It's Stella. Stella Tiggs,' the woman managed between gasps.

Patricia started. She had heard that name before. Hadn't she? She couldn't remember when or where, but the name was familiar.

'Did you – did you have an affair with Luke?' Ade asked, using a kindly tone again, as if he was talking to a child.

'Don't be ridiculous!' Patricia blurted out. 'Luke loves Lucy. And Lucy loves Luke. This is unthinkable.'

Stella's lips were quivering uncontrollably. 'I know. I'm so sorry.'

'You're sorry?' Patricia sounded screechy but she couldn't help it. 'What do you mean, you're sorry?'

'Mum.' Ade put a hand on her arm. 'Calm down.'

'I can't, I can't.' Patricia moved away from Stella, agitated by the sight of her. This couldn't be happening. Her son was lying in a coma and now this woman was saying the most horrible things.

Ade faced Stella again. 'Can you tell us about it?'

'I – I . . .' Stella looked distraught. 'I just feel so awful about this. It must be dreadful for you to hear when Luke is – when he's—' She broke off.

Patricia couldn't believe what she was hearing. 'Are you actually saying something happened between you and Luke?' It was her turn to dizzily grip the edge of the counter. She felt disorientated. This was utterly surreal.

Stella shredded the tissue in her hands and visibly made an effort to compose herself. 'It was just one night. Not an affair. We were drunk and it got out of hand. I tried to explain this to Lucy the other day but, understandably, she couldn't bear to hear the details. I am so deeply ashamed,' she added. Her eyes implored them to believe her, but Patricia could barely make sense of anything. She felt as if she had cotton wool in her throat.

Luke? A one-night stand? It was preposterous. It couldn't be true. Meeting Stella's eyes, she realised that, as far as this woman was concerned, it had happened.

Patricia felt Ade's arm around her; protective, tender, and she felt her insides unravelling. She couldn't tear her eyes away from Stella's bump, as small as it was. Was that Luke's son or daughter in there? Was that her *grandchild*?

Patricia leant into the crook of Ade's arm and allowed her mind to ponder the terrifying but wondrous possibility that Stella might be, just might be, telling the truth. No. No, it wasn't true. She thought of Lucy and steeled herself.

'I really can't handle this,' she said unsteadily.

Stella nodded. 'I totally understand. I'm so terribly sorry. I just wanted to speak to Lucy and now I've upset you both.' A sob caught in her throat. 'I'll leave.'

'Are you – do you feel all right?' Ade asked awkwardly.

Stella gave him a tight smile. 'Don't worry about me. I'm fine. Once again, I am so incredibly sorry about all of this. I wish I hadn't been transferred back here. I tried to stay away, I – I seem to be making a lot of mistakes at the moment.' She turned and left, her head bent down as she made her way down the street.

Patricia's hand fluttered to her mouth and when Ade instantly gathered her up, she fell against him gratefully. Luke, possibly a cheat. A baby on the way when Lucy had just lost one.

Patricia collapsed properly against Ade. Her family. What on earth was happening to her family?

CHAPTER TWENTY-THREE

Lucy and Luke

September, five years earlier
'I can't believe how many things have gone wrong today,'
I groaned, winding my arms around Luke's neck.

'Who cares?' Luke kissed me, tasting of champagne
and cigarettes. 'None of that stuff matters.'

Luke didn't normally smoke, but the kiss was oddly
heady. A sneaky fag with Dan earlier, perhaps. I wondered
if Luke had felt nervous before our vows. I didn't blame
him; getting married had turned out to be a bit like naked
public speaking. Solemn declarations of undying love in
front of a live audience had made both of us feel rather
exposed.

We'd been right about that aspect of marriage, but
every other aspect had been, well, breathtaking, actually.
The quirky vows we'd added to avoid the ceremony
feeling too formulaic, the short, touching speeches and
the romantic first dance to Harry Connick Jnr that had
made us feel like Harry and Sally. Kind of. There were

far too many drunken stumblings on both sides for it to achieve cinematic greatness.

And this – this magical moment where we were finally alone on the outside of the marquee, enjoying the balmy post-rain air, drenched with the scent of summer roses.

Luke stroked my bare shoulder. 'It's like that Alanis Morissette song. It's *supposed* to rain on your wedding day. It's ironic . . . or something.'

'That wasn't *rain*, Harte!' I protested. 'That was a deluge, a flood, a – a *torrent*. "It never rains in September," you said. "We're guaranteed brilliant sunshine," you said.'

'Yeah . . . yeah. I did say that.' He squinted at me sheepishly.

'I believe you also promised that Dan wouldn't drive to the reception like a maniac, allowing our ridiculously expensive wedding cake to fall off the back seat. And that the bottom of my wedding dress wouldn't be destroyed by puddles and mud and—'

'Shhh.' Luke stopped me. 'The cake was magnificent even with a few missing roses and stuff and I don't give a shit about the bottom of your dress. Because later, when it comes off, my eyes will be elsewhere.' Slightly drunk, he leant against me. 'These two, practised fingers will dispense with your dress like *that*.' He held his fingers up, swaying slightly. 'Trust me; I'm a paramedic.'

I gripped his waist to steady him and moulded myself into his body for another reason entirely. Luke's job afforded him a hero status of sorts; saving lives and all that. But I knew him inside out and there was no way he could get me out of this corseted contraption with two fingers, hero or no hero.

'It took Dee half an hour to lace me into this, this *thing*. You'd need to use your thumbs as well, I reckon, because – well, if we're being totally honest here – you're good, but you're not *that* good.'

'Woman, you are so precise.' Luke made a show of sighing. 'Where's your sense of adventure? I might actually be able to de-robe you without having to call for assistance; you never know.'

I held on to him. We were in a bubble, a bubble of happiness that, today, felt indestructible. And why wouldn't it?

'God, do stop it,' Dan said, sidling up behind Luke. 'You two make me want to barf.'

'Leave them alone, Dan.' Dee was bursting at the seams and on the verge of labour. She claimed to have crossed her legs for the past fortnight so as not to miss being a bridesmaid and she had made it. She was rotund and just about pulling it off in Tiffany-blue chiffon.

Dee tipped Dan's straw hat back and grabbed his chin. 'It's their wedding day, you big, drunken idiot. Just because parenthood has caused *you* to forget what passion is doesn't mean anyone else has.'

Dan's eyes were crossing and he belched delicately. 'I have not forgotten what passion is, thank you very much. I've had too much beer, which is something different entirely, darling wife.' He tried to grab her and, not very convincingly, Dee started waddling away from him.

'Stay away from me, you pervert,' she shrieked,

starting to laugh. 'You're not coming near me with that thing . . .'

Waiting until we were alone, Luke laughed and kissed me again. 'I'm so happy,' he said. 'I know I sound sappy, but it's important to say it, right?'

'It's important to say it. And I love that you're so sappy.'

I did. There was a whole lot more to Luke Harte than sappiness, but, in that moment, I realised how much I loved this man.

Pulling Luke in for a hug, I inhaled him, feeling a flood of pure, unadulterated happiness. I caught sight of someone over Luke's shoulder and lifted my head. It was Patricia. She was loitering. Keeping her distance discreetly, but I could tell she wanted to speak to Luke. She looked emotional, as if she had something specific to say.

Ignoring a slight twinge of irritation (it was my wedding day; I thought Patricia might be able to let me have Luke to myself, just for one day), I gave myself a mental slap. Patricia was Luke's mother and she adored him. I had Luke for the rest of my life; I could afford to be generous.

'Go to your mother,' I told Luke.

'What?' He frowned. 'No fair. I want to stay here with you.' He bent his head, nuzzling my neck and I pushed him away, laughing.

'Stop it. She's over there. She – she needs you.'

Luke glanced over his shoulder. 'Yeah. She said she had something of Dad's to give me; think it might be his watch. It never showed the right time, but he loved that old timepiece.'

'Go.' I ushered him away, watching fondly as he sloped over to Patricia. She started crying almost immediately, pressing something – the watch – into Luke's hand as she said a few words. Luke stared at the watch, turned it over in his hands as Patricia tearfully talked, words of wisdom from the lovely Bernard, perhaps. I smiled, moved. Luke broke into a smile, one of the genuine, heart-warming smiles only he seemed capable of; the kind that made the recipient feel sun-drenched. His arms went around Patricia and they hugged tightly, Luke saying something to Patricia, words I knew he would choose carefully, something appropriate to the moment.

I wrapped my arms around myself, loath to intrude upon them but, just then, Luke looked up and flapped his hand at me to join them. I did so, embarrassed when he drew me into the circle with Patricia. Group hugs weren't normally my thing, but it was my wedding day and this was Luke's mother. Patricia looked equally awkward, but we dealt with it, for Luke's sake.

Suddenly, we jumped. It sounded like a thousand fire-crackers had gone off.

'What the hell . . .' Luke turned round incredulously. 'Oh my God. Bloody, *bloody* Dan! I knew he was too pissed to be in charge of fireworks.'

Dan, his straw hat back in place, was whooping and dangerously waving a sparkler too close to the surprise firework display. Dee was standing on the sidelines, her hands clasping her enormous swollen stomach as if she were trying to hold her baby inside her. She was bright red in the face, yelling expletives that a mummy-to-be shouldn't utter.

Another firework went off with a deafening whistle and me and Luke cracked up laughing. Our guests, hearing the commotion, came out to join us and I felt a warm flush inside. Impromptu fireworks let off by our drunken best friend, with the rest of our close friends and family around us. What could be a more picture-perfect end to our wedding? I felt Luke's arm around my shoulders, seeing the other one snake around Patricia.

All three of us turned to face a sky lit up by random rockets and bangers. It was perfection. Utter perfection. Our future was set. Lucy and Luke Harte against the world. We were indestructible.

CHAPTER TWENTY-FOUR

Nell

Nell checked her watch. She was running late, but she figured she had enough time to see Luke before the end of visiting time – enough time to read him another chapter of *Great Expectations*.

Lucy was right about Dickens; he wrote like a dream, Nell decided. Not that they had discussed it. Although she and Lucy had bumped into each other several times at the hospital as they switched shifts with Luke, they hadn't spoken properly since Ade's text about Stella.

Ade had told her what had happened in the florist's shop. It had shocked her to the core. Surely Luke wasn't a cheat? It wasn't possible. Nell didn't want to believe that Luke was capable of such a betrayal in the first place, but, regardless of whether or not it was true, she was struggling to work out how to look Lucy in the eye when she, Luke's sister, was just as bad. She was the other woman – the mistress. The last person Lucy would probably want to speak to if she knew the truth.

Nell swallowed. She still hadn't told Lisa about Cal either. Apart from Ade, no one else knew and it felt like a grubby secret. Nell waited while a gaggle of student doctors propelled a trolley across the corridor, their voices reaching fever pitch as they jostled for theatre duty. Nell's thoughts returned to Luke. There was no way of knowing if Stella was telling the truth, not when Luke couldn't even breathe without help right now. He was hardly in a position to put forward a convincing defence of his ability to stay faithful.

Lucy must be going insane; it must be beyond frustrating not to know who to believe, but to desperately want to trust her gut instincts about her own husband.

About to head into Luke's room, Nell stopped short outside the closed door. Along with the usual nurse in residence, Ade was sitting next to Luke's bed. His head was bent intently almost as if he was listening, but he was talking, his hands moving in the air to illustrate whatever point he was making.

Nell hovered outside, unable to tear her gaze away. It was strange to see Luke and Ade together. It was a sight she had longed to see for years, a sight that had hitherto been denied. They were so alike, it was startling. The golden freckles scattered across noses and the backs of hands, the tawny-brown hair that seemed to arrange itself into a slight quiff, whatever hair product was used.

She edged the door open a fraction, curious to know what Ade was waffling on about. She was only planning to get the gist but, as she listened, she found her feet stuck fast to the floor, as though lodged in clay.

'The thing is, Luke,' Ade was saying, 'is that I've never forgiven you. *I've* never forgiven *you*. Can you believe that?' He sounded troubled, emotional, even. 'You were the one who stepped up when I couldn't and took care of the family, and even now, when you're languishing in a coma, I'm having trouble letting go of how brilliant you are.'

Nell watched Ade rub a hand across the back of his head, feeling voyeuristic. She hadn't a clue Ade felt this way. Ashamed of herself, she acknowledged that she hadn't exactly given him the chance to open up about his feelings. She'd been too busy banging on about her own.

Ade was in full flow. 'Even the medical studies, Luke. I started them then jacked it all in. I couldn't hack it – couldn't handle the study, the exams, the fucking . . . the *pressure* of it all. But you?' He sniffed and shook his head. 'You went the whole hog and became a paramedic. Even better than Dad – even more heroic! I'm the guy who deserts everyone and leaves them hanging and you're the – the superhero who dives in and saves the day.'

Nell heard the break in Ade's voice and she longed to rush in and comfort him. It made him human – it made him real. Ever since he'd come back from Australia, he'd been behaving as though he was taking it all in his stride and, apart from his obvious hurt at their mother's faux pas, Ade had seemed oddly unmoved until this point.

'I envy you, Luke.' Ade made a visible effort to pull himself together. 'Not the coma, obviously. I mean, that's a raw deal right there. But everything else. You succeeded where I failed. I don't know if you did this thing – had this affair with that woman. But it doesn't matter. I mean, it does, but not to me.' He pulled a rueful face at the nurse, in case she was listening and then turned back to Luke. 'I know, I know. I'm a self-absorbed, whiny old woman. That's what you'd call me if you could. And you'd be right.'

He broke down, his head slumping into his hands. The sounds coming from him were unbearable and Nell couldn't hold back any longer.

'Ade, don't.' She dumped her bag on the floor, *Great Expectations* forgotten. 'I had no idea you felt that way.' She sat on the edge of the bed, squashing Luke's leg. 'Sorry, Luke. Ade, why didn't you say any of this before? I always thought you didn't care.'

Ade looked up in surprise, then wiped his eyes. 'I kind of do. I did. It's hard when you're doing your best, but you keep falling short.' He sat back in his chair. 'I spent quite a few years out in Oz seething about him being so amazing, but I got over it.'

'Then you started emailing?'

He nodded. 'There was a fair bit of mutual umbrage going on – I thought he was a goody two shoes for saving the world and he thought I was a prick for not being up to the job of Superman.' Ade rolled his shoulders with a wry smile. 'He's bound to look better in his pants, to be fair.'

Nell laughed. 'Pants and tights, remember. Dan, Luke's friend, calls Luke and his paramedic partner Joe, Batman and Robin. Luke's Batman, obviously.'

'Figures.' Abruptly, Ade reached out and exposed Nell's wrists. He ran his fingers gently over the knobbly skin. 'Nell, sweetheart . . . I'm so sorry about this. So, so sorry.' Tears slid down his face. 'If I'd known this was going to happen, I would never have left, not in a million years.'

'It's okay.' Nell started crying too. 'You didn't know how awful I was feeling; no one did. I'm not sure I did. I mean, I knew I felt abandoned, but I didn't see this coming.' She gestured to her wrists. 'It's not something I planned, Ade. It was impulsive, stupid. I didn't even think about what I was doing – I – I just needed the release.'

Seemingly unable to stand the sight of the still-lurid gashes, Ade turned her wrists over and held on to her hands instead. 'I can't even bear to think about it. This is why I'm so grateful to Luke. I'm glad he was there to pick up the pieces. He told me he sent you to a therapist.'

Nell's gaze shifted to Luke. 'Yeah. I hated her. Called her the c-word once.'

Ade let out a bark of laughter.

'But she was good. She made me talk about "my feelings",' Nell made quote marks in the air, 'until I was sick of them, but it worked. She sorted my head out and untangled all the crap I couldn't make sense of.'

'She sounds great. Do you still have her number?'

'Don't be daft; *you* don't need her.' Pensively, Nell touched her wrist. 'She came up with this weird idea that I could write letters to Dad, so I could tell him how I felt about everything.'

Ade frowned. 'Write letters to our dead father? How did that help?'

'You'd be surprised. It's cathartic – I can say anything to him. He doesn't judge me.'

'He *doesn't* – wait, you still do this?'

Nell flushed. She hadn't meant to own up to that. Fiercely meeting Ade's eyes, she checked them for condemnation. It was absent. He wasn't sneering at her. He was compassionate, accepting.

'I do. Just – just recently. After Luke's accident.' Nell placed a hand on Luke's immobile leg. 'I could always talk to Luke and I wanted to tell him about Cal. I was just about to and then this happened and I felt all panicky again, the way I used to after Dad died.'

She felt Ade wince, but she knew it was important to be honest. 'I get these panic attacks sometimes, this breathless thing where I feel like I might die or something. I have to calm myself, and writing to Dad relaxes me. Recently I've been feeling as though I didn't have anyone else to talk to.'

'You have me,' Ade said soberly. He looked horrified by her admission. 'You have me now. And when Luke gets better, you'll have both of us. I'm not about to desert you again, I promise.'

'Good. I'll slap you if you do.'

'Or call me the c-word.'

'That I might.' Nell leant over and nudged him, almost toppling off the bed. 'Listen, what do you think about this baby thing – do you think this Stella woman is telling the truth? You've met her – you must have formed an opinion of some sort.'

Ade ran a hand through his hair. 'I have no idea. I was just sorting stuff out with Mum and Stella came in looking for Lucy. She obviously didn't want to talk to us about it, but I knew something was up and I kind of pushed her to confess.' He glanced at Luke. 'What can I say? I'm no expert, but she seemed sincere. She doesn't *seem* like a basket case. If she was talking about anyone but Luke, I'd believe her in a heartbeat. I – I called Lucy about it. Was that the right thing to do?'

Nell considered. 'I guess so. I should have done it, really, but she'd probably take it better from you.'

'How so?'

'I'm the "other woman", Ade.' Nell bit her lip. 'How can I sympathise when I'm just as bad?'

'She doesn't know you're the "other woman", as you put it, for starters.' Ade reached out and stroked a lock of Nell's hair out of her eyes. 'But apart from anything else, you love Lucy and you're not a bad person. You must love this . . . Cal, is it? You must love him, because I know you wouldn't be doing this otherwise. You love him, right?'

Nell let out a jerky breath. She did. She must. She did.

'Can't you talk to him about everything – about how you feel?' Ade's eyes betrayed his curiosity.

It was a good point. She should be able to talk to Cal about all of this. Why couldn't she? Was she worried she would sound too needy? Nell picked at her nail polish. She had opened up to him the other day, but generally she was so busy playing the perfect other woman – the woman who doesn't demand, question or apply pressure – that she had emotionally shut down until now.

Ade stood up and gave her a hug. Drawing back, he said, 'I can't imagine how Lucy's feeling right now, can you? She's been so distraught over Luke, but she must be all over the place now that she's dealing with this Stella news. A baby, too.' He picked up his keys and wallet from Luke's bedside table. 'I'd better go. Luke will be missing the latest instalment about Miss Havershall.'

'Miss Havisham,' Nell corrected. She smiled and took the seat he'd vacated. 'Ade . . . I'm glad we've talked.'

'Me too. And, Nell?'

She turned. He stood in the doorway, stricken. 'The next time you have one of those panic attacks, call me, okay? Just pick up the phone and I'll be there. I'll always be there for you now.'

Nell nodded but, choked, she didn't respond. Ade left and Nell slowly drew *Great Expectations* out of her bag. Before she started reading, she leant forward and gripped Luke's hand.

'Did you have an affair with that woman, Luke? Did you get her pregnant? Because if you did, the shit is going to hit the fan in spectacular fashion when you come round.' Nell was conscious that the nurse must be having a field day with all the drama going on. She lowered her voice. 'You have to come round, Luke. I mean, you have to anyway, but you might want to spend your time wherever you are coming up with a bloody good explanation, okay? Because Lucy must be in bits over this, in absolute *bits*.'

Nell smoothed the pages of her book, preparing to read, but when she tried, she found that she couldn't. She watched Luke's chest inflating and deflating, hoping

211

she could trust her gut feeling that her brother was innocent. Otherwise, life as Nell knew it would be turned upside down, even more than it was already.

Later, feeling like a drug addict hiding her guilty secret, Nell began writing.

Dad,
I feel as if I shouldn't be doing this any more. Ade has offered to support me . . . he says I shouldn't need to write to you like this. And he's right, I'm sure he's right. I just don't feel as if I can trust him the way I trust you. He might leave again. Maybe not while Luke is in his coma, but later. He might just leave, like he did last time and then where will I be?
Thanks, Dad. Thanks for always listening to me.

CHAPTER TWENTY-FIVE

Lucy

'Sorry. Run that past me again. My brain is about to explode.' Dee patted her pockets then started opening kitchen cabinets.

I wrapped my cardigan around my body to warm up. The house was boiling hot; Dee always had the heating on, but I couldn't stop shivering. I started to pace, my Converse catching on the wheels of one of the kids' scooters propped up against the fridge.

I had just left the hospital and Ade had taken my place. Usually, when Ade is there I find it hard to look at him, because he makes me long for Luke so badly, but today I was glad of his presence, and it was Luke I could hardly look at. I didn't know what to think or what to say. If it was true that coma victims could hear what was going on around them, he had just spent a boring few hours with me as I sat tightly in silence, trying to make sense of the hideous thoughts in my head.

'Haven't you got any vodka? Or some wine?' I sniffed, wondering if I was about to cry again. Christ. The chat with Stella had hit me harder than I thought it had.

'Yes. Wine. Quicker.' Dee opened the fridge and rooted around. 'Pinot, only about a week old.' She splashed some into brightly coloured plastic tumblers that clearly belonged to the children, not bothering to search out clean glasses. Her tone was breezy, but I could tell that she was wrong-footed and searching for sanity. It was just her way of dealing with a crisis; it was what Dee did.

'Okay. So let me get this straight. You're saying this woman, this Stella, just bowled right up and told you she was having Luke's baby?'

Dee didn't believe it; that much was obvious.

I gulped the wine and carried on pacing. 'She didn't bowl up, no. I saw her outside the hospital and I asked her to come and speak to me.'

'What the hell did you do that for?'

'Because I've got a death wish. Because I'm a bloody idiot and I can't leave well enough alone.' I could feel my cheeks darkening. From the wine, from the fury or maybe from both. 'I don't know why I did it, Dee. I wish I hadn't. I wish I could go back to just feeling totally cut up about Luke being in a coma, rather than feeling utterly devastated that some other woman might be having the baby I couldn't seem to give my husband. It's just too awful. I want him to be okay . . . I want *us* to be okay.' I slammed the plastic tumbler on to the worktop and burst into tears.

Dee's arms were round me before I could take a

breath and she radiated concern. 'Darling, I'm so sorry. You're going through hell. The universe has dumped you right in the middle of a shit storm.' She drew back, still holding me.

'Look, is there any chance she's lying about the baby? About her and Luke?' Her eyes flickered; she was contrite. 'Of course there is. What am I saying? There's *every* chance she's lying.'

Without preamble, I removed myself from Dee's embrace. Sympathy, especially when accompanied by touch, seemed to suffocate me right now. My skin prickled and my chest tightened; it felt akin to drowning. I poured myself another tumbler of wine.

'Believe me, Dee. I've tried to imagine every single scenario that doesn't involve Luke sleeping with this woman. The problem is that I come back to the same point over and over. Why would she do that? What's the point?'

'Fuck knows!' Abruptly changing tack, Dee swung away wildly from the possibility that Luke was a schmuck to fierce defence of him. 'Who knows why people do what they do?'

I said nothing, mentally willing Dee to catch up. I had despaired of finding a credible reason for a woman confessing such a thing to a wife who was struggling to deal with a stillbirth and a husband in a coma. No one was that cruel and insensitive, surely?

Whatever I came up with, however inventive I allowed myself to be, I kept coming back to the same thing. Luke had messages from this woman in his phone and he had given her a nickname. Those two things blew most of my theories out of the water. As a bare minimum, this lent weight to the fact that Luke and Stella had been friends, good friends, who had talked about personal stuff behind my back. That left me with mentally unstable and unhealthy obsession – neither of which seemed wholly believable to me. Dee's expression suddenly became more earnest. 'But Luce, what about Luke? Surely you don't believe he did this to you?'

I exhaled. 'That's where I'm at. Stella is either lying for some unfathomable reason, or she's telling the truth, and I can't even wrap my head around that because I can't bear to think that of Luke.' I edged myself carefully on to a bar stool. 'But maybe that's just wishful thinking, Dee. Maybe I'm being naive. Plenty of men, and women, for that matter, have affairs without the spouses ever having a clue anything is amiss.'

Saying that out loud hurt like hell. The thought that I might have been too trusting of Luke, that I might have been gullible. That our life together might have been a lie.

'Lucy, I'm worried about you.' Dee moved closer. 'You seem so weird and disconnected. If this was me, I'd be raging, climbing the walls.'

'I am. Inside, I am.' I couldn't explain the way I felt. It wasn't quite like being anaesthetised, but I felt dazed. Traumatised, but stupefied, as if I'd been shot but couldn't quite believe it had happened.

'I think you're in shock,' Dee commented, her eyes running over me anxiously. 'You're withdrawn and odd and not yourself at all. It's understandable, it is. I just – I just hate seeing you like this.'

'He's out of my league.' I offered the thought flatly, not really listening to Dee. 'He always has been.'

Dee's expression was incredulous. 'You're joking, right?'

'No. I'm not. I've always thought Luke was too good for me and this proves it.'

'You're being absurd.' Dee sharply dismissed my comment. 'I mean it, Lucy. Luke is a handsome man, but you're beautiful. In a quirky way; granted. But you're lovely. That has nothing to do with what we're talking about because Luke has always been obsessed with the way you look.'

Quirky beautiful. That brought back memories of first meeting Luke. My already-damaged heart was aching now with each little arrow that kept shooting through it. I started to feel panicky. I needed to get my emotions in check again. Numb was better than overwhelmed and destroyed. Numb felt like control. Of sorts.

'Is this Stella stunning or something? Is that what you're getting at?'

I tried hard, but I could barely remember Stella's face. 'She's . . . pretty, yes. I can't say exactly. But I suppose it has crossed my mind that she's prettier than me.'

'Irrelevant. Luke isn't shallow like that. Did she say it was an affair?'

'What?'

'Stella. Did she say it was an affair?'

I rubbed my forehead, pinching the skin between my eyes. 'I don't know. I can't remember. She said something as I ran off . . .' I searched hard, but my mind wasn't playing ball. 'What does it matter?'

Dee let out a sigh. 'I don't know. A one-night stand would be less of a betrayal, wouldn't it?' Her eyes conveyed her apology. 'I'm just trying to think about how I would feel, Luce, if it was me. If it was Dan. I mean, I'd still kill him. I'd kick him in the balls and throw him out of the house. For a while, anyway. But a one-night stand.' Dee's mouth twisted. 'It's not the same as a full-blown affair that's lasted for months and months. It's different. Still sick, but different.'

I put my head in my hands. 'I suppose so. I haven't thought about it.'

'Is it the baby thing you can't get past?' Dee asked carefully. 'That must be awful for you . . . just that thought . . . the possibility.'

I nodded. 'It would be the sickest irony, wouldn't it? Christ.' I glanced at her. 'I'd give anything to be you right now, Dee. Just to be out of my head and out of this situation.'

'It's not as easy as it looks,' Dee told me gently. 'Granted, it's easier than being you right now; that's a given. But generally speaking, I'm like that swan wildly paddling beneath the surface – I look calm enough but, underneath, everything is in chaos.'

I managed a brief, wonky smile, not believing her. 'No, you're not. You have three gorgeous children who are a credit to you.' I carried on, even though I knew I was treading on dangerous ground. 'You fall pregnant immediately each time. I know there have been sleepless nights and illnesses, but you and Dan have coped admirably and life has gone on.' I wondered where I was going with this. My mind was full of Luke and Stella and what

218

it could all mean, but maybe I needed to take a break from it.

'Is that a nice way of saying we've had it easy, Luce?' Dee met my eyes unflinchingly.

Immediately, I felt bad. 'I guess so. I'm sorry. I know that sounds bad.'

Dee sat back. 'Well, if we're laying our cards on the table here, I'm going to be really candid with you, Luce. We didn't fall pregnant straight away, not each time. It took us quite a few months to fall pregnant with Tilly. I also had a miscarriage at fourteen weeks. We were on holiday at the time and we'd missed our scan. As it happened, it didn't matter.'

'What? Why didn't you tell me?'

Dee waved this away. 'Because it seemed insignificant with everything you and Luke were going through. You'd had so many miscarriages and you were so depressed and broken over it. Did you really need me going "Boo hoo, Luce – I've had one – *one* – miscarriage too, and I'm really upset"?'

I was upset by this. Terribly. It felt unfair for Dee to have had to keep such a thing to herself. 'I wish you'd felt you could tell me about it. I'd like to think I could have sympathised.'

I pondered this. Could I have sympathised, honestly? Could I have set aside my own disappointment to share hers? Or was Dee right; had I been in such a state of desolation and self-absorption about my own, multiple, losses that I wouldn't have been able to bring myself to comfort Dee?

'Oh God.' I was mortified. 'Dee, I have this horrible,

horrible feeling you have a point. That I wouldn't have been there for you. Jesus. I'm a shit friend and a whingeing cow for—'

Dee was beside me in a flash. 'Don't say that! That's not what I meant.' She took my face in her hands. 'What you've been through – before all this stuff with Luke's accident – is enough to test *anyone*. You're human, you're normal. You got caught up in your quest for having a baby and rightly so. You want it; you've always wanted it. That doesn't make you a bad person or a bad friend.'

I started to cry, great big sobs that made my whole body shudder. The floodgates were open. Something about the way Dee was holding my face, the distress in her eyes – it was too much. I heard Dee's front door, but I couldn't stop weeping.

'It's Dan. He's just picked Frankie up from nursery.' Dee frantically wiped my face with her sleeve. 'Take a deep breath, act normal – as normal as you can, at any rate. Just until I can get Frankie in front of the TV.' She turned, hiding me, giving me an extra second to pull myself together. 'Darling! How lovely to see you. Did you have a good day at nursery?'

'It was all right.' Frankie was sanguine. 'Lexi said I wasn't her best friend any more and we jumped in muddy puddles like Peppa Pig.'

Dan caught sight of my barbed-wire eyes. 'Franks. Lucy's here. She looks like she needs a hug and yours are better than mine.'

'Awww, don't worry about Uncle Luke.' Frankie cuddled my legs kindly. 'He won't be in hospital forever and when he comes back, his brain won't be funny or anything. He'll still be able to play Swingball.'

I managed a feeble smile and I ruffled her hair. I loved Frankie's simplistic outlook. Dee swiftly ushered her into the lounge with a snack, promising *Peppa Pig* on repeat. When she came back into the kitchen, she rounded on Dan, who was staring at me in horror. I guessed I must look pretty horrendous.

'Did Luke mention a woman called Stella to you?'

'Stella? No.' Dan looked disconcerted. 'Never heard of her. Why? Who is she?'

'She's . . .' Dee seemed at a loss as to how to describe Stella. She did her best, fumbling over the details, and Dan's face became more incredulous as the seconds passed. I wasn't paying much attention because something awful was dawning on me.

Dan put his hand on my shoulder, gripping it sympathetically. 'What? I don't believe it. There's no way Luke would have kept that to himself. He's too honest.' He raised his hands when Dee shot him a withering glance. 'He is! You know it and I know it.'

I watched them and I could see they were both struggling with this information. They saw my relationship with Luke as something to behold, something to aspire to. It was reflected in their eyes. It was strange, the things I was learning since Luke's accident.

'There is no way Luke would cheat on you,' Dan assured me. He was emphatic. 'Believe me, I've heard him talk about you. Endlessly. The man is beyond besotted. Dee would love it if I talked about her that way.'

Dee met Dan's eyes and raised an eyebrow. She said nothing.

'Anyway.' Dan went on, rushing to fill the silence. 'I also know that Luke would have confided in me if he'd done something like that. We're best mates.' There wasn't a trace of doubt in his voice.

'I believe you, Dan. I mean, I want to.' I couldn't even look at them. 'It's just . . . if I shut both of you out – if I was so caught up in my own baby dilemma I couldn't even be trusted to give you a hug when you'd suffered a miscarriage, Dee – how might I have treated Luke? How much did I hurt his feelings, how far did I push him?'

Dan scratched his head and glanced at Dee. Dee stuttered a bit.

'How far? Into another woman's arms?' I silently beseeched, begging for a denial, for reassurance that I was being absurd. They tried – they babbled and blustered and defended but somehow, to me, none of it rang true. To me, it all sounded hollow and empty.

CHAPTER TWENTY-SIX

Lucy and Luke

April, four years earlier

'Right. Let me put you in the picture,' Dee said, halting us outside the front door. 'Linda is one of my "mummy friends" and one of my least favourite.' She pulled a face. 'Before you think I'm being a bitch, let me explain what we're dealing with here.'

Dan started to look restless. 'Come on, Dee. Don't tell them too much. You'll scare them off and I need a drink.'

'Me too,' Luke said. 'I don't care what they're like. You wanted us here for moral support and here we are.'

'Just give me a minute.' Dee gathered her coral pashmina around her shoulders. 'Right, listen up. Linda is American. *Very* American. By this, I mean that she will send the men out into the garden on arrival to play something highly competitive with rules they are unfamiliar with.'

'No fair!' Luke protested. 'You said we were coming

along to drink beer and to stop you wanting to slap the hostess.'

Dan grinned. 'Sorry, mate. Couldn't take a chance on you not coming.'

I already knew from Dee that Linda was the kind of mummy who revelled in her children's (minor) achievements, broadcasting them all over Facebook, accompanied by cute photographs that made the family look like the Waltons. I wasn't sure what was so heinous about this, but Dee had darkly informed me that Linda's offspring were actually a couple of bullying little shits with psychopathic tendencies, and that in reality they bore more resemblance to the Addams family than the Waltons.

Hearing someone approaching the front door, Dee hurriedly hissed a warning. 'And the husband has horribly wandering hands, Luce. Keep your wits about you!'

'Don't worry, I'll biff him if he manhandles you,' Luke said in my ear, his hand sliding over my backside. 'Cor . . . do you think we can sneak off early?'

I wriggled out of his grasp and kissed him, cringing as Dee blithely apologised to the (very) American Linda for bringing two uninvited guests. I soon realised as I was shown around every single room in Linda's house that not only was she supremely house proud, but I was expected to praise and possibly applaud her New England-style furnishings and a lovingly 'distressed' writing bureau in the spare bedroom. I haltingly began to provide praise, if not applause, much to Dee's poorly-concealed amusement.

'Last time I support you when you don't want to go

somewhere,' I sulked later, accepting a glass of Cabernet Sauvignon – Californian, naturally.

'Sorry, darling. You're a star, honestly.' Dee was contrite as she poured herself a glass of wine. 'I really appreciate you coming. I hate these kinds of parties. What sort of party starts in the afternoon then carries on into the evening, anyway?'

I sipped my wine. 'The sort of parties you throw?'

Dee started laughing, realising her error. 'Oh yes, well. Whatever. Let's go and see what the men are being made to do.'

We headed out on to a crowded decking area and Dee warmly introduced me to some of her other mummy friends, the ones she actually liked. I chatted briefly to a few and I felt a pang. There was only so much I had in common with women whose main bonding tool was their young children. It made me long to be one of them.

Were Luke and I ever going to be parents? The longing to become part of this jolly little club who breezily chatted about their children's schooling and toilet habits was overwhelming.

Annoyed to feel tears pricking at my eyelids and desperate to hold them back, I headed to the edge of the decking. Like the house, the garden was beautifully kept and somewhat ostentatious. Sharply-cut flower beds looked as though they'd been measured with a ruler and a very grand fountain took pride of place at the far end of the garden. Luke and Dan had been roped into a game of baseball with Neil (he of the apparent wandering hands), taking unenthusiastic swings of the bat before gamely jogging round the four professional-looking bases.

Luke managed a respectable swing of the bat and a speedy dash before handing over to Dan, who assumed what he obviously believed to be the perfect pose of a baseball player, which essentially meant sticking his backside out and waggling the bat around.

'Go for it!' Neil yelled at Dan after he managed an accidentally brilliant crack of the bat. 'Get to the home plate!'

Clearly having no idea what the 'home plate' was, Dan ran full pelt round each base as the rest of the men weaved across the garden trying to catch the ball.

'Go on, Dan! You can do it!' Dee screamed, jumping up and down on the decking.

I threw her an amused glance. She was the only person yelling and caterwauling from the sidelines, but that was Dee. She tended not to care too much what anyone else did or what they thought of her – not because she wasn't a caring person but because she was sure of herself.

I checked Dee again and noticed that she looked rather pink in the face. The bouncing had caused her to almost burst out of the low-cut black dress she was wearing, an unusually loose creation. Dee normally favoured figure-hugging, busty and leggy all at once, breaking all the rules in one glorious affront.

'Dee.' I put a hand on her shoulder. 'Are you all right? It's a game of baseball, not the Olympics.'

'Good God. Save me.' Luke sloped up the garden and threw himself into my arms. 'It's anarchy out there.' He thrust his bottom lip out in an attempt to garner sympathy.

I patted his back. 'There, there. You made it back unscathed. You'll survive.'

'Only just.'

'Well hello.' Pervy Neil was at Luke's elbow. Close up, he was tall and rather like the Honey Monster. 'Is this Lucy? How lovely to meet you. What did you think of the baseball?'

'Oh, good work, really,' I replied, shaking his hand. Neil had a firm grasp and he did that thing of holding on to my hand for longer than necessary while giving me an intense stare that made my skin crawl. Better to have his hand in mine than on my butt, I reasoned.

'Glad you enjoyed it,' Neil said, giving me a wink. 'Us men like to run around and be a bit macho now and again. Top-up, anyone? Linda seems to be neglecting her hostess duties.' Chuckling, Neil disappeared into the house to berate Linda.

Luke did a mock shudder that made me laugh, then he turned to Dee. 'Are you all right? You look a bit peaky.'

'Thanks,' Dee said. 'Isn't that man-speak for "you look like shit"?'

'No.' Luke put his arm around Dee, shooting me a worried look. 'It's man-speak for "you look a bit peaky".'

Dee swallowed, placing a hand on her stomach. Seeing Dan about to saunter past, she grabbed his arm. 'Could you get me some water please?'

Looking as though he was about to say something sarcastic, Dan paused and lifted Dee's chin. 'Hey. Do I need to be worried or is it just the nausea?'

'I just – I just need some water.' She averted her eyes.

227

I stared at the wine glass in Dee's hand. It hadn't been touched. I began to experience a churning feeling in my stomach. Dee wasn't drinking and she looked peaky. Dan was being sweetly concerned instead of jokingly sarcastic. I glanced at her stomach – it was swollen. How had I missed that? My eyes met Luke's and I could see the same thing mirrored there. We both knew what was coming. I felt Luke's hand reach for mine and I held on to it, tightly.

Please don't let me cry, please don't let me cry, I told myself. These were my best friends. I had to be happy for them, I *would* be happy for them. I could do this. I just knew that the pain was about to cut through me like a chainsaw through a kitten.

Dee started, and her apologetic tone sucked the breath from my throat. 'Listen. We – we . . . have some news for you. And it's . . . I don't know how you're going to react. I can't tell you how awful we feel in the circumstances, but . . .'

'We're having another baby,' Dan blurted out.

'Wow, that's the most wonderful news. You must be so happy.' Mechanically, I put my arms around Dee. I closed my eyes, feeling the tears slide down my cheeks. *It's not her fault*, I told myself. *It's not.*

'I don't know if happy is the right word,' Dee said, pulling back. She wiped the tears from under my eyes. 'Darling, I'm so sorry. I can't tell you how horrible I feel.'

'Horrible? Don't be silly. This is the most wonderful news, truly.'

Dan put his hand on Luke's arm. 'Sorry, mate. Such bad timing. We didn't even – this wasn't exactly—'

'Dan, shut up!' Dee hissed. She met my eyes.

Oh God. Oh God. This was an accident. Dee and Dan hadn't even planned this pregnancy. They were pregnant with their third – their *third* – baby and they hadn't even tried to make it happen.

I felt Luke's arm around my shoulders and I leaned against him for strength.

Luke held his hand out to Dan. 'Congratulations, mate. Really. That's amazing. Wow.'

'Yeah.' Dan shook Luke's hand, his eyes contrite. 'Sorry though. It's – this is . . .'

'It's marvellous news, that's what it is,' Luke insisted brightly. 'I reckon me and Lucy should go and see if Linda has any champagne because this deserves to be celebrated. Excuse us.'

Propelling me into the house, Luke did his genial thing by smiling at everyone and making small talk as he somehow shouldered his way through the crowds of parents. Ducking into the nearest empty room, which turned out to be a dimly-lit mausoleum of a dining room with a marble table and no less than twelve chairs covered in flouncy silk, Luke pulled me into his arms. He put his chin on my head and he hugged me close, wrapping both arms around me.

'It's okay, it's okay,' he kept saying over and over.

But it wasn't. It really wasn't. I couldn't hate Dee and Dan – how could I? They were our best friends. But three pregnancies . . . one an accident? I gasped. God, but that hurt. It *hurt*. I couldn't even describe the pain. Then I felt a flash of anger. How irresponsible of Dee! Why hadn't she taken precautions? If she didn't want another baby, why hadn't she taken steps to prevent it from happening again? I was furious, raging inside. It was so fucking unfair.

But I couldn't even grasp hold of the white-hot pain that was shooting through me. As quickly as the anger had flared up, it dissipated. I collapsed again, holding on to Luke.

'I wish I could make this go away for you,' Luke murmured, drawing back and smoothing my hair away from my face.

The tenderness in his voice caused more sobs. But I knew Luke meant what he said. If he could take this pain away, if he could do anything that meant we had our own child, he would. My mind drifted to adoption. Was I being ridiculous? Should I abandon all hope of having a baby that was part of me and part of Luke? There were so many unwanted children out there. I looked up at Luke and realised that I had to keep trying, just for a bit longer. I wanted a different piece of Luke to love and I couldn't help it.

'I love you, Luce,' Luke said, kissing me. He was crying, which always set me off again. 'And now.' He took my shoulders. 'We have two choices. We can duck out of this party and make our apologies to Dee and Dan later. Or we can go out there, find a bottle of champagne and toast this pregnancy. What can you cope with? Whatever you choose is fine by me.'

I took a deep breath. I wasn't sure I could celebrate, but I also knew I couldn't run away from this. It wouldn't be fair to Dee and Dan. I had to be brave.

'Champagne,' I nodded. 'Let's do it.'

We held hands and left the dining room. And, somehow, we found the strength to whoop and cheer at Dee and Dan's baby news. Dee hugged me apologetically and I had no words. No words. Inside, I died just a bit more that day.

CHAPTER TWENTY-SEVEN

Patricia

Patricia stared at the photo album as she sat with Luke. Each photograph tore at her heart. Luke as a baby. Luke riding a bike. Luke looking adorable in his school uniform on his first day.

Why was she doing this to herself? Because she missed him so much, she supposed. Because reliving his childhood, even through pictures, made him seem real again, more real than the Luke lying in this damned hospital bed. She glanced at his face, watching the way his cheeks moved in and out as the machine sucked and blew air into him. How ridiculous they all were for taking the simple matter of breathing independently for granted.

Patricia slammed the photo album shut. She couldn't make sense of anything. Lucy losing the baby, Luke having his accident. And now this woman – this Stella – saying she was carrying Luke's baby. It was too much.

Patricia frowned. Aside from the whole story seeming

to be preposterous from start to finish, Luke was, and always had been, besotted with Lucy.

Patricia admitted that she didn't always exactly understand why, because Lucy had been difficult to get close to at first. Oddly enough, Luke's accident seemed to be giving her more empathy for Lucy, although they hadn't yet fully connected.

But the fact of the matter was: Luke loved his wife. Patricia couldn't imagine why Stella Tiggs would come out of nowhere and suggest that Luke was the father of her child, but until anything was proven beyond all reasonable doubt, or whatever they said on those police dramas, Patricia felt that she owed it to her son to dismiss this woman out of hand. She owed it to Lucy, too, because she was part of the family – not the way Luke was, but almost. And as much as Patricia yearned for a grandchild, this wasn't the way.

And yet . . . a tiny, horribly guilty part of Patricia couldn't help wanting to know more about Stella, more about the baby she was having. She loathed herself for even feeling that way, but if it was true – if there was even a vague chance that Luke might be connected to this baby . . .

'Patricia. Patricia.'

Patricia looked up. Dee was standing over her, anxiously tugging at Patricia's arm. She had obviously been trying to get her attention for a few seconds and Patricia felt embarrassed that she had been so absorbed.

'I'm sorry, Dee. I was in a world of my own there.'

'Things on your mind,' Dee said sympathetically, removing her coat. 'Come on. Time for a break. It's my turn. I bet Luke can't wait to hear what Peppa Pig's been up to.' She held up one of Frankie's books. 'I promised I'd read this to Luke. Can't hurt . . . thought it might strike a chord because it's the one he always reads to Frankie.'

Dee looked away, tears coming into her eyes. 'Sorry, Patricia. You're going through hell and here I am, falling apart like an idiot.'

'Don't be silly. You love him too.' Patricia squeezed Dee's hand and said goodbye to Luke. 'I'll be back later,' she called in a falsely cheerful tone.

As she left, Patricia's thoughts returned to Lucy and she realised she felt protective of her, something she hadn't felt about her before. Patricia wanted to call her, to find out how she was, but she wasn't sure if that was the right thing to do.

Taking out her mobile phone as she emerged from the hospital, Patricia put it away again. A phone call felt inadequate, insulting. This was too big, too awful, for a phone call. She knew Lucy wasn't at work – she hadn't been at the florists since Luke's accident – and, while they met at the hospital, that was only to swap shifts and Lucy had looked so destroyed the last few times, Patricia hadn't the heart to ask her about Stella. Resolutely, Patricia headed to her car. Without another thought, she drove straight to the house Lucy and Luke shared, doing her best to squash down the pang she felt as she walked up the short pathway. This lovely little house was synonymous with *them*. Not Lucy, not Luke – *them*. Together, as a couple, pre- and post-marriage. They had turned this house from a seventies horror film with casino carpets into a modern, cosy home with enough room for them and all the babies they planned to have.

The babies they would *still* have, Patricia reminded herself firmly. She rang the doorbell and waited. There was no answer, but she was sure Lucy was inside. She took a step back and watched the upstairs curtains. She was right; one shifted slightly before swinging back into place. Patricia rang the doorbell again and called through the letterbox.

'Please, Lucy. I just want to talk. I'm . . . I'm on your side, I promise.' She waited again and, this time, Lucy opened the door a fraction. Her hair showed through, the lank brown lock covering her face.

'Come in,' she said flatly.

Patricia squared her shoulders and followed Lucy inside. Lucy was wearing a brown T-shirt that had seen better days and a pair of grey jogging bottoms. It was debatable if Lucy's hair or body had been acquainted with a shower over the past week, and the remains of make-up she had most likely put on days ago was smudged beneath her reddened eyes. She looked absolutely broken.

Patricia placed her handbag on an armchair and removed her coat. She was walking on eggshells, she knew that. Lucy was vulnerable, damaged. She, Patricia, was probably the last person Lucy wanted to see. *Apart from Stella*, she thought distractedly.

'Shall we have a cup of tea?' Patricia detested the bright tone she kept using around people at the moment. Without waiting for Lucy to answer, Patricia headed into the kitchen and started to fill the kettle. The kitchen seemed quiet and unlived in. Luke's bag of coffee beans sat next to his coffee machine, looking sad and abandoned, no fresh flowers on the windowsill, only a vase with murky-looking water in it and some wilted stalks. Roses. Lucy loved roses, but these ones were long dead.

Patricia glanced over her shoulder as she dealt with the stagnant water in the vase. Lucy was slumped on the sofa, her gaze directed at nothing in particular. She seemed vacant. Patricia made a pot of strong tea and put cups and saucers on a tray, pouring milk into a jug she found in the cupboard. She poured tea silently, pushing a cup towards Lucy. Patricia was surprised when Lucy sat up slightly and reached her hand out towards it.

'Thank you,' she managed. 'Sorry. I must look appalling. I haven't – I've been a bit . . .'

'Of course you have,' Patricia replied soothingly. Her heart contracted. This was a very different Lucy to the one she was used to – more compliant, perhaps, but not the daughter-in-law she was so fond of, even if she found it difficult to communicate this.

'Luke's consultant talked me through his treatment plan yesterday,' Lucy said in a conversational tone. 'He said that if Luke comes out of the coma with good brain activity, we're looking at some fairly intensive physio for his leg and back for starters. He could even be in a wheelchair for a while.'

'He certainly won't be going for runs for a while,' Patricia agreed. 'But if he comes out of this coma with his brain intact, I'll take any of the other stuff we have to go through, won't you?'

Lucy toyed with her saucer. 'For sure. I just hope he's

not incapacitated for long. Luke's never been good at sitting still.'

'Yes, you have a point. Listen, did you – did you hear about that girl coming to the florists?' Patricia was loath to use Stella's name in front of Lucy. It seemed overly familiar, as if they were friends. Lucy nodded. 'Yes. Ade called me.'

'Ade? But . . . that was nice of him.' Patricia had assumed that Nell would have been in touch. Patricia panicked for a moment. She really must keep an eye on Nell . . . just in case.

'Did you believe her?' Lucy asked, cutting across the diplomatic offerings Patricia had been working on during her car journey. 'Stella. Did you believe what she told you? I know Ade had to drag it out of her, I know she didn't go to the florists to tell you about it. It's just so horrible. Luke . . . a baby . . .'

She stumbled over the word and Patricia fought a fierce urge to cuddle her.

'No.'

The word came out decisively, for which Patricia was grateful. It was imperative that she sounded clear and confident on this issue. She was dumbfounded as to why Stella would lie about such a thing, but she still believed Luke was innocent. He was her son and she would stand by him. And she would stand by Lucy.

Lucy nodding, wincing as the hot tea connected with her lips. 'I've been driving myself crazy,' she admitted. 'Trying to work out why Stella would do this, you know? Dee's in favour of the basket case theory, which is obviously possible.' She put her tea down and started to wring her hands. 'I wish he was here to defend himself, but I won't think him capable of this.' She faltered. 'I just can't seem to stop tormenting myself with it, with images of . . . them. Stupid. *Stupid*.'

'It's not stupid.' Patricia appointed herself as the voice of reason. 'I'd do the same in your shoes. I mean, I have.' She felt Lucy's eyes on her and she dipped her head, knowing she needed to explain herself. 'A woman became fixated with Bernard once, you know. A patient. It's true.' Patricia knew Lucy wouldn't believe her, would assume that she was making this up just to make her feel better.

'It happened when Bernard was new to the practice – years ago. Anyway, this woman used to turn up repeatedly; weekly, first of all, then more frequently, her ailments becoming more and more personal and intimate.'

Patricia coloured slightly. 'Poor Bernard was mortified. He had to switch her to another GP and it all went away, but I panicked. I trusted Bernard implicitly, but I wondered. Fleetingly, but enough to drive myself insane. It's the thoughts that appear in your head, isn't it? They're relentless and distressing, even when you don't believe them.'

Lucy smiled, a bitter, tight smile. 'It wouldn't be so bad if there wasn't a – a baby involved. I mean, it would still be horrendous, but somehow, the baby thing. It's just sending my mind into overdrive.'

'I can imagine.' Patricia hesitated. 'Lucy, I don't know exactly what you've been through, so I'm terrified of saying the wrong thing. About the babies, I mean,' she clarified, noting Lucy's confusion. 'I want to help you, but I don't know the facts. I want to understand, I really do.'

'Yes. I know. It's – we made a decision not to – maybe it wasn't the right thing.' Lucy carefully placed her cup on top of its saucer, her hands causing it to clatter. 'I – I can't talk about it easily. Can I . . . show you something?' She stood and headed for the stairs.

Patricia got to her feet and followed Lucy, joining her in front of a wardrobe. She tried not to let the sight of Luke's work T-shirts, still in a heap on the chair in the corner, make her fall apart. She focused her eyes on the cupboard, intrigued, but unnerved.

'These are . . . this is what we've been through.' Lucy lifted a hand and Patricia's eyes travelled to the top of the wardrobe. There were eight shoe boxes stacked tidily next to one another. Eight. Surely these didn't mean – they weren't . . .

'They're memory boxes. A box for each baby we've lost.' Lucy's voice trembled. 'There was this miscarriage forum and they suggested it – it's a way to mark the loss of a baby when you lose it early on. When a – a funeral isn't appropriate.' She coughed and wiped at her face.

Patricia recalled the ghastly funeral they had all attended recently. She was certain she would never get the sight of that tiny white coffin out of her head and, if she was struggling, she was certain the imprint of it must be burnt on Lucy's brain.

'What's inside the boxes?' Patricia managed, sitting down with a thud. Luckily, she connected with the edge of the bed.

'Socks. A goodbye letter and the pregnancy test. A

239

name plaque.' Lucy joined Patricia on the bed, sitting close.

'You didn't . . . you didn't use the names you actually wanted, did you?'

'No.' Lucy sniffed. 'No. We were . . . Luke wanted Jude for a boy. Bryony for a girl. But, for these boxes, we chose unisex names, just to – to give each baby an identity.'

'There are eight of them.'

'Yes.'

Patricia wanted to feel something, but she was so shocked, she felt numb. 'I had no idea. No idea you and Luke had been through such immense tragedy. He – he talked about IVF and some problems, but he didn't go into specifics. I guess I chose to think that it wasn't as bad as all that.'

'We just kept having miscarriages,' Lucy revealed, her shoulders tense, her eyes fixed on the boxes. 'It would take us a while to fall pregnant each time – months and months. And then it would happen and we'd be ecstatic, and then it would be over.'

Patricia no longer felt numb. Several emotions crashed over her at once and she couldn't hold back. 'Lucy, you poor, poor darling.' Without thinking, she turned to Lucy and gathered her up in her arms. She held her tightly, murmuring something, anything, to comfort her. Patricia couldn't imagine the pain of these miscarriages – of what was happening with Luke – but she knew it must be crucifying. She cradled Lucy as if she were Nell, her own flesh and blood.

Lucy, no doubt unsure how she should respond to this sudden, intense display of compassion and love, stiffened initially. She resisted, allowing herself to be cradled, but rigidly only. But after a few moments she let go, giving in, moulding herself to Patricia's embrace. She started crying hysterically, great howls coming from deep within her.

Patricia bent her head to Lucy's, kissing her hair and rubbing her shoulder. She wished she'd known about this; wished she'd known the extent of what Lucy – and Luke – had endured. 'I'm so sorry. So, so sorry. I don't even know what to say.' She almost confessed that she had secretly wanted to blame Lucy for not producing a grandchild, but there was no need, no point. The admission would relieve Patricia's conscience, nothing more.

Lucy slowly extricated herself from Patricia's embrace, as if the proximity was too much. She sniffed and, leaning forward, she closed the wardrobe door. 'I've asked myself if I would be able to forgive Luke if he has done this to me. If he's made that woman pregnant. And I honestly don't know. I feel like half a person without him; that's the problem. Like someone wrenched my right arm off or hobbled my foot. But does feeling paralysed, feeling as though I've been cast adrift – does that excuse the pain of infidelity?'

Patricia ran a hand over the duvet cover, smoothing it. She had asked herself the very same question about Bernard years ago, when the female patient had become obsessed with him. The question – and its answer – had haunted her, but she had come to the conclusion that she would have tried to get past it if she could. Because she, like Lucy, would have felt like half a person without Bernard. Patricia knew this for a fact, because she had

241

felt exactly that since he had died – bereft and diminished. But Lucy had a point; did feeling faded and shrunken without someone cancel out a betrayal?

'I need to speak to Stella,' Lucy said. 'I need to find out the truth. I don't know her – I don't even know if I can trust what she says. But I need to hear what she has to say, all the terrible details she might offer up. Because until he comes out of this coma, that's the only way I will be able to work out if I can view my life the way I always have, or if it's been twisted beyond all recognition.'

'Trust your gut instinct,' Patricia agreed. 'And when Luke can speak for himself, you'll know for sure. But for the record, I don't think he did it. And I won't have some silly girl telling lies and tearing our family apart.'

Lucy slowly lifted her eyes and they were brimming with gratitude. 'It means so much to hear you say that, Patricia.'

Patricia shook her head. 'I mean it, Lucy. And not just because Luke's my son. I don't believe Stella because I know how he felt about you.'

'Thank you. And thank you for making me feel like part of the family.'

The missing word 'finally' hung in the air, but Patricia chose not to be affronted by it. She and Lucy had both made mistakes in the past, and now they needed to pull together.

'I don't know if I have the strength to confront Stella,' Lucy admitted in a small voice.

'You do,' Patricia told her, lifting her chin. 'You are a strong, capable woman and you can do this. You don't believe her, do you?'

'I – I don't know. I don't believe it; I can't. But there's this tiny part of me that doubts. It's small, but it's throbbing like a – like a splinter. I can't ignore it.' Lucy held her chest, as if short of breath. 'But I can't stop feeling the way I feel about Luke. I can't stop loving him. If he's done this? I don't know . . .'

'I read this quote once,' Patricia started, glancing at Lucy's pinched, white face. 'It said: "It's amazing how someone can break your heart, but you still love them with all the little pieces."'

Lucy let out a small, contained sob.

Patricia could tell that Lucy was doing her best to keep it together, to continue to put up a strong front, the way she had since the beginning. She carried on. 'That's how I thought I might feel if Bernard had cheated on me. It doesn't mean I'm saying that Luke did this; I'm just telling you how I would have felt if it happened to me.'

Lucy's hands curled into fists on the duvet. Patricia put her arm round Lucy's heaving shoulders and, feeling her daughter-in-law relax against her like Nell might, she held on. Bridges had been crossed and there was no way Patricia was ever going to let them break down again.

CHAPTER TWENTY-EIGHT

Lucy and Luke

September, three years earlier

'And what, pray tell, is one supposed to wear to a garden party?'

Luke held up a garish Hawaiian shirt. He held his other hand limply in the air.

I turned away from the mirror, my blusher brush in mid-air. 'Could you be any more camp, Harte?'

'Probably. Let's see.' He flung the shirt down and put his hand on his hip, flipping one of his legs out behind him.

I laughed and finished bronzing my cheekbones. 'Stop it. How am I supposed to fancy you when you're acting like one of the Village People?'

Luke picked his shirt up. 'Because I'm hot, hot, hot . . .' He danced around in his boxer shorts, thrusting his groin out. 'Christ, seriously, what do I wear to a garden party? I have a feeling it's not going to be like one of Dee and Dan's drunken barbecues.'

'I know. But it's your boss . . . your potential boss. So we have to make an effort and we have to look right.' I flipped through my wardrobe, searching for something suitable. It was easier for me, because it was arranged by colour, each section organised into short-sleeved, long-sleeved, dresses, trousers. Luke's choice would be more difficult, his clothes arranged on the basis of what had most recently come out of the wash.

'I'm going to wear this.' I held up a cream sundress with spaghetti-thin straps. I slipped off my robe, giving Luke a quick flash of boob and thong before diving into the dress.

Luke groaned. 'Aside from the blatant attention-seeking, you know I always want to roll you back into bed when you wear that. It makes you look like a serving wench.'

'Is that sexist, do you think?'

I wriggled away from his wandering hands. It was a source of constant amazement to me that Luke found me so appealing; I could only imagine that he saw something different to the mirror image I was familiar with. Mostly, I was flattered, but occasionally it troubled me; I worried that the veil would be lifted one day, that he would see me as I truly was and the spell – whatever it was – would be broken.

'Sexist? Hardly.' Luke returned to his wardrobe, feigning a sulk. 'I can say you look like a serving man, if you prefer. So, the Hawaiian shirt isn't the right look then. Maybe this one.' He took out a navy and white striped shirt and grabbed a pair of beige shorts. 'Better?'

'Better. More macho. Me likey.' I kissed him. 'Let's go. You have medical types to impress.'

Luke shrugged his arms into his shirt, spraying antiperspirant at the same time, a time-saving art he had perfected. 'And, maybe later, you'll let me peel that dress off and I can kiss every inch of that gorgeous body.'

'Maybe.' I smiled. Leaning across I checked the diary on my bedside table. 'Or better still . . . we could recreate this in two days' time. I'm due to ovulate, according to this calculator thingy I'm using.'

Luke buttoned his shorts, his brow furrowed. 'Luce, we could just do it today for the hell of it. Not, you know, to make a baby. Haven't we been told to do it all the time, not just when we should?'

'Sure.' I slipped the diary into my bedside drawer. 'I just meant that Tuesday would be the optimum day, or whatever they call it.'

Luke started searching on his hands and knees for something, his shoes most likely. 'I just don't want us to forget to have amazing sex just for the sheer fun of it.' Luke emerged from the side of the bed with a brown deck shoe in his hand. 'Because we do, don't we? Have amazing sex. We always have done.'

I checked my watch. 'We're late. Shall we talk about this later?'

Luke unexpectedly found his shoe in close proximity to the other one, jerkily pulled them on and stood up. 'I don't know. Is there any point?'

His edgy tone put my back up. 'What's that supposed to mean?'

'It means that every now and again, I feel a bit depressed about this whole thing.'

I stared at him. There was more to it than that. Luke was making some sort of point.

'Do *I* make you feel like that?'

Luke started to say something, then fell silent.

I realised my teeth were clenched, but this conversation was becoming irksome. Our most recent miscarriage had happened some time before our wedding and since then, without explanation, we had failed to conceive at all. Baby-making was a touchy topic in our household and I had convinced myself that our failure thus far was my fault, although I wasn't exactly sure why I had come to this conclusion.

We were thinking of seeing some consultants soon to have some tests done – a terrifying thought, because presumably it would prove if this issue could be laid at my door or at Luke's. I wanted to go in armed with information about the number of times we had attempted to conceive during ovulations; I wanted to prove that we were serious about this, especially if the next step might be IVF.

The accusation from Luke that I was making him feel bad about this – however accidentally – wasn't welcome. His eyes had turned a shade or so darker, turning them to a greyish-blue, which meant that he was angry. That made two of us.

'I know you don't realise you're doing it, but some-times—' He faltered. 'Sometimes, I feel like I'm not much more than a . . . I feel like a sperm donor,' he finished.

'A sperm donor?' I sat down on the bed, my knuckles white as I clutched the duvet. 'Jesus.'

'Am I wrong? Isn't that all I am right now?'

'Of course not! Why would you say such a thing?' I sounded defensive. A nerve had been well and truly touched; any fool could see that.

'I just want to show the experts that we're doing everything properly. That we're making a concerted effort to do it at the right times.'

'And I love you for it. I do. You want to do everything properly.' Luke turned my face towards his, using his thumb to smooth an errant tear away. 'I just don't want to lose "us". I don't want to lose what we have together. I want us to have a baby more than anything, but we're important too.'

I knew what he meant. We'd suffered so many miscarriages and so much heartache, but we'd always managed to find one another again and make time for us.

But lately, I had begun to put pressure on myself to make our trysts romantic and meaningful. Well, *effective* might be a more accurate word to describe the way I had systematically set about 'arranging' each assignation.

Oh yes, when the time was right, I found myself to be superbly inventive and focused, but could I honestly say that I bothered to summon up the same level of enthusiasm at any other time? Probably not. I could barely be bothered if sex was on offer at non baby-making times. Part of me felt that there was little point.

How had this happened? When had I stopped thinking about Luke – and about us as a couple? I loved him.

I loved us. Just as I crumbled, Luke gathered me into his arms.

'Don't cry, Luce, please. Look, forget what I said, okay? I'm willing to do whatever it takes to get a baby. It's what you want . . . it's what *we* want.' He smoothed my hair away from my face, stricken. 'I can't believe how selfish I'm being about this.'

'You're not being selfish.' I was heaving now. 'It's me – I'm . . .'

Luke leant forward and kissed my head, tender and forgiving. 'This baby stuff is hard. Anyone would crack up after everything we've been through. And we haven't even started IVF yet.'

'I don't ever want you to think I don't fancy the pants off you. Because I do. A lot.' I put my hand on his calf and tugged at the hair.

Luke gave me a half-smile and held his hand out. 'If you stop yanking my leg hair out, that's a deal. And thank you. For saying all of that.' We shook, solemnly and he stood up, helping me to my feet. 'I love you, Stripes,' he said, his hand resting on my hip. 'Like, to pieces.'

'Ditto.'

It was an in joke. Luke hated the film *Ghost*, but the 'ditto' line always made him laugh because it was pure cheese.

'Now let's go before your prospective boss thinks you're not interested in that promotion.' I checked Luke out. 'And before I forget to mention it, your bum looks seriously sexy in those shorts.' I wasn't just playing nice; I meant it. 'And yes, later. Ravish me. Several times over. Not to make a baby, but just for the sheer hell of it.'

He slung his arm around me, his warm hand gripping my shoulder and, just like that, all was right in our world again.

CHAPTER TWENTY-NINE

Nell

'Cal, do you have a minute?'

'Er, yes. No problem.' Cal glanced up as students sidled out of his office. 'Let me just get organised and then we can talk about your coursework.'

'Thank you.'

Nell waited while Cal collected up his notes. Did anyone suspect anything? She hoped not; she didn't want to get Cal into trouble – that wasn't what this was about. But they needed to talk.

Nell put her folders down on a nearby table and studied him. His green eyes weren't murky today, they were bright and clear, she noted. No alcohol and possibly an early night. Her stomach churned. Do not ask him if he has sex with this wife. Do not ask him if he has sex with his wife.

Nell felt a flicker of panic inside. She needed Cal at the moment, really needed him. He was her solace during this unbearable time . . . well, he should be, shouldn't he? As wrong as she knew it was for her to be with him, Cal was the one thing that was keeping her going. Thinking about him and what they had together stopped her thinking about Luke, stopped her obsessing about what would happen to her family if Luke didn't make it.

Nell nervously chewed her fingernail. The last time she and Cal had spent time together had been two days ago. They had slept together at his city flat and it had been a frantic coupling on her part, as much designed to forget and distract as it was to remind her that she was head over heels in love with him. The sex was always incredible. But this was about more than that, for her, at least. It was Nell's devout belief that Cal felt the same way, but it was difficult to know for sure. Not because he didn't tell her how he felt, because he did – constantly – but because the very fact that he had another life running alongside theirs caused Nell untold insecurity.

Luke flitted into Nell's mind again. She felt selfish for dwelling on her relationship with Cal. Luke. Everything came back to Luke.

Cal sat on the edge of the desk when his office door finally closed. 'Are you okay?'

Nell nodded. 'Yes. No. Yes. Look, Cal. There's been so much going on recently, stuff I haven't had a chance to talk to you about really.' She traced a toe on the floor. 'I've been doing all sorts of thinking.'

'Have you?' Cal looked amused.

'Everything is wrong,' she answered, tearily. Shifting off the desk and throwing a furtive glance at the door in one smooth movement, Cal took her hand. 'Seriously. What's wrong?'

Nell almost lost her nerve. 'The thing is . . .'

Cal gripped her hand. 'God. Are you pregnant?'

'No, no!'

She recoiled from the terror in his eyes. They had turned murky-green again. He radiated relief and she felt inexplicably affronted. She didn't want to be pregnant either, but his reaction was unnerving.

He already has children, Nell reminded herself. He's just not ready for more. Yet.

'It's nothing like that,' she reassured him. 'It's a good thing. Well, it could be a good thing.'

Cal's shoulders lifted impatiently. Now that he had realised there wasn't a pregnancy on the horizon, he seemed to have turned his attention back to practicalities. 'Nell, is this something we can talk about later? I need to grab some lunch and I have a ton of portfolios to wade through . . .'

'I know, right. My timing is off.' Nell grimaced. Should she leave this conversation until later? It wasn't something she could say quickly. Or perhaps it was. Perhaps it was something best blurted out, then left to settle.

No, she decided. It was now or never. 'The thing is, Cal—'

'Fay!'

The name came out like a gunshot and Nell flinched.

Cal stood, abruptly. His eyes darted to Nell's and instinctively she stepped away from him. Fay. Fay was Cal's wife.

Fay had a wide smile; her hair was blonde and flicked

up at the ends. She kissed Cal on the mouth. 'I just popped in to ask you out to lunch. I know we didn't arrange it, but I was out shopping and I thought, what the hell.'

Nell's heart thumped. *Jesus*. This was horrendous. Should she leave? She wanted to leave. The guilt at coming face to face with Cal's wife threatened to suffocate Nell, and she tried to pull herself together.

'Lunch?' Cal glanced at his watch. 'I could squeeze lunch in, I guess. That would be great.'

Nell felt as though she had a golf ball stuck in her throat. Cal and Fay still kissed on the mouth. After two children and several years of marriage, they were intimate enough to kiss on the mouth. What did it mean?

Nell couldn't help staring at Fay. Cal's wife was attractive. Not beautiful, but she had friendly eyes and a good figure, which betrayed no evidence of childbirth, at least on the outside. Nell had no idea, but she rather suspected that Fay might look just as good in underwear. She had never thought of such a thing before, because she hadn't wanted to think of Fay as a real person.

Nell began to feel sick. She had been about to tell Cal that she loved him and here was his stylish wife, wearing a silk jacket and skinny jeans and kissing Cal with genuine love and affection, if not unbridled passion. 'This is Nell, one of my students,' Cal said, by way of an introduction. 'We've just been talking about her coursework.'

'Er . . . nice to meet you,' Nell managed with a nod. How could he be so calm? Why wasn't he freaking out? Apart from some tenseness around the shoulders, which could easily be put down to work stress, he seemed completely at ease. Had he done this before? No. She wouldn't think like that. Cal had told her that this was the first time and she believed him. He was simply better than she was at covering up the abject horror at being found chatting in his office by his wife.

'Nice to meet you, Nell.' Fay gave Nell a brief, casual onceover. 'Is that one of your creations you're wearing?'

Nell glanced down at the black and white shift dress. 'Ummm, yes. It's a bit short, actually, but . . .'

'Don't be silly. You've got fantastic legs. Show them off.' Fay laughed, her eyes creasing at the edges, but she looked no less attractive for it. 'I used to wear mini skirts all the time at your age, but I wouldn't dare these days.' She gave a throaty laugh and caught Cal's eye.

At your age. The comment made Nell feel about twelve, although she was sure that hadn't been Fay's intention. She was also pretty sure Fay could rock a mini skirt even now, if the slender line of her legs in the skinny jeans was anything to go by.

Nell was jolted. If that woman Stella was telling the truth, Lucy was Fay. Fay was Lucy. Lucy was the injured party, innocent, trusting. If Luke *had* cheated on her, Lucy had been oblivious, the way Fay must be. Whatever had gone on between Luke and Lucy, Lucy didn't deserve to be betrayed or lied to. And neither did Fay.

Nell disliked herself intensely at this realisation. What sort of woman was she? Weren't they all supposed to stick together? She was a disgrace to the sisterhood, she was a traitor. If Stella was carrying Luke's baby and they'd had a one-night stand, Nell was just as bad. Worse, in fact, because this wasn't a one-night stand, this was a full-blown affair.

'Er. Right. I should go. Thanks for that,' Nell mumbled, holding her folder up awkwardly. Anything to keep up the pretence of a discussion about coursework.

'You're welcome.' Cal sat on the edge of the desk and met Nell's eyes apologetically. As Fay's mobile rang and she rummaged in her handbag to find it, Cal mouthed something at Nell, but she was too distracted to figure out what he was trying to say.

Once outside, she hurried to the nearest toilets, threw her folders under the sink and turned the taps on, splashing water on to her hot face repeatedly, until her skin felt numb.

God. What an appalling situation. She grabbed some paper towels and dried her face. Gripping the sink, she stared into the age-spotted mirror. I'm a bad person, she told herself. A bad, bad person. She had to stop seeing Cal. She had fallen in love with him, but the affair had to stop. Cal had a wife. A real, live wife who popped into his place of work promising lunch, along with a kiss and a throaty chuckle. Not to mention two children who were likely to be damaged if things went any further.

Nell picked her folders up, hot with shame. The next chance she got, she was going to end it with Cal. Her heart heavy with self-reproach, Nell headed out of the toilets and tried to remember where her next lecture was.

Arriving at the hospital later, Nell came face to face with Lucy, who was just emerging from the double doors. She looked dazed and tearful, not even seeing Nell as she stumbled and nearly tripped over.

'Luce, are you all right?' Nell asked anxiously. Lucy generally looked awful these days, understandably, but today, she looked extra awful.

Lucy nodded, tucking her hair behind her ear. 'I've just been to see Luke. I was begging him to wake up. I was literally begging him, but obviously he can't just shake himself out of it. If he could, he would have done it by now, wouldn't he?'

She stopped, wiping a finger under her eyes. Her fingers were already stained with mascara, the black marks making her look like a student emerging from a difficult exam.

'Not silly at all.' She rubbed Lucy's arm, which felt cold beneath her cardigan. 'It's so one-sided, talking to a coma victim. They just lie there looking beautiful and those machines make loud shhhing noises at you, cutting you off.'

'Off-putting.' Lucy's lip trembled.

Nell wasn't sure if she should ask, but she needed to know what Lucy was thinking about the Stella situation. 'Do you – do you think Luke . . . ?'

'Cheated on me?' Lucy lifted her chin, ever brave. 'I can say it without flinching now. I'm sorry, Nell. I know I've been avoiding talking to you about it. I've been avoiding everyone.' Her eyes were unreadable. 'The honest answer is that I don't know. I don't think so. I don't want to think so. No. Let's go with no.'

'Of course you don't want to think that,' Nell agreed, her head nodding rapidly like that dog in the advert. 'Why would you? You're only human.' She stopped. She sounded sycophantic.

'I just wish I could talk to him about it,' Lucy said, emitting a small, defeated sigh. 'Look, I feel bad talking about him to you in this way, Nell. I know how much you adore him. But . . . I just hate that this has happened and that he's just lying in there with all those machines and he can't tell me to stop being silly, that he would never do this to me in a million years.'

Nell tightened her grip on her folders. 'He wouldn't. I know he wouldn't.'

Clearly troubled, Lucy chewed her lip. 'I think my only option is to speak to that woman Stella again. I can't ignore it, can I? There might be . . . a baby involved. Oh God, it's too awful.'

Nell admired Lucy for being so heroic.

Would she, Nell, do the same thing in Lucy's shoes? She wasn't convinced she would be as brave in the same situation. She favoured the ostrich approach, head firmly rooted in the ground until everything had gone away; it was what she had done when her father died and she was doing the same thing now. About Luke and his recovery, about her relationship with Cal.

'Patricia and I . . . we talked the other day. She – she came round and it was good to talk to her properly about things.' Lucy sniffed. 'We cleared the air a bit.'

Nell was heartened that something positive had come out of what was happening. 'Well, that's something.'

'It is.' Lucy pulled at the sleeves of her cardigan. 'It really is. We had a bit of a breakthrough, I think.' She didn't elaborate. 'Do you think men like Luke cheat?' she asked, out of the blue. 'I know he's your brother, but surely even men like him might . . . succumb?'

Nell shook her head. 'No. I don't.'

'Surely even nice men cheat,' Lucy said, braving a smile. 'You must know some nice guys at college who are having it away with someone they shouldn't be.'

Nell hesitated. A fraction too long. Dammit.

'You do.' Lucy blinked.

'I do,' Nell admitted. She avoided Lucy's eyes. 'Jesus. I don't even know how to tell you this.'

'Tell me what?' Lucy looked concerned. Abruptly, she pulled Nell out of the way of an ambulance crew wielding a trolley with a bloodied body on it. The crew shouted to one another in their own, incomprehensible language – staccato bursts of medical information and directions they all understood, the very definition of teamwork.

The noise died down before being cut off by the automatic doors closing with a swish. Nell leant against the wall. 'I'm . . . in a relationship. He's lovely, he's sweet. He's older than me – quite a bit older than me – but that's not the issue.' She cringed, knowing she was just going to have to say it. 'He's – he's married.'

'What?' Lucy rounded on Nell. 'You – you can't be serious? Jesus, Nell.'

'I know, I know.' Nell recoiled at the anger blazing in Lucy's eyes. 'This is . . . I feel sick just thinking about how you must feel hearing that.'

'*You* feel sick?' Lucy spat the words out. 'God, you have no idea.'

Nell bit her lip. There was nothing she could say, nothing she could do to make things better here.

Lucy turned away from her. 'Christ, Nell. What is it, some sort of default in the family gene? Are you all at it? You, Luke . . . Ade, for fuck's sake? Is that why he's back? Because he's been screwing around and his wife chucked him out?'

Nell inhaled. It was a low blow, but there was no defence, no justification. Not that she could appease Lucy with, at any rate. And Lucy had every right to be angry, considering what she was dealing with.

'Bloody hell!' Lucy rubbed a hand over her eyes. 'I just can't handle this. Why did you tell me that – why did you think I needed to know?'

Nell swallowed. 'I don't know. I just . . . it's . . .' Against her better judgement, she began to cry. 'Shit, sorry. I have no right . . . it's just . . . God, I hate the way you're looking at me.'

Lucy let out another expletive. Then she exhaled, deeply. 'I'm sorry, okay? It's just that this is . . . I can't even get my head round it. I can't actually get my head around anything much these days.'

'I know. And I can understand that, really I can. I guess . . . I wanted to tell you ages ago . . . I almost told Luke, but I was worried he – you – might hate me. And that was before Stella came along. Jesus. Sorry, Lucy.' Nell put her chin on her folders.

Lucy wrapped her arms around her body. 'I wouldn't have hated you. And neither would Luke. I don't hate you now. It's just . . . I'm trying so hard to be strong right now, to hold it all together . . .'

Nell heard the catch in Lucy's voice. 'I know. I know. I'm so, so sorry.' She put her folders down on the ground and put an arm around Lucy's shoulders. They were shaking. She looked so vulnerable and broken, Nell felt even worse than she had when Fay had arrived at college earlier.

Lucy wiped her eyes, trying to compose herself but not managing it remotely. 'Does he . . . does he make you happy, this married guy?'

'He does. I – I think I might love him. Actually, I know I do.' Stricken, Nell turned tortured eyes to Lucy.

'Is he leaving his wife for you?'

'I don't know, but I just met her. She was lovely. Attractive, friendly. She loves Cal, I know she does – I could see it in her eyes. I've never felt like a bigger bitch. I just wanted to run away, but I hated myself for being such a coward. A mistress and a coward.'

Lucy stared straight ahead but she reached for Nell's hand. 'You're not a coward. Or a bitch. Sometimes people just fall in love with the wrong people. Isn't that what they say?'

Despairing, Nell squeezed Lucy's hand. How could she be such a good sister-in-law, such a good friend, when she was going through this horrible situation?

'For what it's worth, I don't believe Luke would do this to you.' Nell meant it. 'I know he's my brother. And I know I love him to distraction. But regardless of that, I don't think he'd do that to you.'

Lucy looked so sad, Nell wanted to gather her up in a hug and not let go. How was she even getting through each day? She watched Lucy drop a hand to her stomach. Nell guessed it was an unconscious gesture – a memory of the baby she'd lost – perhaps thoughts of the one Stella was carrying, too. It was all so ghastly.

261

'I'd better go,' Lucy sighed, looking thoroughly exhausted. 'Thanks for telling me, Nell. I know that must have been hard for you.'

Nell watched Lucy walk away, hating the defeated tilt of her shoulders. Panicked fingers started clawing at Nell's stomach. Should she go and find somewhere to sit down so she could write a letter? Nell reached into her bag, but instead of pulling out her notepad, she pulled out her phone. Terror was setting in again and she could feel anxiety bubbling up in her. She needed a release. She needed something. Someone. Normally she would lean on Luke in a crisis. But Luke couldn't help her now. And neither could Cal. But there was someone else, someone Nell hoped might be there for her this time round.

'Ade. It's me. Have you got a second? I really need to talk.' Nell felt her stomach unwind a fraction and she leant back against the wall. 'I'm at the hospital and I just told Lucy about Cal. She was really nice about it, but yeah, it was bad. Really bad.'

'But you told her?' Ade's voice was reassuring at the other end of the phone. 'That was brave of you.'

'Brave is the last thing I am,' Nell responded glumly. 'I met Cal's wife today, too. I have to finish it, Ade. I have to.' She paused, sucking her breath in.

'You love him,' Ade offered quietly.

'Yeah, I love him. But I can't have him, can I?' Tears rolled down Nell's cheeks and she wondered how she could escape from the unbearable hell she had created. 'He's not mine. And with everything that's happening with Lucy and Luke, I can't do it. It's wrong. It's horrible and it's wrong.'

She glanced down at her wrist, at the gnarled roll of skin that was a repulsive reminder of what had happened when it had all gone wrong last time. Nell started to feel a familiar but terrifying rush of something . . . Panic and overwhelming anxiety, with a dark, stealthy coil of dread, all rolled into one. It was suffocating. She was suffocating.

Without meaning to, Nell let out a whimper. It was happening again, it was happening again.

'Stay where you are,' Ade barked at her. 'Stay where you are, Nell, and I'll come and get you. Don't do anything stupid, will you? Just wait there and everything will be fine. I'm coming to get you. Right now.' He hung up.

Nell felt racking sobs tearing through her and she slid down the wall. She clutched her left wrist, pressing the skin as if she might be able to somehow stop herself from tumbling headlong into despair.

Nell looked around desperately for Ade, wondering why the hell she always needed one of her brothers to save her. Why couldn't she ever seem to save herself?

CHAPTER THIRTY

Lucy

Standing outside the hospital again the following day, I braced myself. I took out Luke's phone and punched Stella's number into my own. I had thought about calling her from Luke's phone because it was easier, but I knew it was twisted. This wasn't the time for childish games. I needed to be adult about this, dignified.

'Hello?'

She sounded cautious.

'It's Lucy.'

I scuffed my shoe on the ground. I was resisting this talk with every part of my being. Unfortunately, it was unavoidable. I pressed on.

'Listen, can we meet? I really think we need to talk.'

'Of course. Yes. We can do that.' She sounded wary.

'Shall we meet in the hospital café?'

'Yes.' Stella paused. 'I'll see you there in five minutes.'

I ended the call. The café wasn't ideal – it was noisy and impersonal – but it was either there or the ICU. I didn't want to move too far from Luke. Ade was with him and I knew he'd get in touch immediately if something happened, but today was one of those days I needed to be close to Luke.

I sat down at a table in the café, horribly on edge.

After this (most likely) hideous meeting, I had another (most likely hideous) meeting – with Luke's consultant. The consultant wanted to talk to me about Luke's condition, about his official treatment plan. I hoped this was a positive sign, a sign that he was soon to be out of ICU and into a ward. But I had given up trying to second-guess the professionals.

One thing at a time, I told myself. *One thing at a time*.

I cradled a cup of weak tea. I wasn't quite sure what Stella might want so I hadn't ordered her anything. That wasn't true; I didn't especially care what Stella wanted. And I didn't want to appear too pally-pally until I knew what the score was.

My stomach was churning. I hadn't had breakfast, because my mouth seemed to be full of dust today, and I was certain even a freshly-baked croissant smothered in butter and apricot jam would taste like cardboard. I hadn't actually enjoyed food for a while now. I couldn't remember what eating something for the sheer hell of it felt like. Food was fuel, nothing more.

My skin prickled, giving me an advanced warning of Stella's arrival. I glanced at the doorway and watched her eyes darting around. She was looking for me and I should stand, I should make it easy for her. But I couldn't, even if I had wanted to, because beneath the table, my legs were shaking too much.

Stella walked over slowly, still reasonably elegant. She must be five months pregnant now, maybe a little more. I felt a wave of sickness again. I couldn't help wondering what had happened at Stella's twenty-week scan. Had she found out the sex of the baby? My stomach clenched and I fought hard to control it. I suddenly noticed how unsteady Stella was on her feet and, in spite of myself, I found myself standing up and guiding her on to a chair, my own jelly legs forgotten. She was pregnant. I'm not a monster.

I reclaimed my seat. 'I didn't get you a drink,' I muttered, feeling the need, for some unfathomable reason, to explain myself on that front, too. 'I wasn't sure what you wanted.'

Stella placed her hands on the table, a gesture my currently cynical mind interpreted as a need to appear open. Had I read that somewhere? Psycho-babble.

'I . . . thank you for calling me,' Stella said. She swallowed, her fingers curling and uncurling on the table.

I noted her nervousness; it was good to see that I wasn't the only one on edge.

'I've been hoping to talk to you again.' Stella clasped her hands together. 'Lucy – I feel so badly about all of this. I couldn't believe it when I was transferred back here for training. I moved away from here on purpose, almost straight after it happened and I haven't been back since . . . not until now.'

I stared at her. She seemed genuine. I believed her, about the work thing, at least.

'I just hoped I wouldn't bump into Luke for the duration of my training assignment. That sounds ridiculous,

I know. But then he had the accident and I wanted to check on him.' She met my eyes and flinched. 'I couldn't believe it when I bumped into you; it was the last thing I wanted. I honestly didn't think any of this would happen.' She made a gesture with her hand that seemed to encompass more than just our current dilemma.

It was my turn to swallow. Stella didn't look crazy or sound crazy. This scared me.

'Tell me about your friendship with Luke,' I said. I believe I was attempting to put across an assertive, non-aggressive, but don't-mess-with-me vibe.

'Sorry – Lucy, are you okay?'

I looked up, startled. It was Nell. Her eyes were fixed on me and she looked concerned.

'I'm fine,' I reassured her. 'This – this is Stella.'

'Right.' Nell clearly felt uncomfortable but she glanced at Stella and gave her a brief nod.

I wasn't entirely happy with my social responsibilities, but I duly introduced Nell. 'This is Luke's sister.'

'Nell.' Stella took a breath. 'I . . . I . . . hello.'

Nell turned away. 'I just wanted to make sure you were all right. That this is . . . what you want to do.'

I let my head nod rapidly. 'It is.' I felt impatient. As much as I appreciated Nell caring and wanting to check up on me, I needed to get to the bottom of things with Stella.

'If you're sure.' Nell left, reluctantly, and I turned back to Stella.

'You and Luke,' I said again, getting straight back to the point.

Stella took a breath. 'Okay. Well. We met a few years

ago, when I first started working here. I didn't really know anyone and I got friendly with Joe.'

'Joe . . . Luke's ambulance partner?' My heart leapt a little. That baby could be Joe's. It was Joe's. Relief. I had wanted to speak to Joe more after Luke's accident, but he had been so cut up about it, he had taken a leave of absence.

Stella nodded. 'Yes. Joe was nice; we used to chat quite a bit. I got to know Luke through Joe and all three of us would meet in this café for coffee sometimes if our shifts matched.'

My skin crawled a little. I was sitting in one of the places Stella and Luke used to meet. Granted, with Joe, but still. It made me feel uncomfortable. This whole thing was making me feel uncomfortable.

Stella placed one hand on her bump. I felt a flash of something unpleasant and I recognised it. It was white-hot jealousy and it pierced my core like a skewer.

As if she sensed me recoiling, Stella placed her hand back on the table. 'Then Joe met Sarah, who works on the maternity ward. They've been going out ever since. Joe dropped off the radar, spent every spare moment with her.'

'Which left you and Luke.' I was beginning to feel sick, but I held on. Hear her out, I told myself.

'We still met up for coffees and we used to text one another.' She rushed to explain. 'Only about meeting up in here. Or about having a shitty day.'

'And then?' I hardly dared ask the question.

Stella scooped her hair away from her neck, taking an audible breath. 'And then we went out for a drink after work one night. I asked Luke, not the other way round.'

She was at pains to stress this, but I still felt queasy. This is it, I told myself. This is what I don't want to hear.

'I'd had a bad day and, as it turns out, Luke was feeling bad too.' Stella bit her lip and looked me in the eye. 'It was a few weeks after you'd lost the baby you conceived naturally.'

She wrinkled her brow apologetically, as if she had an idea how much this utterance might destroy me. She hadn't. My insides shifted again.

'Luke was in bits, saying he had tried to talk to you about it and about hiding it from the IVF team.' Stella shook her head. 'Luke felt guilty, but I could see your point. It would have put you back to square one – or it could have done.'

I stared her down. I didn't need her to side with me. I wanted the truth. That was what I was here for. I recoiled slightly at the thought that our babies – my final IVF one and Stella's – may have been conceived around the same time if something had actually happened.

'So, you went out for a drink with Luke,' I prompted, sounding braver than I felt.

Stella began to look emotional. She was on the brink of tears.

'We had a few drinks. Luke was crying, he was distraught.'

I felt a sob rising in my throat. I didn't want to think about Luke feeling 'distraught'. I didn't want to think about him not being able to discuss his feelings with me.

I tried to remember, tried to focus on those agonising

weeks after the miscarriage. Had he tried to open up? Had he tried to talk to me and I had been incapable of supporting him?

Whilst I thought, Stella pushed ahead. 'I was drinking too. We were both drunk – really drunk. This must be so horrible for you, I don't even want to—'

'Tell me.' I was blunt. We had come this far.

Stella brushed a tear away. 'We went back to mine, just to get a coffee, I swear. Luke was rambling, talking about you. He said he wanted to feel normal again, for you to feel normal again. He said that together, you two were the absolute best, that you had an amazing relationship. Cool, quirky . . . unique.'

Something inside me was starting to unravel. No, no, no. It was like a beat in my head. I wanted to stop Stella now, to stop the pain I knew was hurtling towards me like an oncoming train. I could almost hear Luke as she was speaking – her words were his words, it was how he spoke.

Stella put her hands to her eyes and pressed her palms against them. 'He was being so sweet about you. He loves you so much; it was obvious. And I – I don't even know why I did it, especially then, but I kissed him.'

Bam. My stomach flipped. She kissed him. She kissed Luke. She kissed my husband.

'He didn't kiss me back,' Stella said urgently. 'Not at first. And when he did . . . God, he was barely coherent but he was saying "No, no." I carried on. I'm not proud of it, I'm not.' She was crying openly now, weeping blindly into her hands. 'Since it happened, I've asked myself a million times why I did it. Was I jealous of you? Of what you two had? Did I just fancy him? He's handsome, funny. But honestly, I actually think the attraction came from knowing he was so in love with you.'

I stared at her, revolted. 'What is that supposed to mean? That's so twisted, I can't even fathom . . .'

'He was . . . the way he talked about you, the way he felt about you.' Stella hung her head. 'Hearing him talk about you made me want him to – to want me, the same way. Even with everything you've been through, your marriage was strong. Oh, it was – it *is*,' she stressed, seeing my head shaking.

I was mute. I had nothing. Nothing to say to this woman who was systematically tearing down the secure, beautiful life I thought I had.

Stella's legs were jiggling beneath the table. I could see the tension in her body and I could sense the movement acutely, even though her knees were barely touching mine. She had nothing on me. My nerve endings were screaming, pulsing angrily inside me. I had something in my throat – bile? Vomit? It tasted acrid, the way bitterness and fury and devastation must taste.

'I kissed him, making it clear I wanted more.' Stella's body shuddered.

'Luke didn't want more. I persuaded him. He wasn't in control of himself and he only did it because he was drunk and unhappy and he missed you – the old you, was the way he put it.'

The old me. I was hyperventilating or something. I felt as though someone was pushing my head under water. I was scrabbling, scraping for a full breath, but my lungs were bursting, they were tight, as if they couldn't take in the air I needed.

Stella leant forward. 'Christ. I've said too much. You don't want to know this stuff. All you need to know is that it was over quickly and it was desperate, on his part. He was mortified afterwards. Devastated. He was ashamed and horrified at what he had done. He wanted to tell you, his phone was in his hand. I told him not to do it, not to kill what you had together.'

'How nice of you,' I choked. 'Thoughtful.' My mind was reeling. Images of the two of them together played over and over in my mind. Her leaning in to kiss him, him resisting, then responding, albeit half-heartedly, miserably.

Stella's hands were shaking. 'Sorry. That sounded awful. I just didn't want what had happened to split you up. It was my fault. I initiated it. Luke was hurting and I should have just been a good friend.'

I struggled to act like a normal person. I needed to breathe in and breathe out. I needed to ask this woman what happened after she slept with my husband and watched him break down with guilt. I needed to ask about the baby she was carrying. I had to ask what she wanted, why she was still here. Did she want Luke? Did she want Luke to be involved with this baby? I wanted to open my mouth and say these things, but I couldn't. I couldn't.

Stella started talking again. 'Luke was humiliated afterwards, guilt-stricken and completely full of self-hatred. He staggered out of the door, saying he was going to spend the following day in bed. I think he had the day off.'

My mind processed this information with some detachment. I worked out that this must have been when I had stayed over at Dee's house after a girls' night in watching *Four Weddings and a Funeral*. I would never watch that film again.

'He avoided me for a few days afterwards.' Stella kept her eyes cast down.

I was glad. I didn't want to look at her, not properly.

'We met up a week or so later and he was devastated about what had happened. He said he was very much responsible and that he wasn't about to absolve himself of any blame.'

'Big of him,' I managed, barely able to speak. 'You both seem to be being terribly noble about this whole thing.' I knew I should feel grateful that Luke wanted to tell me. He wanted to talk to me about what had happened, because we had had a pact. He had broken the pact and he had wanted to own up to it. That was something, wasn't it?

Stella continued, her voice suffused with shame. 'He said he was going to write you a letter first, to get his feelings clear and then he was going to tell you. And then two things happened. I found out I was pregnant. And then you found out you were pregnant with your IVF baby.' She tailed off and rubbed her eyes. 'It was all so fucked up. So I told Luke to forget about that night, to put it all behind him. And I left, immediately. I didn't want your lives screwed up because of me. I wanted you and Luke to have your baby and be happy. As for me . . .' Stella gestured to her stomach. 'I figured I'd work that out later. I'm back here to work, because I need to and because I was transferred here. When I heard about Luke's accident, I was worried – not because I love him, but because I care about him. I didn't think you and I would ever meet. You must believe me. I couldn't believe it when we bumped into each other that day in the ICU. I thought you'd gone because a woman walked out just before you. I didn't know what you looked like – I assumed – and I made a mistake. I've made lots of mistakes recently.'

I know I should feel a modicum of gratitude towards her that she had tried to cut ties, that she had stepped aside to let Luke and I have our future together, but I wasn't sure I had it in me.

'How did you know about my recent pregnancy?' I asked. It was a loose end that needed tying up. The thought that Luke and Stella might have been happily texting one another during that much-longed-for pregnancy was nauseating.

'Luke sent me a text,' Stella explained. 'Just one. He told me about your baby, almost, I think, to underline the fact that what had happened with us was wrong. That you and he were moving forwards towards the life you had always planned. He so desperately wanted you to be happy.'

Proper tears came then. Full on racking sobs and streaming tears and horrible, choking noises. The tears streamed down my cheeks uncontrollably and they kept on coming. Luke and Stella hadn't been in contact, but the idea of that one text threatened to undo me all the same. The unbearable poignancy of that one message.

Luke and I had been about to start a new, wonderful chapter in our lives, but somehow, it had all gone wrong.

'Your – your family think the world of you,' Stella offered, unprompted. 'Your mother-in-law – Patricia, is it? And Luke's brother. They were so worried about you, so caring when I spoke to them at the florists.'

I couldn't stand this any longer. I stood, staring at Stella. I tried to work out how I felt about her, but it was all jumbled up.

I hated her. I believed her. I couldn't bear to look at her – her, or her swollen belly that contained a baby that was part of Luke. After this talk, I couldn't deny it any longer. The baby was Luke's. The one-night stand had happened. It was a truth I had pushed away, had denied, because I loved my husband and because of a pact we made one magical morning in bed, buoyed up by Christmas fuzziness and engagement joy.

'I'd like a paternity test,' I said with as much dignity as I could muster. 'I don't know how they work, but as soon as Luke is out of the coma, we need to take steps to get the ball rolling.'

'Of course,' Stella nodded. 'Whatever you want. But Lucy, I promise you.' She was earnest, sincere. And apologetic. 'There's no doubt that this is Luke's baby. I'm so horribly sorry, but I haven't slept with anyone else since my ex-boyfriend. And there is no way I would put you through this if I wasn't sure.'

I suppressed a scream. I believed her, but I didn't want to. Every part of my body was bracing itself against the truth, fighting it like an infection. My insides felt shredded, raw.

'When's the baby due?' I demanded.

'November. I'm nearly seven months now.'

Seven months? While Luke had been in his coma, I had lost track of time.

Not sure what else to say, I turned and walked out of the café, pausing briefly outside to rest against the wall. I leaned my body into it, my hands sliding over the glossy surface as I searched for something to grip on to, a hand hold to steady myself. I couldn't find one, but the surface felt cool against my cheek. I must have looked like a crazy lady, hugging a wall, but it was all I could do.

Once I felt composed, or as close to composed as I could be in the circumstances, I let go of the wall and took a few steps away from it. My progress was unsteady – I must have looked like a patient recovering from an operation, and I was in the right place for that – but I made it from the café to the lift which took me up to Luke's room. I was drowning, but I needed to be with him – Luke, the man who had always bolstered me up when I needed it the most.

I was angry, angrier than I had ever been. I was seething, my insides tight and coiled. This couldn't be true. Could it? Had Luke done this to me? Could he have done this to me? I felt like kicking and screaming in utter fury.

Ade was chatting to Luke, but as soon as he saw me, he stood up.

'Are you all right? What's happened, Luce?'

His concern was too much. I couldn't handle it.

Ade understood at least enough to know that I needed some time with Luke. He put his hand on my shoulder, briefly halting the shaking. 'I'm so worried about you.'

I shook my head, my eyes brimming with tears.

Ade ran his eyes over me nervously. 'Okay. I'll be outside the door, all right? I'm not leaving you like this. So when you're done, come and see me and I'll stay with him if you need me to or I'll call someone else to look after him and I'll stay with you. Whatever you want, all right?'

I nodded gratefully. Suddenly, it was almost as hard to look at Ade as it was to look at Luke.

I sat down in the chair. I had stopped crying. The talk with Stella had released a stream of emotion I had been holding on to since I had first bumped into her in the ICU all those weeks ago, but now I was oddly back in control. Emotions were nudging at me again, threatening to break over my head like a crashing wave, but I wanted to be strong. I wanted to hold things together.

'Oh, Luke.' I rubbed my eyes. They were stinging like hell. 'How did this happen to us? How did we end up here? We were so in love . . . we had such amazing plans.'

I cradled his hand in mine, moved as ever by the touch, as though we were actually holding hands for real. There was something so romantic, so sensual about holding hands and I missed it. I really missed it. And of course he didn't squeeze mine back, but his hand slotted into mine perfectly, the way it always did.

'I thought we were unbreakable, Luke,' I managed in a cracked voice. 'You and me. I thought we could get through anything.' I felt betrayed, but more than anything, I felt heartbroken.

'Was I wrong?' I mumbled, gripping Luke's hand. 'Was

I wrong about us? I don't want to be. I don't want to be.'

Bending my head, I wept, shocked by the amount of tears I had left in me. That wave, the one that had been threatening to crash over me, did so, engulfing me. I had tried so hard to hold it all together, to be resilient, but I couldn't do it any more. I couldn't. I had cried many tears since I had lost my baby and since Luke had ended up here, but I hadn't let go, not properly. I had held something back, something that allowed me to carry on and get through each day. But that something had disintegrated. I literally felt it go inside me, like an elastic band snapping.

I let out a cry of agony as everything came flooding out of me. My life had been shaken up like a snow globe, and nothing looked – or felt – the same.

I cried until I couldn't cry any more, ending up spent, on Luke's bed. Burnt out like a firework that had been doused with water.

I didn't even notice Ade coming back into the room at the sound of my howling, nor did I notice his arm around my shoulders. It was just me and Luke in the room. Me, Luke and a whole lot of heartache.

CHAPTER THIRTY-ONE

Patricia

'Sorry to keep you waiting,' Mr Farrell said, dumping a stack of folders on his desk. 'Thank you both for coming to see me today.'

'You're welcome,' Patricia said, glancing at Lucy, who sat mutely, with her hands clasped together in her lap. Patricia wondered if this new consultant, Mr Farrell, was making Lucy feel as nervous as her with his formal tone and serious expression. Lucy hadn't said a word since she had arrived ten minutes ago and she looked even more wan than usual. Patricia was worried that something else had happened.

'I should introduce myself. I'm Mr Farrell and I'm a neurological consultant. Luke has been referred to me for assessment and I've been monitoring him for a few days now. I asked you both here today to discuss Luke's progress.'

Lucy didn't respond, so Patricia felt obliged to nod. 'Yes. Do you have . . . news?'

'I'm afraid not.' Mr Farrell's mouth tightened apologetically. 'Which is exactly why I thought we should have a chat. Please forgive me if I'm going over old ground here, but I just want to make sure we're all on the same page.' He put his hands together on the desk, the gesture reminding Patricia of lawyers in films when they were about to impart grave news. 'Comas can last for a few seconds, a few weeks or – as we are beginning to see with Luke – months, sometimes. To be clear about what that means, a coma is defined by a state of depressed consciousness, where a person is unresponsive to the outside world.'

Lucy fidgeted in her seat and Patricia shot her another worried glance. Lucy appeared to be on the brink of tears, but Patricia couldn't work out if that was due to what Mr Farrell was saying, or something else.

'Comas aren't fully understood, but we believe them to be associated with activities in the brainstem.' Mr Farrell paused. 'I think we can say that Luke's coma is of the very deep variety and the length of time this has lasted causes me some concern. I don't want to alarm you; not at all. But I do want to make sure that we all understand what we're dealing with here.'

'And w-what are we dealing with?' Patricia asked breathlessly. Lucy wasn't even looking at Mr Farrell; her eyes were cast down to the floor and her shoulders were slumped. As soon as they left Mr Farrell's office, Patricia was going to have to find out what had happened. Something was very wrong with Lucy.

Mr Farrell met Patricia's eyes unswervingly. 'The problem with prolonged comas is that we have no idea of the severity of brain injury. I would have expected – hoped, is perhaps a better word – that Luke would have progressed further by this point. If the brain trauma is severe and continues for years, we describe a patient as being in a PVS – a Persistent Vegetative State.'

Patricia flinched. What a horrible expression. It was involuntary; she reached out and grabbed Lucy's hand.

Lucy clutched at it.

'I don't want to scare either of you, but I do want you to be aware that sometimes coma patients are very different when they come out of this unresponsive state. It can be difficult for loved ones to reconcile themselves to the person who seems much altered from the person they were before.'

Lucy let out a sob. 'God. I can't bear it . . . I can't bear any of this.'

Patricia squeezed Lucy's hand more tightly.

'Listen, you're doing all the right things,' Mr Farrell assured them. 'I know that you hold Luke's hand and that you talk and read to him. The nurses are full of admiration for the daily round of visitors taking turns to sit with Luke, play him music, show him photographs and provide tactile objects so that he can feel different textures. These are all very important. It may not seem as though you are doing much, but you are. Your family and friends are practically providing a coma stimulation programme of your own. It's wonderful to see.'

Patricia managed a watery smile. It was good to hear that they were doing as much as they could for Luke. She just wished she could do more.

'But there are issues we need to think about.' Mr Farrell

cleared his throat. 'I'm afraid I did want to touch on a rather delicate matter while I have you both in the room together.'

Patricia felt an icy trickle down her spine. She looked at Lucy quickly, noticing the terror in her eyes.

'I apologise for saying this, but I feel that I have a duty to be open and honest. Unfortunately, there is always a possibility that Luke might not come out of this coma. Or rather, that something might cause him to have a further cardiac arrest. It's rare, of course,' Mr Farrell held his hands up as if to defend himself against any accusations, 'but it's a possibility with a prolonged coma.

'I'm simply trying to prepare you for the worst,' Mr Farrell added. 'I can't really formulate a plan at this stage because I don't know what we're dealing with. But I feel that it's imperative that I outline the possibilities, so we can all—'

Lucy let go of Patricia's hand and jumped up suddenly. 'Sorry, this is— I can't bear—' Without warning, she pushed her chair out of the way and ran out of the room.

Patricia stared after her. She swallowed and turned back to Mr Farrell. 'I'm so sorry. Lucy is – we're all rather . . .'

'Of course you are,' he agreed. 'It's totally understandable. It's the worst part of my job talking to relatives about these horrible possibilities. But I prefer the family of coma patients to be armed with all the information they need to cope and to move forward.'

Patricia burst into tears. Mortified, she felt Mr Farrell moving round his desk to offer her more tissues. 'Oh, how silly. This isn't part of your job description.'

'It absolutely is.' His tone was firm but his expression was kindly. 'I'm here for Luke, but I'm also here for you and your family.' He frowned in the general direction of the doorway. 'I'm worried about your daughter-in-law, Mrs Harte. Do you think I need to talk to her again? Acceptance – whatever that acceptance relates to – is very much part of this process.'

'Leave it to me.' Patricia knew that for whatever reason, Lucy wasn't capable of dealing with anything much right now. 'Lucy . . . is dealing with some other . . . some personal issues aside from Luke's coma, but I'll make sure she's okay.'

'Good.' Mr Farrell smiled. 'Are *you* all right, Mrs Harte?'

Patricia stood. 'As all right as I'm going to be,' she said.

As right as I'm going to be when a neurological consultant tells me my son might not make it out of his coma – or that he could well be totally different when he does, Patricia thought, stricken.

Once outside the room, Patricia found Lucy sobbing on one of the chairs. Sitting down next to her, she put her arms around Lucy's shoulders and held her.

'Thank you. I – I honestly don't know what I'd do without you.'

Overcome, Patricia almost burst into tears herself. 'I feel the same,' she managed in a choked voice. It was true. She had come to rely on Lucy and she suspected the feeling was mutual. They shared Luke's shifts on a timetable worked out with military precision, they looked after each other, making sure they had both eaten, were drinking enough water – basic things neither of them worried about before but that seemed to have become so important now.

283

'I just hate not knowing what we're dealing with,' Lucy hiccuped.

'I know.' Patricia handed her a tissue. 'And the only way we're going to find out the extent of Luke's injuries is when he wakes up.'

Wake up soon, Luke, Patricia thought to herself. *Please wake up soon.*

CHAPTER THIRTY-TWO

Lucy and Luke

October, a year earlier

'So what do we tell the IVF team?'

I pulled the sleeves of my jumper over my hands and huddled on the bench. It was too chilly to be sitting out in the garden the way we did in the glorious, stretched-out summer we'd recently enjoyed, but sometimes I just felt suffocated. I needed the fresh air.

This recent miscarriage seemed rather more painful than the others, eclipsing even the worst by grinding a firm heel on a little ray of hope we had silently, privately clung on to for eight weeks. We hadn't told a soul – not our IVF team, not our GP. And certainly not friends and family. It was our delicious – short-lived, as it turned out – secret. We had been so overjoyed, so unbearably happy and astonished at this little miracle we had managed. Two bouts of IVF and then – a natural conception! What were the odds? How many times did this happen to anyone in our situation?

We had held our IVF team at arm's length as they asked when we would like to start our third bout, hopeful we had a fantastic surprise for them, a blissful little story of improbable optimism they could regale other clients with.

'Oh, but don't lose faith! We know a couple who struggled for years – *years* – to have a baby and after two failed attempts at IVF, they conceived their baby naturally. That's right – naturally! Without any help or intervention and the pregnancy went without a hitch and the baby was beautiful and healthy . . . I know, right? A miracle. Miracles *do* happen, after all.'

I had lost the baby at home, in the night, when most babies are lost. Why is that? Does the body unwind and allow it to happen? Does the foetus, lying prone within a fluid, relaxed form, feel able to let go? I supposed that, like most of my 'why' questions, there would be woolly, unsatisfying and mostly unspecific answers.

'Luce.' Luke interrupted my thoughts. His gaze was earnest, his hands clasped together. 'What do we tell the IVF team?'

I shrugged. I wasn't sure what Luke was asking me. We hadn't told them anything about the 'miracle' pregnancy to this point, so why would we tell them anything about it now?

'We should update them. About the – the miscarriage.'

I turned to Luke, feeling a headache looming. 'What for? Why do they need to know about it?'

Luke looked taken-aback. 'Because it's something that's happened to us. Something directly relating to our case.'

'But you wanted to keep it a secret from them when I was pregnant.' I didn't have the strength or the inclination for this conversation. 'You were all for it then.'

'Yes, I was. When everything was fine, I agreed with you about keeping it a secret. It was meant to be a lovely surprise for them as well.' Luke stared out across the garden. 'Christ, that lawn really needs sorting and it hasn't rained for a while. I'll get the lawnmower out. Is it too late to mow the lawn, do you think?'

I couldn't fathom why Luke was so engrossed in the state of our lawn all of a sudden. It was irrelevant, both in the scheme of things and right now. 'Forget the lawn. What's changed? Why do we need to tell the IVF people about it now?'

I sounded whiny, but I wasn't going to beat myself up about it. I had done enough of that over the past twenty-four hours. Everything ached – my head, my womb, my back, my heart. I felt that I was in a perpetual state of agony, tormented either by the existence of the useless body I possessed that didn't seem able to manage a function that other women's managed with ease, or by the thoughts that swirled and smarted in my pounding head.

I watched the sun sinking down behind the trees like melting butter oozing out of sight, taking the last of the warmth with it. The trouble was, order and sense no longer had a place in our world. I had spent the afternoon cleaning the house: scrubbing, scouring and wiping. For what? To wipe the slate clean? To pretend to my brain that what had happened could be rationalised in some way? It couldn't. Even for a neat freak like me, cleansing and soaping hadn't provided me with any clarity or insight.

Luke gripped the edge of the bench. 'I think we should tell them,' he said, his eyes fixed on the patio. 'I think it's important that they know we managed to conceive naturally.'

With an effort, I turned to face him, letting go of my legs. 'Why, pray tell? So they can withdraw our last IVF attempt?'

'We don't know they're going to do that.'

Luke sounded whiny now. No, that was mean.

'I think it's pretty much a given that they will,' I snapped, before I could stop myself. 'I've read up on it and I'm fairly certain they would start investigating us again. That it would take us right back to the start – to where we could conceive, but where the baby couldn't quite hang on in there.' I felt rattled, that helpless feeling I had lived with while doctors searched and questioned and assessed curling up into my throat. 'We'd be back to square one. Is that what you want? Is it?'

'No, it bloody well isn't.' Luke's jaw was clenched. Oddly, it was a look that suited him. 'I'd hate to be back there, but we don't know for sure that we would have to start all over again. It's just – it's unethical, Lucy. Isn't it?'

'Unethical?' I put my head in my hands. 'That means immoral, wrong . . . unscrupulous. We're not those things, Luke; we're not. We're a couple, desperate for a baby; that's all.' *A desperate couple*, I thought to myself. A pair of desperate, despairing people who just want something besides themselves to love.

288

It was our identity. We had a label – a few in fact. 'Infertile.' 'Childless couple.' 'Can't have kids . . . what a shame.' It made me want to throw up.

'I know.' Luke looked destroyed. 'I know that. I just . . . it feels wrong.'

I loved Luke, but I couldn't let him destroy the final chance we had of another IVF attempt. I was almost thirty-seven; I didn't have much time left. 'We say nothing, Luke.' I stood up decisively. 'We go back to the IVF team in a few weeks' time and we begin our final bout as planned.'

Luke stood and took my hand. It reminded me of the night we first met, our hands slotting together with smooth precision, as if each one had found its missing mate.

'Can I ask you something?' His voice sounded weak, as if the strength in him had all but ebbed away.

'Go on.'

'If we aren't ever able to have a baby. If, for some reason, we can't do this. I mean, have a baby that's properly ours.' Luke stopped and took a breath. 'You and me, are we enough? Am . . . I enough?'

I looked at him, really looked at him. I adored every inch of his face, from that heart-stopping cleft to those incredible eyes and their clear, expressive depths. Luke's humour, his sensitivity, his – his everything. Was he enough? Could he – without a baby to make us complete – be enough for me for the rest of our lives? I loved Luke. He was part of me, practically. And I wanted a baby that was part of us; that was what my heart yearned for so deeply. Not just a baby. A baby made by him and me, with plenty of him in there.

'Because the thing is, you're enough for me,' Luke said sadly, letting go of my hand. 'You've always been enough for me.'

'I feel the same,' I protested. 'I feel exactly the same. I was just looking at you . . . properly looking at you, to be sure.'

'I guess that's the difference between us, Luce,' Luke replied rigidly. 'I didn't even have to look at you to be one hundred per cent convinced of that.'

Motionless, I watched him take long strides down to the shed. I headed upstairs, bewildered by what had just happened. I had let Luke down, but I hadn't meant to. I probably hadn't needed to look at him for so long to know the answer, and I shouldn't have taken my time.

I wanted to make things right; to smooth this over. The pressure was getting to both of us and, although I felt guilty about the IVF issue, I knew I was right. I had looked it up on the internet endlessly and I knew that to confess to a natural pregnancy could set us back years.

Wondering why I couldn't hear the lawnmower, I glanced out of the bedroom window. Luke sat on a tree stump at the end of the garden, the lawnmower untouched beside him. His elbows rested on his knees and he was looking ahead at something. Nothing. His shoulders were hunched. Was he crying? I hated it when Luke cried. It made me fall apart. God, he looked so horribly forlorn.

My heart ached. For another lost baby and for a dagger in Luke's heart that I appeared to have casually inserted. I lay on the bed waiting for him, but I must have drifted off because by the time I woke up, in the early hours, Luke's side of the bed was ruffled, but empty. The teal

T-shirt on the chair that served as his wardrobe had been removed. On my bedside table lay one of those late, pale pink tea roses – wilted, but fragrant. It was an apology, a peace offering. It was a romantic gesture that told me all I needed to know.

It told me that I was lucky, that I had so much in my life to be thankful for. It told me that I have the best husband, one who wanted only to make me happy and to give me the baby I longed for. The trouble was, that beautiful, wilted rose also told me that Luke would make a wonderful father.

A tear trickled on to my pillow and it was soon joined by another. One final bout of IVF for a baby of our own. That was all it would take to make everything – to make *us* perfect. I started praying to a God I wasn't even sure I believed in.

CHAPTER THIRTY-THREE

Nell

Once Dee had arrived to take over at Luke's bedside, Nell left the hospital and headed to a nearby bar. She needed a drink, just one, to take the edge off.

Her nerves were fraught and Nell knew she was exhausted. She didn't bother finishing her drink. She suddenly didn't have the stomach for it. She really shouldn't drink, anyway; she was such a lightweight. Cal was always telling her that.

Cal. Nell paused by a shop and held on to the door for a second. She had kept her distance from him since Fay had come into college that day. He had called and sent several texts, but she had resisted answering. Cal had a wife and children – a whole life that went on without her, a life that she wasn't part of. She, Nell, had no right to be with him, however happy he made her. He wasn't hers to take.

Nell let out a shuddering, boozy breath. The problem was that Cal was so easy to love. It was like a proper relationship – not like the relationships she had experienced before, which seemed childish by comparison.

Life was cruel, Nell thought, almost twisting her ankle on the cobblestones of a side street. She felt as though she'd met the man of her dreams, but he wasn't hers.

A boy with a pork pie hat grinned at her as he strolled past with his friends.

Nell watched him and felt a stab of envy. She had been like him and his friends not so long ago. Before she had fallen headlong into a relationship that was doomed from the start, and before Luke's accident, she had been a relatively normal student with aspirations of becoming the next big name in fashion.

Nell ran her fingertips over the scars on her wrists. Okay, maybe she hadn't been completely normal. But life hadn't been complicated for a long time until all of this happened. Nell crossed the road, heading homewards. She had to end it with Cal. She stopped dead in the middle of the road. He was never going to leave Fay or his children. And Nell wasn't sure she could stand the guilt – she could barely live with herself as it was. Jolted by the toot of a car, Nell hurried to the kerb. She checked her phone, something she did periodically in case of news about Luke and yes, she admitted it, just in case Cal messaged her.

Just as she was about to snap her phone shut, a message popped up.

Nell. Come and see me at the flat? Promise this isn't a booty call or whatever they call it these days. Just . . . missing you. I know we need to talk. Please. Cal.

Nell stared at her phone. She shouldn't go. She

wouldn't go. It was over between them. There was Fay. There were children involved. Nell swallowed. But she hadn't actually ended it with Cal – she owed him that much, right? It wasn't right to keep ignoring his texts and calls.

Text him, a voice in her head said. Text him. Don't go and see him, you're too weak. Nell shook herself. Could she resist him? She hesitated. Should she call Ade, ask his advice? No. No. She had to start doing things for herself – she had to start standing on her own two feet without relying on her family to prop her up all the time.

Resolutely, Nell changed direction and headed to Cal's flat. She buzzed and he let her in; dejectedly, she climbed the stairs to the first floor.

'Hey.' Cal opened the door and leaned against the frame. He was wearing the dark, soft jeans she loved him in and a grey marl long-sleeved top. His eyes, dark-green in the dim light, softened at the sight of her.

'Come in. It's cold tonight.'

Nell stepped into the flat, but she held herself back. Despite everything she had been thinking earlier, she wanted nothing more than to run into his arms and feel safe again. When she was with him, nothing seemed insurmountable.

'We need to talk,' Cal said softly, standing close. 'Thanks for coming over. Look, I know it was awkward when Fay turned up the other week.' He rubbed his crooked nose, managing to look sheepishly attractive.

'Awkward?' Nell let out a short laugh. 'Cal, that doesn't even cover it.' She moved away from him, conscious of the scent of him, of his proximity. 'I didn't know where to look, what to do with myself. How did you manage to seem so – so calm and normal?' She eyed him, suddenly consumed with suspicion. 'Have you done this before?'

Cal stared at her coldly. 'No, I bloody well haven't done this before. I haven't slept with anyone else since I've been married. And I certainly haven't told any other woman that I love her before now.'

Nell's throat felt dry. She was in desperate need of a glass of water. She needed to tell Cal it was over and then get the hell away from him, fast. She could feel herself relenting, yielding. Her insides were turning to mush with each word.

'Don't leave me,' Cal whispered in her ear, his hand snaking up into her hair. It felt warm, like home. 'I love you so much. I want you, every inch of you.'

Nell's breath became ragged and she could feel Cal's hard body against hers. *No, no, no. Married, married, married.* Tell him it's over, she told herself. Tell him this is dead and buried.

'You're too special,' Cal said, turning her to face him. 'I wouldn't put myself in this position for anyone else but you.'

Nell avoided his eyes, her mind hazy. This had been a big mistake, a huge one. Her head wasn't clear, she wasn't thinking straight. *Please don't touch me, please don't.*

Cal reached out a hand and cupped her face. 'I know this is difficult, Nell. But you and me – we were meant to be together. We're meant to be.'

'Don't.'

She could feel his warm breath against her cheek. She could smell him. His aftershave, toothpaste, whatever he put on his hair. It was too much. He kissed her. His tongue teased hers and his hand smoothed down her tight-fitting skirt so firmly it was as if he was caressing her actual skin.

'I love you. You're in my head, under my skin.' Cal linked his fingers through hers. 'Stay with me here, tonight.'

End it, end it, end it. He kissed her again with intent and the last of Nell's resolve dissolved.

Waking up some hours later, Nell was full of self-loathing. What was wrong with her? She slid out of the bed and reached for her clothes, glancing over her shoulder at Cal. His blonde hair was tousled on the pillow, his eyelids closed. He looked peaceful, guilt-free. How could he be? She was consumed with horror and self-reproach at what had happened and Cal was sleeping like a baby. Something wasn't right if he didn't feel a shred of guilt when he had a wife and kids at home.

Nell wriggled into her skirt and tied her white shirt around her waist. She just needed her shoes and then she would be out of here.

Maybe she should leave a note to explain, Nell thought. No better than the text she should have sent, but it was preferable to leaving without a word.

'Were you about to leave?' Cal asked.

She turned. He had one elbow propped up on a pillow and he was regarding her with amusement.

'Yes,' she admitted in a low voice.

'Why? You don't have to do that.'

'I do. I need to leave and we can't talk any more. Or see each other.'

Cal sat up, shifting his pillow against the headboard. 'Why not? Nell, what's happened? Is it Luke – you haven't had bad news, have you?'

Nell shook her head. She combed her fingers slowly through her hair. 'It's not about Luke. It's about this . . . about you and me. I – I came here to end it, Cal. I can't believe what I've just done.'

He was confused, his expression boyish. 'We've done it before, Nell.'

'I know that. But before I came over, even when I was here, I reminded myself that you have a wife – a woman you proposed to once.' She felt him wince from across the room. 'You have children, Cal. This isn't right. I know Fay doesn't mind you staying in the city when you have late lectures, but the kids must miss you.' Her tone softened, but she wasn't going to compromise again. 'This is goodbye.'

'Goodbye?' Cal sounded angry but he looked devastated. 'What do you mean?'

'I shouldn't have stayed last night. I was stupid . . . weak.'

'No, you weren't,' Cal immediately got up and walked over to her. 'We love each other. What's so bad about that?'

'You're married,' she threw back. 'How many more times do I have to say it?' She held him at arm's length, knowing that she was powerless if he dared to touch her again. 'Let me ask you something, Cal. Do you and Fay still sleep together?'

'What?'

'Just answer me.' Nell had been wrong about her heart. The fractures were fragmenting and soon enough, there was going to be a resounding crack as it split in two. 'Do you still sleep with your wife?'

'That's just . . . what's the point of the question?' Cal started blustering and Nell's heart didn't just crack, it sank into her heels.

'Say it.'

'All right.' The roll of Cal's shoulders was defensive. 'What of it? We're husband and wife. It's part of the job description.'

'Part of the job description,' Nell repeated flatly. 'God, Cal.' She scooped her bag up and slung it over her shoulder. 'That's what I needed to hear. Goodbye. It's over. I'm sorry; I just can't do this any more.'

They both froze as they heard a key in the lock. Nell turned startled eyes to Cal. He grabbed the sheet from the bed and wrapped it round his waist, his movements edgy.

Fay appeared in the doorway. Her face crumpled for a second. 'So, it's you,' she said to Nell.

Nell put a hand to her mouth. The pain in Fay's eyes was obvious; she looked absolutely devastated.

'Fay.' Cal was shocked to the core, his green eyes widening at the sight of her. 'How on earth—'

'I made a spare key from yours,' Fay said to Cal furiously. 'I knew something was up, you've never used this flat as much as you have in the past few months.'

Cal looked flustered. 'It's – it's . . .'

'Please don't insult me by saying that it's not what I think it is. It's exactly what I think it is.' Fay turned to Nell, her jaw rigid. 'I had a feeling about you when I saw you at college a couple of weeks ago, but I wasn't sure. I should have trusted my gut instinct.'

Nell withered beneath her gaze, but she knew she deserved it. She couldn't bear the agonised expression on Fay's face because it proved how much this woman loved her husband.

'It's over,' Nell said hoarsely. 'I came here to finish it and I—'

'Fell into bed with my husband again?' Fay enquired, her breath coming out jerkily. 'That doesn't make this relationship very "over" in my eyes. And it is a relationship, isn't it? This isn't the first time this has happened, by a long shot.'

Nell shook her head miserably, tears trickling down her hot cheeks. She felt so deeply ashamed. She had wrecked a marriage and she had hurt Fay, who really didn't deserve it. 'I'm so, so sorry, Fay. I – I really am. I knew this was wrong and I tried to stay away, but I was weak. I – I thought I loved him, too. I did love him.'

Angry tears came into Fay's eyes and she brushed them away impatiently. 'The thing is, you probably think this is the first time Cal has done this, don't you?' Fay folded her arms. 'Yes, I'm afraid so. I may not have caught him red-handed like this before, but there have definitely been others. Right, Cal?'

Cal couldn't look Fay or Nell in the eye. He hung his head, resembling a little boy being berated for shoplifting.

'I'm an idiot,' Nell whispered, aghast. 'An absolute idiot.'

'I don't think you're half as stupid as I am,' Fay said, her voice cracking with emotion. 'Cal, I'll speak to you at home. It's about time we laid our cards on the table so we can work out if our marriage is actually worth saving. Right now though, I need to get our kids off to school.' She turned on her heel and left, the picture of dignity.

Nell wrapped her arms around her waist, disappointment and regret flooding through her. Cal was a liar and a sleaze ball and not the man she had imagined him to be. And poor Fay. She had built a life with him, she had had children with him, and for better or worse, she still loved him.

Cal gathered the sheet up around him and shuffled over to Nell. 'Listen, Nell, I—'

'Please don't.'

'But you have to hear me out.'

'No, I don't.' Nell wiped her eyes. 'I've heard enough, thank you. Enough to realise how silly and naive I've been. I've hurt your wife and I've hurt myself and you're probably going to be forgiven and I have no doubt you'll do this again.'

'That's so unfair,' Cal protested.

'Unfair?' Nell let out a derisive laugh, but she was so close to the edge, it sounded almost hysterical. 'Cal. Christ, we've both been fooling ourselves here. You do this all the time and as for me . . .' She paused and pressed her fingertips to her forehead. 'I write letters to my father, Cal. My father, who died ten years ago.'

'What?' Cal looked flabbergasted. 'Why on earth would you do that?'

300

Nell gathered up her handbag. 'I write to him because I have things inside that need to come out, Cal, things to say. About me but also about you, ironically. But for some reason, I haven't been able to say those things to you. For fear of you leaving me, for fear of you thinking I'm crazy. I suppose I was worried about being judged . . . by you, by everyone.' She met Cal's eyes unflinchingly. 'I was in love with you, but everything I wanted to say to you spilled out into letters I wrote to my father. I reckon that means we didn't have such a great connection after all.'

'Nell, I—'

She turned and hurried to the door, hurling herself out of the flat, before running home.

Once she got there, she slammed the door shut and dashed into the downstairs bathroom. She sat on the edge of the bath, feeling desperately alone. She should have stopped seeing Cal as soon as she realised he was married. Too many people had been hurt and it was all her fault. Feeling horribly guilty and alone, Nell put her face in her hands and sobbed.

CHAPTER THIRTY-FOUR

Lucy

I stared at Luke. I didn't look my best and I was wearing massive sunglasses to hide the dark half-moons under my eyes. I realised how silly it seemed – unless Luke was about to sit up and have a proper look at me for the first time in two months, I was fairly certain the tell-tale signs of last night's drinking session would go unnoticed. After my conversation with Stella and after the consultant told me Luke might not make it, I had snapped. Something had had to give. And my critical hangover told me that I had gone way too far.

'How are you this morning, Lucy?' Maggie, by far the nicest of Luke's nurses, asked brightly.

'I'm fine,' I muttered, shuffling towards Luke's bed.

'Is it . . . bright in here?' Maggie asked, gesturing to the window. 'I could close the curtains.'

I turned stiffly – I had slept fitfully last night and my neck was aching and sore – and assessed Maggie's expression. Her face radiated innocence, but I sheepishly removed my sunglasses anyway.

'Ah.' Maggie buzzed a colleague who arrived promptly, perhaps anticipating some dramatic emerge-from-coma moment from Luke. She looked disappointed when Maggie put in a brisk order for tea, water and hot toast, but she got on with it, regardless. 'She'll have it outside,' Maggie briskly informed the nurse when she tried to protest that food and drink weren't allowed in the ICU.

'It's perfectly natural,' Maggie told me, plumping Luke's pillows. 'To need an outlet of some kind when a patient has been in a coma for as long as Luke has been,' she continued kindly. 'I've been worried about you. You didn't turn up for your usual shift.'

'I . . . I didn't want to be here. I just needed a bit of time away. I got drunk, as you've obviously guessed.' I passed a hand across my forehead. 'I'm not proud of myself, but I was in a bit of a state. It's—' I faltered. I didn't want to air my dirty linen in public. 'I guess I'm trying to face up to the fact that Luke might not come round at all.'

Maggie let out an audible sigh. 'It's tough to hear. And it's understandable that you cracked under the pressure.'

It wasn't though. I felt so guilty about leaving Luke. Whatever I was feeling towards him, whatever I was dealing with, I hated being away from him.

The trouble was, I felt different. Ever since Stella's confession, my feelings had been all over the place. I couldn't stop thinking about what had happened . . .

what might have happened. The movie reel of the two of them together played over and over in my head invasively, uninvited and unwanted.

I thanked the other nurse who had brought me a tray of tea and toast and went outside to the waiting area. I managed to hook my finger through the tea cup and, almost scalding myself, I took a gulp. Then another. Feeling the heat of the liquid coursing through my body, I felt a fraction more human. I wasn't sure I could face the toast, but I nibbled a corner of it to test my stomach.

I put down the toast and rubbed my pounding forehead. Aside from what the consultant had said, as much as I loved Luke, I could hardly look at him right now. I didn't know him. We had this image as this couple, this cool couple, according to Dee and Dan, who were to be admired and envied. But we weren't. We had allowed a simple enough issue to drive a wedge between us and turn our relationship sour. I just didn't know what to think any more.

I glanced through the door at Luke again. I wanted to yell at him, to pummel his chest and hurt him. I wanted to take the well of throbbing agony my cracked little heart was carrying and I wanted to dump it on Luke. Not because I wanted him to feel what I was feeling – although that wouldn't be a bad thing – but because I was only just coping with the pain. Luke was drugged up to the eyeballs; he could take it. I wasn't remotely anaesthetised and my body was screaming to be given some respite.

'It's all right,' Maggie provided soothingly. 'It's going to be all right, Lucy.'

I felt her hand on my shoulder and I bit back a flood of tears. More bloody tears.

Maggie put her arm around me, tightly. 'Listen. You have to be strong. We don't know what is going to happen. You just have to keep believing in him, believing that whatever is on the horizon can be dealt with.'

Keep believing in him? Tears dripped off my chin. I didn't know what I believed any more. Had we done this to one another? Had our obsession – my obsession? – for a baby done this to us?

'You can do this,' Maggie told me firmly. 'Of course you can. You're strong and you're brave and you can do this.'

Supported by her stocky, capable arm, I gazed at Luke's beautiful – treacherous? – face.

Strong? Brave? Hardly. I was defenceless, exposed and fragmented. But I knew that, at some point, I was going to have to face up to what was going on in my life. It was just a question of letting myself do it.

CHAPTER THIRTY-FIVE

Patricia

Stirring the melted butter, sugar and honey mixture, Patricia tipped oats and dried fruit into the saucepan, mixing it quickly. She tipped everything into a greased cake tin. She had been at the hospital all day but had popped back for a break. It was late evening and Dan often covered this shift, heading straight to Luke's bedside after he and Dee had put the kids down to bed.

The flapjacks in the oven, Patricia set her timer and strolled to the window. Early evening was still an hour or so away but, under a pearly-grey sky that threatened rain, the garden looked extra-bleak. Leaves were scattered over the lawn and the plants appeared neglected. She hadn't touched the garden since Luke's accident. Bernard would be horrified; that garden had always been his pride and joy. In her mind, Patricia could see him gravely shaking his head as he reminded her that that drama was no excuse for laziness.

He'd be right, of course. She had been in to visit Luke

daily, of course – it was where she wanted to be – but she had neglected her house, the garden and anything else that usually kept her ticking over. As soon as the flapjacks were cooked, Patricia planned to bundle herself up in a warm coat and get the garden ship-shape. It was late, but she wanted to get it done.

The doorbell rang. Ade stood outside wearing a new, warmer-looking coat and a striped, university student-style scarf.

'Can I come in? It's freezing out here.'

Patricia waved him in. 'Of course! Don't you have your key any more?'

'I do actually.' Ade ruefully removed his coat and scarf. 'I just didn't want to use it. It'd feel weird after all this time.'

'Yes. I suppose it would.' Patricia headed to the kitchen and put the kettle on. She wanted to keep the conversation light between them. 'Have you seen Luke today?'

'No, I'm heading over tomorrow morning. I saw Lucy there the other day, talking to Luke's consultant. She looked dreadful.' Ade started taking mugs out of the cupboard. 'That sounds rude, but really, she was a mess.'

'She's been through an awful lot,' Patricia shrugged, watching Ade move confidently around the kitchen. He remembered where the mugs were, where she kept the tea and coffee. She returned to the issue of Lucy. 'I can understand how personal grooming can go out of the window. I don't expect Lucy is too worried about her hair and make-up.'

Ade grabbed a teaspoon. 'I didn't mean that, Mum! I

307

meant that she looked . . . devastated. Broken. Luke's coma . . . it's taking its toll on her. And this stuff with that girl Stella must be the final straw.'

Patricia nodded as she checked her flapjacks. 'Yes. It's been a very stressful time for her.' She leant against the counter. 'Me and Lucy, we talked properly about her miscarriages for the first time. I don't know how much you know about our relationship, but it's been . . . let's called it "strained".'

Patricia searched Ade's face, wondering how much he knew. Before all of this had happened, she would have been none the wiser about his level of inside knowledge about any of their relationship issues, but if he and Luke had been in touch for a while, Ade must be privy to at least some information.

Ade stirred the cups of tea impassively. If he knew anything, he wasn't letting on.

Patricia let it pass. The last thing she wanted to do was create another rift between herself and Ade. There were enough fractures in their relationship – it couldn't survive another. She took a breath.

'Lucy opened up quite a bit about the things she and Luke have been through. I had no idea there had been so many miscarriages. I feel awful for them – for Lucy.' She looked stricken. 'In my heart, I blamed her, you know? I can't deny it. It was just easier and I didn't know what had happened, so I just assumed . . .'

'So tough for them,' Ade agreed. 'He emailed me about it a bit. Not much, but a bit,' he added hurriedly. Clearly, he was as wary as she was of putting his foot in it. Talk about walking on eggshells. 'The garden's looking a bit bedraggled.' Ade stood at the window, thrusting his hands into his pockets.

'I know. I haven't had much time to deal with it since . . .' Patricia tailed off, joining him at the window. 'I'm going to deal with it later on.'

'I'll do it,' Ade offered. His expression became grave. 'Listen, Mum, do you think we need to talk about Luke? About the seriousness of this coma?'

Patricia bit her lip. 'Yes. Yes, I should think we do need to do that. It's just that with everything going on with Lucy and Stella—'

'Yes, I know,' Ade interrupted gently. 'But that's a separate issue. We need to think about Luke. About what's going to happen next.' His eyes clouded over. 'The thing is, we all know the implications of Luke's coma dragging on for so long and we need to deal with the possibilities.'

Patricia sat down, her fingers gripping the edge of the armchair. 'A neurological consultant talked to Lucy and me the other day. It didn't go well. Lucy dashed out and I fell apart.'

Ade sank into a nearby armchair with a sigh. 'I don't think any of us wants to confront the reality that Luke might come round and be . . . damaged.'

'I didn't realise you were so pragmatic,' Patricia said. She flushed. 'I didn't mean that as a criticism.'

'I know. How could you possibly be expected to know anything much about me when I haven't been here for nearly a decade? I haven't been here for so long, I'm surprised you can even remember my name.' Ade frowned. 'That was a joke. A bad one. Sorry.'

The cooker timer went off and Patricia busied herself, removing the flapjacks from the oven and scoring them into squares.

'Flapjacks. My favourite,' Ade said as she brought a plateful over. He met her eyes. 'You remembered.'

'Yes. Your favourite, not Luke's. Sorry about the pie.'

Ade waved a hand. 'Don't be. I think we were all a bit touchy that day. And, just for the record, I regret it. I regret leaving. I wanted to man up and hold the family together, but I couldn't do it. I didn't know how.'

He looked like a vulnerable kid again and Patricia's heart squeezed as she felt a rush of love for him.

'You're here now. And that's all that matters, I promise you.' Patricia sighed. 'I expected too much of you, Ade. You and Luke. I was a mess and it's no excuse because you were kids and I expected you to grow up and hold everything, including me, together. It wasn't fair.'

'Can we put it all behind us?' Ade put his flapjack down. 'We've all made mistakes. I'm too worried about Luke to think about what happened all those years ago.'

'Agreed,' Patricia said shakily. 'And you're right . . . we need to think about Luke.

'I love you, Ade,' she blurted out. There was so much she wanted to say, but perhaps that was all that was needed. That and something else. 'And I'm sorry. So sorry for everything that happened back then.'

'I love you, too, Mum.' Ade pulled her into his arms. 'And I'm sorry, too. I wish I wasn't here because of Luke, but I'm glad I'm back.'

'Me too.' Patricia's voice was muffled. 'Even if it's

310

because of Luke. And Luke will be so overjoyed to see you when he comes round.'

Luke, the protector, the carer, the saviour of the family. And now, the dark horse? Patricia didn't know how to handle all this new information about her son. Did any of them really know Luke as well as they thought they did?

As the pearly-grey sky began to darken to a dull charcoal, Patricia knew that, whatever her son had done, she would give anything for him to be out of danger and back where he belonged. The alternative was too horrific to contemplate.

CHAPTER THIRTY-SIX

Lucy and Luke

May, six months earlier
I struggled through the door with several shopping bags, elbowing it shut behind me. A freakishly organised person does their Christmas shopping throughout the year: primarily in the January sales (non-festive items only); in spring, because it's a great time to shop for pretty gifts; and as autumn hits (my favourite) when the shops begin to stock wintry items in rich jewel tones, and all of those special edition beauty and perfume sets.

This was my spring spree, the biggest of the lot. I had gone a bit mad buying Jo Malone candles Patricia probably wouldn't appreciate, an outrageously lavish make-up set that Dee would most assuredly adore and fun, noisy toys for her kids that would have them worshipping me, and Dee and Dan cursing me for enjoying my 'naughty Auntie Lucy' role too much.

I needed a distraction. We'd completed our final bout of IVF a couple of weeks ago and I was seriously on edge. So was Luke. Glancing into the lounge, I made for the kitchen.

Exhausted, I dumped the bags in the kitchen and switched the kettle on. Shopping usually does for me what running does for Luke, I think. It frees my mind and allows me to assemble my thoughts more clearly. Today, that hadn't happened. The shopping spree had been successful and I had distinct ideas of what I needed to buy and where. What was missing was the resulting clarity I normally gained from ticking things off my list and accomplishing what I had set out to achieve.

Shrugging off my coat, I glanced at my watch, wondering where Luke was. I kept a copy of his work schedule on the fridge, which always amused Luke – he said it was like a kid's term dates. Frowning, I checked it quickly and realised that, unless Luke had been asked to work different hours, he should be home right now.

He'd taken a rare day off the other day, had spent it in bed, he told me. I'd stayed over at Dee's house indulging my Hugh Grant fetish (I was a fan of the floppy-haired phase), but staying in bed wasn't really Luke's thing. The man usually ran like a demon when he had some time away from the hospital.

I leant against the kitchen counter and bit my nails as I waited for the kettle to boil. The atmosphere had been strained between us since the last miscarriage. We were talking, but only about non-contentious things that couldn't possibly filter back to babies. We had become experts at discussing the relative benefits of eating oily fish and about whether or not the washing machine might stop leaking water into the fabric softener tray if we ran a ninety-degree cycle with some soda crystals. Luke seemed oddly withdrawn, as if he had shut down. He always seemed on the verge of saying something and would often start, stutter then tail off. I'd even gone off to see my parents in Scotland a few days ago – anything to give us both some space.

Distractedly, I made myself a cup of tea, but I put too much milk into it and had to start over. This happened to me quite a lot lately – mucking up mundane tasks. It was as if my mind was so tangled up with fertility issues, it couldn't assimilate routine processes that didn't normally require thought.

A miscarriage too far, I intoned to myself. Who would have thought there could be such a thing? Luke and I had gone through so much and each tragedy had brought us closer, the way all those earnest, online discussion boards and support groups said it would. But this was different.

I stared down into my cup of tea. I remembered my wedding day all those years ago, so full of hope and happiness. The dreams we had – the *expectations* for our lives. We had anticipated events unfolding with ease – we had assumed that work, houses and babies would come to us. We were ignorant and naive – as we should be at that age. But beyond that? I was assailed by key moments in my relationship with Luke. Moments that underlined how lucky we were to have found each other, how truly blessed we were to love and respect one another so much, to survive all of our losses and crushing disappointments with such heroic courage and determination. For a strange, lucid moment, I could see my life with absolute clarity, played out like a sequence of flashbacks. It ran through my mind like a movie, the peaks and troughs filling out every inch of my body with extremes of emotion. Happiness spiked in my heart as misery swept through my chest. The love, the loss, the longing, the emptiness.

I heard something and looked up towards the ceiling. There it was again. Was Luke home after all? Forgetting my tea, I went upstairs, checking our bedroom first. It was empty. I glanced into the bathroom then made for the spare room, certain Luke couldn't be in there. It was filled with a heap of his old clothes and boxes of his medical books; it was hardly somewhere I could imagine finding Luke if he happened to be home from a shift.

I paused outside the door. The room was a good size with a lovely view of the back garden and it had always been earmarked for a nursery. Unfortunately, we had never reached a stage where we were comfortable enough to decorate it.

I pushed the door open. I found Luke, sitting on the floor, slumped over his knees. He had been crying – he was still crying, racking great sobs that were making his shoulders heave and his hands shake. There was a piece of paper on the floor between his legs, notepaper that was crumpled and tear-stained.

'Luke. My God.' I crouched down. He was wearing this huge grey cardigan, a cardigan I knew he threw on when he felt like shit. It had huge pockets and a big collar and it was comfort-central. 'What happened?'

He started. His eyes were red-raw, agonised. He had

tears streaming down his face and there was such a look of utter hopelessness about him that I started to feel scared.

'Talk to me,' I pleaded.

He took my hands. 'Lucy,' he mumbled, as he fell into my arms.

I held him and I could feel him shuddering. Was it grief? Despair, maybe? Whatever it was, it was heavy and drenched in sorrow. Luke literally felt leaden against my body, and I curled my fingers into his cardigan, pulling him closer.

I was caught off-guard. Luke didn't do this; Luke didn't break down. He was the strong one and I was the weak one. I regularly had emotional episodes that required tea, sympathy and reassuring words and hugs. Luke didn't. He was the solid, reliable rock.

What was this about? I bent my head to Luke's and breathed him in. It's strange how the person you love becomes so identifiable by their scent. It's so evocative of them, just a hint of it takes you right back to that safe place you know you can go to when you need a recharge.

I hoped Luke felt as secure in my arms as I felt in his. I couldn't imagine anything else that could reduce Luke to this state. I felt horrible, just *horrible*. This was my doing. I had forced him to keep quiet about the baby we had conceived naturally and it was killing him.

'Talk to me,' I whispered again. 'Please.'

'I – I can't,' he mumbled into my shoulder. 'I can't even . . .'

I tried to pull away from him, but he wouldn't let me.

His hands were wrapped around me tightly and his head was tucked into my neck.

'I'm sorry,' I said sadly. 'I'm so, so sorry.'

Luke shook his head; I could feel his hair brushing against my neck. 'Don't,' he choked. 'Don't.'

My brow furrowed. What did that mean? I hadn't meant to put Luke in this position. Or myself, for that matter. What I had asked him to do, what I had made myself do, had been born out of madness. Baby madness. Obsession with a dream that persisted in slipping through my fingers like an eel that couldn't wait to slither back into the sea. I hadn't meant to make Luke feel so tortured and trapped.

'But I *am* sorry, Luke.' I forced him to look at me. He looked terrible. 'I know you feel appalling about lying to the IVF team. Lying by omission . . . whatever. I do too. I just . . . I didn't know what else to do.'

Luke nodded and rubbed his eyes. He gazed at me for a second, seemingly about to say something. Then he shook his head and started crying again.

'What's happened to us, Luce?' he said finally, his voice muffled by my shoulder. 'We're in a place . . . I never thought we . . . *I* could end up.'

I let out a slow breath. I knew what he meant. Life had taken a cruel, unexpected turn for us and we were different people as a result. I would never have imagined that I was the kind of person to lie to authorities, to make my husband stand beside me and deceive the hospital he worked at. Who had I become? I had proved myself to be capable of things I couldn't have contemplated years or even months ago.

'You haven't ended up anywhere,' I told him firmly. 'It's

317

me. I've lost it completely recently. Wanting this baby – wanting to have this baby with you – it's turned me into an irrational, emotional wreck.' I kissed the top of Luke's head. Now I was crying. 'I'm just s-sorry you got caught up in all of this. Please don't beat yourself up about it, Luke. It's me. It's all because of me.'

'It's not about the IVF,' Luke blurted out. 'I think about it now and I know it's not a big deal. I mean, it is, but it's not. Not now. There are . . . worse things. And the thing that makes this all so fucked up is that all I ever wanted to do was make you happy.' He stopped. 'It's not about the IVF thing. I promise. I have no right to make you feel bad about that ever again.'

'Okay.' I didn't know what to say. I didn't know what was happening here.

Luke stared straight ahead of him. 'Lucy. I need to say something to you. I – I don't even know how to put it into words.' He sat forward, hunching over his knees.

'Luke, you're scaring me now.'

Something about his total devastation and his air of hopelessness was making me feel that I had more to worry about than the not telling the IVF team about a natural conception. I could feel panic rising inside me and I squashed it down. No. No. It was all right. Everything was all right.

I took his beautiful, cleft chin in my hand and turned his face to mine. 'Listen. Do you still love me?'

'More than anything in the world.' His voice cracked over the words.

'Do you want this baby? I mean, if this baby happens, do you still want it?'

318

Luke took my hand from his face and squeezed it, rather too tightly. I did my best not to wince because I knew Luke needed to say something serious.

He met my eyes. 'You have no idea how much I want this to work. How much I want this baby with you. You mean everything to me, Stripes. Everything.'

I swallowed. 'Then . . . then you have nothing to say to me.'

Luke bit his lip, his eyes filling up again. 'You don't understand—'

'I do.' I kissed him, hard. 'I do understand. This ends here, Luke, okay? Let's stop crying and pull ourselves together, for this baby.' I got to my feet decisively. I gestured to Luke's medical journals. 'This mess needs clearing up before the baby gets here. We need to think positively; we need to get organised. Right?'

Luke let out a jerky breath.

'Right?'

'I . . .' He hesitated and looked away. There was a long pause before he reluctantly nodded. 'Right. Okay.' He still seemed troubled, but he allowed me to pull him to his feet.

'I love you,' I told him. 'And you love me. That's all that matters. That's what you always tell me, isn't it?'

'Yeah.' Luke stared back at me, ashen-faced. 'Yeah. That's what I always tell you.'

Bending down, he picked up the piece of notepaper that he'd left on the floor. Without looking at it, he placed it in the pocket of his chunky cardigan.

I scooped his hand up and led him out of the spare room. 'So, we're fine,' I stated confidently. 'Everything is going to be fine.'

There was a niggling doubt inside me, this queasy feeling that Luke had something to tell me, something earth-shattering. I ignored it because I wanted to, because I had to. Whatever had happened, Luke still loved me and he wanted our baby. We'd been through some horrible shit, but we were back on track. I told myself this a few more times, hearing it more loudly in my head with each resolute statement.

I glanced at Luke. He still seemed shell-shocked, but I hoped he'd be back to his normal self soon enough. This was our final chance for an IVF baby. It was going to work this time; it had to.

CHAPTER THIRTY-SEVEN

Nell

'So, it really is over then?'

'It really is over,' Nell confirmed, wrapping her duvet around herself. 'You didn't have to rush round, Ade. I wasn't going to do anything silly.'

He put a cup of tea in her hand and his eyes flickered to the scars on her wrist. 'I didn't want to take any chances. When you didn't answer your phone for over an hour, I came straight over. You and your phone are surgically attached; I knew something was up.'

'I appreciate it.'

Nell sipped the tea. She supposed she was going to have to accept that attempting to kill herself in her teens was always going to haunt her. People were always going to think she might try and do it again.

'Hey. You're my only sister.' Ade rubbed her head the way brothers do when they don't mind messing up their kid sister's hair. 'I'm here for you, you know that.' He glanced at his watch. 'At least until midday. Dee has a school thing to attend and it's my turn to sit with Luke after that.'

'I'm due over there later,' Nell said, rubbing her eyes. She glanced at Ade. 'He's not getting better, is he?'

Ade put his tea down. 'I don't know, Nell. I mean, nothing has changed, but we won't know what's going on until he comes out of this. The doctors, the consultants, all they can do is keep monitoring him and hope for the best.'

'Do you think he will?' Nell turned to Ade. 'Come round, I mean? I really want to believe it's going to happen, but I can't help panicking, you know? I can't help worrying that the time I saw him when he came to check on me before his shift was the last time I'm ever going to speak to him.'

'You can't think like that,' Ade said firmly, sitting up. 'We have to try and stay positive.' He put his arm around Nell and gave her a squeeze. 'Let's talk about something else.'

'What, like Cal?' Nell let out a derisive laugh. 'No thanks.'

'Maybe we should. Maybe it would be cathartic for you.'

Nell sighed, unpeeling the duvet. 'I don't think so, Ade. I think I'm done talking about him.'

'What would your therapist say to that?' Ade said, wagging a finger. 'Seriously, if you want to, you can.'

Nell pushed her hair out of her eyes. 'There isn't much to say. He's an idiot, I got it wrong, thinking this relationship I had was something special when it wasn't, and now I've managed to hurt his wife in the process. And she's a really nice lady.' Tears started flowing and Nell grabbed a tissue from a box on the table. 'What about their kids? I don't want them to know . . . I don't want Fay to end things with Cal over this . . . over *me*. It's not worth it – her marriage isn't worth losing just because of a silly fling with me.' Nell snorted into the tissue.

'It wasn't silly to *you*,' Ade said gently. 'You fell in love with him; I know you did.'

Nell nodded mutely. 'I did, but it wasn't real. If it was, I'd have been able to talk to him about the stuff I used to say to Dad in those letters. If it was a proper relationship, he would have been there for me when Luke first had his accident, but he wasn't.' She screwed the tissue up in her hands. 'And that's why I hate myself so much, Ade. Cal was escapism for me when everything went wrong for Luke. Losing myself in Cal gave me a release, something else to think about. But I shouldn't have. I should have been thinking about Luke all along.'

'God, Nell!' Ade turned to face her. 'You're being too hard on yourself. You're only human. You loved a man and he was the wrong one. We've all made mistakes, haven't we? Look at me, the way I left all those years ago. My marriage to Tina. Try not to regret so much. Try to think of yourself as doing what you feel to be right at the time. That's what I'm trying to do.'

The doorbell rang and Nell frowned. 'That had better not be Cal.'

'More likely to be Lisa,' Ade said, wincing slightly. 'I popped into her shop on the way over here and asked if she could come and see you during your lunch hour

– is that okay? I didn't want to leave you on your own. Don't worry; I said you were upset about Luke. You don't need to tell her anything about Cal.'

Nell stood up. 'No, it's fine. It's about time I told her about him. I've put it off because I knew she'd tell me I was playing with fire. She's a good friend. I just didn't want to hear what she might say to me.'

'Not everyone is here to judge you, Nell.' Ade ruffled her hair again.

Nell felt a rush of memories. She could have been twelve again, but she wasn't; she was an adult dealing with scary, grown-up stuff. Ade headed to the door and Nell could hear him opening it and chatting in a low voice to Lisa. The door closed again and Lisa came in.

'Hey.'

'Hey.'

'Want to talk about anything?' Lisa sat down next to her on the sofa.

'Yeah. Yeah, I think I do, actually.'

'About Luke?'

'No. Yes. In a bit. But first, I need to tell you about Cal.'

Lisa looked baffled. 'Who's Cal?'

Nell stood up. 'I'll make you a cuppa. It's not a pretty story and I hope you don't think I'm a complete cow by the end of it.'

'Never,' Lisa said cheerfully. 'You're my mate. I'll love you whatever you've done.'

'Don't be too sure.'

'I'm sure,' Lisa confirmed resolutely. 'Hurry up with that tea. I want to hear how Luke is getting on as well.'

Nell paused in the kitchen doorway. She wasn't alone at all. She had plenty of support and it was about time she stopped feeling sorry for herself. From now on, it was all about Luke.

CHAPTER THIRTY-EIGHT

Patricia

December

'Surely if everything was all right, we'd have been given some sort of sign by now?'

Patricia panicked as she stared at Luke. Noting the ashen tone to his skin that had left him with the merest suggestion of freckles and his stillness, something that even now, Patricia struggled to cope with, she wrung her hands anxiously.

It had been over two months since Luke's accident and yet still he lay inert – unresponsive to the various tests and checks that were periodically carried out. Patricia didn't know what she had expected at the outset, but she certainly hadn't envisaged this.

'A sign?' The nurse frowned. 'We don't really deal with signs here, just science.' She smiled kindly, not wishing to offend.

Patricia jerked her hand in frustration then felt guilty. Maggie was the loveliest of the nurses in charge of caring for Luke. She had always been professional, but she had a caring side that made them all feel supported. 'Sorry. I'm not explaining myself very well, Maggie. I don't mean that sort of sign. I'm not talking about a message from God or anything silly. I meant a flicker of his eyelids – a twitch of his hand. Something like that.'

'Yes, of course. It can be so demoralising for family members when a patient stays in a coma for a period of time.' Maggie put her hand over Patricia's, somehow managing not to seem patronising. 'But you must remember that Luke hasn't deteriorated and that's the most important thing. He's stable and his physical wounds have more or less healed. It's just the coma now.' She leant over and, with the utmost sensitivity, quickly tucked a lock of hair out of Luke's eyes. 'Of course, we're all hopeful that he will pull through in the near future, but you mustn't lose hope. We're all very committed to his care.'

'Thank you. I – I know you're all doing your very best.'

Stealing another glance at Luke and knowing he was in safe hands with Maggie, Patricia left the room. She could barely stand being in it for more than a few minutes at a time right now. It felt static, claustrophobic even, purely because nothing ever happened; nothing ever changed. It felt like a time warp, with Luke trapped in a repetitive, agonising cycle of changing catheters and dressings, with a selection of kind-hearted, capable nurses spinning in and out of the room.

'Sorry . . . are you okay?'

Patricia started. A man wearing a chunky navy sweater and jeans stood over her.

'I apologise for coming over, but you looked so sad, I thought I should check that you were all right.'

'Oh.' Patricia hurriedly rubbed her eyes. She hadn't even noticed anyone else in the room when she sat down. 'Yes, I'm fine, thank you. How kind.'

'Are you Luke's mother? Luke Harte, is it?' The man sat down next to her.

'Yes. How did you know that?'

The man raised an eyebrow, reminiscent of Luke. 'I've heard the nurses talking about him. Handsome, is he?'

Patricia smiled fondly. 'I suppose he is. How funny. I didn't think the nurses had even noticed what he looked like.'

'They're only human.' The man held his hand out. 'I'm Larry, by the way. How long has Luke been in a coma?'

'Over two months. I'm Patricia.'

She shook his hand, feeling formal. She gave Larry a discreet onceover. He was in his mid-fifties, she guessed. Attractive, she supposed, with salt-and-pepper hair and good teeth. Patricia smiled to herself. She had just said 'good teeth'. If that wasn't a sign that she was past it, she didn't know what was. Luke would think that was hilarious if he knew. He always said old people judged one another by their teeth and their footwear.

Patricia put Luke out of her mind for a second. Sometimes, as Ade had pointed out, it felt as though every conversation, every thought travelled back to Luke: to what he would think, what he would say and how he would react.

She eyed Larry surreptitiously. She wasn't in an especially chatty mood, but he seemed nice enough. And what else did she have to do? She'd read Luke all the articles in *Woman's Own* later.

'Sorry . . . I'm being rude,' she said to Larry. 'I haven't even asked who you're visiting.'

'My step-daughter. She's only been here for a few weeks, but she's in a coma too, like Luke.' Larry's eyes filled with tears and he rummaged in his pocket. 'How embarrassing. It's only been a few weeks. I can't imagine how you must feel after two months. I apologise.'

'There's no need.' Realising Larry had probably forgotten a handkerchief, Patricia dug a tissue out of her handbag. 'Here. Please don't be embarrassed. Everyone cries around here. Especially me.' She let out a short laugh. 'You're lucky you've caught me on an angry day, not a distraught one.'

Larry took the tissue gratefully. 'I haven't hit the angry stage yet. I'm having trouble moving past the devastated phase at the moment, to be honest. God, I must look like a right idiot, blubbing like this.'

Patricia tried to get comfortable in the rigid chair then gave up. 'Not at all. What happened to your daughter? Sorry, step-daughter, did you say?'

'Yes. My wife and I divorced last year and then my wife died shortly afterwards. All a bit tragic.' Larry snorted into his already sodden tissue. 'But I've always had a great relationship with Alice. I don't have any other children and Alice has lost both her parents now so we only really have each other. That's why this is – this is so—'

'Gosh. It must be horrible for you. I understand.' Patricia dug out another tissue. It was ironic, really. She was providing a shoulder to cry on for once, rather than being the one in need of support. This man was a stranger, but Patricia couldn't help feeling a connection with him.

'Alice was involved in an accident at work. She's an architect and she was in this building . . . it wasn't safe. Part of the ceiling collapsed on to her and her colleague. The colleague is absolutely fine.' His forehead crumpled. 'I have bad thoughts about that.'

'That's perfectly natural. My son's paramedic partner walked away with barely a scratch, too. I had all sorts of horrible thoughts about why Joe hadn't been hurt instead of Luke. And about why axe murderers are walking around scot free.'

Patricia reached out hesitantly, patting Larry's hand briefly before putting her hand back in her lap. 'I find it so hard to see my son like this. He's – he's so funny and so vital and he's just lying there, helpless, with his personality stripped away and his dignity destroyed.' She felt the onset of tears. Perhaps not such an angry day, after all. 'I just want a sign, you know? A sign that he's going to come out of this coma. And that he'll be able to carry on living his life.'

'Christ, yes. I'm trying not to think about that stuff, but I suppose I'll have to. Alice might need specialist care and all sorts.' Larry held up his tissue. 'Do you need this back?'

'No. No, thanks.'

Patricia smiled. Her chat with Larry had proved how reassuring it was to speak to someone else who could at least partly relate to what she was going through.

'I should get back to Luke,' she said abruptly, getting to her feet.

Larry stood, pushing the tissues into his pocket. A gentleman. Even at their age, men with manners were a dying breed.

'I hope Luke comes out of his coma soon,' Larry said, his eyes crinkling sympathetically.

'And Alice, too,' Patricia nodded, keeping the sob in her throat.

'Thanks for the tissues. And the chat. You've made me feel so much better. Just knowing it's not just me going through this is something.' Larry dragged his hair back with his fingers. 'You're coping so well, considering, Patricia.'

Patricia ducked her head and scuttled back into Luke's room. Once in there, she let out a long breath, meeting Maggie's eyes. She couldn't even accept a compliment without wanting to collapse in a hysterical heap these days. She tugged *Woman's Own* out of her handbag, hoping Larry didn't have to wait as long as they had to hear good news about his step-daughter.

'Right, Luke. What shall we have today?' Patricia flipped the magazine open and selected an article she knew Luke would detest. Anything to jerk him out of this coma. Maybe the next time she saw Larry – if she ever saw him again – they'd both have something more upbeat to talk about.

CHAPTER THIRTY-NINE

Lucy

'So. How have you been?' Dee sat down edgily. 'Your head must be all over the place still.'

I looked away. It was unexpectedly peaceful in Dee's house. Dan was at work and the kids were at school and nursery, but there would normally be a sense of frantic energy in the house. Dee would have the TV or some music turned up loud and she was generally doing house-work at high speed or talking frenetically about something. For once, she was quiet and the only noise in the back-ground was MTV, at a muted level. I was relieved; I couldn't handle the likes of Jeremy Kyle right now, although it had occurred to me that I might feel better if I had given Stella a bit of the Jeremy Kyle treatment – but it wasn't my style to make a show of myself. Looking back, had I been too dignified? I had calmly demanded a DNA test and I had been civilised, but behaving in a noble fashion hadn't given me any satisfaction whatsoever.

I turned to find Dee staring at me. 'I'm sorry, Luce. I

just . . . I'm still struggling to get my head round all of this. This Stella thing. Luke. It's not – I can't – I always thought your relationship was per—' She faltered.

Perfect. The word hung, unspoken, between us. That was what Dee and Dan thought – probably what lots of people thought. That Luke and I were perfect. But we weren't. We were just human. Flawed. Way more flawed than we had realised.

I watched Dee's eyes slide away from mine to the framed wedding photographs that adorned the walls of her house. I wondered if she was looking at the ones that included Luke's smiling, handsome face, searching for clues that might give away what he would do five years or so down the line. Or perhaps she was directing her gaze at Dan, wondering if Luke's behaviour had somehow rubbed off on him; if he, too, was a cheat. I flinched. I hated that word. My feelings for Luke were all over the place, but I still hated that word.

'Do you need a drink? I need a drink.' Dee got up.

I nodded and hoped she didn't put a hot cup of tea in my hand. She did, however. I concluded that it was probably for the best. My head was foggy enough without alcohol and, after my drinking session the other week, I had learnt my lesson. Alcohol couldn't solve what I was going through. It deadened the pain for a while, but nothing could assuage it completely.

I closed my eyes. I felt so betrayed, so confused by everything I had learnt about Luke. I couldn't believe he had done this to me, to us.

Dee's words mirrored my thoughts. 'Why on earth would he do it? I mean, I know you told me everything on the phone, but still . . .' Dee paused, wary of hurting my feelings again. 'I just don't understand why he felt he had to talk to her when he had you.'

I had been holding out on Dee. I had told her all the facts but I hadn't told her my thoughts about why Luke had needed to confide in Stella. I took a breath. 'The thing is, Dee, I think Luke needed to talk about me. About what I made him do.'

Dee said nothing and she waited, with admirable constraint. Patience most certainly wasn't her best virtue, but she pulled it out of the bag when it mattered.

'I . . . made him lie about something. Something pretty big.' I clasped my hands together. 'I – I was pregnant, you see. After the second bout of IVF. It was a huge shock, but we were delighted, obviously.'

Dee blinked several times. 'A natural conception. After all those miscarriages and the IVF. Bloody hell, why didn't you tell me?'

'I couldn't. I didn't want to tell anyone. It felt like a miracle baby, like it was actually going to happen.' My fingers felt numb, as if the nerve endings were deadened. My heart had undergone a similar process; it just hurt more. 'We didn't want to jinx it, so we didn't tell anyone.' I shuddered. Thank God. I could feel something again in my fingers, in my heart. I was regaining sensation of something.

'I lost the baby, of course.' I heard an edge of bitterness to my voice, but I didn't think Dee would hold it against me. I hoped I was allowed a degree of cynicism when it came to the babies I had lost.

Dee raked a hand through her hair, leaving it ruffled.

I felt the urge to reach across and smooth it back down again. It wasn't just an OCD thing; Dee didn't look like herself with her blonde hair in disarray. I craved order and normality. It had been months now since I felt in control of anything.

'I don't know what to say,' Dee offered, tugging the sleeves of her jumper down over her hands. She clearly felt vulnerable. I could relate.

'No,' I agreed. 'But anyway, it wasn't that. I – I made Luke lie about it to the IVF team. More accurately, I made him keep quiet about it. He didn't want to, but he did it. He did it for me, but it tore him up inside. He knew why I wanted him to do it . . . he knew I was worried it would jeopardise our chance to have that final bout of IVF. But he hated lying.' I let out a strangled laugh. 'Ironic, I know, in the circumstances.'

'Why did he go along with it if he didn't agree?'

I felt claustrophobic all of a sudden and with some effort, I stood up. Since my discussion with Stella, I felt weighed down with exhaustion. My mind, too, felt heavy and sluggish.

'That's a good question and I've thought about it. I think Luke wanted to keep the peace. I think he wanted to make me happy, even if it meant compromising himself in the process.'

I had done an awful lot of thinking recently. I had forced myself to re-evaluate my life with Luke, to trace back through the steps of our relationship. There had been moments of utter magic, of breathtaking love, of heart-stopping romance, and of innocent hope. But there had also been moments of intense tragedy and sadness, ones that were perhaps more damaging than I had realised.

'Are you saying he was weak?' Dee's stance was aggressive. 'I suppose you are. That's why he betrayed you, after all. I love Luke, but *God*, this is so awful . . .' Her shoulders dropped, the aggression seeping out of her.

Dee was devastated; I could tell. The realisation that me and Luke weren't perfect was hitting her hard; Dan no doubt felt the same.

'I can't say exactly what he did or why, Dee, because only Luke can do that. But I think he felt terribly guilty about everything. I think he tried to talk to me about it and I think I pushed him away. I think he tried to tell me about Stella too, but I shut him down. I didn't want to hear it – I didn't want to deal with whatever was going on with him.'

'You're imagining that!'

'I'm not.' I shook my head sadly. As fatigue threatened to poleaxe me again, I sank down on to the edge of the sofa. 'He tried to talk to me about the IVF thing a few times, but I kept insisting that it was for the best. I – I knew he felt shit about it, but I wasn't listening. All I could think about was the baby we were meant to have together. I was so bloody desperate for a baby that was part of Luke, I pushed the very person that mattered into a corner.'

Dee shifted to face me. 'What's so wrong with wanting that? Luke knew how much you want a baby . . . I mean, how much you both wanted a baby.'

'It's interesting that you've just said that.' I fingered the tassel on a nearby cushion. 'All of this – it's made

336

me wonder how much Luke wanted a baby. I mean, I know he did. But I think he only wanted it so badly because he knew how much it meant to me.'

Dee let out a small, disagreeing sound. 'No. No, I don't believe that. Luke spoke to Dan about a baby all the time – longingly. I genuinely believe he wanted to have children as much as you did. Wants, I mean.'

I ignored her hurried correction. We had all, at one time or another, been guilty of talking about Luke in the past tense – even me – even after I had blasted Patricia for it. Luke had been away for so long now that we had all developed a habit of speaking about him in the past tense. Not all the time, but there were occasional slips.

'I think Luke wanted us to get back to how amazing our relationship was when . . . when everything was normal between us.'

'Normal?'

'Yes, Dee. Before babies. Before babies became ' I faltered. What I wanted to say was before I became so obsessed with the idea, with the reality of having a child. Even early on, when we had suffered miscarriages, I wasn't obsessed. I had longed for a baby, but it wasn't the only thing going on in my life. That had happened later, much later and it had gathered speed stealthily without me even being aware I had let it consume me.

I let out a breath and sat up, my arms resting limply in my lap.

'Oh, Lucy.' Dee reached out a hand and grabbed mine. 'I can't even imagine how you're feeling.'

I didn't know how I was feeling either. I knew that thousands of women had been in my shoes. The only difference, perhaps, is that most women in my situation were able to question their other half, demand answers. Most women were able to scream and shout and accuse.

I wondered if that was why I was feeling so awful, so utterly destroyed. Not just because of what Luke had done, but because I had no outlet for the fury and the desolation I felt inside. Abruptly, Dee was standing beside me, her arm around my shoulders.

'What I don't understand is why he didn't tell you about it,' Dee murmured. 'None of this sounds like Luke . . . but not admitting to it. That's insane.'

'I think he tried. I remember coming home one day back in April, I think it was. I'd been out shopping. Luke was up in the spare room, crying. And I mean sobbing. Having some sort of breakdown. Jesus, he was in such a state, Dee.' I put a shaky hand to my mouth. 'He kept trying to tell me something and I stopped him. I think – I'm sure he was trying to tell me about Stella.'

My throat loosened. I swallowed, then spoke again. 'I thought he was still upset about lying to the IVF team at first, but he said it wasn't that. Luke was talking like a mad man, saying he hated himself. He couldn't stop crying. I've never seen him like that before, not in all the time we've been together.'

'Guilt?'

'For sure. But he wanted to tell me. He wanted to tell me and I cut him off.' I pressed my hands to my eyeballs, which ached unbearably for some reason. 'I think I knew, Dee. Not that he'd slept with someone else, but I knew something was badly, badly wrong with him and I wouldn't let him speak. I brushed him off and told myself – and him – that everything was all right. I had this feeling and I squashed it down. I didn't want to hear what Luke had to say. I couldn't cope, I didn't want to know. I was in such a deep state of denial I couldn't face anything other than getting through each day. All I could deal with was the final bout of IVF. That was all that mattered to me. Even . . . even more than whatever was bothering Luke. Something was very wrong with him, with us. And I knew it; I knew it.'

My voice petered out. It was the first time I had admitted the truth. 'I knew it and I couldn't face it. I didn't have the strength. So I buried it. I buried it deep inside myself in a place I would never look.'

I felt a rush of shock. As the saying went, the truth hurt. The truth had been twisted up inside me like a coil of barbed wire for a long time, but I had refused to give it a voice, even in my head. I felt pain fracturing my heart, but still, tears would not come. Not so for Dee – she was openly blubbering.

'God. *God*. This is so upsetting. I can't believe it.' She wiped her eyes on the sleeve of her jumper. 'I can't believe this, Luce. You and Luke – you were always the most romantic couple out of all of us. You were the couple who were always so obviously in love and destined to last.'

I was only just beginning to realise the full extent of how Dee, and probably Dan, saw Luke and I. I felt heartened and devastated all at once. I wondered how Dan would take the news. Dee was certain Dan knew nothing about Luke's one-night stand and I believed her.

Dan and Dee were so tight there was no way Dan would have been able to keep such a huge secret to himself. I guessed this was why Luke hadn't said anything; why he had felt compelled to lock that skeleton, not just in the cupboard, but inside himself. It had been hidden almost as well as I'd hidden the acute sense that something was wrong, all those months ago when I'd found Luke having his breakdown.

What else had Luke been hiding? Had any one of us really known him, even me? I remembered Stella saying something about Luke writing me a letter. Had he ever done that? I hadn't found a letter, but I hadn't exactly been looking for one either.

Dee gulped and grabbed a tissue. She kept boxes in each room of her house now. It wasn't only children that required a constant flow of tissues.

'Stella's baby,' she said, in between gulps. 'It's definitely Luke's?'

The words were like a body blow – children, my Achilles' heel. Luke's baby. Not *our* baby. Luke's baby . . . with Stella. It was all so disconnected and strange.

'I've asked for a DNA test, but obviously that can't happen whilst Luke is still in his coma. He needs to give permission, sign things.'

I sniffed but I didn't need a tissue yet. I missed the release – it felt as though my sobs were caught inside me like that frozen waterfall I used to carry around in my throat when I yearned for a baby.

'Lucy, I'm so ashamed.' Dee was in bits, sobbing into shreds of sodden tissue. 'Why didn't we realise Luke was feeling so awful? None of us knew – if we had, we could have helped him, we could have stopped this. Me and Dan – we're responsible too. We're his friends.'

'I'm his *wife*,' I reminded her. 'I'm the one who let him down. I was so focused on having a baby, I didn't even consider Luke's feelings most of the time. I mean, it's not okay what he did. I hate what he did. But – but I let him down.'

'He let *you* down,' Dee fired back. 'He didn't need to do this to you.'

I balled up the tissue. 'I know. I – I don't know if I can ever forgive him.'

'I don't blame you. I don't think I can either.' Dee balled up her own tissue. 'If we were in Luke's room now, I'd slap him. Really hard. Coma or no coma.'

I welcomed Dee's devout loyalty and, miserably, I picked at my nails. 'I've tried to speak to him about it, as weird as that sounds. I've been in a few times, but I just keep getting upset and crying. I mean, I'm angry, really angry, but when I go in and see him, I just get overwhelmed and break down.'

I broke down then. Dee gathered me up in a hug and I let her. I let her put her arms around me and hold me close and it felt good.

'I'm so sorry, Lucy. So, so sorry,' Dee kept saying over and over again.

At first I said nothing. I just let her hold me, relaxing into her embrace, the way I had done with Patricia. Maybe I should let people do this to me more often, I thought to myself. Maybe I shouldn't always think I'm strong enough to cope without help.

God knows I've leant on Luke enough over the years,

but since his accident I have kept myself distant from everyone else in my life. I have no idea why. Self-preservation? A misguided coping mechanism? Naivety? Any of those things might explain my behaviour, but I hadn't really had time to work out what my motivations were.

I needed to say something and I held Dee to my chest, tightly. I wanted to look her in the eye and say all that I had to say, but I didn't know if I was quite brave enough for that. I'm not a coward, but it had only just dawned on me how selfish I'd been, and that's hard to face up to sometimes.

'There's still the DNA test,' Dee started to say. 'Nothing is conclusive until we see that DNA test. So we wait for Luke to come out of the coma then he can give his consent . . . if he wants to.'

I loved her at that point, more than I ever had. She was right, of course. There was still the DNA test. The trouble was, even without it, all the pieces of the jigsaw fit together. All the Stella pieces and the Luke pieces and the pieces with my face on them – they fit together perfectly. I was fairly sure I had the whole picture. And it wasn't a pretty one. But I loved Dee for pointing out the one piece of evidence that prevented the picture from being conclusive and heartbreakingly final.

'Dee. I – I need to apologise.'

'Apologise?' She started to pull away.

I couldn't let her. 'Yes. For not being there for you when you had that miscarriage. For thinking you've had it easy with your three kids.' She tried to interrupt me, but I had to say my piece. It was time. 'For being jealous of you. Envious, maybe, not jealous,' I amended. 'You're my best friend and I've resented you for a long time – no, I have, Dee.'

I managed to move away and I looked her in the eye as unflinchingly as I could. 'I love you, but I wanted your life and I couldn't understand why you had so many good things and I didn't. I didn't even realise how lucky I was to have Luke until his accident. Maybe not even until now.' I started to cry.

'It doesn't matter,' Dee stated, shaking her head. 'It doesn't matter. Listen, Luce . . . I've been envious of you at times. No, really,' she added, seeing me frowning. 'You and Luke . . . This is going to sound strange now with – with everything else that might be going on, but you have something special. Whatever happens now, whatever *has* happened, you and Luke are the real deal. I mean that.'

I was sobbing now. *The real deal?*

'You love each other – properly love each other.' Dee was crying now, too. 'Romantically, as friends . . . on every deep level there is. It's . . . It's something I've always been a tiny bit jealous of. Me and Dan joke and have a laugh and we have a good time in bed. But you two have . . . it's different.'

'Oh God.' I wiped my face. 'Do you think so? I suppose I've always thought so, but everything is so screwed up right now.'

'Believe it,' Dee insisted. 'Whatever happens, that's how you feel about Luke and that's how he feels about you – it has always been true love. And I feel terrible for not even knowing what you and Luke were going through, not really. What sort of friend does that make me?'

'My fault again,' I confessed ruefully, sobs racking through my body. 'I didn't tell you what was going on most of the time. Only the big stuff. Me and Luke thought we could handle everything together. We thought we were fucking invincible. Jesus, I can't stop crying now.'

'Neither can I,' Dee said, laughing. 'I'm laughing and crying at the same time. What happens now, does a rainbow come out?' Her expression became sober again. 'Lucy. I hate to even bring this up, but have you . . . have you thought about the possibility of Luke not . . . not . . .'

'Not making it?' I nodded slowly, my heart contracting at the thought. 'Luke's consultant – a neurological one – spoke to Patricia and me about it a few weeks ago. I'm afraid I left – I couldn't take it. It was just after that talk with Stella and I literally couldn't stand hearing it.'

'I can understand that,' Dee nodded, her face pinched and white. 'It's just so horrible . . . Oh God. Tears again . . .'

My mobile phone rang, the shrill noise breaking the moment. Dee rubbed my back then drew back. 'You'd better get that,' she said, wiping her eyes. 'It might be Patricia in a flap or something. But before you do . . . I really am sorry about everything.'

'Don't be. I'm the silly cow here.'

Leaning forward, I kissed her cheek. I had underestimated Dee; she truly was a good friend and she always had been. I checked my phone. I didn't recognise the number but as I listened to the voicemail, cold fingers of shock curled around my body.

'What's happened?' Dee's hand fluttered to her mouth. 'Was that about Luke?'

I mechanically removed the phone from my ear. 'Yes.'

'What's happened?' I shook my head dumbly.

'Lucy, talk to me! What's happened?'

Dee sounded panicked. Tears started spurting out of her eyes again, as if she'd been given those eye drops they used on TV. I wished my emotions were as immediate. Since this had all started, I seemed to react with a strange, stilted, frame-delay, even at the most shocking of revelations.

I spoke, my throat drying up as I said the words we'd all been longing to hear. 'It's . . . Luke's just come out of his coma.'

'What? *What?*'

'Yes.'

'I'm hyperventilating. God. What – is he – what sort of . . . ?'

'I have no idea. They didn't say. They just said that Luke was awake and that I need to get to the hospital as soon as possible.'

My voice sounded flat. I had no idea why, because inside, I felt hyped up and hectic. It was the same sensation I'd felt when I found Luke in his hospital bed. I was aware of the pumping of my blood and the deafening thud of my heart.

'Oh my God.' Dee sat down abruptly.

Luke was awake. Luke was back. After more than two months of saying absolutely nothing whilst a vast, spiky bombshell had exploded all around him, he was back in the land of the living. In God knows what state. I still loved him, I thought to myself. I missed him like crazy. I was furious with him, too. Furious and hurt. But he was awake again. He was back. Excitement mounted.

'I need to run,' I said suddenly. 'I have to get to the hospital.'

'Go, go,' urged Dee. 'I'll call everyone immediately. Just . . . go to him.' She grabbed my arm. 'Are you okay?'

'I don't know. I don't know how I feel.'

Inside, I knew I was petrified. I couldn't wait to see Luke, but I didn't know how he was going to be. I didn't know what to say. I wanted him to be his normal self, I wanted him to be the Luke I knew and loved. But with everything else that had happened . . .

I took a breath and steeled myself. All that mattered for now was that he was back. And I had to be with him. Dialling a cab, I left Dee and hurried to Luke's bedside.

CHAPTER FORTY

Nell

Nell barely recognised the cemetery. She hadn't been here for years, even though it was where her father was buried. She had wanted to come many times before, but something had stopped her. It seemed maudlin to come and stare at a slab of stone that didn't remotely conjure up the amazing, kindly man her father had been.

Nell shivered. A dense mist hung in the air, casting an eerie glow over the headstones. Even the church looked spooky, the windows lit up by the glow of little tea lights that people had lit for lost relatives. Walking towards the centre, she happened upon his gravestone.

Bernard Harte. Loving husband, wonderful father, missed by all, it said. Far from making her feel sad, Nell felt a rush of love and affection. It made her question why she hadn't visited his gravestone before. Had she been in denial all these years? No. She knew her father was dead. But it had hit her so hard perhaps she hadn't been able to properly accept it. Nell felt guilty. Her lovely dad. She hadn't put flowers on his grave once.

She knelt and tidied the grave up a bit, tweaking leaves out of the way and scraping off some moss with her gloved hand. It had been Ade's idea to come here because he thought it might help her. He said he wanted her to realise that, aside from talking to himself or Luke, even chatting to a gravestone could bring some sort of respite.

'Beats writing letters, I reckon,' he had told her before she headed out.

Getting to her feet, Nell stared at the gravestone. It looked tidier, but it still made her feel immeasurably sad. Something caught her eye in the distance. A blonde head. Nell sucked her breath in. Was that Stella at the far end of the grave-yard? She had seen her at the hospital before. She was sure it was her. As the blonde turned and her pregnant stomach came into view, Nell knew for certain.

Taking one last look at her father's gravestone, Nell strolled over. For some reason, she felt that it was import-ant to speak to Stella. After all, they shared at least one thing in common, even if Nell was still struggling to get her head around the idea of Luke cheating on Lucy.

'Oh, Nell!' Stella seemed disconcerted to see her. 'I was just . . . my father is buried here.' She gestured to a gravestone, a more recent-looking one than Bernard's.

'Mine too. It's the first time I've properly visited mine, actually.' Nell wasn't sure why she was admitting this to Stella.

Stella threw her a sympathetic glance. 'Well, it's not a fun place to come to, is it? And it's hard – seeing a grave-stone instead of the person you miss so dearly.'

'Yeah. Think I should have made the effort before now though.' Nell rubbed her hands together, feeling a sudden chill. 'But we all make mistakes.'

'Yes.' Stella looked away.

'That wasn't a dig at you, by the way. I was actually referring to myself. I've made loads of mistakes recently.'

'I bet I can out-mistake you,' Stella replied, her expression wry.

'I wouldn't be too sure. Shall we walk – have you finished here?'

Stella nodded and they strolled in silence.

'We're not so different, you and me,' Nell told Stella.

'Really? I find that pretty hard to believe.'

Nell thrust her hands into her pockets. 'I've been having an affair with a married man. His wife walked in on us . . . not quite in flagrante, but almost.'

'Right.' Stella looked surprised, but non-judgemental.

'I've been such an idiot.'

'Me too. The shame is pretty much overwhelming.'

Nell stopped walking and turned to Stella. 'My brother Ade – says I'm a good person who made a bad choice. As I say, perhaps you and I are more alike than you think.'

'That's a nice way to put it,' Stella mumbled. She placed her hands around her bump and winced.

'Are you all right?' Nell put a hand on her arm. 'Should we get some help?'

'No need,' Stella grimaced. 'They're practice labour pains. I've been having them for the past week or so. Pretty tough, but I reckon I've got a good few weeks of these ahead of me.' She gritted her teeth. 'I'd better go. I need to head into town and grab a few bits. It's time I started to prepare for the baby arriving.'

'If you're sure you're okay . . . ?'

'I'm fine, thank you.' Stella managed a smile. 'And thank you. For being so nice. I – I don't think I've felt like a good person for a very long time. Which I know I deserve, but still. Thank you.'

Nell helped Stella walk to her car and made sure she was safely inside. Nell still wasn't sure Stella was okay, that she should be driving, especially alone, but Stella was insistent. She watched her drive off, feeling strange. Stella was carrying Luke's baby. Her niece or nephew. But Nell just couldn't get her head around the idea. It wasn't how it was supposed to be. None of this should have happened.

Nell's phone rang and she breathlessly dived for it, the way she did whenever it rang at the moment.

'Dee?'

'Nell, it's Luke,' Dee said urgently. 'He's – he's out of his coma.'

Nell gaped. 'What? You're . . . I'm coming. I'm coming right now.' She dashed to her car.

CHAPTER FORTY-ONE

Lucy

I stood next to Luke's bed. I wished I'd been here when he first woke up. But it had been Ade. How strange. Ade had been absent for all this time, yet he was afforded the privilege of being the one who saw Luke open his eyes.

I swallowed. I shouldn't feel that way. At least Luke had someone with him at that crucial moment. And, if anything, Ade seemed to be in a state of shock. We were all in a state of shock. It had been such a long wait and now, with what felt like unexpected abruptness, Luke was out of his coma.

'This is all very normal,' Mr Farrell advised, checking some notes, whilst keeping his eyes on Luke. 'People assume that patients emerge from a coma, open their eyes and start chatting away, like they do in films. They don't, I'm afraid, not for the most part. The speech comes later, in most cases. This phase is what we call PTA.'

'Er . . . PTA?'

'Yes. Nothing to do with parents or schools.' Mr Farrell flashed a brief, humourless smile as if he'd made the joke a hundred times before. 'It actually means Post Traumatic Amnesia, and how long it lasts is a good indicator of brain activity. We start by asking a number of questions to establish awareness of time, place and person.'

'Right.'

I started to get that sinking heart feeling, as if my heart was coldly sliding down inside. It was a sensation I had become accustomed to over the past few months, when positive news hadn't been forthcoming. The point was, how on earth was Luke going to answer any of these questions? He hadn't said a single word yet.

I stared at him. He was awake, but not in the way I had expected. His eyes had opened and closed a few times since I'd been in the room, but I couldn't tell if he recognised me or if he knew what was going on, because that was literally all that had happened. Well, there had been a foot twitch and he had raised his hand, the way people did at the dentists when the drill got too invasive, but nothing more.

What Mr Farrell had said about the way people expected coma patients to react could easily be applied to me. I was obviously one of those dumb people who had assumed that Luke had snapped out of coma by sitting up in bed and demanding lunch. How naive of me. Perhaps I should have read some of the documentation the medical team had given me when Luke had first lapsed into his coma. I had stoutly refused, not imagining for one second that he would remain in it for so long.

Or that so much would happen whilst he lay in this hospital bed, I thought, as Mr Farrell continued.

'Patients can behave strangely during this time, but please don't take too much notice. Patients have been known to be restless and agitated. They sometimes swear and shout. To give you a more positive overview, Luke's eyes are open. He has moved and he has responded to pain. He just hasn't spoken yet.'

'And it makes a difference how long it takes Luke to do these things?'

'Yes, it does. It can determine the level of brain activity. As I mentioned before, we begin with basic questions like "What's your name?" and "What day of the week is it?", and then we move on to memories of the accident and questions of a similar nature.'

I felt a flicker of panic. Surely Luke wouldn't know what day of the week it was after all this time? How on earth would a coma patient be able to distinguish a Saturday from a Wednesday, especially when they had been away from reality for so many weeks?

Patricia arrived.

'Luke!' She burst into the room like a tornado, skidding almost comically to a halt at the end of Luke's bed. I immediately hugged her and we remained in an embrace for a while. This was an emotional moment for both of us.

'What's happening?' Patricia said, pulling away, but gripping my hand tightly. Her voice was shrill, excited. I envied her the ease of her thoughts, the clarity with

353

which she could greet this new development. Whatever he had or hadn't done, Patricia only needed to think about how best to support him. My mind was rather more muddled.

'Nothing too much yet,' Mr Farrell soothed, clearly used to dealing with hysterical relatives. 'This is all very normal. I know how thrilling it can be to receive this news, especially after . . .' he checked Luke's notes, 'after two months. But we all need to be patient and give Luke some time. The next twelve hours are going to be critical, but let's all stay positive.'

I narrowed my eyes at him. What the hell did he think we were going to try and do? I squeezed Patricia's hand before letting it go and edging round the bed to get closer to Luke's head. I don't know why; I hardly expected him to get a whiff of my perfume and do the sitting up in bed thing. I fixed my eyes on his freckles, just for something to focus on. Like him, they seemed faded, but I guess that's what happened after such a long period of time without sunshine and fresh air.

I gingerly took Luke's hand. Touching him felt better than it had done before he had come out of his state of oblivion, even if the response was minimal. At least I could visualise him feeling my touch and maybe knowing it was me. Biting my lip, I resisted the urge to tweak his mussed-up hair into place. He might think I was one of the nurses if I did that.

Luke, *Luke*. What do I feel about you right now? Am I angry? Am I sad? Overjoyed? Overwhelmed? I'm overwhelmed. I just don't know with what. I can't fathom which emotion to apply to the confusion I'm feeling inside. Thinking back to Luke's accident, I tried to remember the person I was then, before everything else exploded. But I couldn't; I couldn't connect to the person I was before Stella arrived. I didn't recognise myself.

Luke's eyes opened again suddenly and I jumped.

Patricia let out a tearful gasp. But, just as suddenly, Luke's eyes closed again. And that was it. Theatrical in one sense, anti-climactic in another. Perhaps Luke couldn't cope with all the female energy around him, I thought, desperate to play down the moment. Perhaps he was trying to delay coming back into the world and facing reality – I reckon I would in his shoes.

We heard the sound of feet pounding down the corridor. Ade and Nell, breathless and eager, bounded in like puppies.

'What's – why isn't he awake?' Nell looked confused. 'Has something gone wrong?'

Before Mr Farrell could open his mouth we all heard a phone buzzing and I exclaimed apologetically, realising I hadn't turned mine off for once. I glanced at it. It was a text from Joe, Luke's ambulance partner. That wasn't so strange; he had sent me texts on and off since Luke's accident to see how I was. What was odd was the fact that Joe's text started with Stella's name.

My heart started doing weird stuff again; not the sinking thing, the jackhammer thing. Why would Joe be sending me texts about Stella?

'Lucy?' Ade came over, concerned.

I braved it and read the text. 'It's from Joe. He was in town and he just saw Stella going into labour.'

Nell gasped. 'That's – isn't that really early?'

355

I nodded, feeling a shiver of horror. 'There's an ambulance on its way and Joe's with her. He wanted to let me know because the baby is in danger. This is too soon.'

Patricia tore her eyes away from Luke momentarily. 'The baby is in danger?'

'She's bleeding. This isn't her due date, not remotely.' I shook my head, feeling numb. 'What's going on here? I can't even cope with what's happening.'

I was feeling bad for Stella, although God only knew why.

'Someone needs to be with her,' I muttered. 'I mean, she's on her own . . .'

Ade put his hand on my shoulder and squeezed it.

'Oh, don't worry; I'm not *that* nice, Ade,' I added wryly. My voice started to wobble and I swallowed, hard. 'The thing is, this might be – it's probably – Luke's . . .' I stopped. I couldn't say it.

'I'll do it.' Patricia turned away from Luke and smoothed her red jumper down.

'What? Mum, you can't!' Nell looked aghast.

'I can and I will.' Patricia met my eyes. 'She's alone . . . she doesn't have her mum here, right? Or many friends? I can do it.'

For you, was the unspoken inference. I will do it for you.

Bloody hell. I couldn't believe it. The woman was a saint. She might have been desperate for a grandchild at one time, but all I could see in her eyes was . . . duty. Patricia wasn't doing this for Stella – she wasn't even doing it for Luke. She was doing it for me because she knew I wasn't up to it, that I needed to be with Luke.

I was about to lose it, big time, but I couldn't afford to collapse in a heat of snot and gratitude, not right now. I struggled to say something, but my throat was oddly dry.

'If anything happens with Luke, I'll run down and get you straight away,' Ade promised.

'Thank you.' Patricia took one last glance at Luke and I knew she was mentally willing him to get it together in her absence. 'Listen, I'm going to do my duty, but no more. I feel that I have no choice, especially if . . .'

She touched my hand as she walked past clutching her handbag primly, a mannerism I had come to find rather endearing. God, it was all so weird. Everything I had thought about my mother-in-law before Luke's accident had pretty much been turned on its head.

'This isn't how I thought it would be,' Nell confessed, coming up beside me and slipping her arm through mine.

'No,' I agreed wearily.

'What do we do now?' she asked. She looked vulnerable, lost. I wondered if she had looked this way when Bernard had died.

'We wait, I guess. We wait and we hope, and we do all the other stuff we've been doing since Luke got here.'

Nell put her head on my shoulder. 'I finished with Cal,' she offered in a small voice. 'But his wife came in and caught us so it was all just horrible. And he's done this tons of times, not just with me.'

I kissed the top of her head. 'I'm sorry. That sounds really grim.'

'Don't be sorry,' Nell said.

Her teeth were gritted and I sensed there was more to Nell's predicament. Wearily, I dismissed the thought. I had enough to deal with. If Nell needed help with something, she was going to have to ask.

'What I mean is,' Nell continued, 'is that I made those choices. As Ade says, we're all in charge of our own destiny. We just sometimes don't realise we're hurting people when we take a particular path.'

I stared at Luke. I had hurt him with my blindly obsessive baby plans and he had hurt me with Stella. Not in a tit-for-tat way, but in a desperate, I-just-want-everything-to-be-all-right kind of a way.

I gulped. Everything was about to change. And maybe it had to. None of us could go back now. Now, it was all about moving forward.

'I have to tell you that, apart from the lack of speech, I'm very pleased with Luke's progress,' Mr Farrell informed me in an aside. 'His obs are good and his heartbeat is strong. His lungs seem fine, too – he's breathing perfectly well without the machinery.'

I turned to him eagerly. 'Does that mean that you're hopeful he's going to be back to normal?'

Mr Farrell smiled kindly. 'I wish I could give you a more definite prognosis, but I'm afraid it's all about Luke now. I have learnt that the human body responds in its own time and there isn't anything we can do to hurry it.' He patted my arm. 'I know this is difficult. You've been waiting so long for this moment and you must be feeling very impatient and anxious now. But everything looks positive right now; that's all I can say.'

I nodded, biting my lip. I felt scared, but hopeful. Luke was properly back in the room, and surely it was only a matter of hours before he was going to say something?

CHAPTER FORTY-TWO

Patricia

'All you need to do is breathe. Or rather pant . . . one, two, three, one, two, three . . .'

Patricia had no idea what she was saying, but that might be because her brain was all over the place – a combination of exhaustion and extremes of emotion. Patricia had torn herself in half somehow, allowing one half to worry about Luke and what was happening with his recovery and the other half to support Stella. In some shape or form.

Patricia wiped a hand across her forehead, then hurriedly stroked a damp flannel over Stella's forehead, lest anyone presume her to be self-indulgent. Stella had only been in labour for two hours. It felt like days to Patricia because she was away from Luke, but she imagined that Stella must be feeling a whole lot worse.

Patricia didn't blame Stella for being scared; giving birth was a frightening experience, especially the first time around – especially alone. Especially when the baby was trying to arrive early, Patricia thought worriedly.

Patricia's own experiences of giving birth three times were so long ago, she couldn't even recall the details. Patricia remembered factually that it had hurt in a unique way, in a kind of unbearable-bearable way, but, even back then, she wouldn't have been able to exactly define the pain.

Patricia felt that she should be encouraging Stella more, that she should be more useful, but she didn't have a clue how to connect with her or what to say. She had also ducked out of the room four times already to check on Luke, but nothing had changed so far with him. Awkwardly, Patricia tried again with Stella. 'It's – it's all about the breathing. Well, the panting.'

With a grim smile, Stella did her best to oblige.

'Just work through the contraction,' the midwife advised, throwing Patricia a wink. 'Work through it and get to the other side. That's it. Well done. Okay, I'm going to check how many centimetres dilated you are again now.'

Patricia allowed Stella to take her hand, wincing as Stella squeezed and braced herself for the invasion. Patricia dug deep inside, it was the most surreal situation she had ever been in. She barely knew this woman and yet here she was urging her to deliver a baby that may or may not be Luke's.

'Thank you so much for this,' Stella panted, looking up at Patricia gratefully. 'My mum lives so far away, she'd never make it here on time.'

'Don't you have any friends nearby?' Patricia asked. She flushed. 'Sorry, that sounded rude. I just wondered . . .'

'No. It's fine.' Stella gritted her teeth. 'I do have a few friends, but we're not close. A few have moved to other hospitals, but to be honest, I've always been so career-minded.' She let out a short laugh. 'I know. Look at me now. God, that hurts!'

The midwife emerged from between Stella's legs with an apologetic smile. 'I'm sorry; I know that can sting.'

Stella lay back, sweating. 'Yes. It feels like a hot spoon scooping at your insides.'

The midwife patted her knee with a grin. 'Good description. Right. You're nearly ten centimetres dilated now, so we're almost there. Soon, you should be ready to push.'

Patricia felt a thrill shudder through her and she pushed it away. She grabbed a cup of ice chips, offering them to Stella.

'Thank you,' Stella said, popping a few in her mouth. Her eyes met Patricia's and Patricia sensed the gratitude there. She patted Stella's arm and hoped she wasn't a bad person for wishing that this birth would hurry up a bit. Stella let out a suppressed gasp of pain. 'I don't know if I can do this.' She turned her head to Patricia. 'I didn't – this isn't what I – I'm so sorry . . .'

'Don't be sorry. Everything is all right. I'm – I'm here.'

Patricia felt tears pricking at her eyelids, but she held them back. It would never do if she fell apart just when Stella needed her the most. A wave of emotion almost made her come undone and she struggled to hold herself in check. A baby was about to be born. Maybe her grandchild. A baby. Luke's baby.

Despite her earlier reticence, Stella let out an almighty

362

scream. 'The head is out,' the midwife announced a few minutes later.

Patricia let out a gasp. 'Come on, Stella,' she cried, gripping her hand. 'Let's get this baby out!'

After a few hours of intense labour pains, Stella gave an energetic push. She yelled and Patricia heard a wet, whooshing sound that transported her back several years to Ade's birth, Nell's . . . Luke's. It was a sound unlike any other, the sound of new life bursting forth. Suddenly, the room got busy.

'You have a son,' the midwife said, making a frantic gesture with her hand.

Patricia caught sight of a tiny, blue-ish body before the umbilical cord was cut and the baby was whisked away and swaddled in towels.

'Five pound, four,' one of the nurses called out.

Five pound, four? Patricia bit her lip. Okay, so it wasn't drastic. This baby was a little premature, but not exactly underweight.

Then Patricia noticed that there were suddenly a few more staff in the room and they started calling out numbers to each other as two of them rubbed the baby with towels. Paralysed with fear, Patricia listened to the numbers. She heard a zero. Was that good or bad? It was bad; she was sure of that. She remembered this now; it was called the Apgar score. She couldn't remember what the letters meant or what the numbers signified, but she knew it was a way to check if a baby was healthy or not. She heard the number one called out a few times and she didn't know if she should panic or not. One was

363

better than a zero; that much made sense. Patricia took strength from that until she realised that the baby was still not making a sound. The lack of noise was chilling. And the little body was still. So, so still.

'Is – is he all right?' Patricia could barely breathe. She glanced at Stella who, mercifully, seemed too weary to take in what was happening.

'Try not to worry,' the midwife told her, her expression direct and kind. 'Let us get him breathing. This often happens, so please stay positive.'

'Where's the baby?' Stella asked groggily, her head lifting from the pillow. 'I can't hear the baby.'

Patricia wished Stella had remained out of it for a little longer. Just a little longer. Now, her words hung tensely in the air. Nothing happened. Nothing changed. Then the baby coughed. He coughed and started to cry, his tiny fingers curling into fists. Patricia let out a sob and the midwife and nurses clapped.

'Heart rate normal,' one of them called out. 'Grimace and Activity checked . . . all at twos now . . .'

'Good boy,' another said, gathering the baby up. She swaddled him snugly in a blanket and stroked his forehead. 'Good boy. That's better, isn't it? We can all relax again now you've properly joined us.' She turned to Stella. 'Would you like to hold him?'

Stella let out a shuddering breath. She lifted her arms then let them fall back on to the sheet.

'Shall I?' Patricia offered impulsively. 'It's all so overwhelming for you. But no . . . you should hold him first.'

'No.' Stella's eyes brimmed over with tears. 'Thank you,

Patricia. I'll hold him in a minute. I'd – I'd like you to hold him.'

Patricia held her arms out, feeling her throat constrict. She hadn't held a baby for a long time but when she had him in her arms, it felt natural. He was warm and he made a few cute snuffly noises. When Patricia looked down at him, her heart nearly stopped. He looked like Luke. She stared. She wasn't imagining it. She wasn't. It would be natural of her to visualise her son, to want to see him somehow reflected in this baby, even though it had bad connotations. But she wasn't being fanciful; she knew she wasn't. When Patricia looked into this baby's eyes, she knew she was looking into an echo of her own son. He had a cleft chin . . . the dimple rather more pronounced than Luke's. She couldn't tell if his eyes were the same colour or not at this stage, but the eyelashes were long like his.

Patricia tweaked the blanket back and caught her breath. They had always joked about Luke's weird, crooked toes. This little boy had those toes – longish, slightly bent, the second toe proud of the big toe.

Oh, Lucy, she thought to herself miserably. What has my son done to you?

'I don't even know what to call him,' Stella murmured.

'You haven't thought of names?' Patricia rocked the baby, inhaling his scent. 'I . . . this probably sounds funny, but do you think you've been in denial about the baby a bit?'

Stella jerked her head. 'Totally. I haven't got as far as thinking about the baby arriving, about what his – or her – name might be. I've been so worried about Luke . . .' She faltered.

Patricia glanced down at the little boy who was turning instinctively towards her breast.

'Are . . . are there names that you like?'

Patricia remembered the conversation with Lucy that day in her bedroom. She had mentioned a few names. She recalled Bryony. Bryony, for a girl. What was the boy's name? Jamie? Judd? No. Jude. But she wouldn't offer it up, not in a million years. Lucy would hate for Stella to choose that name, surely?

'Jude,' Stella said, out of nowhere. 'He liked the name Jude.' She faltered. 'No. I can't do that to Lucy, not without asking first. Or maybe when Luke comes round . . . Shit, this is all so screwed up.'

Patricia didn't know what to say.

'I'll think of another name,' Stella decided with a sigh. 'I – I've hurt Lucy enough.' She burst into tears suddenly and turned her head away.

Patricia stared down at Luke's son. She swallowed a lump in her throat. Patricia was absolutely certain that whatever happened with Luke, Lucy's pain hadn't ended just yet.

CHAPTER FORTY-THREE

Lucy

Four days had passed. Agonising days, that yielded small changes, but at such a stumbling, limping pace that each improvement seemed hard-earned.

I checked with the nurse and she nodded, so I climbed up on to the bed next to Luke and lay down next to him. It was something I had taken to doing over the past four days; it comforted me and I had this vague idea that it might spur Luke into . . . something.

I held Luke's hand, yearning to feel him hold my hand back. Such a simple thing, the concept of holding hands. But almost as intimate as kissing. Warm fingers slotted together, that secret squeeze that gives you a fuzzy feeling inside and the sheer pleasure of physical contact.

I sighed as Luke's freckled hand lay inert in mine. The expectation for Luke's recovery was immense, more so than when he was in the coma. That had been a no-man's-land . . . an oasis we had all been residing in that had felt suffocating and airless. But somehow, incredibly, this felt worse. I felt caught in the crescendo of a wave, trapped in the deafening climax as I waited for the break and release that must surely come soon.

I looked up, sensing someone else coming into the room. It was Dee, looking flushed from the chilly air outside, clinging on to Dan, who had clearly dashed out of work. He looked shattered and his pale-grey suit was crumpled. I don't think any of us were too fussed about our appearance those days.

'How are you doing, Luce?' Dan bent down and kissed my cheek.

I clung to him for a few seconds. 'Not great.'

'You look pretty good, considering,' Dee said kindly, fiddling with the button on the huge winter coat she was wearing. 'Any change?' She glanced at Luke, her eyes softening.

'Not much, unfortunately. Do you mind if I stay up here?'

'Fill your boots.' Dee smiled. 'It's kind of nice to see you like that.'

I nodded. I wondered if Dee and Dan were surprised that I felt able to do this, assuming it meant I had forgiven Luke.

The truth of it was that I wasn't sure how I felt. But I wanted to be close to him, I wanted to be here for every tiny development.

As Dee and Dan chattily updated Luke on their day, watching eagerly for a reaction the way I had every time I'd spoken to him since he'd 'woken up', I realised how grateful I was for the long stream of visitors that ducked in and out of Luke's room. Sometimes, when I found myself alone with Luke (bar the obligatory nurses, naturally), I began to feel edgy. Not all the time, but there were moments, flashes, where I found myself plagued by worries about what I would say to Luke if he suddenly started talking to me. How would I respond? I wanted to show compassion for what he had been through; I wanted him to know I was there for him. But I had this anger, this resentment that I couldn't find a place for.

We had things to talk about. Large, prickly things that needed to be discussed and pulled apart and put back together again. Post-coma wasn't the time and I knew that, but the problem was, I wasn't sure I was equal to hiding the intense sadness and pain I felt inside.

'Has he . . . has he spoken yet?' Dan asked.

'Nope.' I sat up and stretched, careful not to lean on any of Luke's injured limbs. 'But he's breathing properly on his own. And he followed me with his eyes earlier.'

Dan scratched his head. 'That's good. I'm sure that's good.'

I stood up and turned back to look at Luke. 'Oh, it is, definitely. It's just the speech now. Amazing, for someone as loud as he has always been.'

'It . . . it will come back, won't it?' Dee cradled her coat as she exchanged a worried glance with Dan.

'They hope so.'

I hoped so; fervently. I couldn't bear the thought of a Luke that didn't speak. He was all about making jokes and saying the right thing. He placated, he encouraged, he caused people to break out in spontaneous laughter. His words meant more to me than anything else and I knew that the longer it took for Luke to speak, the worse it might be, that it was possible that he might need speech therapy and rehabilitation. Another mountain to climb. Well, a hill, perhaps, compared to everything else, but still.

'So. Nell said that Stella had the baby.' Dee made the statement carefully, her eyes watchful for my reaction.

Beside her, Dan looked strained. By all accounts, he had taken the news about Luke's one-night stand with Stella extremely badly, repeatedly beating himself up for being a bad friend to Luke, for not being there for him.

'Yes.' I answered Dee finally. My voice sounded mechanical. 'It's . . . a boy. There were some complications early on – the baby didn't breathe for a few minutes.'

'God. How terrifying. Sorry.' Dee added the apology, lest I thought her disloyal.

I expelled some air. 'Yes. But he's fine now; healthy and feeding well, by all accounts.'

Dee met my eyes. I knew what she was thinking. Did the baby look like Luke? Was it definitely his? I couldn't answer that. Patricia had been cautious with the details she provided and I appreciated that. As long as the baby was well and Stella was okay, I didn't need more information than that.

I turned back to check on Luke. Since he had come out of the coma, I seemed to have developed some sort of sixth sense for each time his eyes opened. Maggie, the nurse, told me it was one of those intuitive things that partners of coma victims often experienced.

'Can we . . . can we talk to him?' Dan seemed uncharacteristically child-like, not able to cope with seeing his best friend in such a weird state, I supposed.

'Yes. We're meant to talk to Luke – even more so now. He . . . he can hear us, apparently . . . as long as everything is all right with his hearing.'

'We've come to say hi,' Dan started, awkwardly.

Luke made a gargling sound. He was trying to talk. At last! I felt a rush of exhilaration. I watched the nurse in the room put a call out for the consultant to return. He arrived swiftly, out of breath, but with a sense of purpose. I caught sight of Ade and Nell in the waiting room and I gestured for them to come in. Dee and Dan, excited and rather bewildered, shuffled back to stand on the other side of the door, aware that there were too many of us.

'He looks like himself again,' Nell said in delight.

Ade put his arm around Nell's shoulders. 'I can't believe it.'

'Can someone get Patricia?' I said, over my shoulder, urgently. 'She nipped downstairs quickly to check on Stella . . . an infection, or something.'

I wasn't sure how I felt about Patricia checking on Stella. As far as I was concerned, she had done her duty. I wanted her to be here for any new development with Luke. Here with Luke. With me.

'I'll go.' Dan was already heading off.

The consultant picked up a clipboard and leaned in towards me. 'I'm going to start asking Luke some questions. Please don't be distressed if he can't answer them or if his responses are garbled. It's very normal, especially after such a long time.'

Frightened, I bit down on my fingernail. Speak properly, Luke, I pleaded in my head. Speak properly, please. All

of a sudden, I wasn't worried about what to say to him.
I would say whatever came out and it would be right. I
just wanted him back. We could work everything out; I
was sure of that.

'Luke, I'm about to ask you some questions. Is that
all right?'

There was a pause. Luke nodded his head. He actually
nodded his head. Nell clapped her hands to her face and
started to laugh. Ade was shaking his head over and over
again, but he was grinning widely. Patricia rushed into
the room, her cheeks flushed.

'What's happening? Luke, can you hear me? It's
Mum—'

'Mrs Harte,' the consultant cautioned her, trying to
contain her hysteria. 'I know this feels hugely exciting,
but you must let me go through my questions. It's really
important.'

Patricia's eyes darted from Luke to the consultant and
back to Luke again, but she calmed down obediently and
took her place next to me. I took her hand.

The consultant returned to his clipboard. 'Can you tell
me your name?'

Luke's eyes worked the room, but he said nothing.

The consultant tried again. Luke remained silent. 'Do
you know what day of the week it is?' Silence again.

'Do you remember the accident?'

Luke jerked his head and found me in the room. He
seemed fully alert and connected. His eyes were on mine.
I could see torment, distress . . . grief. He knew. He knew
that I knew and he was distraught.

'It's okay,' I whispered. I saw him shake his head

slightly and I wanted to run to him, to gather him up in my arms so he would know that I meant it, that everything was truly all right. Or at least, that it *would* be. I glanced at the consultant who gave a brief nod, and I rushed to Luke's side and put my hand on his cheek.

'It's okay,' I repeated tearfully in his ear. 'Everything is okay, Luke. I promise.'

I heard Patricia let out a strangled sob.

Luke said something incomprehensible, his hand on mine. He was trying to say something to me. I bent my head to hear him, but he made a weird gargling sound again.

'I have to ask him the questions, Lucy.' The consultant's tone was kind, but firm.

I swallowed. Without turning round, I jerked my head in acknowledgement. I let go of Luke's hand; he needed to concentrate.

The consultant continued. 'Can you tell me your name?'

'L-Luke.' He croaked the word out, but it was clear.

There was a collective gasp in the room. I think the loudest one came from me. I was thrilled. I felt absurdly proud, the way a parent presumably did when their child performed a hitherto insurmountable task. In this moment, not much else mattered apart from Luke saying the right things. And he had always been so good at saying the right things.

'Do you remember the accident?'

'Yes.' Luke looked at me urgently. 'Stri . . . Stri . . .'

I let out a breath, overwhelmed. I snatched up his hand again.

The consultant looked over his clipboard. 'I think Luke might be getting tired now.'

'He's not.' I shook my head and started to cry. 'He's not.'

'Stri . . .' Luke tried again. His eyelids flickered and the hand holding mine pulsed.

'I'm here,' I told him. I tried to make my voice sound firm and reassuring, like Maggie's, but it came out a bit wobbly and unsure. I wanted to tell him that nothing mattered but us, that the stuff with Stella didn't matter. The words didn't come, even though I wanted them to.

The consultant's eyes sharply watched Luke. His shoulders moved slightly and he glanced at the machines.

'It's a nickname,' Nell blurted out. 'He's talking to Lucy. He's trying to say "Stripes".'

I stroked Luke's hair out of his face. I wasn't aware of anyone else in the room, just me and him. Tears were dripping down my cheeks, but my heart was full and fit to burst. He looked like Luke again, not the empty shell he had been for the past few months.

I love him. I *love* him. I knew this, with absolute conviction. We could make things right. I started to speak, but he met my eyes and spoke urgently. He was alert, connected.

'Stripes. I . . . you're . . . p-please . . .' His eyes slid away from mine, flipping back into his head. His eyelids fluttered like tiny bird wings, then abruptly closed.

I touched his face again, feeling a flicker of alarm. 'Luke? Luke, can you hear me?'

I sensed the consultant putting his clipboard down and I turned to him, confused. His eyes were on the machines, watching the figures and the lines and, after a second, he was shouting for a crash team. One of the machines shrieked out a flat-line as the crash team, including Maggie, came rushing in with a trolley.

Oh my God. No. No.

'Get the paddles ready,' Maggie called. 'Lucy, sweetheart, move! Everyone out, please.'

I couldn't move, but I felt someone pulling me backwards. This couldn't be happening.

'He was fine,' I said in a small voice.

Maggie gripped my quivering shoulders. 'Luke has suffered a cardiac arrest. We're going to try and save him. Stay out here.'

I nodded numbly. We had all shuffled out of the room, but I stood in the doorway, watching. Patricia groped for my hand and I squeezed it, not taking my eyes off Luke. His gown had been pulled down and he was shocked, once, twice, three times. Could anyone take that much electricity? Surely they were going to kill him?

Stop killing him. Make him live.

They pushed at Luke's chest, breathing into his mouth, counting, counting. One of them scrambled on to the bed at one point, thumping Luke hard between the ribs.

It didn't make any difference. Nothing was happening.

My head spun wildly but Patricia was frozen with terror, still gripping my hand and all I could see of Ade, Nell, Dee and Dan were their eyes, wide with shock and horror and disbelief.

Nurses handed things deftly to one another and there was a chorus of voices as they all battled. They all battled to save Luke's life, a whole team of them. But they couldn't. They couldn't save him. He had gone.

Staggered, I gripped the doorframe. As quickly as the room had become active, lively and full of movement, just as quickly it slowed and stilled and became quiet. Heads were bent reverentially, voices were hushed and the only sound in the room was that shrill machine that let us all know that Luke was dead.

Someone reached out and gently switched the machine off. The acute silence that followed was worse. It rang in my ears like one of those stupid whistles must for dogs; a hideous screaming noise that wouldn't let up, piercing my brain.

In the background, I heard a noise like an animal being strangled. I guessed it must be Patricia, falling apart at the seams. She had torn her hand from mine at some point, but I hadn't noticed. I could hear Nell crying, Dee crying. I could hear Dan angrily denying reality and I thought I could hear Ade making a noise that was surely the personification of incredulity and grief combined.

'No,' I said simply. 'No.' I said it louder. My body felt rigid. Shock? Was that shock?

'I'm so sorry.' It was Maggie. 'Lucy, I am so terribly sorry.'

'There's no need,' I replied. I heard myself say that. What did I mean? 'It's . . . it's . . .'

'The heart attack that Luke suffered at the scene of the accident, his ruptured spleen – these can cause permanent damage to the heart.' Maggie put her hand on my arm. 'The worse the damage, the more likely a further attack is.'

I shook Maggie's arm off. 'Why didn't you tell me this? You made me believe he was going to live. You gave me false hope . . .'

My voice petered out. They *had* told me all of this. They had. I just hadn't listened. I hadn't wanted to listen.

I shivered. Coldness seeped through me and life shifted on its axis. A life without Luke in it. A world, an existence, without Luke. Only ten minutes before, I had been holding Luke's hand as he looked at me with love and apology and hope in his eyes. Half an hour before, I had lain next to his warm body, trying to figure out how we would move forward when he came home. But he was never coming home.

My vision swam. I couldn't see for tears. I couldn't bear it. There was a pain in my chest, a horrible, horrible pain. I glanced down at my chest, clasping my hands to it. My heart was breaking. I swear I could feel it fracturing inside my body, splintering into useless pieces that didn't mean anything any more, not without the person that heart lived for.

I collapsed against someone wordlessly. Luke had died. He had died.

There was a funeral. It hadn't occurred to me before now how incredible it was that funerals actually took place at all when family members were so hysterical and grief-stricken they could barely put one foot in front of the other, let alone wade through a series of sensible phone calls and organise a suitable, fitting send-off for the person in question.

When a funeral needs arranging, everyone needs a

facilitator, a person who is able to keep their emotions in check for long enough to take control and get the job done. Ade was our facilitator. Such a situation separates the men from the boys, as they say, and in this scenario, I was the boy and Ade was very much the man. Thank God.

Luke and I hadn't got round to writing wills. We always meant to, don't people always mean to? But we hadn't done it. It hadn't been a priority. We weren't meant to die in our thirties. I think we'd always thought we'd sort out wills when we had a child; when there was a reason to put our affairs in order, or whatever the expression was.

Without a will to guide him, Ade had sorted the entire funeral out, checking details with me when he had to, his voice patient and slow as though he was talking to a vague child with an attention disorder. I didn't blame him. I was about as much use.

Ade didn't moan about it, nor did he harass me. He just got on with it. Perhaps he felt he owed it to Luke or something. Or maybe he just knew that the rest of us were incapable, too poleaxed with grief to even answer our phones, let alone anything else.

The day itself was horrific. I remembered waking up groggily. I didn't experience that thing that people talked about, those few seconds of thinking everything was okay before I realised that nothing was ever going to be okay again because Luke was dead. I knew that Luke was dead. I could feel it in the coldness of my bones and the heavy, leaden emptiness in my heart. I had been sedated for a few days after I left the hospital, but I refused further medication. I needed to feel, I needed to face this. I didn't want to, but I had to. I had to find some way of pushing myself through today and through the rest of my life.

I was looked after by Dee and Nell before the funeral. When I say looked after, I mean that they took complete charge of me. They slept at the house the night before. They got me out of bed, they bathed me, they did my make-up. Dee put me in a black dress she found in my wardrobe that I didn't have the heart to tell her reminded me of Luke because I wore it when he cooked me a celebratory 'The IVF worked!' dinner the first time round. No matter. Everything reminded me of Luke. My feet were pushed into court shoes and I was fed a corner of buttered toast and some bitter coffee that made my stomach heave. Nell got me into the funeral car, a huge, shiny monstrosity that smelt of leather and death.

I must confess that I collapsed when I saw Luke's coffin. Not quite on to the floor – looking back, that would have been shamefully dramatic – but I did slump into Dan's arms and he held me up, even though he must have been a mess himself. His face was streaming with tears as he gripped me tightly and I had never felt more grateful for his strong presence, or for his loyalty and friendship.

The flowers were magnificent, I had noted vaguely. Not arranged by myself or Patricia, naturally (who would have had the strength for such a poignant farewell?) but they looked good. I'm not sure Luke would have minded either way, but I understood that it was part of the process, part of the etiquette of a funeral.

There was a great photo of him at the front of the crematorium – a lovely photo. He looked tanned, happy, handsome. The music was very Luke, chosen by Nell and Ade, with some help from Dan. 'There Goes My Hero' – Dave Grohl from the Foo Fighters' song for Kurt Cobain – 'Time of Your Life' by Green Day and 'Ho Hey' by the Lumineers, the song that Luke always said would be our theme tune as a family when our baby arrived. That one almost had me on the floor. It was heartbreaking. I would never have a family with Luke. I would never again have *Luke*.

I thought Patricia would hate the music choices, but she didn't. She moved gently and leant her shoulder on Ade's throughout, giving me the occasional glance. People made speeches. Ade, Dan, Joe, Luke's paramedic partner. How do people make speeches? I wanted to because it felt disrespectful not to acknowledge Luke and the incredible way I felt about him. But I couldn't. There wasn't a way that I could coherently arrange my feelings about Luke into a concise speech fit for public consumption. Love, anger, heartbreak, despair, regret, fury, more love. Passionate, never-ending, romantic, beautiful, heart-wrenching, wonderful love that I would never have with another person for as long as I lived.

As they did that hideously theatrical thing with the curtain, I walked out of the crematorium. I walked away from the flowers and the people and, most of all, away from the oppressive feeling inside.

I couldn't make small talk, however well-meant everyone was. Ade had arranged a wake at a hall, but I wasn't sure if I could go. I heard my parents calling after me and I hurried away. I couldn't deal with them, mostly because the obvious love and concern in their eyes had shocked and touched me earlier that morning. They loved me and they had loved Luke, more than I had realised. But the timing of this reveal was a little more than I could bear. Too agonising, too sharp.

I was relieved to be outside in the bracing air, away from people I might be rude to. Beneath the surface of the careful, waterproof make-up Dee had applied, I was seething, bubbling with molten lava, furious at the God or whoever it was that had taken Luke away from me.

And that's when I caught sight of her. She was hiding, standing some distance away by a tree, but she was there. Stella was here. She had a car seat cradled over her arm and she was doing her best not to be seen, but it was too late.

Don't do it, I told myself, feeling my breath quickening. *Don't do it. Not today. Walk away. Go home.* She saw me. Our eyes connected and she started. I made for her. *Go home,* I told myself. *Don't do this.* But I couldn't stop myself. It was as if something had taken over my body. I was out of control, on a mission.

'What are you doing here?'

'Lucy . . .' Stella swallowed. Her eyes were bloodshot. She looked shattered. 'I'm so sorry. Joe told me the funeral was today. I wasn't going to come because I knew you'd hate it, but it felt wrong. The baby . . .' She glanced down at the car seat.

The baby? Hadn't she given him a name?

'You're right. I hate it. I hate that you're here.'

I was being rude and I was being aggressive. I noticed that her lip was bleeding, as if she'd bitten down hard on it, worrying about whether she had made the right decision. I didn't care. My insides were bleeding uncontrollably; her lip was nothing to me. There was still the matter of the DNA test, and I felt a surge of panic. Luke had just been cremated; how on earth would we prove that the baby wasn't his now?

Stella nodded. 'I understand. I – I just wanted to say goodbye. For him to say goodbye.' She glanced down at the baby.

'Him?' I snarled the word out. I must have hit the angry stage of grief already. Or maybe I just wanted to punch this woman for daring to turn up at Luke's funeral. My eyes were blazing in Stella's direction.

'Doesn't your baby have a name?'

She hoisted the car seat up protectively. 'Not – not yet. I wasn't sure . . . it seems—'

'What?'

Stella hesitated. 'I know Luke liked the name Jude. But I don't know . . . I wanted . . .'

'My permission?'

My throat was choking me. I was livid, *livid*. How dare she? How dare Stella turn up here today, flaunting her baby, begging for me to say that she could have the name Luke had wanted for our child?

I caught sight of the baby. My mind reeled. He looked like Luke. My *God* he looked like Luke. The nose, the shape of the eyes . . . the chin. The chin almost made me come undone. The dent was more pronounced than Luke's. But it was undoubtedly his. Luke couldn't have left a clearer imprint of himself if he'd tried. This baby was Luke's. No DNA test required.

Suddenly, the fight went out of me. I felt deflated like a balloon that had been punctured and slowly let down, its squeal a torturous death cry.

'Call him Jude.' The words came out abruptly, but I meant them.

I sensed Ade dashing towards me and I held a hand up to halt him. I didn't need him to do his hero thing, the thing he was doing so brilliantly at, finally. I didn't need saving. I just wanted to rewind my life to two or three months or so ago, when it had more or less made sense.

'W-what?' Stella's eyes creased with shock.

'Call him Jude. It's . . . it's what Luke would have wanted. Just do me a favour, Stella?' Wearily, I stared at the ground, marvelling at the way the frost had turned each blade of grass into a stiff little tuft. 'Just – just go away, will you? Live your life, be good to – to Jude.' My voice broke. Saying the name killed me. 'But . . . leave me alone, please. I – I can't bear this . . .'

I walked away from her, from Ade, heading home. I wanted to shut everyone out and be on my own. I wanted a moment to be cocooned with Luke – my memories of Luke – without anyone butting in.

I heard Ade calling out to me, but I shook my head, thrusting my hands into the pockets of my coat. My court shoes kept slipping on the icy pavements and I took them off in the end, feeling my way in stocking-clad feet, welcoming the icy pin prick of numbness on my soles. Inside the house, I felt like a ghost drifting through it. I wished I hadn't put the Christmas decorations up in preparation for Luke's return. I felt as if I'd walked into a winter wonderland at the wrong time of year, like accidentally happening upon Miss Havisham's spooky wedding room with the decaying cake and the cobwebs draped all over the furniture.

I wrapped my arms around myself for comfort, wondering what I should do next. My head throbbed and every muscle felt weary, as though I'd run a marathon. I couldn't work out if I'd been thrashing around in bed or if this was simply a result of grief and exhaustion.

Suddenly, I remembered something. I forced myself to climb the stairs, wincing as my muscles protested. In the bedroom, I resolutely looked away from the bed we'd shared that make me weep with sorrow every time I caught sight of it, and I opened Luke's wardrobe. I gazed at his clothes. At some point soon, I would be forced to sort them out. I would need to send them away to charity, so that someone else could wear his things and smell like him. His paramedic's uniforms would go back to the hospital, but I thought I might sneak one set away, just so I could look at it now and again. I started pulling at the jumpers and cardigans Luke kept in a higgledy-piggledy stack, eventually finding the one I wanted. It was the huge, grey one he'd been wearing the day he'd had his horrible breakdown in the spare room.

Holding the soft wool to my face, I inhaled the faint smell of him. How long would I do this for, how long would I yearn for this reminder of him? I turned the cardigan over in my hands, wondering if I was being silly. That day, Luke had sat on the floor, with some crumpled pages between his legs. I felt inside the pockets and my fingers touched notepaper. It was there. Whatever Luke had been upset about was in my hands.

The pages were crumpled, the way I remembered, but they had been smoothed out, almost lovingly, as though the contents were too precious to sully. My heart began to thump and I wondered if I was making a mistake. What if whatever was in here made me feel worse? I let out a small sound. Nothing could make me feel worse than I did now; I was sure of that. I was alive, but only just.

Holding my tears at bay for as long as I could, I opened the pages and started reading.

CHAPTER FORTY-FOUR

Luke

18th May
Lucy. I don't even know how to start this letter. I
want to tell you how much I love you and how
much you mean to me. And I will. Because, what-
ever happens, you have to know that, Stripes. You're
my girl and I hope, more than anything, that you'll
believe me when I say that you're my whole life.

I need to be brave and I need to do this.
Something happened. Something terrible. I . . . I
slept with someone else. Jesus. I'm looking at
those words now and I can't even believe them.
This isn't something I ever thought I would write
down, that I would read back or – most import-
antly – that I would ever, ever do. I slept with
someone. Her name is Stella. She works at the
hospital and she's a trainee doctor. We became
friends. Not close friends, just coffee-chat friends.
In all honesty, I think I used her as a sounding

board. She's not like Dan or Joe or any of my other friends. Not because she's female but because she's like a therapist. I talked *at* her.

I talked *to* her mostly about the baby stuff. About the stuff you and me talk about, but also some of the stuff we don't. Like . . . is this my fault? Why can't I make this happen for you? Can you be happy without a baby? Can I make you happy?

Please don't think that these were cosy chats. Please don't think it was a meeting of minds or an emotional connection. These were angry, self-indulgent rants about patronising consultants and prolonged disappointment. As odd as it must sound, I honestly feel that there is little physical or mental attraction between us.

Fuck, I can't even remember the night I spent with Stella. I wish I could tear it from my life because it is the single most heinous thing I have ever done. I guess I'm not quite the hero you thought I was, Stripes.

I'm a fucking idiot. A man. An idiot-man who wanted to escape from his life and his problems for a night. It happened and I can't make it un-happen. I wish I could, but I can't. I've tried to erase it but that's just cowardly. All I can say is that I am sorry. So, so sorry. I cannot even find the words to make that inadequate little phrase more meaningful.

The only other thing for me to say, the most important thing to say, is that I love you, Stripes. I *love you. With every single piece of this shitty, wretched heart of mine. I hope I can find the courage to tell you all of this to your face one day, if it's right for me to do so. At the moment, I am shot with terror every time the memory – or rather, the knowledge of my behaviour – seeps into my soul. I want to make you happy, to have the future we always dreamt of. You're my girl. My girl, Stripes. You truly are all I ever wanted. You were and you are everything I want from life. Our baby will be the cherry on the cake. You will be the best mother. The best. You are amazing and funny and perfect and I hope our baby – babies, if we're lucky enough – look just like you. Quirky-beautiful. I hope they grow up to arrange their books in alphabetical order and buy Christmas presents in April.*

You and me, it's always been this huge romance. A proper love story. And this is kind of like my love letter to you. An apologetic, fucked-up, unconventional love letter that probably doesn't even communicate an iota of how awful I feel about what happened and about how happy I am that I have you in my life.

Now it's about you and me and our baby. And that's all I have ever wanted. Please remember that you are the love of my life. I feel absolutely blessed to have loved you with all my heart and soul since I met you. Yes. Since I met you. What does that poem 'Captive' say? 'Twas but for half an hour.' Yes that. Thirty minutes with you and I was smitten, as they say. And just like that poem says, I have no will and no power. And that's just the way I have always wanted it.

Yours forever, if you'll still have me.

Luke.

CHAPTER FORTY-FIVE

Nell

May, the following year
'Are you sure you want these up in the window?'

Nell turned to Lisa, doubting herself.

Lisa nodded. 'Yes! That was the deal. You work here at the weekends and I let you put your designs in the window. Go on, they're going to look great.'

Nell hesitated. 'God, I hope so. This is the first one I've actually had the guts to show.' She started dressing the dummy clumsily, pulling the mint-green dress over its head. She pulled the hem down and did up the tiny buttons on the back, standing back to take a better look at it. The dress looked good. No, it looked great. It really looked great.

'Fabulous,' Lisa said admiringly. 'I really love it, Nell. I have a good feeling about this.'

Nell smiled. She had a good feeling about it, too. She had initially taken the weekend job to keep herself busy. After Luke had died, she had gone into a state of shock. It had taken everything she had not to start spiralling again and Nell thanked God for Ade's steady presence. He had been her rock, the way Luke had been when Ade had headed off to Australia all those years ago. In a kind of neat role reversal, everything had come full circle, but Nell had spent months wishing that it hadn't. But on reflection, perhaps she and Ade had been there for each other. Ade had seemed to need her almost as much as she had needed him, which felt like some kind of progress to Nell. It made a change for her to be supporting someone, to be a shoulder to cry on.

Nell glanced at Lisa. Lisa had met Ade all those months ago, when he had first arrived, and Nell was convinced that she had been attracted to him. And Nell was sure that Ade must have noticed how pretty Lisa was. He hadn't said anything, but Lisa was surely his type? But Ade seemed completely disinterested in women right now. He was all about the business side of things, probably trying to protect himself after Luke's death and his divorce. He had gone back to Australia to sort some things out. Nell missed him badly.

'So when is your swoonsome brother back?' Lisa asked, slotting some hangers into some cute T-shirts.

Nell felt a pang in her heart. Ade. Lisa meant Ade. 'I just can't get used to only having one brother.'

'Gosh, sorry, Nell.' Lisa looked stricken.

'Don't be silly. I – it's – it's strange without Luke, that's all.' Nell straightened the dress on the dummy and stepped back for a better look. 'Ade's back in a few days' time, I think.'

'For good?'

'For good. He's selling his business to his partner and his apartment has already been snapped up, so it's just the divorce now.'

Lisa hung the T-shirts up. 'It must be really hard for him to let go of his wife and everything they had together. They were married for a long time, weren't they?'

'Just less than a decade, I suppose.'

'What's he going to do when he's back here?'

Nell studied the dummy, realising it needed some accessories. 'I think he's going to work on opening another florist, if Mum will let him. She's resisting, but I think she's rather excited by the whole idea. She's better, by the way,' she added, anticipating Lisa's next question. 'She was obviously a total mess for the first few months, but she's picking herself up again and she's trying to help Lucy do the same.'

Nell had been feeling a profound fondness for her mum of late. She appreciated her, more than she had done in the past. Sometime after Luke's death, she had confided in her about Cal – not the full details, but some of them – and Nell had been surprised at how understanding her mother had been about everything. Even the fact that Cal had been married.

'Poor Lucy.' Lisa leant on the counter. 'I can't even imagine how I would feel if I had been through what she's been through over the past few months.'

Nell bent and picked up a trilby hat. 'She's . . . okay. I mean, she's been living like a hermit, not going out at all, really. We've all been so worried about her. She wouldn't talk to me or Mum or Dee for ages, but I think she just needed to be on her own.' Nell balanced the hat on the dummy's head. 'She found some letter from Luke and it knocked her for six. She realised how awful he'd been feeling about the baby stuff and how guilty he felt about what happened with Stella.'

'A letter? That Luke wrote to her before he died?'

'Yes. It was pretty much a love letter.'

'Wow. That's romantic. Well, sad, but romantic, too.'

'Yeah. Luke talked about sleeping with Stella in the letter, about how devastated he was. Lucy was absolutely inconsolable. I think she'd more or less forgiven him, you know. I think they would have been all right if Luke had survived.'

'That is so sad.' Lisa looked upset.

'I know. Heartbreaking. But I've been spending quite a bit of time with Lucy recently. I don't know if she'll ever want to be with anyone else, but I'm trying to get her out more. Just for drinks. Round to Dee and Dan's for dinner, stuff like that.'

'That's good. I really feel for her. And what about . . . have you . . . seen Luke's baby?' Lisa asked the question with some discomfort.

Nell stepped out of the window display and shook her head. 'No. I don't know if Stella has moved away or if she's due back at the hospital when she's finished her maternity leave.'

'That must be weird for you. Or is it? Do you want to see the baby?'

Nell's eyes filled with tears. 'Of course I do. I know it's horrible for Lucy, but that's my nephew. That's a part of Luke.'

Lisa squeezed Nell's shoulder and changed the subject. 'Have you heard from Cal recently?'

'Not recently.' Nell took out her phone. 'After all those messages after Luke died, he gave up. I think he had hopes of getting back together, but I reckon he's finally got the message.'

'He's an idiot.' Lisa was openly disdainful. 'I can't believe he contacted you like that after Luke died. I know he made out he cares about you, but you were vulnerable. He's so inappropriate.'

Nell hid a smile. Lisa had made her thoughts about Cal extremely clear, and he wasn't welcome in Lisa's shop, that was for sure.

Truthfully, it had taken Nell a while to get over Cal. Luke's death had taken up almost all of her time, but a part of Nell's heart had ached for Cal. She hated him for what he'd done, but she hadn't found it easy to switch her feelings off. It had taken huge strength to resist him, to ignore his texts and phone calls. But losing Luke had clarified Nell's mind. She was no longer in love with Cal and the relationship with him had been toxic and wrong.

'Who's that?' Lisa nodded towards the window. 'Someone's waving at me. No. Not me. I think he's waving at you.'

Nell frowned and took a peek. He was nice-looking, with dark eyes, a winsome smile. And a pork pie hat. The penny dropped. This guy was at her college. She had seen him around.

'Do you know him?' Lisa gave him a full onceover. 'He's *hawt.*'

'He goes to my college. Hey, I thought you only had eyes for Ade?'

Lisa shrugged. 'I do, but he's not interested, honey. Trust me. I know when a guy is into me and Ade is most definitely not into me.'

Nell felt a thump of disappointment. She really thought she had had Ade's love life tied up. 'I don't think he's into anyone, to be fair,' she admitted. 'I think he just wants to throw himself into all the business stuff.'

'And that's his right,' Lisa replied lightly. If she was concerned about Ade's disinterest, she was hiding it well. 'Anyway, don't worry about me. Go and talk to your man out there. See if you can talk him out of the untrendy hat.'

'I like the hat,' Nell protested. 'It's "hawt", as you would say.' About to head outside, she floundered. Was she ready for this? She hadn't been with anyone since Cal and her heart still felt bruised. But wasn't it about time she started living again?

'How do I look?' she asked Lisa, giving her hair a quick rake with her fingers.

'Ready,' Lisa said with a supportive smile. 'You look ready.'

Nell flipped her a thumbs up and took a deep breath before she headed outside.

CHAPTER FORTY-SIX

Patricia

Patricia put the phone down and made a final note on her pad. She paused for a second, collecting herself. Perhaps she would never be able to take a message about funeral flowers without thinking about Luke. It had happened with Bernard and now Luke swam into her mind every time someone made that call.

Patricia drifted to the front of the shop. It had been five months now. Five months since Luke's shocking death. She still thought about him every day. Her boy. Her baby. Patricia knew it was silly to think about him as a baby when he had been in his thirties, but he *had* been *her* baby. It was true what people said; however much time had passed – and that included marriages, children of their own, divorce, illness – your babies were still your babies. Even when they had gone.

Patricia often found herself poleaxed by a sudden wave of grief that flooded her mind with memories of

Luke. His birth, his first day at school, his graduation, his first day as a qualified paramedic, his wedding to Lucy. All the key moments that had punctuated Luke's life and made him real and important.

God, she missed him. Patricia caught her breath, stunned as tears pricked at her eyelids for the umpteenth time. He had been such a huge part of her life, and her heart was bereft without him. She tried to pull herself together, but it was difficult. Luke had gone and she had to get her head round that.

Patricia's mind swam to Jude as she wandered back inside the shop. None of them had seen Luke's son since the day of the funeral.

Deep inside, Patricia longed to see Luke's child. Jude was her grandson – he was part of the family in his own way. But Patricia was terrified of hurting Lucy's feelings. Lucy couldn't take any more pain, and none of them were willing to put pressure on her to do anything.

Patricia bit her lip, feeling a fresh wave of tears coming. They were all going to have to wait until Lucy was ready would she ever be ready? Ade had already sternly, but quite rightly, warned her that that time might never come. Lucy might not ever want Jude to be a part of their lives and they needed to respect that. It was a desolate thought and one that Patricia was struggling with, but Lucy was her daughter in law. She was Luke's wife – widow – and Patricia had far too much respect for her to overstep the mark.

'Er, hello again.'

Patricia turned round. She stared at the man who was hovering in the doorway. Early fifties, salt-and-pepper hair, good teeth. Good teeth. She hid a smile. That was what she had thought about him the first time she had met him.

'Larry. It's Larry, isn't it? How nice to see you again.'

'And you.' Larry puffed up a bit when she remembered his name.

'I haven't seen you . . . since that day in the hospital.'

'No.' Larry nodded awkwardly, proffering a hand before letting it drop to his side again. 'I . . . I heard about your son, Luke. I'm so sorry.'

Patricia ducked her head and slowly counted to five. It was a technique she had adopted since Luke died. When people mentioned his name, she counted. To five, to ten, if necessary. It usually stopped the embarrassing onslaught of tears the mere mention of his name dredged up. Usually. God, how humiliating. She was sobbing. After five months, the mention of Luke's name had her crying a river.

'Please don't be embarrassed,' Larry said, pulling a clean handkerchief from his pocket. He handed it to her. 'You were my shoulder to cry on last time, remember.'

'It's . . . it's just so . . .'

'It's just so incredibly sad. I know.'

Larry put his hand on her shoulder and waited, saying nothing.

Patricia collected herself, feeling the warmth of Larry's palm on her shoulder. It was reassuring. She dabbed at her eyes, leaving mascara smudges all over Larry's handkerchief. Her hands were trembling, but she took some deep breaths and managed to calm down.

Larry gave her a kind smile. 'I can't tell you how

shocked I was when they told me at the hospital. That kind nurse Maggie spoke to me.'

'Aaah, the lovely Maggie.' Patricia sniffed. 'Now there's a lady in the right job.' She remembered something suddenly. 'Larry. Your step-daughter – is she . . . ?'

'Alice is fine. She came out of her coma a few days after we had that chat.' He plucked a dark-red rose from a nearby tub and stared at it uncomfortably. 'She started work again a couple of months ago. She's . . . unbelievably, everything is . . . Well. Everything is back to normal. For me, anyway.'

Patricia wondered why Larry was behaving so strangely. He seemed edgy and he couldn't stop fiddling with the rose he was holding. It was going to shed all of its scarlet petals all over the floor in a minute. Suddenly, she realised that he must be feeling guilty that Alice had survived when Luke had died. She felt contrite; crying in front of him like that must have made him feel even worse.

'Larry. I'm delighted for you that Alice is well again.'

'Thank you. Thank you. That's so kind.' His eyes crinkled at the edges, but he clearly felt awkward. 'It still must be hard for you to hear.'

'Don't be silly,' Patricia lied. She placed her hands on the counter and took a cleansing breath. 'It's not your fault, is it, about Luke? It's not anyone's fault. It's sad and it's horrible, but please don't feel bad. It's wonderful news about Alice, really.'

'I was in two minds about coming here,' Larry admitted, slotting the rose back into the tub with its petals intact. 'I didn't want you to think I was . . . I just felt a bit . . .'

'I understand.' Patricia smiled. 'So . . . why did you come here?' She blushed. She hadn't meant to be so direct.

Larry met her eyes. 'Umm. Well, I'm not sure I should . . .'

'You came for some flowers?'

He scratched his head. 'Well, yes. Yes, I did want to buy some flowers. But it's . . . I don't know if . . .'

Patricia felt her heart slump just a little. How silly of her. What had she been thinking – that Larry had come here to ask her out? She lifted her chin.

'Come on. Let me help you. What sort of flowers did you have in mind? Who are they for?'

'They're for . . . someone special.' Larry went a little pink. 'I, er, I don't know this person very well, but I'd like to make it clear that I like this person. If you get my drift.'

'I think I do. You're after some flowers that say . . . romance?'

Patricia was annoyed at herself. She was hardly ready to date anyone. No one was ever going to compare to Bernard, and Luke was still very much in her thoughts. Her heart was far too bruised to contemplate allowing space for anyone else.

'Yes. Shall we say, cautiously romantic,' Larry decided after some thought. 'Something that says . . . no hurry, but one day, it would be er, nice to go out for dinner. So, umm, what would you recommend?'

Patricia cleared her throat. The best thing to do was to detach herself from the situation. Larry needed her help and she was going to provide it. 'Well, there are red roses, of course. But they can seem a little obvious. These pale pink ones are very pretty . . . or perhaps these?' She gestured to a pot of lilac freesias with fragrant, funnel-shaped flowers. 'Pretty, highly scented and to me, they suggest some thought, as well as letting someone know that you're romantically interested in them – but in a gentle way. But that's just my opinion.' She turned away quickly.

'Perfect.' Larry selected a large bunch and brought them to the counter.

'Shall I wrap them in paper?'

'If you like.'

'I mean, are you sending them to someone or . . . ?'

'They'll be fine like that, thank you.' Larry gave her a smile and handed over some money.

Patricia wished he'd stop beaming at her. She was distracted by his lovely teeth and the way his eyes looked like he was on the edge of laughter. She bundled the freesias in some cream paper patterned with sprigs of lavender and twisted the bottom.

'These will last for about six to ten days in water,' she told Larry, irked at the prim tone she seemed to have adopted. 'A bright, sunny location is best to open the petals but then they should be moved to a darker spot. They'll last longer then.' She thrust the freesias into his hands.

'I see.' Larry looked amused as he took the flowers. 'So where are you going to put them then?'

'What?'

'The flowers. Where are you going to put them?'

Patricia's mouth fell open and she clamped it shut again.

'You know these flowers are for you, don't you?' Larry held them out.

'I . . . I . . .'

Larry put the flowers down on the counter. 'Patricia,' he started softly. 'I sort of like you. I mean, I like you. Not sort of. Wow.' He stopped, in wonder. 'How about that? I sound like a teenage boy.'

Patricia let out a relieved laugh.

'Okay. Let me try again. I know that you're vulnerable and that you're hurting. And I wish I could take that away. But I can't.' Larry sighed. 'But we could chat and laugh and we could go out and I'm not trying to replace anyone in your life because I know—'

'Yes.' Patricia blurted the word out.

'Sorry?'

'Yes.' Patricia knew she was scarlet. 'I'd like to chat. I'd like to laugh. With you. I just might need some . . .'

'Time,' Larry finished. 'Of course. So here's my number.' He scribbled it down on Patricia's orders notepad. 'And I have yours,' he gestured to the work phone. 'And that's all we need to get started. According to Alice, anyway. She's very much a fan of exchanging numbers and leaving it at that. She says that if it's meant to happen, it'll happen.' He thrust his hands into his pockets. 'She knows about me coming here today, you see. She . . . she thought it was a good idea.'

'She was right.' Patricia picked up the flowers. 'Thank you for these.'

'You have good taste. I might have gone for the red roses. Way too obvious.' Larry flashed her a grin and

402

moved towards the door. 'I'll call you. Or you call me. Apparently, it's all very free and easy these days.'

Patricia felt her heart lift a fraction as she waved goodbye to Larry. Something had shifted. For the better. Who would have thought it?

Patricia headed into the office to find a vase for her flowers and as she plucked one down from the shelf, she caught sight of a photo of Lucy and Luke pinned to the wall. It instantly made her think of Jude again.

My grandson, Patricia thought to herself sadly. The last piece of Luke. She shook herself. That wasn't her decision to make. She loved Lucy far too much to interfere.

'Pleased to see me?'

Patricia turned. It was Ade, tanned and vital-looking, wearing jeans with a navy and white striped shirt. He was holding up a bottle of champagne and he looked relaxed and happy.

'You're early! I was going to come and collect you—'

'I know.' Ade put the bottle of champagne on the counter. 'I sorted everything out with Tina, wrapped up my business. So it was time to say goodbye to Australia. Goodbye to the sunshine.' He cast a rueful glance outside.

'Champagne?' Patricia couldn't believe how pleased she was to see him.

'We're celebrating the fact that I'm back for good. Home again, where I belong,' Ade added, undoing the foil on the champagne. 'Do you have any glasses?'

'I have mugs.' Patricia grabbed two from the kitchen and held them out. There was a loud pop and Ade struggled to pour the bubbles neatly into the mugs.

'To absent friends,' Ade said, meeting her eyes for a moment. 'To Luke. And Dad.'

Patricia nodded, but she couldn't say the words out loud.

Feeling Ade's arm around her shoulders, Patricia leant her head against him. She had plenty to feel grateful for.

CHAPTER FORTY-SEVEN

Lucy

I gripped the front door handle and took a breath. Leaving the house still presented a problem, but I was getting better at it. It felt like leaving a safe haven, as if the outdoors was out of my comfort zone, but apparently that was quite normal after a shock. Especially after the death of a loved one. 'The death of a loved one' – such a neat little phrase, one that didn't quite convey the bleakness it entailed.

I glanced at the hallway table. It was organised and tidy, with a new cream lamp in one corner, the telephone in the other. Keys hung in an ordered line on a wooden key plaque studded with butterflies, and I could actually see beneath the table because it was free of shoes.

I felt forlorn. It looked great, but it was all wrong. As much as I have always deplored clutter and chaos, the memory of the disarray was so reminiscent of Luke, I was tempted to shove the phone to one side and knock

405

the keys on to the table just so it looked the way it did when he was alive.

I stared at the door handle again. I could do it. I had done it before and I wanted to go outside. I needed some air. I pulled the door open and stepped outside, taking a big breath of air. It was May, warmer than expected, but I was dressed in skinny jeans, a T-shirt and a worn pair of Converse, so I'd cope.

I started walking without any particular agenda, glancing into the odd front garden. I wondered if I would end up like the elderly, widowed types who lived in my road, adorning my garden with whimsical stone figures because I had nothing much else to do. Errol, my kindly neighbour, had the most magnificent gnome by his front door, lying in repose like a glamorous movie star, a pipe clutched in one hand, which at least revealed a touch of humour.

I don't know why there are supposed to be five stages of grief, I thought to myself. I seemed to be firmly stuck between anger and depression. Denial didn't really work for me – Luke died right in front of me; I was under no illusion about that one – and I wasn't into doing deals with God, so they were both off the list. The only one left was acceptance. Me and acceptance weren't exactly on good terms yet. It felt a bit too hopeful an emotion for me to embrace right now.

I kept walking, feeling – as I always did these days – conspicuous, as if I had 'widow' stamped on my head. It was silly; everyone around me was simply getting on with their lives, but I had changed irrevocably.

Before Luke had died, spring had been the perfect time to begin my Christmas shopping. Spring would now be associated with fresh starts because, a couple of weeks ago, just as our garden had started to flower and burst into bright, uncoordinated colour, I had finally found the courage to sort through Luke's things. I told myself I would be strict, that I would only keep one box of his stuff so that when I was feeling maudlin, I could look through it and have a good cry. Of course I couldn't manage just one box and I ended up with three, rammed full of things that made my mind reel, they reminded me so much of Luke. Chunky cardigans, smelly trainers, bottles of aftershave. A bundle of cards, holiday photos and Post-it notes I used to leave on Luke's pillow that I didn't even know he'd squirrelled away. His hideous Hawaiian shirt. The packet of coffee he could never seem to put away in the cupboard, tied up in a bag to retain the rich aroma that, for me, was synonymous with him.

I know, it probably wasn't healthy. But it was all I could do – all I knew how to do. And it was, in its own twisted way, my attempt at moving on. It was a start, I reminded myself. It was better than having a house like a shrine that I couldn't bear to live in.

I found myself at the park and, taking a breath of fresh air, I decided to go for a wander. It had occurred to me that I should have learnt something from Luke's death or that something momentous should have happened. Perhaps I should turn my back on floristry and use my English degree for something more fabulous, like becoming a journalist or writing a novel. But it wasn't what I wanted.

I hadn't ever been especially ambitious; Luke's death hadn't changed that.

Frankly, the only thing I had learnt about life without Luke was that it was practically unbearable. That quote Patricia told me Bernard used to bang on about (something about someone breaking your heart but you still found yourself loving them with every little piece) was spot on. Despite everything, I still loved Luke. My heart did feel rather like it had been shattered, but I had come to realise that it was no less resilient when it came to feeling and knowing.

I hadn't yet learned to cope with the awkwardness that Luke's shining self-confidence and love had erased during our relationship, but I knew I was going to have to try. I kind of owed it to him to make an effort on that front, although it wasn't an immediate issue.

I had, however, realised one other, crucial thing. I had realised it too late, but I now knew that having a baby was about being a mother, not about being pregnant. I had been so hell-bent on having a baby of our own, that I had denied myself, *us*, the chance to use an egg donor, to adopt, to use a surrogate. I had blindly stumbled along the natural conception path, dragging Luke unwillingly behind me in the quest for a 'normal' pregnancy, when all I should have been thinking about was a baby that both of us could love and cherish, however it had come about.

I carried on walking, feeling the weight of my mistake on my shoulders. It was almost as heavy as my grief.

Reaching the central part of the park, I glanced around, deciding which way to turn. But instead of choosing a path, I stopped dead where I was, unable to believe my eyes. It couldn't be. I rarely came into the park and the first time I had, I bumped into Stella. Not literally; she was sitting on one of the benches that ring-fenced the lake with a black and red pram next to her. Jude. Jude was in the pram. Luke's son. The baby I had put out of my mind since the funeral.

Ha. Not above denial after all, my subconscious told me loftily. Jude was the one thing I couldn't make sense of in my mind. Luke, I had managed to forgive, more or less. Stella, I had written off as someone who had just been at the right place, at the right time (or wrong place and time, depending on your perspective). But Jude . . .

I scuffed the toe of my Converse on the ground. On the one hand, I couldn't bear the thought that Luke had a baby, a son with someone else. Especially after the heartache we had been through together trying to make our own family. On the other, Jude was a part of Luke. Luke was a part of Jude. It was the one topic I avoided like the plague. Nell and Patricia had both tried to broach it, but I had cut them off sharply. How dare they? How *dare* they talk to me about Jude? But deep down, I felt a stirring of guilt. Jude wasn't just a part of Luke. He was Nell and Ade's nephew and he was Patricia's grandchild. But God, the reality of that was like a razor to my throat.

I glanced at Stella again, hoping I could turn round without her seeing me and scurry back home to safety. What was she doing here? Had she stayed in Bath after Jude was born? Shouldn't she have done the decent thing and moved as far away from me as possible?

Frowning, I noticed that Stella wasn't cooing into the pram. She wasn't even paying attention to the baby. She was staring straight ahead of her and her shoulders were shaking. She was crying. Not just a few tears, but great big, racking sobs. I was familiar with those. Quite an expert, in fact.

I let out a breath. Like I had on the day of Luke's funeral, I told myself to leave well alone. To turn around, the way I had planned and get the hell out of that park. But, just as I had at the funeral, I found myself walking towards Stella doggedly, despite my misgivings, with a kind of stubborn determination.

She looked staggered to see me. She rubbed her face frantically with her hands as if to disguise her emotional breakdown, but she was still a mess. Close up, I could see that she was wearing her white coat with her stethoscope draped around her neck. The coat had a few stains on it and her blonde hair was tied back, but it still looked dishevelled. Stella looked to me like a mum. A harassed, not very together mum, but still. I felt horribly envious of her, but I wasn't about to beat myself up about that.

'How are things?' Stella asked me. She was clearly stunned to see me, but she was doing her best to sound calm and normal.

'Oh, you know.' I shrugged. 'I've been better. Yourself?'

Stella placed a hand on her forehead, her shoulders slumping. 'Me? I'm . . . I'm . . .'

She was in a massive state, that's what she was. I knew a breaking point when I saw one. I sat down gingerly, my brain telling me to run, run far away from this mental situation. I must have a death wish.

'Is it . . . Luke?' I asked cautiously, not sure I wanted to hear the answer.

'Luke?' Stella shook her head vigorously. 'No. No, it's not Luke. Obviously it was shocking, him – him dying, but no. I told you and I meant it – I haven't ever thought of him that way. I'm terribly sorry though, really. For you. For you all.'

'Thank you.' It was an automatic response. Lots of well-meaning people told me they were sorry these days; it was part of the job description. I didn't mind; it was nice that people cared.

'Then what's wrong?' I pressed gently.

She shot an involuntary glance at the pram.

'Jude?'

She nodded.

I felt a stab of defensiveness, although God only knew why. Perhaps because he was only a baby. Perhaps because he was part of Luke.

'Yes. No. I mean, it's not him, exactly.' Stella removed her stethoscope. 'It's juggling work and Jude and working when I've been up all night. Sorry, I shouldn't be saying this stuff to you. You don't want to hear me whining about my problems. You can't stand the sight of me and I don't blame you.'

'That's a bit strong,' I protested, knowing it was partly true. I was finding Stella difficult to look at, because I have an imagination and I don't like the way it drifts off when I see her face and hear her voice. 'I didn't even know you were still here.'

'I've been keeping my distance,' Stella admitted. 'I have an apartment here and they asked me to carry on working at the hospital, so I accepted and I went back early. Because I need to work. I wasn't sure it was the right thing to do, but I've gone out of my way not to bump into you or any of your family.'

I stared past Stella. I appreciated that.

'But really, it's about me,' Stella said with a sniff. 'It's about me being a complete failure at this, I mean.' Her face twisted contemptuously. 'The irony. I get to have the baby and I'm crap at being a mother.'

'I'm sure you're not—'

'I'm terrible, Lucy. I can assure you of that. I'm not organised when it comes to this stuff.'

We both heard a squeak from the pram and Stella sighed and grabbed the handle. She started rocking the pram and I wanted to tell her to slow it down a bit, to give it a bit of rhythm. But what did I know? I certainly wasn't about to speak up, not when she'd just told me she thought she was a rubbish mother.

'I'm . . . I'm not coping,' Stella admitted, starting to cry again. 'I'm so sorry to break down like this in front of you; it's just such a shock seeing you again after all these months.'

'Yes,' I said. It probably was. My mind was firing off in several different directions right now, so I could only imagine what Stella must be thinking.

Still jiggling the pram, Stella watched Jude. 'I'm still trying to complete my training at the hospital, but I keep missing my shifts because I'm sleeping through my alarm or I can't get cover for Jude.'

'Who's looking after him?'

'A child-minder someone recommended at the hospital. But she can only spare a few hours here and there because she's pretty much got a full quota of children. And all the other ones have waiting lists, as do all the nurseries in the area.' Stella shook her hair out of her face ruefully. 'I didn't get anything sorted before Jude was born. I didn't even get as far as thinking about how I was going to look after him and then I went into labour early and I wasn't prepared – for any of this.'

I found myself hugging her. It was a knee-jerk re-action and I couldn't explain it if I tried. But Stella was on the edge. And I knew what that felt like. I could tell her that she'd brought it on herself, I could tell her that it was karma, that you shouldn't dick around with the Buddha or whoever. But sometimes, I think it's best to say nothing and try and find it in yourself to be the bigger person. I had spent a long time despising Stella. But seeing her like this reduced her to a mere human being, one that made mistakes.

We jumped as Jude let out a loud cry. Self-consciously, I started to pull back and Stella reluctantly let go of me. I guessed she hadn't had much human contact for a while, Jude aside.

'He's hungry,' Stella stated glumly, checking her watch. 'I'll get him out. I actually remembered to bring his bottle this time.'

I had a feeling she wasn't joking. I watched her lift Jude out, marvelling at how much he had grown in five months. He had chubby arms and thighs and lots of

413

hair. Blonde, like Stella's, but even fairer. Most babies have less hair than he has, I thought, but he looked cute with his mop of blonde curls.

'Could you . . . ?' Stella gestured to the bag next to me.

I dug around in it, finding a baby bottle full of water. I tried again, finding a pot of powdered formula. I almost advised Stella that she might find a change bag from a maternity shop easier to use because they have special pockets for bottles and stuff like that, but I knew it would sound critical. None of this was anything to do with me.

'You just tap it in there and shake it up,' she said, putting a bib around Jude's neck.

She tried to put the bottle in his mouth but Jude turned away. He did it repeatedly and Stella eventually gave up, irritated beyond belief.

'He usually feeds at this time. Well, sometimes. Sometimes he does this, as if I've given him something vile to drink.'

Jude grabbed my hair suddenly. He didn't yank it; he turned it over in his hands, examining it. I found myself watching him in fascination.

'Whoops, sorry. He's really into hair at the moment. He pulled a man's hair at the hospital the other day and it was a wig. The poor man was mortified and I didn't have a clue what to say.'

I laughed. I surprised myself by doing it, but it came out before I could stop it. I was rusty when it came to the whole laughing thing, but I guess widows aren't known for their guffaws.

'Do you . . . no, you probably don't. That would be weird.' Stella shook her head.

'What?'

'Would you . . . want to hold him? Just say no if it's weird,' she added quickly.

'I . . . I'm not . . .'

I wasn't sure what to do. It would be rude to say no, but I wasn't altogether comfortable with the idea. Could my heart take it?

Almost as if he had heard what his mother had said, and not giving me any choice in the matter, Jude leaned in towards me. To stop him falling, I thrust my arms forward and took him under the armpits. Before I had even thought about what I was doing, I had lifted Jude off Stella's lap. My heart started beating, frantically. This was Luke's son – the son we should have had. The son he shouldn't have had with someone else.

But when I looked down at Jude and held him in my arms, none of that seemed to matter. His body was warm and solid and he held his head well. His eyes connected with mine and his eyelashes fluttered as he took me in. I did the same back, examining every inch of his face, every smooth line, each delicate eyebrow, the slope of his beautiful, tiny nose. God, he looked so much like Luke it hurt. At the same time, it was kind of lovely, like Luke hadn't properly gone. No, that sounded wrong. I knew Luke had gone. I mean that Jude was like an extension of him, a fragment he had left behind.

I remembered the last baby I had lost, the last IVF baby. If only, if only, if only. Had that baby managed to stick around, I would have had her by now and I would have my own reminder of Luke – a pure one that didn't make my heart sting the way this reminder did.

Jude smelt good. No different to any other baby I had held over the years (and there had been many), he had that freshly washed, talcum powder smell that couldn't be bottled. Stella was protesting too much; Jude wasn't spotless by any means (show me a baby that was), but he was more or less clean and he had obviously been well-fed over the past few months.

'How . . . how do you feel?' Stella wanted to know. She was tentative, but I couldn't blame her for asking.

Honestly, I couldn't put it into words. Just as I had been at Luke's funeral, there wasn't a chance I was going to be able to articulate the way holding Jude was making me feel. Tearfully joyous. Gutted, but unbearably moved. But I wasn't sure I wanted Stella to know how affected I was. I felt I needed to protect myself, to keep those feelings hidden. Without Luke, I was vulnerable enough.

The baby grabbed my cheeks.

'Ow, Mister. How would you feel if I did that to you?' I pretended to squeeze his cheeks back and he let out a delighted squeal.

'He likes you,' Stella said, giving me a wide smile. 'Honestly, he doesn't do that with everyone.'

Jude didn't know who I was. How could he know? But somehow, the fact that he had instantly warmed to me made me feel good. Seemingly impressed, Stella held up the bottle and I nodded and took it. After pushing it away several times as he had before, Jude finally conceded and glugged the bottle down. He puked on my jeans a bit, but it didn't bother me; it was only formula.

We sat together for some time. Stella put Jude on his tummy on a blanket and we laughed as he unintentionally mimed a front crawl.

That afternoon, something changed inside me and, without even knowing what it was, I grabbed it with both hands.

Stella needed help. She didn't have time to look after Jude every hour of the day. Time was something I had in abundance. I would probably go back to the florists at some point, but Patricia was being supremely patient and I wasn't sure I could stand the sweet concern of our regular customers, not for a while.

But . . . there was something I could offer Stella. Was the idea of looking after Jude for a few afternoons a week more than I could bear? I wasn't sure yet, but I knew I wanted to know him. And I knew that Nell, Ade and Patricia would want to be a part of Jude's life, too.

I missed Luke and I knew I would never stop wishing that what had happened with Stella could be erased. I also knew I would always long for a child, the child I was meant to have with Luke.

But there was this baby, this bittersweet gift Luke had left behind. Jude was a reminder of him, a living, breathing piece of Luke that had his cleft chin and his eyes and yes, I double-checked. He had Luke's freaky toes. What were the odds? Tears came into my eyes, but for the first time in a long while, they were happy ones. I smiled, knowing that I was making the right decision. There were people who wanted to hold Jude and love him and be a part of his life.

And I was one of them. I was definitely one of them.

Did *PIECES OF YOU*
make you want to talk?

Turn the page for some
reading group questions . . .

Reading Group Questions for
PIECES OF YOU

1. If you had to choose between having a baby or the love of your life, which would you choose?

2. The role of motherhood becomes the most important thing to Lucy in *Pieces of You*. Can you understand her feelings?

3. Can you empathise with Lucy for lying about her IVF attempts? Can you understand her obsession and why she is unable to move on?

4. Is a one-night stand a more forgivable infidelity than a drawn-out affair?

5. Do you think fatherhood is less crucial than motherhood?

6. Do you feel any sympathy for Luke when he talks about his once-passionate relationship with Lucy being reduced to that of a sperm donor?

7. Examine Patricia and Ade's relationship. At the start of the novel we see it in a delicate state. Can you understand why Ade felt he had to move to Australia? And why Patricia found it so hard to forgive him?

8. How is the theme of morality explored in the book?

9. How much of Nell's behaviour can be attributed to the fact that she lost her father at a young age?

10. Every character in the novel has something to hide. What are the repercussions of their respective secrets?

11. Consider the role of truth within the novel. How would the story be different had people chosen to tell the truth at all times?

12. Were you able to forgive Luke?